Lick
& Play

Kylie Scott

St. Martin's Paperbacks

This is a work of fiction. All of the characters, organizations, and events portrayed in this novel are either products of the author's imagination or are used fictitiously.

LICK & PLAY

Copyright © 2016 by Kylie Scott.

All rights reserved.

For information address St. Martin's Press, 175 Fifth Avenue, New York, NY 10010.

ISBN: 978-1-250-10371-0

Our books may be purchased in bulk for promotional, educational, or business use. Please contact your local bookseller or the Macmillan Corporate and Premium Sales Department at 1-800-221-7945, ext. 5442, or by e-mail at MacmillanSpecialMarkets@macmillan.com.

Printed in the United States of America

"Lick" St. Martin's Griffin trade paperback edition / May 2014
"Play" St. Martin's Griffin trade paperback edition / September 2014
St. Martin's Paperbacks edition / November 2016

St. Martin's Paperbacks are published by St. Martin's Press, 175 Fifth Avenue, New York, NY 10010.

10 9 8 7 6 5 4 3 2

Lick

For Hugh.

And also for Mish,
who wanted something without zombies.

ACKNOWLEDGMENTS

First up, all lyrics (with the exception of the final song) are used courtesy of Soviet X-Ray Record Club. You can learn more about the band at www.sovietxrayrecordclub .com. The term "topless cuddles" comes courtesy of the writer Daniel Dalton.

Much love to my family, who suffered as always while I wandered around in a story daze working on this. Your patience is legendary, thank you so much. To my invaluable friends who give me feedback and support (in no particular order because you are all Queens in my eyes): Tracey O'Hara, Kendall Ryan, Mel Teshco, Joanna Wylde, Kylie Griffin, and Babette. A big thank-you to all book bloggers for doing what you do, especially my friends Angie from *Twinsie Talk*, Cath from *Book Chatter Cath*, Maryse from *Maryse's Book Blog*, and Katrina from *Page Flipperz*. Thanks to Joel, Anne, and Mark at Momentum for being so supportive. And special thanks to my editor, Sarah JH Fletcher.

Last but not least, to the lovely folk who chat with me on Twitter and Facebook, and send me e-mails saying kind things about my books. To the people who enjoy my stories and take the time to write a review, THANK YOU.

CHAPTER ONE

I woke up on the bathroom floor. Everything hurt. My mouth felt like garbage and tasted worse. What the hell had happened last night? The last thing I remembered was the countdown to midnight and the thrill of turning twenty-one—legal, at last. I'd been dancing with Lauren and talking to some guy. Then BANG!

Tequila.

A whole line of shot glasses with lemon and salt on the side.

Everything I'd heard about Vegas was true. Bad things happened here, terrible things. I just wanted to crawl into a ball and die. Sweet baby Jesus, what had I been thinking to drink so much? I groaned, and even that made my head pound. This pain had not been part of the plan.

"You okay?" a voice inquired, male, deep, and nice. Really nice. A shiver went through me despite my pain. My poor broken body stirred in the strangest of places.

"Are you going to be sick again?" he asked.

Oh, no.

I opened my eyes and sat up, pushing my greasy blond hair aside. His blurry face loomed closer. I slapped a hand over my mouth because my breath had to be hideous.

"Hi," I mumbled.

Slowly, he swam into focus. He was built and beautiful and strangely familiar. Impossible. I'd never met anyone like him.

He looked to be in his mid to late twenties—a man, not a boy. He had long, dark hair falling past his shoulders and sideburns. His eyes were the darkest blue. They couldn't be real. Frankly, those eyes were overkill. I'd have swooned perfectly fine without them. Even with the tired red tinge, they were a thing of beauty. Tattoos covered the entirety of one arm and half his bare chest. A black bird had been inked into the side of his neck, the tip of its wing reaching up behind his ear. I still had on the pretty, dirty white dress Lauren had talked me into. It had been a daring choice for me on account of the way it barely contained my abundance of boobage. But this beautiful man easily had me beat for skin on show. He wore just a pair of jeans, scuffed black boots, a couple of small silver earrings, and a loose white bandage on his forearm.

Those jeans . . . he wore them well. They sat invitingly low on his hips and fit in all the right ways. Even my monster hangover couldn't detract from the view.

"Aspirin?" he asked.

And I was ogling him. My gaze darted to his face and he gave me a sly, knowing smile. Wonderful. "Yes. Please."

He grabbed a battered black leather jacket off the floor, the one I'd apparently been using as a pillow. Thank God I hadn't puked on it. Clearly, this beautiful half-naked man had seen me in all my glory, hurling multiple times. I could have drowned in the shame.

One by one he emptied the contents of his pockets out onto the cold white tiles. A credit card, guitar picks, a phone, and a string of condoms. The condoms gave me pause, but I was soon distracted by what emerged next. A multitude of paper scraps tumbled out onto the floor.

All had names and numbers scrawled across them. This guy was Mr. Popularity. Hey, I could definitely see why. But what on earth was he doing here with me?

Finally, he produced a small bottle of painkillers. Sweet relief. I loved him, whoever he was and whatever he'd seen.

"You need water," he said, and got busy filling a glass from the sink behind him.

The bathroom was tiny. We both barely fit. Given Lauren's and my money situation, the hotel had been the best we could afford. She'd been determined to celebrate my birthday in style. My goal had been a bit different. Despite the presence of my hot new friend, I was pretty sure I'd failed. The pertinent parts of my anatomy felt fine. I'd heard things hurt after the first couple of times. They sure as hell had after the first. But my vagina might have been the only part of my body not giving me grief.

Still, I took a quick peek down the front of my dress. The corner of a foil package could still be seen, tucked into the side of my bra. Because if it was sitting there, strapped to me, no way would I be caught unprepared. The condom remained whole and hearty. How disappointing. Or maybe not. Finally plucking up the courage to get back on the horse, so to speak, and then not remembering it would have been horrible.

The man handed me the glass of water and placed two pills into my hand. He then sat back on his haunches to watch me. He had an intensity to him that I was in no condition to deal with.

"Thanks," I said, then swallowed the aspirin. Noisy rumbles rose from my belly. Nice, very ladylike.

"Are you sure you're okay?" he asked. His glorious mouth twitched into a smile as if we shared a private joke between us.

The joke being me.

All I could do was stare. Given my current condition,

he was just too much. The hair, face, body, ink, all of it. Someone needed to invent a word superlative enough to describe him.

After a long moment it dawned on me that he expected an answer to his question. I nodded, still unwilling to unleash my morning breath, and gave him a grim smile. The best I could do.

"Okay. That's good," he said.

He was certainly attentive. I didn't know what I'd done to deserve such kindness. If I'd picked up the poor guy with promises of sex and then proceeded to spend the night with my head in the toilet, by rights he should be a bit disgruntled. Maybe he hoped I'd make good on the offer this morning. It seemed the only plausible explanation for why he'd linger.

Under normal conditions, he was light-years out of my league and (for the sake of my pride) worlds away from my type. I liked clean-cut. Clean-cut was nice. Bad boys were highly overrated. God knows, I'd watched enough girls throw themselves at my brother over the years. He'd taken what they'd offered if it suited him, and then moved on. Bad boys weren't the stuff serious relationships were made of. Not that I'd been chasing forever last night, just a positive sexual experience. Something not involving Tommy Byrnes being mad at me for getting a smear of blood on the backseat of his parents' car. God, what a horrible memory. The next day the douche had dumped me for a girl on the track team half my size. He then added insult to injury by spreading rumors about me. I hadn't been made bitter or twisted by this event at all.

What had happened last night? My head remained a tangled, throbbing mess, the details hazy, incomplete.

"We should get something into you," he said. "You want me to order some dry toast or something?"

"No." The thought of food was not fun. Not even

coffee appealed, and coffee always appealed. I was half tempted to check myself for a pulse, just in case. Instead, I pushed my hand through my crappy hair, getting it out of my eyes. "No . . . ow!" Strands caught on something, tugging hard at my scalp. "Crap."

"Hang on." He reached out and carefully disentangled my messy do from whatever was causing the trouble. "There we go."

"Thanks." Something winked at me from my left hand, snagging my attention. A ring, but not just any ring. An amazing ring, a stupendous one.

"Holy shit," I whispered.

It couldn't be real. It was so big it bordered on obscene. A stone that size would cost a fortune. I stared, bemused, turning my hand to catch the light. The band beneath was thick, solid, and the rock sure shone and sparkled like the real deal.

As if.

"Ah, yeah. About that . . ." he said, dark brows drawn down. He looked vaguely embarrassed by the ice rink on my finger. "If you still wanna change it for something smaller, that's okay with me. It is kinda big. I do get your point about that."

I couldn't shake the feeling I knew him from somewhere. Somewhere that wasn't last night or this morning or anything to do with the ridiculous beautiful ring on my finger.

"You bought me this?" I asked.

He nodded. "Last night at Cartier."

"Cartier?" My voice dropped to a whisper. "Huh."

For a long moment he just stared at me. "You don't remember?"

I really didn't want to answer that. "What is that, even? Two, three carats?"

"Five."

"Five? Wow."

"What do you remember?" he asked, voice hardening just a little.

"Well . . . it's hazy."

"No." His frown increased until it owned his handsome face. "You have got to be fucking kidding me. You seriously don't know?"

What to say? My mouth hung open, useless. There was a lot I didn't know. To my knowledge, however, Cartier didn't do costume jewelry. My head swam. Bad feelings unfurled within my stomach and bile burnt the back of my throat. Worse even than before.

I was not puking in front of this guy.

Not again.

He took a deep breath, nostrils flaring. "I didn't realize you'd had that much to drink. I mean, I knew you'd had a bit, but . . . shit. Seriously? You don't remember us going on the gondolas at the Venetian?"

"We went on gondolas?"

"Fuck. Ah, how about when you bought me a burger? Do you remember that?"

"Sorry."

"Wait a minute," he said, watching me through narrowed eyes. "You're just messing with me, aren't you?"

"I'm so sorry."

He physically recoiled from me. "Let me get this straight, you don't remember anything?"

"No," I said, swallowing hard. "What did we do last night?"

"We got fucking married," he growled.

This time, I didn't make it to the toilet.

I decided on divorce while I brushed my teeth, practiced what I would say to him as I washed my hair. But you couldn't rush these things. Unlike last night, when I'd apparently rushed into marriage. Rushing again would be wrong, foolish. That, or I was a coward taking the world's longest shower. Odds were on the latter.

Holy, holy hell. What a mess. I couldn't even begin to get my head wrapped around it. Married. Me. My lungs wouldn't work. Panic waited right around the corner.

No way could my desire for this disaster to go away come as a surprise to him. Puking on the floor had to have been a huge hint. I groaned and covered my face with my hands at the memory. His look of disgust would haunt me all my days.

My parents would kill me if they ever found out. I had plans, priorities. I was studying to be an architect like my father. Marriage to anyone at this stage didn't fit into those plans. In another ten, fifteen years, maybe. But marriage at twenty-one? Hell no. I hadn't even been on a second date in years and now I had a ring on my finger. No way did that make sense. I was doomed. This crazy wedding caper wasn't something I could hide from.

Or could I?

Unless my parents could not find out. Ever. Over the years I had made something of a habit of not involving them in things that might be seen as unsavory, unnecessary, or just plain stupid. This marriage quite possibly fell under all three categories.

Actually, maybe no one need know. If I didn't tell, how would they find out? They wouldn't. The answer was awe-inspiring in its simplicity.

"Yes!" I hissed and punched the air, clipping the shower head with the side of my fist. Water sprayed everywhere, including straight in my eyes, blinding me. Never mind, I had the answer.

Denial. I'd take the secret to my grave. No one would ever know of my extreme drunken idiocy.

I smiled with relief, my panic attack receding enough so that I could breathe. Oh, thank goodness. Everything would be okay. I had a new plan to get me back on track with the old one. Brilliant. I'd brave up, go and face him, and set things straight. Twenty-one-year-olds with grand life plans didn't marry complete strangers in Vegas, no matter how beautiful those strangers happened to be. It would be fine. He'd understand. In all likelihood, he sat out there right now, working out the most efficient method to dump and run.

The diamond still glittered on my hand. I couldn't bring myself to take it off just yet. It was like Christmas on my finger, so big, bright, and shiny. Though, upon reflection, my temporary husband didn't exactly appear to be rich. His jacket and jeans were both well-worn. The man was a mystery.

Wait. What if he was into something illegal? Maybe I'd married a criminal. Panic rushed back in with a vengeance. My stomach churned and my head throbbed. I knew nothing about the person waiting in the next room. Absolutely not a damn thing. I'd shoved him out the bathroom door without even getting his name.

A knock on the door sent my shoulders sky-high.

"Evelyn?" he called out, proving he at least knew my name.

"Just a second."

I turned off the taps and stepped out, wrapping a towel around myself. The width of it was barely sufficient to cover my curves, but my dress had puke on it. Putting it back on was out of the question.

"Hi," I said, opening the bathroom door a hand's length. He stood almost half a head taller than me, and I wasn't short by any means. Dressed in only a towel, I found him rather intimidating. However much he'd had to drink the previous night, he still looked gorgeous, as opposed to me—pale, pasty, and sopping wet. The aspirins hadn't done nearly as much as they should have.

Of course, I'd thrown them up.

"Hey." He didn't meet my eyes. "Look, I'm going to get this taken care of, okay?"

"Taken care of?"

"Yeah," he said, still avoiding all eye contact. Apparently the hideous green motel carpeting was beyond enticing. "My lawyers will deal with all this."

"You have lawyers?" Criminals had lawyers. Shit. I had to get myself divorced from this guy now.

"Yeah, I have lawyers. You don't need to worry about anything. They'll send you the paperwork or whatever. However this works." He gave me an irritated glance, lips a tight line, and pulled on his leather jacket over his bare chest. His T-shirt still hung drying over the edge of the tub. Sometime during the night I must have puked on it too. How gruesome. If I were him, I'd divorce me and never look back.

"This was a mistake," he said, echoing my thoughts.

"Oh."

"What?" His gaze jumped to my face. "You disagree?"

"No," I said quickly.

"Didn't think so. Pity it made sense last night, yeah?" He shoved a hand through his hair and made for the door. "Take care."

"Wait!" The stupid, amazing ring wouldn't come off my finger. I tugged and turned it, trying to wrestle it into submission. Finally it budged, grazing my knuckle raw in the process. Blood welled to the surface. One more stain in this whole sordid affair. "Here."

"For fuck's sake." He scowled at the rock sparkling in the palm of my hand as if it had personally offended him. "Keep it."

"I can't. It must have cost a fortune."

He shrugged.

"Please." I held it out, hand jiggling, impatient to be rid of the evidence of my drunken stupidity. "It belongs to you. You have to take it."

"No. I don't."

"But—"

Without another word, the man stormed out, slamming the door shut behind him. The thin walls vibrated with the force of it.

Whoa. My hand fell back to my side. He sure had a temper. Not that I hadn't given him provocation, but still. I wish I remembered what had gone on between us. Any inkling would be good.

Meanwhile my left butt cheek felt sore. I winced, carefully rubbing the area. My dignity wasn't the only casualty, it seemed. I must have scratched my behind at some stage, bumped into some furniture or taken a dive in my fancy new heels. The pricey ones Lauren had insisted went with the dress, the ones whose current whereabouts were a mystery. I hoped I hadn't lost them. Given my recent nuptials, nothing would surprise me.

I wandered back into the bathroom with a vague memory of a buzzing noise and laughter ringing in my ear, of him whispering to me. It made no sense.

I turned and raised the edge of my towel, going up on tippy-toes to inspect my ample ass in the mirror. Black ink and hot pink skin.

All the air left my body in a rush.

There was a word on my left butt cheek, a name:

David

I spun and dry-heaved into the sink.

CHAPTER TWO

Lauren sat beside me on the plane, fiddling with my iPhone. "I don't understand how your taste in music can be so bad. We've been friends for years. Have I taught you nothing?"

"To not drink tequila."

She rolled her eyes.

Above our heads the seat belt sign flashed on. A polite voice advised us to return our seats to the upright position as we'd be landing in a few minutes. I swallowed the dregs of my shitty plane coffee with a wince. Fact was, no amount of caffeine could help me today. Quality didn't even come into it.

"I am deadly serious," I said. "I'm also never setting foot in Nevada ever again so long as I live."

"Now, there's an overreaction."

"Not even a little, lady."

Lauren had stumbled back to the motel a bare two hours before our flight was due to leave. I'd spent the time repacking my small bag over and over in an attempt to get my life back into some semblance of order. It was good to see Lauren smiling, though getting to the airport in time had been a race. Apparently she and the cute waiter she'd met would be keeping in touch. Lauren had always been great with guys, while I was more closely related to your standard garden-variety wallflower. My plan to get laid in Vegas had been a deliberate attempt to get out of that rut. So much for that idea.

Lauren was studying economics, and she was gorgeous, inside and out. I was more kind of unwieldy. It was why I made a habit of walking everywhere I could in Portland and trying not to sample the contents of the cake display case at the café where I worked. It kept me manageable, waist-wise. Though my mom still saw fit to give me lectures on the subject because God forbid I dare put sugar in my coffee. My thighs would no doubt explode or something.

Lauren had three older brothers and knew what to say to guys. Nothing intimidated her. The girl oozed charm. I had one older brother, but we no longer interacted outside of major family holidays. Not since he moved out of our parents' home four years back leaving only a note. Nathan had a temper and a gift for getting into trouble. He'd been the bad boy in high school, always getting into fights and skipping classes. Though blaming my lack of success with guys on my nonexistent relationship with my brother was wrong. I could own my deficiencies with the opposite sex. Mostly.

"Listen to this." Lauren plugged my earphones into her phone, and the whine of electric guitars exploded inside my skull. The pain was exquisite. My headache roared back to sudden, horrific life. Nothing remained of my brain but bloody red mush. Of this I was certain.

I ripped out the earphones. "Don't. Please."

"But that's Stage Dive."

"And they're lovely. But, you know, another time maybe."

"I worry about you sometimes. I just want you to know that."

"There is nothing wrong with country music played softly."

Lauren snorted and fluffed up her dark hair. "There is nothing right with country music played at any volume. So what did you get up to last night? Apart from spending quality time heaving?"

"Actually, that about sums it up." The less said the better. How could I ever explain? Still, guilt slid through me and I squirmed in my seat. The tattoo throbbed in protest.

I hadn't told Lauren about my grand having-good-sex plan for the night. She'd have wanted to help. Honestly, sex didn't strike me as the sort of thing you should have help with. Apart from what was required from the sexual partner in question, of course. Lauren's assistance would have involved foisting me on every hottie in the room with promises of my immediate leg-open availability.

I loved Lauren, and her loyalty was above question, but she didn't have a subtle bone in her body. She'd punched a girl in the nose in fifth grade for teasing me about my weight, and we'd been friends ever since. With Lauren, you always knew exactly where you stood. Something I appreciated the bulk of the time, just not when discretion was called for.

Happily, my sore stomach survived the bumpy landing. As soon as those wheels hit the tarmac, I let out a sigh of relief. I was back in my hometown. Beautiful Oregon, lovely Portland, never again would I stray. With mountains in the distance and trees in the city, she was a singular delight. To limit myself to the one city for life might indeed be going overboard. But it was great to be home. I had an all-important internship starting next week that my father had pulled strings to get for me. There were also next semester's classes to start planning for.

Everything would be fine. I'd learned my lesson. Normally, I didn't go past three drinks. Three drinks were good. Three got me happy without tripping me face-first into disaster. Never again would I cross the line. I was back to being the good old organized, boring me. Adventures were not cool, and I was done with them.

We stood and grabbed our bags out of the overhead lockers. Everyone pushed forward in a rush to disembark. The hostesses gave us practiced smiles as we tramped up the aisle and out into the connecting tunnel. Next came security, and then we poured out into the baggage claim. Fortunately, we only had carry-on, so no delays there. I couldn't wait to get home.

I heard shouting up ahead. Lights were flashing. Someone famous must have been on the plane. People ahead of us turned and stared. I looked back too but saw no familiar faces.

"What's going on?" Lauren asked, scanning the crowd.

"I don't know," I said, standing on tippy-toes, getting excited by all the commotion.

Then I heard it, my name being called out over and over. Lauren's mouth pursed in surprise. Mine fell open.

"When's the baby due?"

"Evelyn, is David with you?"

"Will there be another wedding?"

"When will you be moving to LA?"

"Is David coming to meet your parents?"

"Evelyn, is this the end for Stage Dive?"

"Is it true that you got tattoos of each other's names?"

"How long have you and David been seeing each other?"

"What do you say to accusations that you've broken up the band?"

My name and his, over and over, mixed into a barrage of endless questions. All of which merged into chaos. A wall of noise I could barely comprehend. I stood gaping in disbelief as flashbulbs blinded me and people pressed in. My heart hammered. I'd never been great with crowds, and there was no escape that I could see.

Lauren snapped out of it first.

She shoved her sunglasses onto my face and then grabbed my hand. With liberal use of her elbows, she dragged me through the mob. The world became a blur, thanks to her prescription lenses. I was lucky not to fall on my ass. We ran through the busy airport and out to a waiting taxi, jumping the queue. People started yelling. We ignored them.

The paparazzi were close behind.

The motherfucking paparazzi. It would have been surreal if it wasn't so frantic and in my face.

Lauren pushed me into the backseat of the cab. I scrambled across, then slumped down, doing my best to hide. Wishing I could disappear entirely.

"Go! Hurry!" she shouted at the driver.

The driver took her at her word. He shot out of the place, sending us sliding across the cracked vinyl seating. My forehead bounced off the back of the (luckily padded) passenger seat. Lauren pulled my seat belt over me and jammed it into the clasp. My hands didn't seem to be working. Everything jumped and jittered.

"Talk to me," she said.

"Ah . . ." No words came out. I pushed her sunglasses up on top of my head and stared into space. My ribs hurt, and my heart still pounded so hard.

"Ev?" With a small smile, Lauren patted my knee. "Did you somehow happen to get married while we were away?"

"I . . . yeah. I, uh, I did. I think."

"Wow."

And then it just all blurted out of me. "God, Lauren. I screwed up so badly and I barely even remember any of it. I just woke up and he was there and then he was so pissed at me and I don't even blame him. I didn't know how to tell you. I was just going to pretend it never happened."

"I don't think that's going to work now."

"No."

"Okay. No big deal. So you're married." Lauren nodded, her face freakily calm. No anger, no blame. Meanwhile, I felt terrible I hadn't confided in her. We shared everything.

"I'm sorry," I said. "I should have told you."

"Yes, you should have. But never mind." She straightened out her skirt like we were sitting down to tea. "So, who did you marry?"

"D-David. His name is David."

"David Ferris, by any chance?"

The name sounded familiar. "Maybe?"

"Where we going?" asked the cabdriver, never taking his eyes off the traffic. He wove in and out among the cars with supernatural speed. If I'd been up to feeling anything, I might have felt fear and more nausea. Blind terror, perhaps. But I had nothing.

"Ev?" Lauren turned in her seat, checking out the cars behind us. "We haven't lost them. Where do you want to go?"

"Home," I said, the first safe place to come to mind. "My parents' place, I mean."

"Good call. They've got a fence." Without pausing for breath, Lauren rattled off the address to the driver. She frowned and pushed the sunglasses back down over my face. "Keep them on."

I gave a rough laugh as the world outside turned back into a smudge. "You really think it'll help, now?"

"No," she said, flicking back her long hair. "But people in these situations always wear sunglasses. Trust me."

"You watch too much TV." I closed my eyes. The sunglasses weren't helping my hangover. Nor was the rest of it. All my own damn fault. "I'm sorry I didn't say something. I didn't mean to get married. I don't even remember what happened exactly. This is such a . . ."

"Clusterfuck?"

"That word works."

Lauren sighed and rested her head on my shoulder. "You're right. You really shouldn't drink tequila ever again."

"No," I agreed.

"Do me a favor?" she asked.

"Mm?"

"Don't break up my favorite band."

"Ohmygod." I shoved the sunglasses back up, frowning hard enough to make my head throb. "Guitarist. He's the guitarist. That's where I know him from."

"Yes. He's the guitarist for Stage Dive. Well spotted."

The David Ferris. He'd been on Lauren's bedroom wall for years. Granted, he had to be the last person I'd expect to wake up with, on a bathroom floor or otherwise. But how the hell could I not have recognized him? "That's how he could afford the ring."

"What ring?"

Shuffling farther down in the seat, I fished the monster out of my jeans pocket and brushed off the lint and fluff. The diamond glittered accusingly in the bright light of day.

Lauren started shaking beside me, muffled laughter escaping her lips. "Mother of God, it's huuuuge!"

"I know."

"No, seriously."

"I know."

"Fuck me. I think I'm about to pee myself," she squealed, fanning her face and bouncing up and down on the car seat. "Look at it!"

"Lauren, stop. We can't both be freaking out. That won't work."

"Right. Sorry." She cleared her throat, visibly struggling to get herself back under control. "How much is that even worth?"

"I really don't want to guess."

"That. Is. Insane."

We both stared at my bling in awed silence.

Suddenly Lauren started bopping up and down in her seat again like a kid riding a sugar high. "I know! Let's sell it and go backpacking in Europe. Hell, we could probably circle the globe a couple of times on that sucker. Imagine it."

"We can't," I said, as tempting as it sounded. "I've got to get it back to him somehow. I can't keep this."

"Pity." She grinned. "So, congratulations. You're married to a rock star."

I tucked the ring back in my pocket. "Thanks. What the hell am I going to do?"

"I honestly don't know." She shook her head at me, her eyes full of wonder. "You've exceeded all of my expectations. I wanted you to let your hair down a little. Get a life and give mankind another chance. But this is a whole new level of crazy you've ascended to. Do you really have a tattoo?"

"Yes."

"Of his name?"

I sighed and nodded.

"Where, might I inquire?"

I shut my eyes tight. "My left butt cheek."

Lauren lost it, laughing so hard that tears started streaming down her face.

Perfect.

CHAPTER THREE

Dad's cell rang just before midnight. My own had long since been switched off. When the home phone wouldn't stop ringing, we'd unplugged it from the wall. Twice the police had been by to clear people out of the front yard. Mom had finally taken a sleeping pill and gone to bed. Having her neat, ordered world shot to hell hadn't gone down so well. Surprisingly, after an initial outburst, Dad had been dealing all right with the situation. I was suitably apologetic and wanted a divorce. He was willing to chalk this one up to hormones or the like. But that all changed when he looked at the screen of his cell.

"Leyton?" He answered the call, his eyes drilling into me from across the room. My stomach sank accordingly. Only a parent could train you so well. I had disappointed him. We both knew it. There was only one Leyton and only one reason why he'd be calling at this hour on this day.

"Yes," my father said. "It's an unfortunate situation." The lines around his mouth deepened, turning into crevices. "Understandably. Yes. Good night, then."

His fingers tightened around the cell and then he tossed it onto the dining room table. "Your internship has been canceled."

All of the air rushed out of me as my lungs constricted to the size of pennies.

"Leyton rightly feels that given your present situation . . ." My father's voice trailed away to nothing. He'd called in years-old favors to get me the internship with one of Portland's most prestigious architectural firms. It'd had taken only a thirty-second phone call, however, to make it disappear.

Someone banged on the door. Neither of us reacted. People had been hammering on it for hours.

Dad started pacing back and forth across the living room. I just watched in a daze.

Throughout my childhood, times such as this had always followed a certain pattern. Nathan got into a fight at school. The school called our mother. Our mother had a meltdown. Nate retreated to his room or, worse, disappeared for days. Dad got home and paced. And there I'd be among it all, trying to play mediator, the expert at not making waves. So what the hell was I doing standing in the middle of a fucking tsunami?

As kids went, I'd always been pretty low maintenance. I'd gotten good grades in high school and had gone on to the same local college as my father. I might have lacked his natural talent at design, but I put in the hours and effort to get the grades I needed to pass. I had been working part-time in the same coffee shop since I was fifteen. Moving in with Lauren had been my one grand rebellion. I was, all in all, fantastically boring. My parents had wanted me to stay home and save money. Anything else I'd achieved had been done through subterfuge so my parents could sleep soundly at night. Not that I'd gotten up to much. The odd party. The Tommy episode four years back. There'd been nothing to prepare me for this.

Apart from the press, there were people crying on the front lawn and holding signs proclaiming their love for

David. One man was holding an old-style boom box high in the air, blasting out music. A song called "San Pedro" was their favorite. The yelling would reach a crescendo every time the singer made it to the chorus, "But the sun was low and we'd no place to go . . ."

Apparently, later they were planning on burning me in effigy.

Which was fine, I wanted to die.

My big brother Nathan had been over to collect Lauren and take her back to his place. We hadn't seen each other since Christmas, but desperate times and desperate measures. The apartment Lauren and I shared was likewise surrounded. Going there was out of the question, and Lauren didn't want to get her family or other friends involved. To say Nathan enjoyed my predicament would be unkind. Not untrue, but definitely unkind. He'd always been the one in trouble. This time, however, it was all on me. Nathan had never gotten accidentally married and inked in Vegas.

Because of course some asshat reporter had asked my mother how she felt about the tattoo, so that secret was out. Apparently now no decent boy from a good family would ever marry me. Previously, I'd been unlikely to land a man due to my various lumps and bumps. But now it was all on the tattoo. I'd decided to forgo pointing out to her that I was already married.

More banging on the front door. Dad just looked at me. I shrugged.

"Ms. Thomas?" a big voice boomed. "David sent me."

Yeah, right. "I'm calling the cops."

"Wait. Please," the big voice said. "I've got him on the phone. Just open the door enough so I can hand it in to you."

"No."

Muffled noises. "He said to ask you about his T-shirt."

The one he'd left behind in Vegas. It was in my bag, still damp. Huh. Maybe. But I still wasn't convinced. "What else?"

More talking. "He said he still didn't want the . . . excuse me, miss . . . 'fucking ring' back."

I opened the door but kept the chain on. A man who resembled a bulldog in a black suit handed me a cell phone.

"Hello?"

Loud music played in the background and there were lots of voices. Apparently this marriage incident hadn't slowed down David at all.

"Ev?"

"Yes."

He paused. "Listen, you probably want to lie low for a while until this all dies down, okay? Sam will get you out of there. He's part of my security team."

Sam gave me a polite smile. I'd seen mountains smaller than this guy.

"Where would I go?" I asked.

"He'll, ah . . . he'll bring you to me. We'll sort something out."

"To you?"

"Yeah, there'll be the divorce papers and shit to sign, so you may as well come here."

I wanted to say no. But taking this away from my parents' front doorstep was wildly tempting. Ditto with getting out of there before Mom woke up and heard about the internship. Still, with good reason or not, I couldn't forget the way David had slammed his way out of my life that morning. I had a vague backup plan taking shape. With the internship gone, I could return to work at the café. Ruby would be delighted to have me full-time for the summer and I loved being there. Turning up with this horde on my heels, however, would be a disaster.

My options were few and none of them appealed, but still I hedged. "I don't know . . ."

He gave a particularly pained-sounding sigh. "What else are you gonna do? Huh?"

Good question.

Out past Sam, the insanity continued. Lights flashed and people yelled. It didn't seem real. If this was what David's everyday life was like, I had no idea how he handled it.

"Look. You need to get the fuck out of there," he said, words brisk, brittle. "It'll calm down in a while."

My dad stood beside me, wringing his hands. David was right. Whatever happened, I had to get this away from the people I loved. I could do that much at least.

"Ev?"

"Sorry. Yes, I'd like to take you up on that offer," I said. "Thank you."

"Hand the phone back to Sam."

I did as asked, also opening the door fully so the big man could come inside. He wasn't overly tall, but he was built. The guy took up serious space. Sam nodded and said some "yes, sirs." Then he hung up. "Ms. Thomas, the car is waiting."

"No," said Dad.

"Dad—"

"You cannot trust that man. Look at everything that's happened."

"It's hardly all his fault. I played my part in this." The whole situation embarrassed me. But running and hiding was not the answer. "I need to fix it."

"No," he repeated, laying down the law.

The problem was, I wasn't a little girl anymore. And this wasn't about me not believing that our backyard was too small for a pony. "I'm sorry, Dad. But I've made my decision."

His face pinked, eyes incredulous. Previously, on the

rare occasions he'd taken a hard stance, I'd buckled (or quietly gone about my business behind his back). But this time . . . I was not convinced. For once my father seemed old to me, unsure. More than that, this problem was mine, all mine.

"Please, trust me," I said.

"Ev, honey, you don't have to do this," said Dad, trying a different tack. "We can figure something out on our own."

"I know we could. But he's got lawyers on the job already. This is for the best."

"Won't you need your own lawyer?" he asked. There were new lines on his face, as if just this one day had aged him. Guilt slunk through me.

"I'll ask around, find someone suitable for you. I don't want you being taken advantage of here," he continued. "Someone must know a decent divorce lawyer."

"Dad, it's not like I have any money to protect. We're going to make this as straightforward as possible," I said with a forced smile. "It's okay. We'll take care of it, and then I'll be back."

"We? Honey, you barely know this guy. You cannot trust him."

"The whole world is apparently watching. What's the worst that can happen?" I sent a silent prayer to the heavens that I'd never find out the answer to that.

"This is a mistake . . ." Dad sighed. "I know you're as disappointed over the internship as I am. But we need to stop and think here."

"I have thought about it. I need to get this circus away from you and Mom."

Dad's gaze went to the darkened hallway heading toward where Mom lay in her drug-induced slumber. The last thing I wanted was for my father to feel torn between the two of us.

"It'll be okay," I said, willing it to be true. "Really."

He hung his head at last. "I think you're doing the wrong thing. But call me if you need anything. If you want to come home, I'll organize a flight for you right away."

I nodded.

"I'm serious. You call me if you need anything."

"Yes. I will." I wouldn't.

I picked up my backpack, still fresh from Vegas. No chance to refresh my wardrobe. All of my clothes were at the apartment. I smoothed back my hair, tucking it neatly behind my ears, trying to make myself look a little less like a train wreck.

"You were always my good girl," Dad said, sounding wistful.

I didn't know what to say.

He patted me on the arm. "Call me."

"Yeah," I said, my throat tight. "Say bye to Mom for me. I'll talk to you soon."

Sam stepped forward. "Your daughter is in safe hands, sir."

I didn't wait to hear Dad's reply. For the first time in hours I stepped outside. Pandemonium erupted. The instinct to turn tail, run, and hide was huge. But with Sam's big body beside me it wasn't quite so crazy frightening as before. He put an arm loosely around my shoulder and hustled me out of there, down the garden path, and toward the waiting crowd. Another man in a sharp black suit came toward us, making a way through the mob from the other side. The noise level skyrocketed. A woman yelled that she hated me and called me a cunt. Someone else wanted me to tell David that he loved him. Mostly, though, it was more questions. Cameras were shoved in my face, the flashbulbs glaring. Before I could stumble, Sam was there. My feet barely touched the ground as he and his friend hurried me into the waiting car. Not a limousine. Lauren would be disappointed. It was a fancy new sedan with an all-leather interior. The door slammed shut behind me and Sam and his friend climbed in. The driver nodded to me in the rearview mirror, then carefully accelerated. People banged on the windows and ran alongside. I huddled down in the middle of the seat. Soon we left them behind.

I was on my way back to David.

My husband.

CHAPTER FOUR

I slept on the short flight to LA, curled up in a super-comfortable chair in a corner of the private jet. It was a level of luxury above anything I'd ever imagined. If you had to turn your life upside down, you might as well enjoy the opulence while you were at it. Sam had offered me champagne and I'd politely declined. The idea of alcohol still turned me inside out. It was entirely possible I'd never drink again.

My career path had been temporarily shot to hell, but never mind, I had a new plan. Get divorced. It was breathtakingly simple. I loved it. I was back in control of my own destiny. One day, when I got married, if I got married, it would not be to a stranger in Vegas. It would not be a terrible mistake.

When I woke up, we were landing. Another sleek sedan stood waiting. I'd never been to LA. It looked every bit as wide-awake as Vegas, though less glam. Plenty of people were still out and about despite the hour of night.

I had to brave turning on my phone sometime. Lauren would be worried. I pushed the little black button and the screen flashed bright lights at me, coming to life. A hundred and fifty-eight text messages and ninety-seven missed calls. I blinked stupidly at the screen but the number didn't change. Holy hell. Apparently everyone I knew had heard the news, along with quite a few people I did not.

My phone pinged.

> Lauren: You okay? Where r u???
>
> Me: LA. Going to him till things calm down. You all right?
>
> Lauren: I'm fine. LA? Living the dream.
>
> Me: Private jet was amazing. Though his fans are crazy.
>
> Lauren: Your brother is crazy.
>
> Me: Sorry about that.
>
> Lauren: I can handle him. Whatever happens, do not break up the band!!!
>
> Me: Got it.
>
> Lauren: But break his heart. He wrote San Pedro after what's-her-face cheated on him. That album was BRILLIANT!
>
> Me: Promise to leave him a broken quivering mess.
>
> Lauren: That's the spirit.
>
> Me: xx

It was after three in the morning by the time we reached the massive 1920s-era Spanish-style mansion in Laurel Canyon. It was lovely. Though Dad would not have been impressed—he preferred clean, contemporary lines with minimal fuss. Four-bedroom, two-bathroom houses for Portland's well-to-do. But I don't know, there was something beautiful and romantic about such extravagance. The decorative black wrought iron against the bare white walls.

A gaggle of girls and the obligatory pack of press milled about outside. News of our marriage had apparently stirred things up. Or maybe they always camped here. Ornate iron gates swung slowly open at our approach. Palm trees lined the long, winding driveway, large fronds waving in the wind as we drove by. The place looked like something out of a movie. Stage Dive were big business, I knew that much. Their last two albums had spawned numerous hit songs. Lauren had driven all over the countryside last summer, attending three of their shows in the space of a week. All of them had been in stadiums.

Still, that was a damn big house.

Nerves wound me tight. I wore the same jeans and blue top I'd had on all day. Dressing for the occasion wasn't an option. The best I could do was finger-brush my hair and spray on some perfume I had in my handbag. I might be lacking in glamour, but at least I'd smell all right.

Every light in the house blazed bright, and rock music boomed out into the warm night air. The big double doors stood open, and people spilled out of the house and onto the steps. It seemed the party to end all others was taking place.

Sam opened the car door for me and I hesitantly climbed out.

"I'll walk you in, Ms. Thomas."

"Thank you," I said.

I didn't move. After a moment Sam got the message. He forged ahead and I followed. A couple of girls were making out just inside the door, mouths all over each other. They were both slender and beyond gorgeous, dressed in tiny, sparkly dresses that barely hit their thighs. More people milled about drinking and dancing. A chandelier hung overhead and a grand staircase wound around an interior wall. The place was a Hollywood palace.

Thankfully, no one seemed to notice me. I could gawk to my heart's content.

Sam stopped to talk to a young man slouched against

a wall, a bottle of beer to his lips. Long, blond hair stuck out every which way and his nose was pierced with a silver ring. Lots of tattoos. In ripped black jeans and a faded T-shirt, he had the same über-cool air as David. Maybe rock stars brought their clothes artfully aged. People with money were a pack apart.

The man gave me an obvious looking-over. I steadfastly resisted the urge to shrink back. Not happening. When he met my eyes, his gaze seemed curious but not unfriendly. The tension inside me eased.

"Hey," he said.

"Hi." I braved a smile.

"It's all good," he said to Sam. Then he tipped his chin at me. "Come on. He's out this way. I'm Mal."

"Hi," I said again, stupidly. "I'm Ev."

"Are you all right, Ms. Thomas?" asked Sam in a low voice.

"Yes, Sam. Thank you very much."

He gave me a polite nod and headed back the way we'd come. His broad shoulders and bald head soon disappeared among the crowd. Running after him and asking to be taken home wouldn't help, but my feet itched to do so. No, enough with the pity party. Time to pull up my big-girl panties and get on with things.

Hundreds of people had been packed into the place. The only thing in my experience that came close was my senior prom, and it paled significantly. None of the dresses here tonight compared. I could almost smell the money. Lauren was the dedicated celeb-watcher, but even I recognized a few of the faces. One of last year's Oscar winners and a lingerie model I'd seen on billboards back home. A teen pop queen who shouldn't have been swilling from a bottle of vodka, let alone sitting on the lap of a silver-haired member of . . . damn, what was that band's name?

Anyway.

I shut my mouth before someone noticed I had stars

in my eyes. Lauren would have loved all this. It was amazing.

When a woman who most closely resembled a half-dressed Amazonian goddess sideswiped me, Mal stopped and frowned after her. "Some people, no manners. Come on."

The sluggish beat of the music moved through me, re-awakening the dregs of my headache and putting a taint on the glitter. We weaved our way through a big room filled with plush velvet lounges and the people draped over them. Next came a space cluttered with guitars, amps, and other rock 'n' roll paraphernalia. Inside the house the air was smoky and humid, despite all the open windows and doors. My top clung beneath my arms. We moved outside onto the balcony, where a light breeze was blowing. I raised my face to it gratefully.

And there he was, leaning against a decorative iron railing. The strong lines of his face were in profile. Holy shit, how could I have forgotten? There was no explaining the full effect of David in real life. He fit in with the beautiful people just fine. He was one of them. I, on the other hand, belonged in the kitchen with the waitstaff.

My husband was busy talking to the leggy, enhanced-breasted brunette beside him. Perhaps he was a tit man and that's how we'd wound up wed. It was as good a guess as any. Dressed in only a teeny white bikini, the girl clung to him like she'd been surgically attached. Her hair was artfully messed in a way that suggested a minimum of two hours at a top-notch salon. She was beautiful and I hated her just a little. A trickle of sweat ran down my spine.

"Hey, Dave," Mal called out. "Company."

David turned, then saw me and frowned. In this light, his eyes looked dark and distinctly unhappy. "Ev."

"Hi."

Mal started to laugh. "That's about the only word I've

been able to get out of her. Seriously, man, does your wife even speak?"

"She speaks." His tone of voice made it obvious he wished I wouldn't, ever again. Or at least not within his hearing.

I didn't know what to say. Generally, I wasn't after universal love and acceptance. Open hostility, however, was still kind of new to me.

The brunette tittered and rubbed her bountiful boobs against David's arm as if she was marking him. Sadly for her, he didn't seem to notice. She gave me a foul look, red mouth puckered. Charming. Though the fact that she saw me as competition was a huge boost to my ego. I stood taller and looked my husband in the eye.

Big mistake.

David's dark hair had been tied back in a little ponytail with strands falling around his face. What should have reeked of scummy drug dealer worked on him. Of course it did. He could probably make a dirty back alleyway seem like the honeymoon suite. A gray T-shirt molded to his thick shoulders and faded blue jeans covered his long legs. His black army-style boots were crossed at the ankles, easy as you please, because he belonged here. I didn't.

"You mind finding her a room?" David asked his friend.

Mal snorted. "Do I look like your fucking butler? You'll show your own wife to a room. Don't be an asshole."

"She's not my wife," David growled.

"Every news channel in the country would disagree with you there." Mal ruffled my hair with a big hand, making me feel all of eight years old. "Check you later, child bride. Nice to meet you."

"Child bride?" I asked, feeling clueless.

Mal stopped and grinned. "You haven't heard what they're saying?"

I shook my head.

"Probably for the best." With a last laugh, he wandered off.

David disentangled himself from the brunette. Her plump lips pursed in displeasure, but he wasn't looking. "Come on."

He put his hand out to usher me on, and there, spread across the length of his forearm, was his tattoo:

Evelyn

I froze. Holy shit. The man sure had chosen a conspicuous place to put my name. I didn't know how I felt about that.

"What?" His brows drew down and his forehead wrinkled. "Ah, yeah. Come on."

"Hurry back, David," cooed Bikini Girl, primping her hair. I had nothing against bikinis. I owned several despite my mom believing I was too big boned for such things. (I'd never actually worn them, but that was beside the point.) No, what I minded were the sneers and snarly looks Bikini Girl shot me when she thought David wasn't looking.

Little did she know he didn't care.

With a hand to the small of my back, he ushered me through the party toward the stairs. People called out and women preened, but he never slowed. I got the distinct feeling he was embarrassed to be seen with me. Being with David, I sure caught some scrutiny. Any money, I didn't fit the bill of a rock star's wife. People stopped and stared. Someone called out, asking if he could introduce us. No comment from my husband as he hurried me through the crowd.

Hallways spread out in both directions up on the second floor. We went left, down to the end. He threw open a door and there my bag sat, waiting on a big king-size bed. Everything in the sumptuous room had been done in white: the bed, walls, and carpets. An antique white love seat sat in the corner. It was beautiful, pristine. Nothing like my small, cramped room back at the apartment I shared with Lauren, where between the double bed and my desk, you had just enough room to get the cupboard door open, no more. This place went on and on, a sea of perfection.

"I'd better not touch anything," I mumbled, hands tucked into my back pockets.

"What?"

"It's lovely."

David looked around the room with nil interest. "Yeah."

I wandered over to the windows. A luxurious pool sat below, well lit and surrounded by palm trees and perfect gardens. Two people were in the water, making out. The woman's head fell back and her breasts bobbed on the surface. Oh, no, my mistake. They were having sex. I could feel the heat creep up my neck. I didn't think I was a prude, but still. I turned away.

"Listen, some people are going to come to talk to you about the divorce papers. They'll be here at ten," he said, hovering in the doorway. His fingers tapped out a beat on the doorframe. He kept casting longing looks down the hall, clearly impatient to be gone.

"Some people?"

"My lawyer and my manager," he told his feet. "They're rushing things, so . . . it'll all be, ah, dealt with as fast as it can."

"All right."

David sucked in his cheeks and nodded. He had killer cheekbones. I'd seen men in fashion magazines that couldn't have compared. But pretty or not, the frown never lifted. Not while I was around. It would have been nice to see him smile, just once.

"You need anything?" he asked.

"No. Thank you for all this. For flying me down here and letting me stay. It's very kind of you."

"No worries." He took a step back and started closing the door after him. "Night."

"David, shouldn't we talk or something? About last night?"

He paused, half hidden behind the door. "Seriously, Ev. Why fucking bother?"

And he was gone.

Again.

No door slam this time. I counted that as a step forward in our relationship. Being surprised was stupid. But disappointment held me still, staring around the room, seeing nothing. It wasn't that I suddenly wanted him to fall at my feet. But antipathy sucked.

Eventually I wandered back over to the window. The lovers were gone, the pool now empty. Another couple stumbled along the lit garden path, beneath the huge swaying palm trees. They headed toward what had to be the pool house. The man was David, and Bikini Girl hung off him, swishing her long hair and swaying her hips, working it to the nth degree. They looked good together. They fit. David reached out and tugged on the tie of her bikini top, undoing the neat bow and baring her from the waist up. Bikini Girl laughed soundlessly, not bothering to cover herself.

I swallowed hard, trying to dislodge the rock in my throat. Jealousy felt every bit as bad as antipathy. And I had no damn right to be jealous.

At the door to the pool house, David paused and looked back over his shoulder. His eyes met mine. Oh, shit. I ducked behind the curtain and idiotically held my breath. Caught spying—the shame of it. When I checked a moment later, they were gone. Light peeked out from the sides of the curtains in the pool house. I should have brazened it out. I wished I had. It wasn't like I was doing anything wrong.

The immaculate grandeur of the white room spread out before me. Inside and out, I felt a mess. The reality of my situation had apparently sunk in, and what a clusterfuck it was. Lauren had been right on with the word choice.

"David can do what he wants." My voice echoed through the room, startlingly loud even over the thumping of the music downstairs. I straightened my shoulders. Tomorrow I would meet with his people and the divorce would be sorted. "David can do what he wants and so can I."

But what did I want to do? I had no idea. So I unpacked my few items of clothing, settling in for the night. I hung David's T-shirt over a towel rail to finish drying. It was probably going to be needed for sleepwear. Organizing myself took five minutes, max. You could refold a couple of tank tops only so many ways before you just looked pathetic.

What now?

I hadn't been invited to the party downstairs. No way did I want to think about what might be happening in the pool house. Doubtless David was giving Bikini Girl everything I'd wanted in Vegas. No sex for me. Instead, he had sent me to my room like a naughty child.

What a room it was. The adjoining bathroom had a tub larger than my bedroom back home. Plenty of space to splash around. It was tempting. But I never had been much good at getting sent to my room. On the few occasions it happened at home, I used to climb out the window and sit outside with a book. As rebellions went, it lacked a lot, but I'd been satisfied. There was a lot to be said for being a quiet achiever.

Screw staying in the room of splendor. I couldn't do it. No one noticed me as I crept back down the stairs.

I slunk into the closest corner and settled in to watch the beautiful people at play. It was fascinating. Bodies writhed on an impromptu dance floor in the middle of the room. Someone lit up a cigar nearby, filling the air with a rich, spicy scent. Puffs of smoke billowed up toward the ceiling, a good twenty feet above. Diamonds glittered and teeth sparkled, and that was just some of the men. Open opulence fought grunge among the mixed crowd. You couldn't get better people-watching if you tried. No sign of Mal, sadly. At least he'd been friendly.

"You're new," a voice said from beside me, startling the crap out of me. I jumped a mile, or at least a few inches.

A man in a black suit lounged against the wall, sipping a glass of amber liquor. This slick black suit was something else. In all likelihood Sam's had come off the rack, but not this one. I'd never understood the appeal of a suit and tie before, but this man wore them incredibly well. He looked to be about David's age and he had short dark hair. Handsome, of course. Like David, he had the whole divine cheekbones thing going on.

"You know, if you move another foot over you'll disappear entirely behind that palm." He took another sip of his drink. "Then no one would see you."

"I'll give it some thought." I didn't bother denying I was in hiding. Apparently it was already obvious to all.

He smiled, flashing a dimple. Tommy Byrnes had dimples. He'd inured me to their power. The man leaned closer, so as to be heard more easily over the music, most likely. The fact that he backed it up by taking a decent-sized step toward me seemed unnecessary. Personal space was a wonderful thing. Something about this guy gave me the creeps, despite the swanky suit.

"I'm Jimmy."

"Ev."

He pursed his lips, staring at me. "Nope, I definitely don't know you. Why don't I know you?"

"You know everyone else?" I surveyed the room, highly dubious. "There are a lot of people here."

"There are," he agreed. "And I know them all. Everyone except you."

"David invited me." I didn't want to drop David's name, but I was being pushed into a corner, figuratively and literally as Jimmy closed in on me.

"Did he now?" His eyes looked wrong, the pupils pinpricks. Something was up with this guy. He stared down at the small amount of cleavage I had on display like he intended to plant his face there.

"Yeah. He did."

Jimmy didn't exactly seem pleased by the news. He threw back his drink, finishing it off in one large mouthful. "So, David invited you to the party."

"He invited me to stay for a few days," I said, which was not a lie. Happily, hopefully, he had somehow missed the news about David and me. Or maybe he was just too stoned to put two and two together. Either way, I wasn't filling him in.

"Really? That was nice of him."

"Yes, it was."

"What room did he put you in?" He stood in front of me and dropped his empty glass into the potted plant with a careless hand. His grin looked manic. My need to get away from him gained immediate urgency.

"The white one," I said, looking for a way around him. "Speaking of which, I'd better get back."

"The white room? My, my, aren't you special."

"Aren't I just? Excuse me." I pushed past him, giving up on social niceties.

He mustn't have expected it because he stumbled back a step. "Hey. Hold up."

"Jimmy." David appeared, earning my instant gratitude. "There a problem here?"

"Not at all," said Jimmy. "Just getting to know . . . Ev."

"Yeah, well, you don't need to know . . . Ev."

The guy's smile was expansive. "Come on. You know how I like pretty new things."

"Let's go," David said to me.

"It's not like you to cockblock, Davie," said Jimmy. "Didn't I see the lovely Kaetrin with you earlier out on the balcony? Why don't you go find her, get her to do what she's so damn good at? Me and Ev are busy here."

"Actually, no, we're not," I said. And why was David back so soon from his playtime with Bikini Girl? He couldn't possibly have been concerned about his little wife's well-being, surely.

Neither of them appeared to have heard me.

"So you invited her to stay in my house," said Jimmy.

"I was under the impression Adrian rented the place for all of us while we're working on the album. Something changed I don't know about?"

Jimmy laughed. "I like the place. Decided to buy it."

"Great. Let me know when the deal's going through and I'll be sure to get out. In the meantime, my guests are none of your business."

Jimmy looked at me, face alight with malicious glee. "It's her, isn't it? The one you married, you stupid son of a bitch."

"Come on." David grabbed my hand and dragged me toward the staircase. His jaw was clenched tight enough to make a muscle pop out on the side.

"I could have had her against a wall at a fucking party and you married her?"

Bullshit he could have.

David's fingers squeezed my hand tight.

Jimmy chortled like the cretin he was. "She is nothing, you sorry fuck. Look at her. Just look at her. Tell me this marriage didn't come courtesy of vodka and cocaine."

It wasn't anything I hadn't heard before. Well, apart from the marriage reference. But his words still bit.

Before I could tell Jimmy what I thought of him, how-ever, the iron-hard hold on my hand disappeared. David charged back to him, grabbing hold of his lapels. They were pretty evenly matched. Both were tall, well built. Neither looked ready to back down. The room hushed, all conversation stopping, though the music thumped on.

"Go for it, little brother," hissed Jimmy. "Show me who the star of this show really is."

David's shoulders went rigid beneath the thin cotton of his T-shirt. Then with a snarl he released Jimmy, shoving him back a step. "You're as bad as Mom. Look at you, you're a fucking mess."

I stared at the two of them, stunned. These two were the brothers in the band. Same dark hair and handsome faces. I clearly hadn't married into the happiest of fami-lies. Jimmy looked almost shamefaced.

My husband marched back past me, collecting my arm along the way. Every eye was on us. An elegant brunette took a step forward, hand outstretched. Distress lined her lovely face. "You know he doesn't mean it."

"Stay out of it, Martha," said my husband, not slowing down at all.

The woman shot me a look of distaste. Worse yet, of blame. With the way David was acting, I had a bad feel-ing that was going around.

Up the steps he dragged me, then down the hallway toward my room. We said nothing. Maybe this time he'd lock me in. Jam a chair under the door handle, perhaps. I could understand him being mad at Jimmy. That guy was a dick of epic proportions. But what had I done? Apart from escaping my plush prison, of course.

Halfway along the long hallway I liberated my limb from his tender care. I had to do something before he cut off the blood supply to my fingers.

"I know the way," I said.

"Still wanna get some, huh? You should have said

something, I'd be more than happy to oblige," he said with a false smile. "And hey, you're not even shit-faced tonight. Chances are you'd remember."

"Ouch."

"Something I said untrue?"

"No. But I still think it's fair to say you're being an ass."

He stopped dead and looked at me, eyes wide, startled, if anything. "I'm being an ass? Fucking hell, you're my wife!"

"No, I'm not. You said so yourself. Right before you went off to play in the pool house with your friend," I said. Though he hadn't stayed long in the pool house, obviously. Five, six minutes maybe? I almost felt bad for Bikini Girl. That wasn't service with a smile.

Dark brows descended like thunderclouds. He was less than impressed. Bad luck. My feelings toward him were likewise at an all-time low.

"You're right. My bad. Should I take you back to my brother?" he asked, cracking his knuckles like a Neanderthal and staring back down the hallway from where we'd come.

"No, thank you."

"That was real nice, making fuck-me eyes at him, by the way. Out of everyone down there, you had to be flirting with Jimmy," he sneered. "Classy, Ev."

"That's honestly what you think was happening?"

"What with you and him getting all fucking cozy in the corner?"

"Seriously?"

"I know Jimmy and I know girls around Jimmy. That's definitely what it looked like, baby." He held his arms out wide. "Prove me wrong."

I wasn't even certain I knew how to make fuck-me eyes. But I definitely hadn't been making them at that tool downstairs. No wonder so many marriages ended in divorce. Marriage sucked and husbands were the worst. My shoulders were caving in on me. I didn't think I'd ever felt so small.

"I think your brother issues might be even worse than your wife issues, and that's saying something." Slowly, I shook my head. "Thank you for offering me the opportunity to defend myself. I really appreciate it. But you know what, David? I'm just not convinced your good opinion is worth it."

He flinched.

I walked away before I said something worse. Forget anything amicable. The sooner we were divorced, the better.

CHAPTER FIVE

Sunlight poured in through the windows when I woke the next morning. Someone was hammering on the door, turning the handle, trying to get in. I'd locked it after the scene with David last night. Just in case he was tempted to return to trade some more insults with me. It had taken me hours to get to sleep with the music thrumming through the floor and my emotions running wild. But exhaustion won out in the end.

"Evelyn! Hello?" a female voice yelled from out in the hallway. "Are you in there?" I crawled across the ginormous bed, tugging on the hem of David's T-shirt. Whatever he'd used to wash it in Vegas, it didn't smell of puke. The man had laundry skills. Fortunate for me, because apart from my dirty party dress and a couple of tops, I had nothing else to wear

"Who is it?" I asked, yawning loudly.

"Martha. I'm David's PA."

I cracked open the door and peered out. The elegant brunette from last night stared back at me, unimpressed. From being made to wait or the sight of my bed hair, I didn't know. Did everyone in this house look like they'd just slunk off the cover of *Vogue*? Her eyes turned into slits at the sight of David's shirt.

"His representatives are here to meet with you. You might want to get your ass into gear." The woman spun on her heel and strode off down the hallway, heels clacking furiously against the terra-cotta tiled floor.

"Thanks."

She didn't acknowledge me, but, then, I didn't expect her to. This part of LA was clearly a colony for ill-mannered douches. I rushed through a shower, pulled on my jeans and a clean T-shirt. It was the best I could do.

The house stayed silent as I rushed down the hallway. There were no signs of life on the second level. I'd slapped on a little mascara, tied my wet hair back in a ponytail, but that was it. I could either hold people up or go without makeup. Politeness won. If coffee had been in the offering, however, I'd have left David's representatives hanging for at least two cups. Running on zero caffeine seemed suicidal given the stressful circumstances. I hurried down the stairs.

"Ms. Thomas," a man called, stepping out of a room to the left. He wore jeans and a white polo shirt. Around his neck hung a thick, gold chain. So who was this? Another of David's entourage?

"Sorry I'm late."

"It's fine." He smiled, but I didn't quite believe him despite the big white teeth. Nature had clearly played no part in his teeth or tan. "I'm Adrian."

"Ev. Hello."

He swept me into the room. Three men in suits sat waiting at an impressively long dining table. Overhead, another crystal chandelier sparkled in the morning light. On the walls were beautiful, colorful paintings. Originals, obviously.

"Gentlemen, this is Ms. Thomas," Adrian announced. "Scott Baker, Bill Preston, and Ted Vaughan are David's legal representatives. Why don't you sit here, Ev?"

Adrian spoke slowly, as if I were a feeble-minded child.

He pulled a chair out from the table for me directly opposite the team of legal eagles, then walked around to sit on their side. Wow, that sure told me. The lines had been drawn.

I rubbed my sweaty palms on the sides of my jeans and sat up straight, doing my best not to wilt beneath their hostile gazes. I could definitely do this. How hard could it be to get a divorce, after all?

"Ms. Thomas," the one Adrian had identified as Ted started. He pushed a black leather folder full of papers toward me. "Mr. Ferris asked us to draw up annulment papers. They'll cover all issues, including details of your settlement from Mr. Ferris."

The size of the stack of papers before me was daunting. These people worked fast. "My settlement?"

"Yes," Ted said. "Rest assured Mr. Ferris has been very generous."

I shook my head in confusion. "I'm sorry. Wha—"

"We'll deal with that last," Ted rushed on. "You'll notice here that the document covers all conditions to be met by yourself. The main issues include your not speaking to any member of the press with regard to this matter. This is nonnegotiable, I'm afraid. This condition remains in force until your death. Do you fully understand the requirement, Ms. Thomas? Under no circumstances may you talk to any member of the press regarding Mr. Ferris in any way while you're alive."

"So I can talk to them after I die?" I asked with a weak little laugh. Ted was getting on my nerves. I guess I hadn't gotten enough sleep after all.

Ted showed me his teeth. They weren't quite as impressive as Adrian's. "This is a very serious matter, Ms. Thomas."

"Ev," I said. "My name is Ev and I do realize the seriousness of this issue, Ted. I apologize for being flippant. But if we could get back to the part about the settlement? I'm a little confused."

"Very well." Ted looked down his nose at me and tapped a thick, gold pen on the paperwork in front of me. "As I said, Mr. Ferris has been very generous."

"No," I said, not looking at the papers, "you don't understand."

Ted cleared his throat and looked down at me over the top of his glasses. "It would be unwise of you to try and press for more given the circumstances, Ms. Thomas. A six-hour marriage in Las Vegas entered into while you were both heavily under the influence of alcohol? Textbook grounds for annulment."

Ted's cronies tittered and I felt my face fire up. My need to accidentally kick the prick under the table grew and grew.

"My client will not be making another offer."

"I don't want him to make another offer," I said, my voice rising.

"The annulment will go ahead, Ms. Thomas," said Ted. "There is no question of that. There will be no reconciliation."

"No, that's not what I meant."

Ted sighed. "We need to finalize this today, Ms. Thomas."

"I'm not trying to hold anything up, Ted."

The other two lawyers watched me with distaste, backing up Ted with sleazy, knowing smiles. Nothing pissed me off faster than a bunch of people trying to intimidate someone. Bullies had made my life hell back in high school. And really, that's all these people were.

Adrian gave me a big-toothed, faux-fatherly grin. "I'm sure Ev can see how kind David's being. There are not going to be any delays here, are there?"

These people, they blew my mind. Speaking of which, I had to wonder where my darling husband was. Too busy banging bikini models to turn up to his own divorce, the poor guy. I pushed back my fringe, trying to figure out the right thing to say. Trying to get my anger managed. "Wait—"

"We all just want what's best for you given the unfortunate situation," Adrian continued, obviously lying through his big, bright teeth.

"Great," I said, fingers fidgeting beneath the table. "That's . . . that's really great of you."

"Please, Ms. Thomas." Ted tapped his pen imperiously alongside a figure on the paperwork and I dutifully looked, though I didn't want to. There were lots of zeros. I mean, really a lot. It was insane. In two lifetimes I couldn't earn that kind of money. David must have wanted me gone something fierce. My stomach rumbled nervously but my puking days were over. The whole scene felt horrific, like something out of a bad B movie or soap opera. Girl from the wrong side of the tracks hijacks hot, rich guy and tricks him into marriage. Now all that was left was for him to use his people to chase me off into the sunset.

Well, he won.

"This was all just a mistake," said Adrian. "I'm sure Ev is every bit as keen to put it behind her as David is. And with this generous financial settlement she can move forward to a bright future."

"You'll also never attempt to make contact with Mr. Ferris ever again, in any manner. Any attempt on your part to do so will see you in breach of contract." Ted withdrew his pen, sitting back in his seat with a false smile and his hands crossed over his belly. "Is that clear?"

"No," I said, scrubbing my face with my hands. They actually thought I'd fall over myself to get at that money. Money I'd done nothing to earn, no matter how tempting accepting it was. Of course, they also thought I'd sell my story to the press and harass David every spare moment I got for the rest of my life. They thought I was cheap, trashy scum. "I think I can honestly say that nothing about this is clear."

"Ev, please." Adrian gave me a disappointed look. "Let's be reasonable."

"I'll tell you what . . ." I stood and retrieved the ring from my jeans pocket, throwing it onto the sea of paperwork. "You give this back to David and tell him I don't want any of it. None of this." I gestured at them, the table, the papers, and the entire damn house. The lawyers looked nervously among themselves as if they'd need more paperwork before they could allow me to go waving my arms about in such a disorderly fashion.

"Ev . . ."

"I don't want to sell his story, or stalk him, or whatever else you have buried in subclause 98.2. I don't want his money."

Adrian coughed out a laugh. Fuck him. The phony bastard could think what he liked.

Ted frowned at my big sparkly ring lying innocently among the mess. "Mr. Ferris didn't mention a ring."

"No? Well. Why don't you tell Mr. Ferris he can shove it wherever he feels it might best fit, Ted."

"Ms. Thomas!" Ted stood, his puffy face outraged. "That is unnecessary."

"Going to have to disagree with you there, Ted." I bolted out of the dining room of death and made straight for the front door as fast as my feet could carry me. Immediate escape was the only answer. If I could just get the hell away from them long enough to catch my breath, I could come up with a new plan to deal with this ridiculous situation. I'd be fine.

A brand new-black Jeep pulled up as I tore down the front steps.

The window lowered to show my guide from last night, Mal, sitting in the driver's seat. He smirked from behind black sunglasses. "Hey there, child bride."

I flipped him the finger and jogged down the long, winding driveway toward the front gates. Toward liberty and freedom and my old life, or whatever remained of it. If only I'd never gone to Vegas. If only I'd tried harder to convince Lauren that a party at home would be fine, none of this would have happened. God, I was such an idiot. Why had I drunk so much?

"Ev. Hold up." Mal pulled up alongside me in his Jeep. "What's wrong? Where're you going?"

I didn't answer. I was done with all of them. That and I had the worst feeling I was about to cry, damn it. My eyes felt hot, horrible.

"Stop." He pulled the brake and climbed out of the Jeep, running after me. "Hey, I'm sorry."

I said nothing. I had nothing to say to any of them.

His hand wrapped around my arm gently, but I didn't care. I swung at him. I'd never hit anyone in my life. Apparently, I wasn't about to start now. He dodged my flying fist with ease.

"Whoa! Okay." Mal danced back a step, giving me a wary look over the top of his shades. "You're mad. I get it."

Hands on hips, he looked back toward the house. Ted and Adrian stood on the front steps, staring after us. Even from this distance the dynamic duo did not appear happy. Evil bastards.

Mal hissed out a breath. "You're fucking joking. He sicced that ball sucker Ted onto you?"

I nodded, blinking, trying to get myself under control.

"Did you have anyone with you?" he asked.

"No."

He cocked his head. "Are you going to cry?"

"No!"

"Fuck. Come on." He held out his hand to me and I stared at in disbelief. "Ev, think. There're photographers and shit waiting out front. Even if you get past them, where are you going to go?"

He was right. I had to go back, get my bag. So stupid

of me not to have thought of it. Just as soon as I had myself under control I'd go in and retrieve it, then get the hell out of here. I fanned my face with my hands, took a big breath. All good.

Meanwhile, his hand hovered, waiting. There were a couple of small blisters on it, situated in the join between thumb and finger. Curious.

"Are you the drummer?" I asked with a sniff.

For some reason he cracked up laughing, almost doubling over, clutching at his belly. Maybe he was on drugs or something. Or maybe he was just one more lunatic in this gigantic asylum. Batman would have had a hard time keeping this place in check.

"What is your problem?" I asked, taking a step away from him. Just in case.

His snazzy sunglasses fell off, clattering on the asphalt. He swiped them up and shoved them back on his face. "Nothing. Nothing at all. Let's get out of here. I've got a house at the beach. We'll hide out there. Come on, it'll be fun."

I hesitated, giving the jerks on the front steps a lethal look. "Why would you help me?"

"Because you're worth helping."

"Oh, really? Why would you think that?"

"You wouldn't like my answer."

"I haven't liked a single answer I've had all morning, why stop now?"

He smiled. "Fair enough. I'm David's oldest friend. We've gotten drunk and out of control more times than I can remember. He's had girls angling to snare him for years, even before we had money. He never was the slightest bit interested in marriage. It was never even on his radar before. So the fact that he married you, well, that suggests to me you're worth helping. Come on, Ev. Stop worrying."

Easy for him to say, his life hadn't been skewered by a rock star.

"I need to get my stuff."

"And get cornered by them? Worry about it later." He held his hand out, fingers beckoning for mine. "Let's get out of here."

I put my hand in his and we went.

CHAPTER SIX

"So, hang on, this song isn't about his dog dying or something?"

"You're not funny." I laughed.

"I so am." Mal sniggered at the opposite end of the couch as Tim McGraw let rip about his kind of rain on the flat-screen TV taking up the opposite wall. "Why do they all wear such big hats, do you think? I have a theory."

"Shush."

The way these people lived blew my tiny little mind. Mal, short for Malcolm, lived in a place at the beach that was mostly a three-story architectural feat of steel and glass. It was amazing. Not ridiculously huge like the place in the hills, but awe-inspiring just the same. My dad would have been in raptures over the minimalism of it, the cleanliness of the lines, or some such. I just appreciated having a friend in my time of need.

Mal's house was clearly a bachelor pad–slash–den of iniquity. I'd had a vague notion to make lunch to thank him for taking me in, but there wasn't a single speck of food in the house. Beer filled the fridge and vodka the freezer. Oh, no, there was a bag of oranges used as wedges to go with shots of vodka, apparently. He'd ruled out touching those. His super-slick coffee machine, however, made everything right. He even had decent beans. I wowed him by busting out a few of my barista moves. After drinking three cups in the space of an hour, I felt a lot more like my old well-planned, caffeinated self.

Mal dialed for pizza and we watched TV late into the night. Mostly he found his joy in mocking my taste in pretty much everything: movies, music, the lot. At least he did it good-naturedly. We couldn't go outside because a couple of photographers were waiting on the beach. I felt bad about it but he'd just shrugged it off.

"What about this song?" he asked. "You like this?"

Miranda Lambert strode on screen in a cool '50s frock and I grinned. "Miranda is mighty."

"I've met her."

I sat up straight. "Really?"

More sniggering from Mal. "You're impressed I've met Miranda Lambert but you didn't even know who I was. Honestly, woman, you are hard on the ego."

"I saw the gold and platinum records lining the hall-way, buddy. I'm thinking you can take it."

He snorted.

"You know, you remind me a lot of my brother." I al-most managed to duck the bottle cap he flicked at me. It bounced off my forehead. "What was that for?"

"Can't you at least pretend to worship me?"

"No. Sorry."

With total disregard for my Lambert love, Mal started surfing the channels. Home shopping, football, *Gone with the Wind,* and me. Me on TV.

"Wait," I said.

He groaned. "Not a good idea."

First my school pictures paraded past, followed by one of Lauren and me at our senior prom. They even had a reporter standing across the road from Ruby's, prattling on about my life before being elevated to the almighty status of David's wife. And then there was the man himself in some concert footage, guitar in his hands as he sang backup. The lyrics were your typical my-woman-is-mean, "She's my one and only, she's got me on my knees . . ." I wondered if he'd write songs about me. If so, odds were they'd be highly uncomplimentary. "Shit." I hugged a couch cushion tight to my chest.

Mal leaned over and fluffed my hair. "David's the favorite, darlin'. He's pretty, plays guitar, and writes the songs. Girlies faint when he walks by. Team that with your being a young 'un and you've got the news of the week."

"I'm twenty-one."

"And he's twenty-six. It's enough of a difference if they hype it just right." Mal sighed. "Face it, child bride. You got married in Vegas by an Elvis impersonator to one of rock 'n' roll's favorite sons. It was always bound to cause a shitstorm. Given there's also been some crap going on with the band lately . . . what with Jimmy partying like it's 1999 and Dave losing his music-writing mojo. Well, you get the picture. But next week, someone else will do something wacky and all the attention will move on."

"I guess so."

"I know so. People are constantly fucking up. It's a glorious thing." He sat back with his hands behind his head. "Go on, smile for Uncle Mal. You know you want to."

I smiled halfheartedly.

"That's a bullshit smile and I'm ashamed of you. You're not going to fool anyone with that. Try again."

I tried harder, smiling till my cheeks hurt.

"Damn. Now you just look like you're in pain."

Banging on the front door interrupted our merriment.

Mal raised his brows at me. "Wondered how long he'd take."

"What?" I trailed him to the front door, lurking behind a divider just in case it was more press.

He opened the door and David charged in, face tight and furious. "You piece of shit. You better not have touched her. Where is she?"

"The child bride is otherwise occupied." Mal cocked his head, taking David in with a cool glance. "Why the fuck do you even care?"

"Don't start with me. Where is she?"

Quietly, Mal shut the door, facing off against his friend. I hesitated, hanging back. All right, so I skulked in a cowardly fashion. Whatever.

Mal crossed his arms. "You left her to face Adrian and three lawyers on her own. You, my friend, are most definitely the piece of shit in this particular scenario."

"I didn't know Adrian would go at her with all that."

"You didn't want to know," said Mal. "Lie to everyone else out there, Dave. Not me. And sure as fuck not to yourself."

"Back off."

"You need some serious life advice, friend."

"Who are you, Oprah?"

Coughing out a laugh, Mal slumped against the wall. "Hell, yeah. Soon I'm gonna be giving out cars, so stick around."

"What did she say?"

"Who, Oprah?"

David just scowled at him. He didn't even notice me spying. Sad to say, even a scowling David was a thing of rare beauty. He did things to me. Complicated things. My heart tripped about in my chest. The anger and emotion in his voice couldn't be concern for me. That made no sense, not after last night and this morning. I had to be projecting, and it sucked that I even wanted him to care. My head made no sense. Getting away from this guy was the safest option all round.

"Dave, she was so upset she took a swing at me."

"Bullshit."

"I kid you not. She was nearly in tears when I found her," said Mal.

I banged my forehead in silent agony against the wall. Why the hell did Mal have to tell him that?

My husband hung his head. "I didn't mean for that to happen."

"Seems you didn't mean for a shitload to happen." Mal shook his head and tutted. "Did you even mean to marry her, dude? Seriously?"

David's face screwed up, his brow doing the wrinkly James Dean thing again. "I don't know anymore, okay? Fuck. I went to Vegas because I was so sick of all this shit, and I met her. She was different. She seemed different that night. I just . . . I wanted something outside of all this fucking idiocy for a change."

"Poor Davey. Did being a rock god get old?"

"Where is she?"

"I feel your manpain, bro. Really, I do. I mean, all you wanted was a girl who wouldn't kiss your ass for once and now you're pissed at her for the same damn reason. It's complicated, right?"

"Fuck you. Leave it alone, Mal. It's done." My husband huffed out a breath. "Anyway, she's the one who wanted the fucking divorce. Why aren't you giving her the third degree, huh?"

With a dramatic sigh, Mal flung out his arms. "Because she's really busy hiding around the corner, listening. I can't disturb her now."

David's body stilled and his blue eyes found me. "Evelyn."

Huh. Busted.

I stepped away from the wall and tried to put on a happy face. It didn't work. "Hi."

"She says that so well." Mal turned to me and winked. "So did you really ask the mighty David Ferris for a divorce?"

"She threw up on me when I told her we were married," my husband reported.

"What?" Mal dissolved into laughter, tears leaking from his eyes. "Are you serious? Fucking hell, that is fantastic. Oh, man, I wish I'd been there."

I gave David what I hoped to be the meanest look in all of time and space. He stared back, unimpressed.

"It was the floor," I clarified. "I didn't throw up on him."

"That time," said David.

"Please keep going," said Mal, laughing harder than ever. "This just gets better and better."

David didn't. Thank God.

"Seriously, I fucking love your wife, man. She's awesome. Can I have her?"

The look I got from David spoke of a much more reluctant affection. With the line between his brows, it was closer to outright irritation. I blew him a kiss. He looked away, hands fisted like he was barely holding himself back from throttling me. The feeling was entirely mutual.

Ah, marital bliss.

"You two are just the best." A chiming sound came from Mal's pocket and he pulled out a cell phone. Whatever he saw on the screen stopped his laughter dead. "You know, you should take her to your house, Dave."

"I don't think that's a good idea." David's mouth pulled wide in a truly pained expression.

I didn't think it was a good idea either. I'd happily go through life without setting foot inside the house of horrors ever again. Maybe if I asked Mal nicely he'd fetch my stuff for me. Imposing on him further didn't appeal, but I was running low on options.

"Whoa." With a grim face, Mal shoved his cell at David.

"Fuck," David mumbled. He wrapped his hand around the back of his neck and squeezed. The worried glance he gave me from beneath his dark brows set every alarm ringing inside my head. Whatever was on that screen was bad.

Really bad.

"What is it?" I asked.

"Oh, you, ah . . . you don't need to worry about it." His gaze dropped to the phone again, then he passed it back to Mal. "My place would be cool, actually. We should do that. Fun. Yeah."

"No." For David to be so nice to me it had to be something truly bad. I held out my hand, fingers twitching from impatience or nerves or a bit of both. "Show me."

After a reluctant nod from David, Mal handed it over.

There could be no doubting what it was, even on the small screen. There was a lot of skin on account of my being bare from the waist down. My naked butt sat front and center in all its pale, dimpled glory. God, it looked huge. Had they used a wide-lens camera or something? The party dress had been pushed up and I stood, bent over a table while a tattoo artist worked hard inking my rear. My panties had been cinched down, barely covering the basics. Shit. Talk about a compromising position. Taking part in a porn shoot was definitely not part of the plan.

At the other end of the frame, our faces were close together and David was smiling. Huh. So that was what he looked like when he smiled.

I remembered it then, the buzz of the needle, and him talking to me, holding my hands. At first, that needle had stung. "You were pretending to bite my fingers. The tattoo artist got mad at us for messing around."

David tipped his chin. "Yeah. You were s'posed to be keeping still."

I nodded, trying to remember more but coming up empty.

People would see this picture. People had seen this. People I knew and strangers both. Anyone and everyone.

My head spun woozily, the same as it had then. Only alcohol wasn't at fault this time.

"How did they get it?" I asked, my voice wavering and my heart at my toes. Or maybe that was just what remained of my tattered dignity.

David gave me sad eyes. "I don't know. We were in a private room. This should never have happened, but people get offered a lot of money for this sort of thing."

I nodded and handed Mal back his phone. My hand shook. "Right. Well . . ."

They both just looked at me, faces tense, waiting for me to burst into tears or something. Not happening.

"It's okay," I said, doing my best to believe it.

"Sure," said Mal.

David shoved his hands into his pockets. "It's not even that clear a picture."

"No, it's not," I agreed. The pity in his eyes was more than I could take. "Excuse me a minute."

Fortunately, the closest bathroom was only a short dash away. I locked the door and sat on the edge of the Jacuzzi, trying to slow my breathing, trying to be calm. There was nothing I could do. The picture was already out there. This was no death and dismemberment. It was a stupid picture of me in a compromising position showing more skin than I liked. But so what? Big deal. Accept it and move on. Despite the fact that everyone I knew would likely see it. Worse things had happened in the history of the world. I just needed to put it in context and stay calm.

"Ev?" David tapped lightly on the door. "Are you okay?"

"Yep." No. Not really.

"Let me in?"

I gave the door a pained look.

"Please."

Slowly, I stood and flicked the lock. David wandered in and shut the door behind him. No ponytail today. His dark hair hung down, framing his face. He had three small silver earrings in one ear playing peekaboo behind his hair. I stared at them because meeting his eyes was out of the question. I was not going to cry. Not about this. What the hell was even wrong with my eyes lately? Letting him in had been dumb.

With a heavy frown he stared down at me. "I'm sorry."

"It's not your fault."

"Yeah, it is. I should have looked after you better."

"No, David." I swallowed hard. "We were both drunk. God, this is all so horrifically, embarrassingly stupid."

He just stared at me.

"Sorry."

"Hey, you're allowed to be upset. That was a private moment. It shouldn't be out there."

"No," I agreed. "I . . . actually, I'd like to be alone for a minute."

He made a growly noise and suddenly his arms wrapped around me, pulling me in against him. He caught me off guard and I stumbled, my nose bumping into his chest. It hurt. But he smelled good. Clean, male, and good. Familiar. Some part of me remembered being this close to him and it was comforting. Something in my mind said "safe." But I couldn't remember how or why.

A hand moved restlessly over my back.

"I'm sorry," he said, "so fucking sorry."

The kindness was too much. Stupid tears flowed. "I'd hardly even shown anyone my ass and now it's all over the Internet."

"I know, baby."

He rested his head against the top of mine, holding on tight as I blubbered into his T-shirt. Having someone to hold on to helped. It would be okay. Deep down I knew it would be. But right then I couldn't see my way clear. Standing there with his arms around me felt right.

I don't know when we started swaying. David rocked

me gently from side to side as if we were dancing to some slow song. The overwhelming temptation to stay like that with my face pressed into his shirt was what made me step back, pull myself together. His hands sat lightly on my hips, the connection not quite broken.

"Thanks," I said.

"S'okay." The front of his shirt had a damp patch, thanks to me.

"Your shirt's all wet."

He shrugged.

I ugly-cried. It was a gift of mine. The mirror confirmed it, demon-red eyes and flushed fluoro-pink cheeks. With an awkward smile I stepped away from him, and his hands fell back to his sides. I splashed my face with water and dried it on a towel while he stood idly by, frowning.

"Let's go for a drive," he said.

"Really?" I gave him a dubious look. David and me alone? Given the marriage situation and our previous sober encounters, it didn't seem the wisest plan.

"Yeah." He rubbed his hands together, getting all enthused. "Just you and me. We'll get out of here for a while."

"David, like you said out there, I don't think that's a good idea."

"You want to stay in LA?" he scoffed.

"Look, you've been really sweet since you stepped through that door. Well, apart from telling Mal about me puking on you. That was unnecessary. But in the preceding twenty-four hours you dumped me alone in a room, went off with a groupie, accused me of trying to get it on with your brother, and sicced your posse of lawyers onto me."

He said nothing.

"Not that you going off with a groupie is any of my business. Of course."

He turned on his heel and paced to the other end of the bathroom, his movements tight, angry. Despite it being five times the size of the one back home, it still didn't leave enough room for a showdown like this. And he was between me and the door. Because suddenly exiting seemed a smart move.

"I just asked them to sort out the paperwork," he said.

"And they sure did." I put my hands on my hips, standing my ground. "I don't want any of your money."

"I heard." His face was carefully blank. My statement prompted in him none of the disbelief or mockery it had in the suited bullies. Lucky for him. I doubt he believed me, but at least he was willing to pretend. "They're drawing up new papers."

"Good." I stared him down. "You don't have to pay me off. Don't make assumptions like that. If you want to know something, ask. And I was never going to sell the story to the press. I wouldn't do that."

"Okay." He slumped against the wall, leaning his head back to stare up at nothing. "Sorry," he told the ceiling. I'm sure the plasterwork appreciated it immensely.

When I made no response, his gaze eventually found me. It had to be wrong, or at the very least immoral, to be so pretty. Normal people didn't stand a chance. My heart took a dive every time I looked at him. No, a dive didn't cover it. It plummeted.

Where was Lauren to tell me I was being melodramatic when I needed her most?

"I'm sorry, Ev," he repeated. "I know the last twenty-four hours have been shit. Offering to get out of here for a while was my way of trying to make things better."

"Thank you," I said. "And also for coming in here to check on me."

"No problem." He stared at me, eyes unguarded for once. And the honesty in his gaze changed things for me, the brief flash of something more. Sadness or loneliness,

I don't know. A kind of weariness that was there and gone before I could understand. But it left its mark. There was a lot more to this man than a pretty face and a big name. I needed to remember that and not make my own assumptions.

"You really want to go?" I asked. "Really?"

His eyes were bright with amusement. "Why not?"

I gave him a cautious smile.

"We can talk over whatever we need to, just you and me. I need to make a couple of calls, then we'll head off, okay?"

"Thank you. I'd like that."

With a parting nod he opened the door and strode back out. He and Mal talked quietly about something in the lounge room. I took the opportunity to wash my face once more and finger-brush my hair for luck. The time had come to take control. Actually, it was well overdue. What was I doing, bouncing from one disaster to the next? That wasn't me. I liked being in control, having a plan. Time to stop worrying about what I couldn't change and take decisive action on what I could. I had money saved up. One of these days my poor old car would die and I'd been planning accordingly. Because once winter hit, and things turned cold, gray, and wet, walking wouldn't always appeal. The thought of using my savings didn't fill me with glee, but emergency measures and all that.

David's lawyers would draw up papers minus the money and I would sign them. No point worrying about that side of things. However, getting out of the public eye for a couple of weeks was well within my capabilities. I just needed to stop and think for a change instead of reacting. I was a big girl and I could take care of myself. The time had come to prove it. I'd go for the drive with him, sort out the basics, and get gone, first on a hideaway holiday, and then back to my very ordinary, well-ordered life devoid of any rock-star interventions.

Yes.

"Give me the keys to the Jeep," said David, squaring off against Mal in the lounge.

Mal winced. "I was joking about giving away cars."

"Come on. Quit bitching. I rode over on the bike and I don't have a helmet for her."

"Fine." With a sour face, Mal dropped his car keys into David's outstretched hand. "But only 'cause I like your wife. Not a scratch, you hear me?"

"Yeah, yeah." David turned and saw me. A hint of a smile curled his lips.

Except for that first day on the bathroom floor, I'd never seen him smile, never even seen him come close. This bare trace of one made me light up inside. My knees wobbled. That couldn't be normal. I shouldn't be feeling all warm and happy just because he was. I couldn't afford to have any feelings for him at all. Not if I wanted to get out of this in one piece.

"Thanks for putting up with me today, Mal," I said.

"The pleasure was all mine," he drawled. "Sure you wanna go with him, child bride? Fucktard here made you cry. I make you laugh."

David's smile disappeared and he strode to my side. His hand sat lightly against the base of my spine, warm even through the layer of clothing. "We're out of here."

Mal grinned and winked at me.

"Where are we going?" I asked David.

"Does it matter? Let's just drive."

CHAPTER SEVEN

My neck had seized up. Pain shot through me as I slowly straightened and blinked the sleep from my eyes. I rubbed at the offending muscles, trying to get them to unlock. "Ow."

David took one hand off the steering wheel and reached out, rubbing the back of my neck with strong fingers. "You okay?"

"Yeah. I must have slept funny." I shuffled up in the seat, taking in our surroundings, trying not to enjoy the neck rub too much. Because of course he was crazy good with his hands. Mr. Magic Fingers cajoled my muscles back into some semblance of order with seemingly little effort. I couldn't be expected to resist. Impossible. So instead I moaned loudly and let him have his way with me.

Being barely awake was my only excuse.

The sun was just rising. Tall, shadowy trees rushed by outside. Trying to get out of LA, we'd gotten caught in a traffic jam the likes of which this Portland girl had never seen. For all my good intentions, we hadn't really talked. We'd stopped and gotten food and gas. The rest of the time, Johnny Cash had played on the stereo and I'd practiced speeches in my head. None of the words made it out of my mouth. For some reason, I was reluctant to call a halt to our adventure and go off on my own. It had nothing to do with pulling up my big-girl panties and everything to do with how comfortable I'd begun to feel with him. The silence wasn't awkward. It was peaceful. Refreshing, even, given the last day's worth of drama. Being with him on the open road . . . there was something freeing about it. At around two in the morning, I'd fallen asleep.

"David, where are we?"

He gave me a sidelong look, his hand still massaging my muscles. "Well . . ."

A sign flew past outside. "We're going to Monterey?"

"That's where my place is," he said. "Stop tensing up."

"Monterey?"

"Yeah. What've you got against Monterey, hmm? Have a bad time at a music festival?"

"No." I backpedaled fast, not wanting to appear ungrateful. "It's just a surprise. I didn't realize we were, umm . . . Monterey. Okay."

David sighed and pulled off the road. Dust flew and stones pinged off the Jeep. (Mal wouldn't be pleased.) He turned to face me, resting an elbow on the top of the passenger seat, boxing me in.

"Talk to me, friend," he said.

I opened my mouth and let it all tumble out. "I have a plan. I have some money put away. I was going to go someplace quiet for a couple of weeks until this blew over. You didn't have to put yourself out like this. I just need to get my stuff from back at the mansion and I can be out of your hair."

"All right." He nodded. "Well, we're here now and I'd like to go check out my place for a couple of days. So why don't you come with me? Just as friends. No big deal. It's Friday now, the lawyers said they'd have the new papers sent to us Monday. We'll sign them. I've got a show early next week back in LA. If you want, you can lie low at the house for a few weeks till things calm down. Sound like a plan? We spend the weekend together, then go our separate ways. All sorted."

It did sound like a solid idea. But still, I deliberated for a second. Apparently, it was a second too long.

"You worried about spending the weekend with me or something? Am I that scary?" His gaze held mine, our faces a bare hand's breadth apart. Dark hair fell around his perfect face. For a moment I almost forgot to breathe. I didn't move. I couldn't. Outside a motorcycle roared past then all fell quiet again.

Was he scary? The man had no idea.

"No," I lied, throwing in some scoff for good measure.

I don't think he believed me. "Listen, I'm sorry about acting like a creep back in LA."

"It's okay, really, David. This situation would do anyone's head in."

"Tell me something," he said in a low voice. "You remembered about getting the tat. Anything else come back to you?"

Reliving my drunken rampage wasn't somewhere I wanted to go. Not with him. Not with anyone. I was paying the consequences by having my life upended and splashed about on the Internet. Ridiculous, given nothing in my past was even mildly sordid. Well, apart from the backseat of Tommy's parents' car. "Does this even matter? I mean, isn't it a bit late to be having this conversation?"

"Guess so." He shifted back in his seat and put a hand on the wheel. "You need to stretch your legs or anything?"

"A restroom would be great."

"No worries."

We pulled back out onto the road, and silence ensued for several minutes. He'd turned off the stereo sometime while I slept. The quiet was awkward now and it was all my doing. Guilt sucked first thing in the morning. It probably didn't improve later in the day, but first up, without even a drop of caffeine to fortify me, it was horrible. He'd been nice to me, trying to talk, and I'd shut him down.

"Most of that night is still a blur," I said.

He lifted a couple of fingers off the steering wheel in a little wave. Such was the sum total of his response.

I took a deep breath, fortifying myself to go further. "I remember doing shots at midnight. After that, it's hazy. I remember the sound of the needle at the tattoo parlor, us laughing, but that's about it. I've never blacked out in my life. It's scary."

"Yeah," he said quietly.

"How did we meet?"

He exhaled hard. "Ah, me and a group of people were leaving to go to another club. One of the girls wasn't looking where she was going, bumped into a cocktail waitress. Apparently the waitress was new or something and she crashed her tray. Luckily, it was only a couple of empty beer bottles."

"How did I get involved?"

He darted me a glance, taking his eyes off the road for a moment. "Some of them started giving the poor waitress shit, telling her they were going to get her fired. You just swooped in and handed them their asses."

"I did?"

"Oh, yeah." He licked his lips, the corner of his mouth curling. "Told them they were evil, pretentious, overpriced assholes who should watch where they were walking. You helped the girl pick up the beer bottles and then you insulted my friends some more. It was pretty fucking classic, actually. I can't remember everything you said. You got pretty creative with the insults by the end."

"Huh. And you liked me for that?"

He shut his mouth and said nothing. A whole wide world of nothing. Nothing could actually cover a lot of ground when you put that much effort into it.

"What happened next?" I asked.

"Security came over to throw you out. Not like they were gonna argue with the rich kids."

"No. I guess not."

"You looked panicky, so I got you out of there."

"You left your friends for me?" I watched him in amazement.

He did a one-shoulder shrug. As if it meant nil.

"What then?"

"We took off and had a drink in another bar."

"I'm surprised you stuck with me." Stunned was closer.

"Why wouldn't I?" he asked. "You treated me like a normal person. We just talked about everyday stuff. You weren't angling to get anything out of me. You didn't act like I was a different fucking species. When you looked at me it felt . . ."

"What?"

He cleared his throat. "I dunno. Doesn't matter."

"Yes, you do. And it does."

He groaned.

"Please?"

"Fuck's sake," he muttered, shifting around in the driver's seat all uncomfortable-like. "It felt real, okay? It felt right. I don't know how else to explain it."

I sat in stunned silence for a moment. "That's a good way to explain it."

Suddenly, he got decidedly smirky. "Plus, I'd never been propositioned quite like that."

"Yeeeah. Okay, stop now." I covered my face with my hands, and he laughed.

"Relax," he said. "You were very sweet."

"Sweet?"

"Sweet is not a bad thing."

He pulled the Jeep into a gas station, stopping in front of a pump. "Look at me."

I lowered my fingers.

David stared back at me, beautiful face grinning. "You said that you thought I was a really nice guy. And that it would be great if we could go up to your room and have sex and just hang out for a while, if maybe that was something I'd be interested in doing."

"Ha. I have all the moves." I laughed. There might have been more embarrassing conversations in my life. Doubtful, though. Oh, good God, the thought of me trying out my smooth seduction routine on David. He who had groupies and glamour models throwing themselves at him on a daily basis. If there'd been enough room under the car seat, I'd have hid down there. "What did you say?"

"What do you think I said?" Without taking his gaze off me, he popped the glove box and pulled out a baseball cap. "Looks like the restrooms are around the side."

"This is so mortifying. Why couldn't you have forgotten too?"

He just looked at me. The smirk was long gone. For a long moment he held my gaze captive, unsmiling. The air in the car seemed to drop by about fifty degrees.

"I'll be right back," I said, fingers fumbling with the seat belt.

"Sure."

I finally managed to unbuckle the stupid thing, heart galloping inside my chest. The conversation had gotten crazy heavy toward the end. It had caught me unawares. Knowing he'd stood up for me in Las Vegas, that he'd chosen me over his friends . . . it changed things. And it made me wonder what else I needed to know about that night.

"Wait." He rifled among the collection of sunglasses, pulled out a pair of designer aviator shades, and handed them to me. "You're famous now too, remember?"

"My butt is."

He almost smiled. He fit the baseball cap to his head and rested an arm on the steering wheel. The tattoo of my name was right there, in all its glory. It was pink around the edges and some of the letters had small scabs on them. I wasn't the only one permanently marked by this.

"See you in a bit," he said.

"Right." I opened the door and slowly climbed out of the car. Tripping and landing on my ass in front of him must be avoided at all costs.

I saw to the necessities, then washed my hands. The girl in the restroom mirror looked wild-eyed and then some. I splashed water on my face and did a little damage control on my hair. What a joke. This adventure I was on was undoing any and all attempts at keeping control. Me, my life, all of it seemed to be in a state of flux. That shouldn't have felt as strangely good as it did.

When I got back he was standing by the Jeep, signing an autograph for a couple of guys, one of whom was busy doing an enthusiastic air guitar performance. David laughed and clapped him on the back and they talked for a couple of minutes more. He was kind, gracious. He stood smiling, chatting with them, until he noticed me hovering nearby. "Thanks, guys. If you could keep this quiet for a couple of days I'd appreciate it, hey? We could do with a break from the fuss."

"No worries." One of the guys turned and grinned at me. "Congratulations. You're way prettier in person than in your pictures."

"Thanks." I waved a hand at them, not quite knowing what else to do.

David winked at me and opened the passenger door for me to hop in.

The other man pulled out a cell phone and started snapping pictures. David ignored him and jogged around to the other side of the vehicle. He didn't speak till we were back out on the road.

"It's not far now," he said. "We still going to Monterey?"

"Absolutely."

"Cool."

Hearing David talk about our first meeting had put a new spin on things. That conversation had aroused my curiosity. That he'd chosen me to some degree that night . . . I don't think the possibility had occurred to me before. I'd figured we'd both let tequila do the thinking and somehow fallen into this mess together. I was wrong. There was more to the story. Much more. David's reluctance to answer certain questions made me wonder.

I wanted answers. But I needed to tread carefully.

"Is it always like that for you?" I asked. "Being recognized? Having people approach you all the time?"

"They were fine. The crazies are a worry, but you handle it. It's part of my job. People like the music, so . . ."

A bad feeling crept through me. "You did tell me who you were that night, didn't you?"

"Yeah, of course I did." He gave me a snarky look, his brows bunched up.

My bad feeling crept away, only to be replaced by shame. "Sorry."

"Ev, I wanted you to know what the fuck you were getting into. You said you really liked me, but you weren't that keen on my band." He fiddled with the stereo, another half smile on his face. Soon some rock song I didn't know played quietly over the speakers. "You felt pretty bad about it, actually. You kept apologizing over and over. Insisted on buying me a burger and shake to make up for it."

"I just prefer country."

"Believe me, I know. And stop apologizing. You're allowed to like whatever the hell you want."

"Was it a good burger and shake?"

He gave me a one-shoulder shrug. "It was fine."

"I wish I remembered."

He snorted. "There's a first."

I don't know what exactly came over me. Maybe I just wanted to see if I could make him smile. With a knee beneath me I pulled out a length of seat belt, raised myself up, and kissed him quick on the cheek. A surprise attack. His skin was warm and smooth against my lips. The man smelled so much better than he had any right to.

"What was that for?" he asked, shooting me a look out of the corners of his eyes.

"For getting me out of Portland and then LA. For talking to me about that night." I shrugged, trying to play it off. "For lots of things."

A little line appeared above the bridge of his nose. When he spoke, his voice was gruff. "Right. No problem."

His mouth stayed shut and his hand went to his cheek, touching where I'd been. The frown-faced side-on looks continued for quite some time. Each one made me wonder a bit more if David Ferris was just as scared of me as I was of him. This reaction was even better than a smile.

The log-and-stone house rose out of the trees, perched on the edge of a cliff. The place was awe-inspiring on a whole different level from the mansion back in LA. Below, the ocean went about its business of being spectacular.

David climbed out of the car and walked up to the house, fiddling with a set of keys from his pocket. He opened the front door, then stopped to punch numbers into a security system.

"You coming?" he yelled.

I lingered beside the car, looking up at the magnificent house. Him and me alone. Inside there. Hmm. Waves crashed on the rocks nearby. I swore I could hear the swell of an orchestral accompaniment not too far off in the distance. The place was decidedly atmospheric. And that atmosphere was pure romance.

"What's the problem?" David came back down the stone path toward me.

"Nothing . . . I was just—"

"Good." He didn't stop. I didn't know what was going on until I found myself hanging upside down over his shoulder in a fireman's hold.

"Shit. David!"

"Relax."

"You're going to drop me!"

"I'm not going to drop you. Stop squirming," he said, his arm pressing against the back of my legs. "Show some trust."

"What are you doing?" I battered my hands against the ass of his jeans.

"It's traditional to carry the bride across the threshold."

"Not like this."

He patted my butt cheek, the one with his name on it. "Why would we wanna start being conventional now, huh?"

"I thought we were just being friends."

"This is friendly. You should probably stop feeling my ass, though, or I'm gonna get the wrong idea about us. Especially after that kiss in the car."

"I'm not feeling your ass," I grumbled, and stopped using his butt cheeks for a handhold. Like it was my fault the position left me no alternative but to hold on to his firm butt.

"Please, you're all over me. It's disgusting."

I laughed despite myself. "You put me over your shoulder, you idiot. Of course I'm all over you."

Up the steps we went, then onto the wide wooden patio and into the house. Hardwood floors in a rich brown and moving boxes, lots and lots of moving boxes. I couldn't see much else.

"This could be a problem," he said.

"What could be?" I asked, still upside down, my hair obscuring my view.

"Hang on." Carefully, he righted me, setting my feet

on the floor. All the blood rushed from my head and I staggered. He grabbed my elbows, holding me upright.

"Okay?" he asked.

"Yeah. What's the problem?"

"I thought there'd be more furniture," he said.

"You've never been here before?"

"I've been busy."

Apart from boxes there were more boxes. They were everywhere. We stood in a large central room with a huge stone fireplace set in the far wall. You could roast a whole cow in the thing if you were so inclined. Stairs led to a second floor above and another level below this one. A dining room and open-plan kitchen came next. The place was a combination of floor-to-ceiling glass, neat lines of logs, and gray stonework. The perfect mix of old and new design techniques. It was stunning. But then all the places he lived in seemed to be.

I wondered what he'd make of my and Lauren's tiny bedraggled apartment. A silly thought. As if he'd ever see it.

"At least they got a fridge." He pulled one of the large stainless steel doors open. Every inch of space inside had been packed with food and beverages. "Excellent."

"Who are 'they'?"

"Ah, the people that look after the place for me. Friends of mine. They used to look after it for the previous owner too. I rang them, asked them to sort some stuff out for us." He pulled out a Corona and popped the lid. "Cheers."

I smiled, amused. "For breakfast?"

"I've been awake for two days. I want a beer, then I want a bed. Man, I hope they thought to get a bed." Beer in hand, he ambled back through the lounge and up the stairs. I followed, curious.

He pushed open one bedroom door after another. There were four all up and each had its own bathroom because cool, rich people clearly couldn't share. At the final door at the end of the hall he stopped and sagged with relief. "Thank fuck for that."

A kingdom of a bed made up with clean, white sheets waited within. And a couple more boxes.

"What's with all the boxes?" I asked. "Did they only get one bed?"

"Sometimes I buy stuff on my travels. Sometimes people give me stuff. I've just been sending it all here for the last few years. Take a look if you want. And yes, there's only one bed." He took another swig of beer. "You think I'm made of money?"

I huffed out a laugh. "Says the guy who got Cartier to open so I could pick out a ring."

"You remember that?" He smiled around the bottle of beer.

"No, I just assumed given what time of night it must have been." I wandered over to the wall of windows. Such an amazing view.

"You tried to pick some shitty little thing. I couldn't believe it." He stared at me, but his gaze was distant.

"I threw the ring at the lawyers."

He flinched and studied his shoes. "Yeah, I know."

"I'm sorry. They just made me so mad."

"Lawyers do that." He took another swig of the beer. "Mal said you took a swing at him."

"I missed."

"Probably for the best. He's an idiot but he means well."

"Yeah, he was really kind to me." Crossing my arms, I checked out the rest of his big bedroom, wandering into the bathroom. The Jacuzzi would have made Mal's curl up in shame. The place was sumptuous. Yet again the feeling of not belonging, of not fitting in with the décor, hit me hard.

"That's some heavy frown, friend," he said.

I attempted a smile. "I'm just still trying to figure things out. I mean, is that why you took the plunge in Vegas?

Because you're unhappy? And apart from Mal you're surrounded by jerks?"

"Fuck." His let his head fall back. "Do we have to keep talking about that night?"

"I'm just trying to understand."

"No," he said. "It wasn't that, okay?"

"Then what?"

"We were in Vegas, Ev. Shit happens."

I shut my mouth.

"I don't mean . . ." He wiped a hand across his face. "Fuck. Look, don't think it was just all drinking and partying and that's the only reason anything happened. Why we happened. I wouldn't want you to think that."

I flailed. It seemed the only proper response. "But that's what I do think. That's exactly what I think. That's the only way this fits together in my head. When a girl like me wakes up married to a guy like you, what else can she possibly think? God, David, look at you. You're beautiful, rich, and successful. Your brother was right, this makes no sense."

He turned on me, face tight. "Don't do that. Don't run yourself down like that."

I just sighed.

"I'm serious. Don't you ever give what that asshole said another thought, understood? You are not nothing."

"Then give me something. Tell me what it was like between us that night."

He opened his mouth, then snapped it closed. "Nah. I don't want to dredge it all up, you know, water under the bridge or whatever. I just don't want you thinking that the whole night was some alcohol-fueled frenzy or something, that's all. Honestly, you didn't even seem that drunk most of it."

"David, you're hedging. Come on. It's not fair that you remember and I don't."

"No," he said, his voice hard, cold, in a way I hadn't

heard it. He loomed over me, jaw set. "It's not fair that I remember and you don't, Evelyn."

I didn't know what to say.

"I'm going out." True to his word, he stormed out the door. Heavy footsteps thumped along the hallway and back down the stairs. I stood staring after him.

I gave him awhile to cool off, then followed him out onto the beach. The morning light was blinding, clear blue skies all the way. It was beautiful. Salty sea air cleared my head a little. David's words raised more questions than they answered. Puzzling that night out consumed my thoughts. I'd reached two conclusions. Both worried me. The first was that the night in Vegas was special to him. My prying or trivializing the experience upset him. The second was, I suspected, he hadn't been all that drunk. It sounded like he knew exactly what he was doing. In which case, how the hell must he have felt the next morning? I'd rejected him and our marriage out of hand. He must have been heartsore, humiliated.

There'd been good reasons for my behavior. I'd still, however, been incredibly thoughtless. I didn't know David then. But I was beginning to now. And the more we talked, the more I liked him.

David sat on the rocks with a beer in hand, staring out to sea. A cool ocean wind tossed his long hair about. The fabric of his T-shirt was drawn tight across his broad back. He had his knees drawn up with an arm wrapped around them. It made him seem younger than he was, more vulnerable.

"Hi," I said, squatting beside him.

"Hey." Eyes squinted against the sun, he looked up at me, face guarded.

"I'm sorry for pushing."

He nodded, stared back out at the water. "S'okay."

"I didn't mean to upset you."

"Don't worry about it."

"Are we still friends?"

He huffed out a laugh. "Sure."

I sat down next to him, trying to figure out what to say next, what would set things right between us. Nothing I could think of saying was going to make up for Vegas. I needed more time with him. The ticking clock of the annulment papers grew louder by the minute. It unnerved me, thinking our time would be cut short. That it would soon all be over and I wouldn't see or talk to him again. That I wouldn't get to figure out the puzzle that was us. My skin grew goose pimples from more than the wind.

"Shit. You're cold," he said, wrapping an arm around my shoulders, pulling me in closer against him.

And I got closer, happily. "Thanks."

He put down the beer bottle, wrapping both arms around me. "Should probably get you inside."

"In a bit." My thumbs rubbed over my fingers, fidgeting. "Thank you for bringing me here. It's a lovely place."

"Mm."

"David, really, I'm so sorry."

"Hey." He put a finger beneath my chin, raising it. The anger and hurt were gone, replaced by kindness. He gave me one of his little shrugs. "Let's just let it go."

The idea actually sent me into a panic. I didn't want to let go of him. The knowledge was startling. I stared up at him, letting it sink in. "I don't want to."

He blinked. "All right. You want to make it up to me?"

I doubted we were talking about the same thing, but I nodded anyway.

"I've got an idea."

"Shoot."

"Different things can jog your memory, right?"

"I guess so," I said.

"So if I kiss you, you might remember what we were like together."

I stopped breathing. "You want to kiss me?"

"You don't want me to kiss you?"

"No," I said quickly. "I'm okay with you kissing me."

He bit back a smile. "That's very kind of you."

"And this kiss is for the purposes of scientific research?"

"Yep. You want to know what happened that night and I don't really want to talk about it. So, I figure, easier all around if you can maybe remember some of it yourself."

"That makes sense."

"Excellent."

"How far did we go that night?"

His gaze dropped to the neck of my tank top and the curves of my breasts. "Second base."

"Shirt on?"

"Off. We were both topless. Topless cuddles are best." He watched as I absorbed the information, his face close to mine.

"Bra?"

"Absolutely not."

"Oh." I licked my lips, breathing hard. "So, you really think we should do this?"

"You're overthinking it."

"Sorry."

"And stop apologizing."

My mouth opened to repeat the sentiment but I snapped it shut.

"S'okay. You'll get the hang of it."

My brain stuttered and I stared at his mouth. He had the most beautiful mouth, with full lips that pulled up slightly at the edges. Stunning.

"Tell me what you're thinking," he said.

"You said not to think. And honestly, I'm not."

"Good," he said, leaning even closer. "That's good."

His lips brushed against mine, easing me into it. Soft but firm, with no hesitation. His teeth toyed with my bottom lip. Then he sucked on it. He didn't kiss like the boys I knew, though I couldn't exactly define the difference. It was just better and . . . more. Infinitely more. His mouth pressed against mine and his tongue slipped into my mouth, rubbing against mine. God, he tasted good. My fingers slid into his hair as if they'd always wanted to. He kissed me until I couldn't remember anything that had come before. None of it mattered.

His hand slid around the nape of my neck, holding me in place. The kiss went on and on. He lit me up from top to toe. I never wanted it to end.

He kissed me till my head spun, and I hung on for dear life. Then he pulled back, panting, and set his forehead against mine once again.

"Why did you stop?" I asked when I could form a coherent sentence. My hands pulled at him, trying to bring him back to my mouth.

"Shh. Relax." He took a deep breath. "Did you remember something? Anything about that familiar to you?"

My kiss-addled mind came up blank. Damn it. "No. I don't think so."

"That's a pity." A ridge appeared between his brows. The dark smudges beneath his beautiful blue eyes seemed to have darkened. I'd disappointed him again. My heart sank.

"You look tired," I said.

"Yeah. Might be time to get some shut-eye." He planted a quick kiss on my forehead. Was it a friend's kiss, or more? I couldn't tell. Maybe it too was just for scientific purposes.

"We tried, huh?" he said.

"Yeah. We did."

He rose to his feet, collecting his beer bottle. Without him to warm me, the breeze blew straight through me, shaking my bones. It was the kiss, though, that had really shaken me. It had blown my ever-lovin' mind. To think I'd had a night of kisses like that and forgotten it. I needed a brain transplant at the earliest convenience.

"Do you mind if I come with you?" I asked.

"Not at all." He held out a hand to help me to my feet.

Together, we wandered back up to the house, up the stairs into the master bedroom. I tugged off my shoes as David dealt with his own footwear. We lay down on the mattress, not touching. Both of us staring at the ceiling like there might be answers there.

I kept quiet. For all of about a minute. My mind was wide awake and babbling at me. "I think I understand a little better now how we ended up married."

"Do you?" He turned his head to face me.

"Yes." I'd never been kissed like that before. "I do."

"C'mere." A strong arm encircled my waist, dragging me into the center of the bed.

"David." I reached for him with a nervous smile. More than ready for more kisses. More of him.

"Lie on your side," he said, his hands maneuvering me until he lay behind me. One arm slipped beneath my neck and the other was slung over my waist, pulling me in closer against him. His hips fit against my butt perfectly.

"What are we doing?" I asked, bewildered.

"Spooning. We did it that night for a while. Until you felt sick."

"We spooned?"

"Yep," he said. "Stage two in the memory rehab process, spooning. Now go to sleep."

"I only woke up an hour ago."

He pressed his face into my hair and even threw a leg over mine for good measure, pinning me down. "Bad luck. I'm tired and I wanna spoon. With you. And the way I figure it, you owe me. So we're spooning."

"Got it."

His breath warmed the side of my neck, sending shivers down my spine.

"Relax. You're all tense." His arms tightened around me.

After a moment, I picked up his left hand, running the pads of my fingers over his calluses. Using him for my fidget toy. The tips of his fingers were hard. There was also a ridge down his thumb and another slight one along the bottom of his fingers where they joined the palm of his hand. He obviously spent a lot of time holding guitars. On the back of his fingers the word *Free* had been tattooed. On his right hand was the word *Live*. I couldn't help but wonder if marriage would impinge on that freedom. Japanese-style waves and a serpentine dragon covered his arm, the colors and detail impressive.

"Tell me about your major," he said. "You're doin' architecture, right?"

"Yes," I said, a little surprised he knew. I'd obviously told him in Vegas. "My dad's one."

He meshed his fingers with mine, putting the kibosh on my fidgeting.

"Did you always want to play guitar?" I asked, trying not to get too distracted by the way he was wrapped around me.

"Yeah. Music's the only thing that ever really made sense to me. Can't imagine doing anything else."

"Huh." It must be nice, having something to be so passionate about. I liked the idea of being an architect. Many of my childhood games had involved building blocks or drawing. But I didn't feel driven to do it, exactly. "I'm pretty much tone deaf."

"That explains a lot." He chuckled.

"Be nice. I was never particularly good at sports either. I like drawing and reading and watching movies. And I like to travel, not that I've done much of it."

"Yeah?"

"Mm."

He shifted behind me, getting comfortable. "When I travel, it's always about the shows. Doesn't leave much time for looking around."

"That's a pity."

"And being recognized can be a pain in the ass sometimes. Now and then, it gets ugly. There's a fair bit of pressure on us, and I can't always do what I want. Truth is, I'm kind of ready to slow things down, hang out at home more."

I said nothing, turning his words over inside my head.

"The parties get old after a while. Having people around all the damn time."

"I bet." And yet, back in LA he'd still had a groupie hanging off him, cooing at his every word. Obviously parts of the lifestyle still appealed. Parts that I wasn't certain I could compete with even if I wanted to. "Won't you miss some of it?"

"Honestly, it's all I've done for so long, I don't know."

"Well, you have a gorgeous home to hang out in."

"Hmm." He was quiet for a moment. "Ev?"

"Yeah?"

"Was being an architect your idea or your dad's?"

"I don't remember," I admitted. "We've always talked about it. My brother was never interested in taking up the mantle. He was always getting into fights and skipping class."

"You said you had a tough time at high school too."

"Doesn't everyone?" I wriggled around, turned over so I could see his face. "I don't usually talk about that with other people."

"We talked about it. You said you got picked on because of your size. I figured that's what set you off with my friends. The fact that they were bullying that girl like a pack of fucking schoolkids."

"I guess that would do it." The teasing wasn't a subject I liked to raise. Too easily, it brought back all of the crappy feelings associated with it. David's arms didn't allow for any of that to slip through, however. "Most of the teachers just ignored it. Like it was an extra hassle they didn't need. But there was this one teacher, Miss Hall. Anytime they started in on me or one of the other kids, she'd intercede. She was great."

"She sounds great. But you didn't really answer my question. Do you want to be an architect?"

"Well, it's what I've always planned to do. And I, ah, I like the idea of designing someone's home. I don't know that being an architect is my divine calling, like music is for you, but I think I could be good at it."

"I'm not doubting that, baby," he said, his voice soft but definite.

I tried not to let the endearment reduce me to a soggy mess on the mattress. Subtlety was the key. I'd hurt him in Vegas. If I was serious about this, about wanting him to give us another go, I needed to be careful. Give him good memories to replace the bad. Memories we could both share this time.

"Ev, is it what you want to do with your life?"

I stopped. Having already trotted out the standard responses, extra thought was required. The plan had been around for so long I didn't tend to question it. There was safety and comfort to be had there. But David wanted more and I wanted to give it to him. Maybe this was why I'd spilled my secrets to him in Vegas. Something about this man drew me in, and I didn't want to fight it. "Honestly, I'm not sure."

"That's okay, you know." His gaze never shifted from mine. "You're only twenty-one."

"But I'm supposed to be an adult now, taking responsibility for myself. I'm supposed to know these things."

"You've been living with your friend for a few years, yeah? Paying your own bills and doing your classes and all that?"

"Yes."

"Then how are you not taking responsibility for yourself?" He tucked his long dark hair behind an ear, getting it out of his face. "So you start out in architecture and see how you go."

"You make it sound so simple."

"It is. You either stick with that or try something else, see how it works for you. It's your life. Your call."

"Do you only play guitar?" I asked, wanting to know more about him. Wanting the topic of conversation to be off me. The knot of tension building inside me was not pleasant.

"No." A smile tugged at the corner of his mouth—he knew exactly what I was about. "Bass and drums too. Of course."

"Of course?"

"Anyone passable at guitar can play bass if they put their mind to it. And anyone who can pick up two sticks at the same time can play drums. Be sure to tell Mal I said that next time you see him, yeah? He'll get a kick out of that."

"You got it."

"And I sing."

"You do?" I asked, getting excited. "Will you sing something for me? Please?"

He made a noncommittal noise.

"Did you sing to me that night?"

He gave me a small pained smile. "Yeah, I did."

"So it might bring back a memory."

"You're going to use that now, aren't you? Anytime you want something you're going to throw it at me."

"Hey, you started it. You wanted to kiss me for scientific purposes."

"It was for scientific purposes. A kiss between friends for reasons of pure logic."

"It was a very friendly kiss, David."

A lazy smile lit his face. "Yes, it was."

"Please sing me something?"

"Okay," he huffed. "Turn back around, then. We were in spoon position for this."

I snuggled back down against him and he shuffled closer. Being David's cuddle toy was a wonderful thing. I couldn't imagine anything better. Pity he was sticking with the scientific rationale. Not that I could blame him. If I were him, I'd be wary of me.

His voice washed over me, deep, rough in the best way possible as he sang the ballad.

I've got this feeling that comes and goes
Ten broken fingers and one broken nose
Dark waters very cold
I know I'll make it home
This sorry sun has burned the sky
She's out of touch and she's very high
Her bed was made of stone
I know I'll break her throne
These aching bones won't hold me up
My swollen shoes they have had enough
These smokestacks burn them down
This ocean let it drown

When he finished I was quiet. He gave me a squeeze, probably checking I was still alive. I squeezed his arms right back, not turning over so he couldn't see the tears in my eyes. The combination of his voice and the moody ballad had undone me. I was always making a mess of myself around him, crying or puking. Why he wanted anything to do with me, I had no idea.

"Thank you," I said.

"Anytime."

I lay there, trying to decipher the lyrics. What it might mean that he'd chosen that song to sing to me. "What's it called?"

" 'Homesick.' I wrote it for the last album." He rose up on one elbow, leaning over to check out my face. "Shit, I made you sad. I'm sorry."

"No. It was beautiful. Your voice is amazing."

He frowned but lay back down, pressed his chest against my spine. "I'll sing you something happy next time."

"If you like." I pressed my lips to the back of his hand, to the veins tracing across, and the dusting of dark hair. "David?"

"Hmm?"

"Why don't you sing in the band? You have such a great voice."

"I do backup. Jimmy loves the limelight. It was always more his thing." His fingers twined with mine. "He wasn't always the asshole he is now. I'm sorry he hassled you in LA. I could have killed him for saying that shit."

"It's okay."

"No, it's not. He was off his face. He didn't have a fucking clue what he was talking about." His thumb moved restlessly over my hand. "You're gorgeous. You don't need to change a thing."

I didn't know what to say at first. Jimmy had said some horrible things and it had stayed with me. Funny how the bad stuff always did.

"I've both puked and cried on you. Are you entirely sure about that?" I joked, finally.

"Yes," he said simply. "I like you the way you are, blurting out whatever shit crosses your mind. Not trying to play me, or use me. You're just . . . being with me. I like you."

I lay there speechless for a moment, taken aback. "Thank you."

"You're welcome. Anytime, Evelyn. Anytime at all."

"I like you too."

His lips brushed against the back of my neck. Shivers raced across my skin. "Do you?"

"Yes. Very much."

"Thanks, baby."

It took a long time for his breathing to even out. His limbs got heavier and he stilled, asleep against my back. My foot went fuzzy with pins and needles, but never mind. I hadn't slept with anyone before, apart from the occasional platonic bed-sharing episode with Lauren. Apparently, sleeping was all I'd be doing today.

In all honesty, it felt good, lying next to him.

It felt right.

CHAPTER EIGHT

"Hey." David padded down the stairs seven hours later, wearing a towel wrapped around his waist. He'd slicked his wet hair back and his tattoos were displayed to perfection, defining his lean torso and muscular arms. There was a lot of skin on show. The man was a visual feast. I made a conscious effort to keep my tongue inside my head. Keeping the welcoming grin off my face was beyond my abilities. I'd planned to play it cool so as not to spook him. That plan had failed.

"Whatcha doin'?" he asked.

"Nothing much. There was a delivery for you." I pointed to the bags and boxes waiting by the door. All day I'd pondered the problem of us. The only thing I'd come up with was that I didn't want our time to end. I didn't want to sign those annulment papers. Not yet. The idea made me want to start puking all over again. I wanted David. I wanted to be with him. I needed a new plan.

The pad of my thumb rubbed over my bottom lip, back and forth, back and forth. I'd gone for a long walk up the beach earlier, watching the waves crash on the shore and reliving that kiss. Over and over again, I'd played it inside my mind. The same went for our conversations. In fact, I'd picked apart every moment of our time together, explored every nuance. Every moment I could remember, anyway, and I'd tried damn hard to remember all of it.

"A delivery?" He crouched down beside the closest package and started tearing at the wrapping. I averted my eyes before I caught a glimpse up his towel, despite being wildly curious.

"Would you mind if I used your phone?" I asked.

"Ev, you don't need to ask. Help yourself to whatever."

"Thanks." Lauren and my folks were probably freaking out, wondering what was going on. It was time to brave up to the butt-picture repercussions. I groaned on the inside.

"This one's for you." He handed me a thick brown-paper parcel done up with string, followed by a shopping bag with some brand I'd never heard of printed on the side. "Ah, this one too, by the look."

"It is?"

"Yeah. I asked Martha to order some stuff for us."

"Oh."

"Oh? No." David shook his head. Then he kneeled down in front of me and tore into the brown package in my hands. "No 'oh.' We need clothes. It's really simple."

"That's very kind of you, David, but I'm fine."

He wasn't listening. Instead he held up a red dress the same thigh-baring length as those girls at the mansion had worn. "What the fuck? You're not wearing this." The designer dress went flying, and he ripped into the shopping bag at my feet.

"David, you can't just throw it on the ground."

"Sure I can. Here, this is a little better."

A black tank top fell into my lap. At least this one looked the right size. The thigh-high red dress had been a size-four joke. Quite possibly a mean one, given Martha's dislike of me back in LA. No matter.

A tag dangled from the tank. The price. Shit. They couldn't be serious.

"Whoa. I could pay my rent for weeks with this top."

In lieu of a response he threw a pair of skinny black jeans at me. "Here, they're okay too."

I put the jeans aside. "It's a plain cotton tank top. How can this possibly cost two hundred dollars?"

"What do you think of this?" A length of silky blue fabric dangled from his hand. "Nice, huh?"

"Do they sew the seams with gold thread? Is that it?"

"What are you talking about?" He held up the blue dress, turning it this way and that. "Hell no, it's backless. The top of your ass will probably show in that." It joined the red dress on the floor. My hands itched to rescue them, fold them away nicely. But David just ripped into the next box. "What were you saying?"

"I'm talking about the price of this top."

"Shit, no. We're not talking about the price of that top because we're not talking about money. It's an issue for you, and I'm not going there." A micromini denim skirt came next. "What the fuck was Martha thinking ordering you this sort of stuff?"

"Well, to be fair, you do normally have girls in bikinis hanging off you. In comparison, the backless dress is quite sedate."

"You're different. You're my friend, aren't you?"

"Yes." I didn't entirely believe the tone of my own voice.

His forehead wrinkled up with disdain. "Damn it. Look at the length of this. I can't even tell if it's meant to be a skirt or a fucking belt."

Laughter burst out of me and he gave me a hurt look, big blue puppy-dog eyes of extreme sadness and displeasure. Clearly, I had hurt his heart.

"I'm sorry," I said. "But you sound like my father."

He shoved the micromini back into its bag. At least it wasn't on the floor. "Yeah? Your dad and I should meet. I think we'd get along great."

"You want to meet my father?"

"Depends. Would he shoot me on sight?"

"No." Probably not.

He just gave me a curious look and burrowed into the next box. "That's better. Here."

He passed me a couple of sedate T-shirts, one black and one blue.

"I don't think you should be selecting nun's clothing for me, friend," I said, amused at his behavior. "It's vaguely hypocritical."

"They're not nun's clothes. They just cover the essentials. Is that too much to ask?" The next bulging bag was passed to me in its entirety. "Here."

"You do admit it's just a tiny bit hypocritical, though, right?"

"Admit nothing. Adrian taught me that a long time ago. Look in the bag."

I did so and he burst out laughing, whatever expression I wore being apparently hilarious.

"What is this?" I asked, feeling all wide-eyed with wonder. It might have been a thong if the makers had seen fit to invest just a little more material into it.

"I'm dressing you like a nun."

"La Perla." I read the tag, then turned it over to check out the price.

"Shit. Will you not look at the price, please, Ev?" David dived at me and I lay back, trying to make out the figures on the crazily swaying tag that was bigger than the scrap of lace. His larger hand closed over mine, engulfing the thong. "Don't. For fuck's sake."

The back of my head hit the edge of a step and I winced, my eyes filling with tears. "Ow."

"You all right?" His body stretched out above mine. A hand rubbed carefully at the back of my skull.

"Um, yeah." The scent of his soap and shampoo was pure heaven, Lord help me. But there was something more

than that. His cologne. It wasn't heavy. Just a light scent
of spice. There was something really familiar about it.

The tag hanging down in front of my face momentarily
distracted me however. "Three hundred dollars?"

"It's worth it."

"Holy shit. No, it's not."

He hung the thong from the tip of a finger, a crazy cool
smile on his face. "Trust me. I'd have paid ten times that
amount for this. No questions asked."

"David, I could get the exact same thing for less than
a tenth of that price in a normal store. That's insane."

"No, you couldn't." He balanced his weight on an elbow set on the step beside my head and started reading
from the tag. "See, this exquisite lace is handmade by local artists in a small region of northern Italy famous for
just such craftsmanship. It's made from only the finest of
silks. You can't get that at Walmart, baby."

"No, I guess not."

He made a pleased humming sound and looked at me
with eyes soft and hazy. Then his smile faded. He pulled
back and scrunched the thong up in his hand. "Anyway."

"Wait." My fingers curled around his biceps, keeping
him in place.

"What's up?" he asked, his voice tightening.

"Just, let me . . ." I lifted my face to his neck. The scent
was strongest there. I breathed him deep, letting myself
get high off the scent of him. I shut my eyes and remembered.

"Evelyn?" The muscles in his arms flexed and hardened. "I'm not sure this is a good idea."

"We were in the gondolas at the Venetian. You said you
couldn't swim, that I'd have to save you if we capsized."

His Adam's apple jumped. "Yeah."

"I was terrified for you."

"I know. You hung on to me so tight I could barely
breathe."

I drew back so I could see his face.

"Why do you think we stayed on them for so long?" he asked. "You were practically sitting in my lap."

"Can you swim?"

He laughed quietly. "Of course I can swim. I don't even think the water was that deep."

"It was all a ruse. You're tricky, David Ferris."

"And you're funny, Evelyn Thomas." His face relaxed, his eyes softening again. "You remembered something."

"Yes."

"That's great. Anything else?"

I gave him a sad smile. "No, sorry."

He looked away, disappointed, I think, but trying not to let it show.

"David?"

"Mm?"

I leaned forward to press my lips to his, wanting to kiss him, needing to. He pulled back again. My hopes dived. "Sorry. I'm sorry."

"Ev. What are you doing?"

"Kissing you?"

He said nothing. Jaw rigid, he looked away.

"You're allowed to kiss me and cuddle me and buy me insanely priced lingerie and I can't kiss you back?" My hands slid down to his and he held them. At least he wasn't rejecting me totally.

"Why do you wanna kiss me?" he asked, his voice stern.

I studied our entwined fingers for a moment, getting my thoughts in order. "David, I'm probably not ever going to remember everything about that night in Vegas. But I thought we could maybe make some new good memories this weekend. Something we can both share."

"Just this weekend?"

My heart filled my throat. "No. I don't know. It just . . . it feels like there's meant to be more between us."

"More than friends?" He watched me, eyes intent.

"Yes. I like you. You're kind and sweet and beautiful and you're easy to talk to. When we're not always arguing about Vegas. I feel like . . ."

"What?"

"Like this weekend is a second chance. I don't want to just let it slip by. I think I'd regret that for a long time."

He nodded, cocked his head. "So what was your plan? Just kiss me and see what happened?"

"My plan?"

"I know about you and your plans. You told me all about how anal you are."

"I told you that?" I was an idiot.

"Yeah. You did. You especially told me about the big plan." He stared down at me, eyes intense. "You know . . . finish school then spend three to five years establishing yourself at a midrange firm before moving up the ranks somewhere more prestigious and starting your own small consultancy business by thirty-five. Then there'd maybe time to get a relationship and those pesky 2.4 kids out of the way."

My throat was suddenly a dry, barren place. "I was really chatty that night."

"Mm. But what was interesting was the way you didn't talk about that plan like it was a good thing. You talked about it like it was a cage and you were rattling the bars."

I had nothing.

"So, come on," he said softly, taunting me. "What's the plan here, Ev? How were you going to convince me?"

"Oh. Well, I was um . . . I was going to seduce you, I guess. And see what happened. Yeah . . ."

"How? By complaining about me buying you stuff?"

"No. That was just an added bonus. You're welcome."

He licked his lips, but I saw the smile. "Right. Come on, then, show me your moves."

"My moves?"

"Your seduction techniques. Come on, time's a-wasting." I hesitated and he clicked his tongue, impatient. "I'm only wearing a towel, baby. How hard can this be?"

"Fine, fine." I held his fingers tight, refusing to let go. "So, David?"

"Yes, Evelyn?"

"I was thinking . . ."

"Hmm?"

I was so hopelessly outclassed with him. I gave him the only thing I could think of. The only thing that I knew had a track record of working. "I think you're a really nice guy and I was wondering if you'd maybe like to come up to my room and have sex with me and maybe hang out for a while. If that's maybe something you'd be interested in doing . . ."

His eyes darkened, accusing and unhappy. He started to pull back again. "Now you're just being funny."

"No." I slipped my hand around the back of his neck, beneath his damp hair, trying to bring him back to me. "No, I'm very, very serious."

Jaw tensed, he stared at me.

"You asked me this morning in the car if I thought you were scary. The answer is yes. You scare me shitless. I don't know what I'm doing here. But I hate the thought of leaving you."

His gaze searched my face, but still he said nothing. He was going to turn me down. I knew it. I'd asked for too much, pushed him too far. He'd walk away from me, and who could blame him after everything?

"It's okay," I said, gathering what remained of my pride up off the floor.

"Ah, man." He sighed. "You're kinda terrifying too."

"I am?"

"Yeah, you are. And wipe that smile off your face."

"Sorry."

He angled his head and kissed me, his lips firm and so

good. My eyes closed and my mouth opened. The taste of him took me over. The mint of his toothpaste and the slide of his tongue against mine. All of it was beyond perfect. He lay me back against the stairs. The new bruise at the back of my head throbbed in protest when I bumped it yet again. I flinched but didn't stop. David cupped the back of my skull, guarding against further injury.

The weight of his body held me in place, not that I was trying to escape. The edge of the steps pressed into my back and I couldn't care less. I'd have happily lain there for hours with him above me, the warm scent of his skin making me high. His hips held my legs wide open. If not for my jeans and his towel, things would get interesting fast. God, I hated cotton just then.

We didn't once break the kiss. My legs wrapped around his waist and my hands curved around his shoulders. Nothing had ever felt this good. My ache for him increased and caught fire, spreading right through me. My legs tightened around him, muscles burning. I couldn't get close enough. Talk about frustrating. His mouth moved over my jaw and down my neck, lighting me up from inside. He bit and licked, finding sensitive spots below my ear and in the crook of my neck. Places I hadn't known I had. The man had magic. He knew things I didn't. Where he'd learned his tricks didn't matter. Not right then.

"Up," he said in a rough voice. Slowly he stood, one hand beneath my ass and the other still protecting my skull.

"David." I scrambled to tighten my hold on his back.

"Hey." He drew back just enough to look into my eyes. His pupils were huge, almost swallowing the blue iris whole. "I am not going to drop you. That's never going to happen."

I took a deep breath. "Okay."

"You trust me?"

"Yes."

"Good." His hand slid down my back. "Now put your arms around my neck."

I did, and my balance immediately felt better. Both of David's hands gripped my butt and I locked my feet behind his back, holding on tight. His face showed no sign of pain or imminent back breakage. Maybe he was strong enough to carry me around after all.

"That's it." He smiled and kissed my chin. "All good?"

I nodded, not trusting myself to speak.

"Bed?"

"Yes."

He chuckled in a way that did bad things to me. "Kiss me," he said.

Without hesitation, I did so, fitting my mouth to his. Sliding my tongue between his lips and getting lost in him all over again. He groaned, his hands holding me hard against him.

Which was when the doorbell rang, making a low, mournful sound that echoed in my heart and groin. "Nooo."

"You're fucking joking." David's face screwed up and he gave the tall double doors the foulest of looks. At least I wasn't alone. I groaned and gave him a tight full-body hug. It would have been funny if it didn't hurt so much.

A hand rubbed at my back, sliding beneath the hem of my tank to stroke the skin beneath. "It's like the universe doesn't want me inside you or something, I swear," he grumbled.

"Make them go away. Please."

He chuckled, clutching me tighter.

"It hurts."

He groaned and kissed my neck. "Let me answer the door and get rid of them, then I'll take care of you, okay?"

"Your towel is on the floor."

"That's a problem. Down you hop."

I reluctantly loosened my hold and put my feet back

on firm ground. Again the gonglike sound filled the house. David grabbed a pair of black jeans out of a bag and quickly pulled them on. All I caught was a flash of toned ass. Keeping my eyes mostly averted might have been the hardest thing I'd ever done.

"Hang back just in case it's press." He looked into a small screen embedded beside the door. "Ah, man."

"Trouble?"

"No. Worse. Old friends with food." He gave me a brief glance. "If it makes you feel any better, I'll be hurting too."

"But—"

"Anticipation makes it sweeter. I promise," he said, then threw open the door. A hand tugged down the front of his T-shirt, trying to cover the obvious bulge beneath his jeans. "Tyler. Pam. Hey, good to see you."

I was going to kill him. Slowly. Strangle him with the overpriced thong. A fitting death for a rock star.

A couple about my parents' age came in, laden down with pots and bottles of wine. The man, Tyler, was tall, thin, and covered in tats. Pam looked to have Native American in her heritage. Beautiful long black hair hung down her back in a braid, thick as my wrist. They both wore wide grins and gave me curious glances. I could feel my face heat when they took in the lingerie and clothing strewn about on the floor. It probably looked like we'd been about to embark on a two-person orgy. Which was the truth, but still.

"How the hell are ya?" Tyler roared in an Australian accent, giving David a one-armed hug on account of the Crock-Pot he held in the other. "And this must be Ev. I have to read about it in the damn paper, Dave? Are you serious?" He gave my husband a stern look, one brow arched high. "Pam was pissed."

"Sorry. It was—ah, it was sudden." David kissed Pam on the cheek and took a casserole dish and a laden bag from her. She patted him on the head in a motherly fashion.

"Introduce me," she said.

"Ev, this is Pam and Tyler, old friends of mine. They've also been taking care of the house for me." He looked relaxed standing between these people. His smile was easy and his eyes were bright. I hadn't seen him looking so happy before. Jealousy reared its ugly head, sinking its teeth in.

"Hello." I put out my hand for shaking, but Tyler engulfed me in a hug.

"She's so pretty. Isn't she pretty, hon?" Tyler stepped aside and Pam came closer, a warm smile on her face.

I was being a jerk. These were nice people. I should be profoundly grateful not every female David knew rubbed her boobs on him. Damn my screaming hormones for making me surly.

"She sure is. Hello, Ev. I'm Pam." The woman's coffee-brown eyes went liquid. She seemed ready to burst into tears. In a rush, she took my hands and squeezed my fingers tight. "I'm just so happy he found a nice girl, finally."

"Oh, thank you." My face felt flammable.

David gave me a wry grin.

"Okay, enough of that," Tyler said. "Let's let these lovebirds have their privacy. We can visit another time."

David stood aside, still holding the casserole dish and bag. When he saw me watching, he winked.

"I'll have to show you the setup downstairs sometime," Tyler said. "You here for long?"

"We're not sure," he said, giving me a glance.

Pam clung to my hands, reluctant to leave. "I made chicken enchiladas and rice. Do you like Mexican? It's David's favorite." Pam's brows wrinkled. "But I didn't think to check if that was all right with you. You might be vegetarian."

"No, I'm not. And I love Mexican," I said, squeezing

her fingers back, though not as hard. "Thank you so much."

"Phew." She grinned.

"Hon," called Tyler.

"I'm coming." Pam gave my fingers a parting pat. "If you need anything at all while you're here, you give me a call. Okay?"

David said nothing. It was clearly my decision if they stayed or went. My body was still abuzz with need. That, and we seemed to do better alone. I didn't want to share him because I was shallow and wanted hot sex. I wanted him all to myself. But it was the right thing to do. And if anticipation made it sweeter, well, maybe this once the right thing to do was also the best thing to do.

"Stay," I said, stammering out the words. "Have dinner with us. You've made so much. We could never possibly finish it all."

David's gaze jumped to me, a smile of approval on his face. He looked almost boyish, trying to contain his excitement. Like I'd just told him his birthday had been brought forward. Whoever these people were, they were important to him. I felt as though I'd just passed some test.

Pam sighed. "Tyler is right, you're newlyweds."

"Stay. Please," I said.

Pam looked to Tyler.

Tyler shrugged but smiled, obviously delighted.

Pam clapped her hands with glee. "Let's eat!"

CHAPTER NINE

Warm hands pushed up my tank top as the sun rose. Next came hot kisses down my back, sending a shiver up my spine. My skin came to immediate goose-pimpled attention, despite the truly horrible time of day.

"Ev, baby, roll over." David whispered in my ear.

"What time is it?"

We'd all gone downstairs to the recording studio after dinner for a "quick look." At midnight Pam had bailed, saying Tyler could call her when they were done. No one anticipated that being anytime soon, since they'd opened a bottle of bourbon. I'd stretched out on the big couch down there while David and Tyler messed around, moving between the control room and the studio. I'd wanted to be close to David, to listen to him play guitar and sing snippets of songs. He had a beautiful voice. What he could do with a six-string in his hands blew my mind. His eyes would take on this faraway look and he was gone. It was like nothing else existed. Sometimes, I actually felt a little lonely, lying there watching him. Then the song would end and he'd shake his head, stretch his fingers, returning to earth. His gaze would find me and he'd smile. He was back.

At some stage I'd dozed off. How I'd gotten up to bed

I had no idea. David must have carried me. One thing was certain: I could smell booze.

"It's almost five in the morning," he said. "Roll over."

"Tired," I mumbled, staying right where I was.

The mattress shifted as he straddled my hips and put an arm either side of my head, bending down over me, covering me.

"Guess what?" he asked.

"What?"

Gently he pushed my hair back off my face. Then he licked my ear. I squirmed, ticklish.

"I wrote two songs," he said, his voice a little slurred, soft around the edges.

"Mm." I smiled without opening my eyes. Hopefully he'd take that as being supportive. I couldn't manage much more on fewer than four hours' sleep. I simply wasn't wired that way. "That's nice."

"No, you don't understand. I haven't written anything in over two years. This is fucking amazing." He nuzzled my neck. "And they're about you."

"Your songs?" I asked, stunned. And still dazed. "Really?"

"Yeah, I just . . ." He breathed deep and nipped my shoulder, making my eyes pop open.

"Hey!"

He leaned over so I could see his face, his dark hair hanging down. "There you are. So, I think of you and suddenly I have something to say. I haven't had anything I wanted to say in a long time. I didn't give a fuck. It was all just more of the same. But you changed things. You fixed me."

"David, I'm glad you got your mojo back, but you're incredibly talented. You were never broken. Maybe you just needed some time off."

"No." From upside down, he frowned at me. "Roll over. I can't talk to you like this." I hesitated and he slapped my butt. The nontattooed cheek, lucky for him. "Come on, baby."

"Watch it with the biting and spanking, buddy."

"So move already," he growled.

"Okay. Okay."

He climbed off me onto the other side of the mammoth mattress and I sat, drawing my knees up to my chest. The man was shirtless, staring back at me with only a pair of jeans on. How the hell did he keep losing his shirt? The sight of his bare chest brought me to the dribble point. The jeans pushed me right over. No one wore jeans like David. And having caught a glimpse of him without them only made it worse. My imagination went into some sort of sexual berserker rage. The pictures that filled my head . . . I have no idea where they all came from. The images were surprisingly raw and detailed. I was quite certain I wasn't flexible enough to achieve some of them.

All of the air left the room. Truth was, I wanted him. All of him. The good and the bad and the bits in between. I wanted him more than I'd ever wanted anything before in my life.

But not when he'd been drinking. We'd already been there, made that mistake. I didn't know quite what was going on between us, but I didn't want to mess it up.

So, right. No sex. Bad.

I had to stop looking at him. So I took a deep breath and studied my knees. My bare knees. I'd gone to sleep wearing jeans. Now I had only panties and my tank top on. My bra had also mysteriously disappeared. "What happened to the rest of my clothes?"

"They left," he said, face serious.

"You took them?"

He shrugged. "You wouldn't have been comfortable sleeping in them."

"How on earth did you manage to get my bra off without waking me?"

He gave me a sly smile. "I didn't do anything else. I swear. I just . . . removed it for safety reasons. Underwire is dangerous."

"Riiiight."

"I didn't even look."

I narrowed my eyes on him.

"That's a lie," he admitted, rolling his shoulders. "I had to look. But we are still married, so looking is okay."

"It is, huh?" It was pretty much impossible to be mad at him when he looked at me like that. My foolish girl parts got giddy.

No. Sex.

"What are you doing up that end of the bed? That's not going to work," he said, totally unaware of my wakening hormones and distress at same.

Faster than I'd have thought possible given the amount of booze on his breath, he grabbed my feet and dragged me down the bed. My back hit the mattress and my head bounced off the pillow. David sprawled out on top of me before I could attempt any more evasive maneuvers. His weight pressed me into the mattress in the best possible way. Saying no under these conditions was a big ask.

"I don't think we should have sex now," I blurted out.

The side of his mouth kicked up. "Relax. There's no way we're fucking right now."

"No?" Damn it, I actually whined. My patheticness knew no end.

"No. When we do it the first time we'll both be stone-cold sober. Trust me on that. I'm not waking up in the morning again to find you're freaking out because you don't remember or you've changed your mind or something. I'm done being the asshole here."

"I never thought you were an asshole, David." Or at least, not exactly. A jerk maybe, and definitely a bra thief, but not an asshole.

"No?"

"No."

"Not even in Vegas when I started swearing at you and slamming doors?" His fingers slid into my hair, rubbing at my scalp. Impossible not to push into his touch like a happy kitty. He had magic hands. He even made mornings bearable. Though five o'clock was pushing it.

"That wasn't a good morning for either of us," I said.

"How about in LA with that girl hanging off me?"

"You planned that?"

He shut one eye and looked down at me. "Maybe I needed some armor against you."

I didn't know what to say. At first. "It's none of my business who you have hanging off you."

His smile was one of immense self-satisfaction. "You were jealous."

"Do we have to do this right now?" I pushed against his hard body, getting nowhere. "David?"

"Can't own up to it, can you?"

I didn't reply.

"Hey, I couldn't bring myself to touch her. Not with you there."

"You didn't?" I calmed down a lot at that statement. My heart palpitations eased. "I wondered what happened. You came back so fast."

He grunted, got closer. "Seeing you with Jimmy . . ."

"Nothing was going on. I swear."

"No, I know. I'm sorry about that. I was out of line."

My pushing hands turned to petting. Funny that. They slid over his shoulders, around his neck to fiddle with his hair. I just wanted to feel the heat of his skin and keep him near. He made for an emotional landslide, turning me from sleep deprived and cranky to adoring in under eight seconds. "It's great that you wrote some songs."

"Mm. How about when I left you with Adrian and the lawyers? Were you mad at me then?"

I huffed out a breath. "Fine. I might admit to being a bit upset about that."

He nodded slowly, his eyes never leaving mine. "When I got back and they told me what had happened, that you'd taken off with Mal, I lost it. Trashed my favorite guitar, used it to take apart Mal's kit. Still can't believe I did that. I was just so fucking angry and jealous and mad at myself."

I could feel my face scrunch up in disbelief. "You did?"

"Yeah." His eyes were stark, wide. "I did."

"Why are you telling me this now, David?"

"I don't want you hearing it from someone else." He swallowed, making the line of his throat move. "Listen, I'm not like that, Ev. It won't happen again, I promise. I'm just not used to this. You get to me. This whole situation does. I dunno, I'm fucking rambling. Do you understand?"

Later, he mightn't even remember any of this. But right now, he looked so sincere. My heart hurt for him. I looked into his bloodshot eyes and smiled. "I think so. It definitely won't happen again?"

"No. I swear." The relief in his voice was palpable. "We're okay?"

"Yes. Are you going to play the songs for me later?" I asked. "I'd love to hear them."

"They're not done yet. When they're done, I will. I want them perfect for you."

"Okay," I said. He'd written songs about me. How incredible, unless they were the uncomplimentary kind, in which case we needed to talk. "They're not about how much I annoy you sometimes, are they?"

He seesawed his hand in the air. "A little. In a good way, though."

"What?" I cried.

"Trust me."

"Do you actually state what a pain in the ass I am in these songs?"

"Not those words exactly. No." He chuckled, his good humor returned. "You don't want me to lie and say everything's always fucking unicorns and rainbows, do you?"

"Maybe. Yes. People are going to know these are about me. I have a reputation as a constant delight to protect."

He groaned. "Evelyn, look at me."

I did so.

"You are a constant fucking delight. I don't think anyone could ever doubt that."

"You're awful pretty when you lie."

"Am I, now? They're love songs, baby. Love isn't always smooth or straightforward. It can be messy and painful," he said. "Doesn't mean it isn't still the most incredible thing that can ever happen to you. Doesn't mean I'm not crazy about you."

"You are?" I asked, my voice tight with emotion.

"Of course I am."

"I'm crazy about you too. You're beautiful, inside and out, David Ferris."

He lay his forehead against mine, closing his eyes for a moment. "You're so fucking sweet. But, you know, I like that you can bite too. Like you did in Vegas with those assholes. I like that you cared, standing up for that girl. I even kind of like it when you piss me off. Not all the time, though. Shit. I'm rambling again . . ."

"It's okay," I whispered. "I like you rambling."

"So you're not angry at me for losing my temper?"

"No, David. I'm not angry at you."

Without another word, he crawled off me and lay at my side. He pulled me into his arms, arranging an arm beneath me and another over my hip. "Ev?"

"Hmm?"

"Take your shirt off. I wanna be skin to skin," he said. "Please? Nothing more, I promise."

"Okay." I sat up and pulled the tank top off over my head, then snuggled back down against him. Topless had a lot going for it. He tucked me in beneath his chin, and the feel of his warm chest was perfect, thrilling and calming all at once. Every inch of my skin seemed alive with sensation. But being like this with him soothed the savage storm within or something. It never occurred to me to worry about my belly or hips or any of that crap.

Never mind the lingering scent of booze on his skin, I just wanted to be close to him.

"I like sleeping with you," he said, his hand stroking over my back. "Didn't think I'd be able to sleep with someone else in the bed, but with you it's okay."

"You've never slept with anyone before?"

"Not in a long time. I need my space." His fingers toyed with the band on my boy-leg shorts, making me squirm.

"Huh."

"This with you is torture, but it's good torture."

Everything fell quiet for a few minutes and I thought he might have fallen asleep. But he hadn't. "Talk to me, I like hearing your voice."

"All right. I had a nice time with Pam, she's lovely."

"Yeah, she is." His fingers trailed up and down along my spine. "They're good people."

"It was really kind of them to bring us dinner." I didn't know what to say. I wasn't ready to confess I'd been thinking about what he'd said about my becoming an architect. That I'd started questioning the almighty plan. Saying I was scared I'd mess up and somehow ruin things between us didn't seem smart either. Maybe the fates would be listening and screw me over first chance they got. God, I hoped not. So instead I chose to talk trivial. "I love how you can hear the ocean here."

"Mm," he hummed his agreement. "Baby, I don't want to sign those papers on Monday."

I held perfectly still, my heart pounding. "You don't?"

"No." His hand crept up, fingers stroking below my breast, tracing the line of my rib cage. I had to remind myself to breathe. But he didn't even seem to be aware he did it, like he was just doodling on my skin the same way you would on paper. His arms tightened around me. "There's no reason it can't wait. We could spend some time together, see how things went."

Hope rushed through me, hot and thrilling. "David, are you serious about this?"

"Yeah, I am." He sighed. "I know I've been drinking. But I've been thinking it over. I don't . . . shit, I didn't even like having you out of my sight the last few hours, but you looked like you needed to sleep. I don't want us to sign those papers."

I squeezed my eyes tight and sent up a silent prayer. "Then we won't."

"You sure?"

"Yes."

He pulled me in tight against him. "Okay. Okay, that's good."

"We're going to be fine." I sighed happily. The relief made me weak. If I hadn't been lying down I'd have landed on the floor.

Suddenly he sniffed at his shoulder and underarms. "Shit, I stink of bourbon. I'm going to have a shower." He gave me a quick kiss and rolled out of the bed. "Kick me out of bed next time I try to come in smelling like this. Don't let me cuddle up to you."

I loved that he was talking about our being together like it would be an everyday thing. I loved it so much, I didn't even care how bad he smelled.

True love.

CHAPTER TEN

The gong of the doorbell echoed through the house just after ten. David slept on against my back. He didn't stir at all. With a couple more hours' sleep I felt happily half human. I crawled out from beneath his arm, trying not to disturb him. I pulled my top and jeans back on and dashed down the stairs, doing my best not to break my neck in the process. In all likelihood it would be more deliveries.

"Child bride! Let me in!" Mal hollered from the other side of the door. He followed it up with an impressive percussive performance, banging his hands against the solid wood. Definitely the drummer. "Evvie!"

No one called me Evvie. I'd stamped out that nickname years ago. However, it might be better than child bride.

I opened the door and Mal barreled in, Tyler dragging himself along after. Considering Tyler had sat up drinking and playing music with David until the wee small hours, I wasn't really surprised at his condition. The poor man clearly suffered with the hangover from hell. He looked like he'd been punched in both eyes, the bruises from lack of sleep were so bad. An energy drink was attached to his lips.

"Mal. What are you doing here?" I stopped, rubbed the sleep from my eyes. Wake-up call, it wasn't even my house. "Sorry, that was rude. It's just a surprise to see you. Hi, Tyler."

I'd been hoping to have my husband to myself today, but apparently it wasn't to be.

Mal dropped my backpack at my feet. He was so busy looking around the place he didn't even seem to have heard my question, rude or not.

"David is still asleep," I said, and rifled through the contents of my bag. Oh, my stuff. My wonderful stuff. My purse and phone in particular were a delight to lay eyes on. Many text messages from Lauren, plus a few from my dad. I hadn't even known he could text. "Thank you for bringing this."

"Dave called me at four in the morning and told me he'd written some new stuff. Figured I'd come up and see what was going on. Thought you'd like your gear." Hands on hips, Mal stood before the wall of windows pondering the magnificence of nature. "Man, check out that view."

"Nice, huh?" said Tyler from behind his drink. "Wait till you see the studio."

Mal cupped his hands around his mouth. "Hipster King. Get down here!"

"Hi, sweetie." Pam wandered in, twirling a set of keys on her finger. "I tried to make them leave it a few more hours, but as you can see, I lost. Sorry."

"Never mind," I said. I'm not much of a hugger normally. We didn't do a lot of it in my family. My parents preferred a more hands-free method. But Pam was so nice that I hugged her back when she threw her arms around me.

We'd talked for hours the night before down in the recording studio. It had been illuminating. Married to a popular session player and producer, she'd lived the lifestyle for over twenty years. Touring, recording, groupies . . . she'd experienced the whole rock 'n' roll shebang. She and Tyler had attended a music festival and fallen in love with Monterey with its jagged coastline and sweeping ocean views.

"The lounge and another couple of beds are on their way, should be here soon. Mal, Tyler, help move the boxes. We'll stack them against the fireplace." Suddenly Pam stopped, giving me a cautious smile. "Hang on. You're the woman of the house. You give the orders here."

"Oh, against the fireplace sounds great, thanks," I said.

"You heard her, boys. Get moving."

Tyler grumbled but put down his can and lumbered toward a box, dragging his feet like the walking dead.

"Hold up." Mal smacked his lips at Pam and me. "I haven't gotten my hello kisses yet." He caught Pam up in a bear hug, lifting her off her feet and twirling her around until she laughed. Arms wide, he stepped toward me next. "Come to daddy, bed-head girl."

I put a hand out to halt him, laughing. "That's actually really disturbing, Mal."

"Leave her be," said David from the top of the stairs, yawning and rubbing the sleep from his eyes. Still wearing just the jeans. He was my kryptonite. All the strength of my convictions to be careful disappeared. My legs actually wobbled. I hated that.

Were we married or not today? He'd had a hell of a lot to drink last night. Drunk people and promises did not go well together—we'd both learned that the hard way. I could only hope he remembered our conversation and still felt the same way.

"What the fuck are you doing here?" growled my husband.

"I want to hear the new stuff, asswipe. Deal with it." Mal stared up at him, his jaw set in a hard line. "I should beat the living crap out of you. Fuck, man. That was my favorite kit!"

Body rigid, David started down the stairs. "I said I'm sorry. I meant it."

"Maybe. But it's still time to pay, you dickwad."

For a moment David didn't reply. Tension lined his face but there was a look of inevitability in his weary eyes. "All right. What?"

"It's gotta hurt. Bad."

"Worse than you turning up when Ev and me are having time alone?"

Mal actually looked a little shamefaced.

David stopped at the foot of the steps, waiting. "You wanna take this outside?"

Pam and Tyler said nothing, just watched the byplay. I got the feeling this wasn't the first time these two had faced off. Boys will be boys and all that. But I stood beside Mal, every muscle tensed. If he took one step toward David, I'd jump him. Pull his hair or something. I didn't know how, but I'd stop him.

Mal gave him a measuring look. "I'm not hitting you. I don't want to mess up my hands when we've got work to do."

"What, then?"

"You already trashed your favorite guitar. So it's going to have to be something else." Mal rubbed his hands together. "Something money can't buy."

"What?" asked David, his eyes suddenly wary.

"Hi, Evvie." Mal grinned, and slung an arm around my shoulder, pulling me in against him.

"Hey," I protested.

In the next moment his mouth covered mine, entirely unwelcome. David shouted a protest. An arm wrapped around my back and Mal dipped me, kissing me hard, bruising my lips. I grabbed at his shoulders, afraid I'd hit the floor. When he tried to put his tongue in my mouth, however, I didn't hesitate to bite him.

The idiot howled.

Take that.

Just as fast as he'd dipped me, he set me to rights. My

head spun. I put a hand to the wall to stop from stumbling. I rubbed at my mouth, trying to get rid of the taste of him, while Mal gave me a wounded look.

"Damn it. That hurt." He carefully touched his tongue, searching for damage. "I'm bleeding!"

"Good."

Pam and Tyler chuckled, highly amused.

Arms wrapped around me from behind and David whispered in my ear, "Nice work."

"Did you know he was going to do that?" I asked, sounding distinctly pissy.

"Fuck no." He rubbed his face against the side of my head, mussing my bed hair. "I don't want anyone else touching you."

It was the right answer. My anger melted away. I put my hands on top of his, and the grip on me tightened.

"You want me to beat the shit out of him?" asked David. "Just say the word."

I pretended to consider it for a moment while Mal watched us with interest. We obviously looked a lot friendlier than we had in LA. But it was nobody's business. Not his friend's, not the press's, nobody's.

"No," I whispered back, my belly doing backflips. I was falling so fast for him it scared me. "I guess you'd better not."

David turned me in his arms and I fit myself against him, wrapping my arms around his waist. It felt natural and right. The scent of his skin made me high. I could have stood there breathing him in for hours. It felt like maybe we were together, but I no longer trusted my own judgment, if I ever had to begin with.

"Malcolm is joining you on your honeymoon?" Pam's voice was heavy with disbelief.

David chuckled. "No, this isn't our honeymoon. If we have a honeymoon it'll be somewhere far away from everyone. Sure as hell, he won't be there."

"If?" she asked.

I really did love Pam.

"When," he corrected, holding me tight.

"This is all real cute, but I came to make music," Mal announced.

"Then you're just going to have to fucking wait," said David. "Ev and I have plans this morning."

"We've been waiting two years to come up with something new."

"Tough shit. You can wait a few more hours." David took my hand and led me back toward the stairs. Excitement ran rife through me. He'd chosen me and it felt wonderful.

"Evvie, sorry about the mouth mauling," Mal said, sitting himself down on the nearest box.

"You're forgiven," I said with a queenly wave, feeling magnanimous as we headed up the stairs.

"You going to apologize for biting me?" Mal asked.

"Nope."

"Well, that's not very nice," he called out after us.

David sniggered.

"Okay, people, we need to move boxes." I heard Pam say.

David rushed us down the hallway, then closed and locked the bedroom door behind us.

"You put your clothes back on," he said. "Get them off."

He didn't wait for me to do it, grabbing the hem of my shirt and lifting it up over my head and raised arms.

"I didn't think answering the door mostly naked was a good idea."

"Fair enough," he murmured, pulling me in against him and backing me up against the door. "You looked worried about something downstairs. What was it?"

"It was nothing."

"Evelyn." There was something about the way he said

my name. It made me a quivering mess. Also the way he cornered me, pressing his body against mine. I put my hands flat on his hard chest. Not pushing him away, just needing to touch him.

"I was wondering," I said. "After our talk this morning, when we, um, discussed signing the papers on Monday."

"What about it?" he asked, staring straight at me. I couldn't have looked away if I'd tried.

"Well, I wasn't sure if you still felt the same way. About not signing them, I mean. You'd had a lot to drink."

"I haven't changed my mind." His pelvis aligned with mine and his hands swept up my sides. "You changed yours?"

"No."

"Good." His warm hands cupped my breasts, and I lost all ability to think straight.

"You okay with this?" He gave his hands a pointed look.

I nodded. Talking had gone with thinking, apparently.

"Then here's the plan. Because I know how you like your plans. We're going to stay in this room until we're both satisfied we're on the same page when it comes to us. Agreed?"

I nodded again. Without a doubt, the plan had my full support.

"Good." He placed the palm of one hand between my breasts, flat against my chest. "Your heart's beating real fast."

"David."

"Hmm?"

Nope, I still had no words. So instead, I covered his hand with my own, holding it against my heart. He smiled.

"This is a dramatic reenactment of the night we got married," he announced, looking at me from beneath dark brows. "Hang on. We were sitting on the bed in your motel room. You were straddling me."

"I was?"

"Yeah." He led me to the bed and sat at the edge. "Come on."

I climbed onto his lap, my legs wrapped around him. "Like this?"

"That's it." His hands gripped my waist. "You refused to go back to my suite at the Bellagio. Said I was out of touch with real life and needed to see how the little people lived."

I groaned with embarrassment. "That doesn't sound the least bit arrogant of me."

His mouth curved into a small smile. "It was fun. But also, you were right."

"Better not tell me that too often or it'll go to my head."

His chin rose. "Stop making jokes, baby. I'm being serious. I needed a dose of reality. Someone who'd actually say no to me occasionally and call bullshit on that scene. That's what we do. We push each other out of our comfort zones."

It made sense. "I think you're right . . . Is it enough?"

He held his hand to my heart again and bumped the tip of his nose against mine. "Can you feel what we're doing here? We're building something."

"Yes." I could feel it, the connection between us, the overwhelming need to be with him. Nothing else mattered. There was the physical, the way he went to my head faster than anything I'd ever experienced. How wonderful he smelled all sleep warm first thing in the morning. But I wanted more from him than just that. I wanted to hear his voice, hear him talk about everything and anything.

I felt all lit up inside. Like a potent mix of hormones was racing through me at light speed. His other hand curled around the back of my neck, bringing my mouth to his. Kissing David threw kerosene on the mix within me. He slid his tongue into my mouth to stroke against my own, before teasing over my teeth and lips. I'd never felt anything so fine. Fingers caressed my breast, doing wonderful things and making me gasp. God, the heat of his bare skin. I shuffled forward, seeking more, needing it. His hand left my breast to splay across my back, pressing me against him. He was hard. I could feel him through both layers of denim. The pressure that provided between my legs was heavenly. Amazing.

"That's it," he murmured as I rocked against him, seeking more.

Our kisses were fierce, hungry. His hot mouth moved over my jaw and chin, my neck. Where my neck met my chest, he stopped and sucked. Everything in me drew tight.

"David—"

He pulled back and looked at me, his eyes dilated. Every bit as affected as I was. Thank God I wasn't alone with the panting. A finger traced a slow path between my breasts down to the waistband of my jeans.

"You know what happened next," he said. His hand slipped beneath. "Say it, Ev." When I hesitated, he leaned forward and nipped at my neck. "Go on. Tell me."

Biting had never appealed to me before, neither in thought nor in action. Not that there'd been much action. But the sensation of David's teeth pressing into my skin turned me inside out. I shut my eyes tight. A bit from the bite and a lot from having to say the words he wanted.

"I've only done this once before."

"You're nervous. Don't be nervous." He kissed me where he'd just bitten. "So, anyway, let's get married."

My eyelids opened and a startled laugh flew out of me. "I bet that's not what you said that night."

"I might have been a little concerned by your inexperience. And we might have had words about it." He gave me a faint smile and kissed the side of my mouth. "But everything worked out fine."

"What words? Tell me what happened."

"We decided to get married. Lie back on the bed for me."

He grasped my hips, helping me climb off him and onto the mattress. My hands slid over the smooth, cool cotton sheet. I lay on my back and he swiftly undid my jeans and disposed of them. The bed shifted beneath me as he knelt above me. I felt ready to implode, my heart hammering, but he seemed perfectly calm and in control. Nice that one of us was. Of course, he'd done this dozens of times.

Probably more, what with groupies and all that. Hundreds? Thousands, even?

I really didn't want to think about it.

His gaze rose to meet mine as he hooked fingers into my panties. In no rush at all, he dragged the last of my clothing down my legs. The urge to cover myself was overwhelming. But I fisted the sheet instead, rubbing the fabric between my fingers.

He undid his jeans. The rustles of his clothing were the only sounds. We didn't break eye contact. Not until he turned to the bedside table and retrieved a condom, discreetly tucking it underneath the pillow next to me.

David naked defied description. Beautiful didn't begin to cover it, all the hard lines of his body and the tattoos covering his skin, but he didn't give me much time to look.

He climbed back onto the bed, lying at my side, raised up on one elbow. His hand curled over my hip. Dark hair fell forward, blocking his face from view. I wanted to see him. He leaned down, kissing me gently this time on my lips, my face. His hair brushed against my skin.

"Where were we?" he asked, his voice a low rumble in my ear.

"We decided to get married."

"Mm, because I'd just had the best night of my life. First time I hadn't felt alone in so fucking long. The

thought of not having you with me every other night . . .
I couldn't do it." His mouth traveled up my neck. "I
couldn't let you go. Especially once I knew you'd only
been with one other guy."

"I thought that bothered you?"

"It bothered me, all right," he said, and kissed my chin.
"You were obviously ready to give sex another try. If I was
stupid enough to let you go, you might have met someone else. I couldn't stand the thought of you fucking anyone but me."

"Oh."

"Oh," he agreed. "Speaking of which, any second
thoughts about what we're doing here?"

"No." Lots of nerves but no second thoughts.

The hand on my hip traced over my stomach. It circled
my belly button before dipping lower, making me shiver.

"You are so damn pretty," he breathed. "Every piece
of you. And when I dared you to put aside your plan and
run away with me, you said yes."

"I did?"

"You did."

"Thank God for that."

Fingers stroked over the top of my sex before moving
on to my thigh muscles clenched tight together. If I wanted
this to go any further I was going to need to open my legs.
I knew this. Of course I did. Memories of the pain from
last time made me hesitate. My toes were curled and a
cramp was threatening to start up in my calf muscle from
all of the tensing. Ridiculous. Tommy Byrnes had been a
thoughtless prick. David wasn't like that.

"We can go as slow as you want," he said, reading me
just fine. "Trust me, Ev."

His warm hand smoothed over my thigh as his tongue
traveled the length of my neck. It felt wonderful, but it
wasn't enough.

"I need . . ." I turned my face to him, searching for his

mouth. He fit his lips to mine, making everything right. Kissing David healed every ill. The knot of tension inside me turned into something sweet at the taste of him, the feel of his body against mine. One arm was trapped underneath me, but the other I made full use of, touching all of him within reach. Kneading his shoulder and feeling the hard, smooth planes of his back.

When I sucked on his tongue, he moaned in the back of his throat and my confidence soared. His hand slipped between my legs. Just the pressure of his palm had me seeing stars. I broke off the kiss, unable to breathe. He touched me gently at first, letting me get used to him. The things his fingers could do.

"Elvis couldn't be with us today," he said.

"What?" I asked, mystified.

He stopped and put two fingers into his mouth, wetting them or tasting me I didn't know. Didn't matter. What was important was him putting his hand back on me, fast.

"I didn't want to share this with anyone." The tip of his finger pushed into me, easing inside just a little. Pulling back before pressing in again. It didn't have the same thrill attached to it that came with him stroking me, but it didn't hurt. Not yet.

"So, no Elvis. I'll have to ask the questions," he said.

I frowned at him, finding it hard to focus on what he was saying. It couldn't be as important as him touching me. The pursuit of pleasure ruled my mind. Maybe he babbled during foreplay. I didn't know. If he wanted, I was more than willing to listen to him later.

His gaze lingered on my breasts until finally he dipped his head, taking one into his mouth. My back bowed, pushing his finger further inside. The way his mouth drew on me erased any discomfort. He stroked me between my legs and the pleasure grew. I tingled in the best way possible. When I did this, it was nice. When David did it, it reached the heights of spectacular, stellar. I knew he was crazy good at guitar, but this had to be where his true talent lay. Honestly.

"God, David." I arched against him when he moved to my other breast. Two fingers worked inside me, a little uncomfortable but nothing I couldn't handle. Not so long as he kept his mouth on me, lavishing my breasts with attention. His thumb rubbed around a sweet spot and my eyes rolled back into my head. So close. The strength of what was building was staggering. Mind-blowing. My body was going to be blown to dust, atoms, when this hit.

If he stopped, I'd cry. Cry, and beg. And maybe kill.

Happily, he didn't stop.

I came, groaning, every muscle drawn taut. It was almost too much. Almost. I floated, my body limp, satiated for all time. Or at least until the next time.

When I opened my eyes again, he was there waiting. He ripped open the condom with his teeth and then put it on. I'd barely caught my breath when he rose over me, moved between my legs.

"Good?" he asked, with a smile of satisfaction.

A nod was the best I could do.

He took the bulk of his weight onto his elbows, his body pressing me into the bed. I'd noticed he enjoyed using his size to the advantage of both of us. It worked. Certainly, there was nothing boring or claustrophobic about the position. I don't know why I'd thought there would be. In the back of Tommy Byrnes's parents' car I'd been cramped and uncomfortable, but this was nothing like that. Lying underneath him, feeling the heat of his skin against mine was perfect. And there could be no doubting how much he wanted this. I lay there, waiting for him to push into me.

Still waiting.

He brushed his lips against mine. "Do you, Evelyn Jennifer Thomas, agree to stay married to me, David Vincent Ferris?"

Oh, that was the Elvis he'd been talking about. The one who'd married us. Huh. I held back his hair, needing to see his eyes. I should have asked him to tie it back. It made it hard to try and gauge his seriousness.

"You really want to do this now?" I asked, a little thrown. I'd been so busy worrying about the sex I hadn't seen this coming.

"Absolutely. We're doing our vows again right now."

"Yes?" I said.

He cocked his head, narrowing his eyes at me. The look on his face was distinctly pained. "Yes? You're not sure?"

"No. I mean, yes," I repeated, more definitely. "Yes. I'm sure. I am."

"Thank fuck for that." His hand rifled under the pillow next to me, returning with the ring of stupendousness sparkling between his fingers. "Hand."

I held my hand between us and he slid the ring on. My cheeks hurt, I was smiling so hard. "Did you say yes too?"

"Yes." He took my mouth in a hard kiss. His hand slid down my side, over my stomach to cup me between my legs. Everything there was still sensitive and no doubt wet. The hunger in his kisses and the way he touched me assured me he certainly didn't mind.

He fit himself to me and pushed in. This was it. And suddenly, shit, I couldn't relax. The memory of pain from the last time I'd attempted this messed with my mind. Wet didn't matter when my muscles wouldn't give. I gasped, my thighs squeezing his hips. David was hard and thick and it hurt.

"Look at me," he said. The blue of his eyes had darkened and his jaw was set. His damp skin gleamed in the low lighting. "Hey."

"Hey." My voice sounded shaky even to my own ears.

"Kiss me." He lowered his face and I did so, pressing my tongue into his mouth, needing him. Carefully, he rocked against me, moving deeper inside me. The pad of his thumb played around my clit, counteracting the hurt. The pain eased, coming closer to being plain old discomfort with an edge of pleasure. No problem. This I could handle.

Fingers wrapped around my leg before sliding down to cup a butt cheek. He pulled me in against him and moved deeper inside me. Rocking against me until I'd taken him all. Which was a problem, because there wasn't enough damn room in me for him.

"It's okay," he groaned.

Easy for him to say.

Shit.

Bodies flush against each another, we lay there, unmoving. My arms were around his head so tight, clinging to him, that I'm not certain how he breathed. Somehow he managed to turn his face enough to kiss my neck, lick the sweat from my skin. Up, over my jaw to my mouth. The death grip I had on him eased when he kissed me.

"That's it," he said. "Try and relax for me."

I nodded jerkily, willing my body to unwind.

"You are so damn beautiful and, God, you feel fucking amazing." His big hand petted my breast, calloused fingers stroking down my side, easing me. My muscles began to relax incrementally, adjusting to his presence. The hurt faded more every time he touched me, whispering words of praise.

"This is good," I said at last, my hands resting on his biceps. "I'm okay."

"No, you're better than okay. You're amazing."

I gave him a giddy smile. He said the best things.

"You mean I can move?" he asked.

"Yes."

He started rocking against me again, moving a little more each time. Gradually gaining momentum as our bodies moved slickly together. We fit, mostly. And we were actually doing it, the deed. Talk about feeling close to someone. You couldn't get physically closer. I was so profoundly glad it was him. It meant everything.

Tommy had lasted two seconds. Long enough to break my hymen and hurt me. David touched me and kissed me and took his time. Slowly, the sweet heat, that sensation of pressure building, came again. He tended to it with care, feeding me long, wet kisses. Stroking himself into me in a way that brought only pleasure. He was incredible, watching me so closely, gauging my reactions to everything he did.

Eventually, I clung onto him and came hard. It felt like the New Year's fireworks display inside me, hot and bright and perfect. So much more with him inside and over me, his skin plastered to mine. I stuttered out his name and he pressed hard against me. When he groaned, his whole body shuddered. He buried his face in my neck, his breath heating my skin.

We'd done it.

Huh.

Wow.

Things did ache a little. People were right about that. But nothing like last time.

Carefully, he moved off me, collapsing on the bed at my side.

"We did it," I whispered.

His eyes opened. His chest was still heaving, working to get more air into him. After a moment, he rolled onto his side to face me. There'd never been a better man. Of this I was certain.

"Yeah. You okay?" he asked.

"Yes." I shuffled closer, seeking out the heat of his body. He slid an arm over my waist, drawing me in. Letting me know I was wanted. Our faces were a bare hand's width apart. "It was so much better than last time. I think I like sex after all."

"You have no idea how relieved I am to hear that."

"Were you nervous?"

He chuckled, shuffling closer. "Not as nervous as you were. I'm glad you liked it."

"I loved it. You're a man of many talents."

His smile took on a certain glow.

"You're not going to get all cocky on me now, are you? All puns intended."

"I wouldn't dare. I trust you to keep me grounded, Mrs. Ferris."

"Mrs. Ferris," I said, with no small amount of wonder. "How about that?"

"Hmm." His fingers stroked my face.

I caught his bare hand, inspecting it. "You don't have a ring."

"No, I don't. We'll have to fix that."

"Yes, we will."

He smiled. "Hey, Mrs. Ferris."

"Hey, Mr. Ferris."

There wasn't enough room in me for all the feelings he inspired.

Not even close.

CHAPTER ELEVEN

We spent the afternoon back down in the recording studio with Tyler and Mal. When David wasn't playing, he pulled me onto his lap. When he was busy on guitar, I listened, in awe of his talent. He didn't sing, so I remained in the dark about the lyrics. But the music was beautiful in a raw, rock 'n' roll sort of way. Mal seemed pleased with the new material, bopping his head along in time.

Tyler beamed behind the splendid board of buttons and dials. "Play that lick again, Dave." My husband nodded and his fingers moved over the fretboard, making magic.

Pam had been busy while we'd been upstairs, starting on unpacking the collection of boxes. When she made a move to return to the job in the early evening, I went with her. Asked or not, it wasn't fair that she got lumped with the task on her own. Plus, it pleased my inner need to organize. I snuck back downstairs now and then as the hours passed, stealing kisses, before heading back up to help Pam again. David and company remained immersed in the music. They'd come up seeking food or drink but returned immediately to the studio.

"This is what it's like when they're recording. They lose track of time, get caught up in the music. The number of dinners Tyler has missed because he simply forgot!" said Pam, hands busy unpacking the latest box.

"It's their job, but it's also their first love," she continued, dusting off an Asian-style bowl. "You know that one old girlfriend that's always hanging around the fringes, drunk-dialing them at all hours and asking them to come over?"

I laughed. "How do you deal with never getting to come first?"

"You have to strike a balance. Music's a part of them that you have to accept, hon. Fighting it won't work. Have you ever been really passionate about something?"

"No," I answered in all honesty, eyeing up another stringed instrument I'd never seen the likes of. It had intricate carving encircling the sound hole. "I enjoy college. I love being a barista, it's a great job. I really like the people. But I can't sling coffee for the rest of my life." I stopped, grimaced. "God, those are my father's words. Forget I ever said that."

"You can totally sling coffee for the rest of your life, if you so choose," she said. "But sometimes it takes time to find your thing. There's no rush. I was a born and bred photographer."

"That's great."

Pam smiled, her gaze going distant. "That's how Tyler and I met. I went on tour for a couple of days with the band he was in at the time. I ended up going right around Europe with them. We got married in Venice at the end of the tour and we've been together ever since."

"That's a wonderful story."

"Yeah." Pam sighed. "It was a wonderful time."

"Did you study photography?"

"No, my father taught me. He worked for National Geographic. He put a camera in my hand at age six and I refused to give it back. The next day he brought me an old secondhand one. I carried it everywhere I went.

Everything I saw was through its lens. Well, you know what I mean . . . the world made sense when I looked at it that way. Better than that, it made everything beautiful, special." She pulled a couple of books out of a box, adding them to the shelves built into one wall. We'd already managed to half fill them with various books and mementoes.

"You know, David's dated a lot of women over the years. But he's different with you. I don't know . . . the way he watches you, I think it's adorable. It's the first time he's brought anyone here in six years."

"Why was the place empty so long?"

Pam's smile faded and she avoided my eyes. "He wanted it to be his place to come home to, but then things changed. The band was just hitting it big. I guess things got complicated. He could explain it to you best."

"Right," I said, intrigued.

Pam sat back on her haunches, looking around the room. "Listen to me rabbiting on. We've been at this all day. I think we deserve a break."

"I second that."

Nearly half the boxes were open. The contents we couldn't think of an immediate home for were lined up along one wall. A big plush black couch had been delivered. It fit the house and its owner perfectly. With various rugs, pictures, and instruments strewn about, the place had almost begun to look like a home. I wondered if David would approve. Easily, I could picture us spending time here when I wasn't in classes. Or maybe holidays would be spent touring. Our future was a beautiful, dazzling thing, filled with promise.

In the here and now, however, I still hadn't caught up with Lauren. A fact that caused me great guilt. Explaining this situation didn't appeal, nor did confessing my fast-growing feelings for David.

"Come on, let's go grab some food from down the road.

The bar does the best ribs you've ever tasted. Tyler goes crazy for them," said Pam.

"That's a brilliant idea. I'll just let him know we're going. Do I need to change?" I had on the black jeans and tank top, a pair of Converses. The only shoes I'd been able to find among Martha's buys that didn't feature four-inch-plus heels. For once, I looked almost rock 'n' roll– associated. Pam wore jeans and a white shirt, a heavy turquoise necklace around her throat. It was casual in theory, but Pam was a striking woman.

"You're dressed fine," she said. "Don't worry. It's very relaxed."

"All right."

The sound of music still drifted up from downstairs. When I went down there, the door was shut and the red light shining. I could see Tyler with headphones on, busy at the console. I'd forgotten to charge my phone with all the recent excitement. But I didn't have David's phone number so I couldn't have texted him anyway. I didn't want to interrupt. In the end, I left a note on the kitchen bench. We wouldn't be gone long. David probably wouldn't even notice.

The bar was a traditional wooden wonderland with a big jukebox and three pool tables. Staff called out "hel-los" to Pam as we walked in. No one even blinked at me, which was a relief. The place was packed. It felt good to be back out among people, just part of the crowd. Pam had phoned ahead, but the order wasn't ready yet. Apparently the kitchen was every bit as busy as the bar. We grabbed a couple of drinks and settled in to wait. It was a nice place, very relaxed. There was lots of laughter, and country music blared from the jukebox. My fingers tapped along in time.

"Let's dance," said Pam, grabbing my hand and tugging me out of my chair. She bopped and swayed as I followed her onto the crowded dance floor.

It felt good to let loose. Sugarland turned into Miranda Lambert and I raised my arms, moving to the music. A guy came up behind me and grabbed my hips, but he backed up a step when I shook my head with a smile. He grinned back at me and kept dancing, not moving away. A man spun Pam and she whooped, letting him draw her into a loose hold. They seemed to know each other.

When the guy beside me moved a little closer, I didn't object. He kept his hands to himself and it was all friendly enough. I didn't know the next song, but it had a good beat and we kept right on moving. My skin grew damp with sweat, my hair clinging to my face. Then Dierks Bentley came on. I'd had a terrible crush on him since age twelve, but it was all about his pretty blond hair and nothing to do with his music. My love for him was a shameful thing.

Dude One moved away and another took his place, slipping an arm around my waist and trying to pull me in against him. I planted my hands on his chest and pushed back, giving him the same smile and headshake that had worked on the last. He might have been only about my height, despite the huge hat, but he was built solid. He had a big barrel of a chest and he stank of cigarette smoke.

"No," I said, still trying to push him off me. "Sorry."

"Don't be sorry, darlin'," he yelled in my ear, knocking me in the forehead with the brim of his hat. "Dance with me."

"Let go."

He grinned and his hands slapped down hard on both my butt cheeks. The jerkoff started grinding himself against me.

"Hey!" I pushed against him, getting nowhere. "Get off me."

"Darlin'." The letch leaned in to kiss me, smacking me in the nose with the brim of his hat again. It hurt. Also, I hated him. If I could just wiggle my leg between his and knee the asswipe in the groin, I'd be able to even the playing field. Or leave him writhing on the floor crying for his mommy. An outcome I was fine with.

I shoved my foot between the two of his, getting closer to my objective. Closer . . .

"Let her go." David miraculously appeared out of the crowd beside us, a muscle jumping in his jaw. Oh, shit. He looked ready to kill.

"Wait your turn," the cowboy yelled back, pushing his pelvis into me. God, it was disgusting. Puking could happen. It would be no less than he deserved.

David snarled. Then he grabbed the man's hat and sent it flying off into the crowd. The man's eyes went round as plates and his hands dropped away from me.

I skipped back a step, free at last. "David—"

He looked to me, and in that moment, the cowboy swung. His fist clipped David's jaw. David's head snapped back and he stumbled. The cowboy dove at him. They landed hard, sprawled across the dance floor. Fists flew. Feet kicked. I could barely see who did what. People formed a circle around them, watching. No one doing anything to stop it. Blood spurted, spraying the floor. The pair rolled and pushed, and David came out on top. Then just as fast he fell aside. My pulse pounded behind my ears. The violence was startling. Nathan used to get into fights regularly after school. I'd hated it. The blood and the dirt, the mindless rage.

But I couldn't just stand by, caught in a cold stupor. I wouldn't.

A strong hand grabbed my arm, halting my forward momentum.

"No," said Mal.

Then he and another couple of guys stepped in. Relief poured through me. Mal and Tyler wrestled David off the cowboy. Another pair restrained the bloody-faced fool who bellowed on and on about his hat. Goddamn idiot.

They hustled David out of the bar, dragging him backward. Through the front doors and down the steps they went while his feet kicked out, trying to get back into it. And he kept right on fighting until they threw him up against Mal's big black Jeep.

"Knock it off!" Mal yelled in his face. "It's over."

David slumped against the vehicle. Blood seeped from one nostril. His dark hair hung in his face. Even in the shadows he looked swollen, misshapen. Not half as bad as the other guy, but still.

"Are you okay?" I stepped closer to check the extent of his wounds.

"I'm fine," he said, shoulders still heaving as he stared at the ground. "Let's go."

Moving in slow motion, he turned and opened the passenger-side door, climbing in. With a mumbled goodbye, Pam and Tyler headed for their own car. A couple of people stood on the steps leading into the bar, watching. One guy held a baseball bat as if he expected further trouble.

"Ev. Get in the car." Mal opened the door to the backseat and ushered me in. "Come on. Cops could be coming. Or worse."

Worse was the press. I knew that now. They'd be all over this in no time.

I got in the car.

CHAPTER TWELVE

Mal disappeared as soon as we got home. David stomped up the stairs to our bedroom. Was it really ours? I didn't have a clue. But I followed. He turned and faced me as soon as I entered the room. His expression was fierce, dark brows down and his mouth a hard line. "You call that giving us a chance?"

Whoa. I licked my lips, giving myself a moment. "I call it going out to pick up some food. The kitchen was running late so we got a beer. We liked the music so we decided to get up to dance for a couple of songs. Nothing more."

"He was all over you."

"I was about to knee him in the balls."

"You left without a fucking word!" he shouted.

"Don't yell at me," I said, searching for a calm I didn't have in me just then. "I left you a note in the kitchen."

He shoved his hands through his hair, visibly fighting for calm. "I didn't see it. Why didn't you come talk to me?"

"The red light was on. You were recording and I didn't want to disturb you. We weren't supposed to be gone for long."

Bruised face furious, he walked a few steps away, then turned and marched back. No calmer from what I could

tell despite the pacing. But at least he seemed to be trying. His temper was the third person in the room, and it
took up all the damn space. "I was worried. You didn't
even have your phone on you, I found it on the fucking
table. Pam's phone kept ringing out."

"I'm sorry you were worried." I held out my hands, out
of excuses for both of us. "I forgot to charge my phone. It
happens sometimes. I'll try to be more careful in the
future. But David, nothing was going on. I'm allowed to
leave the house."

"Fuck. I know that. I just . . ."

"You're doing your thing, and that's great."

"This was some sort of fucking punishment?"
He forced the hard words out through gritted teeth. "Is
that it?"

"No. Of course not." I sighed. Quietly.

"So you weren't trying to get picked up?"

"I'm going to pretend you didn't say that." Slapping
him upside the head wasn't out of the question. I kept my
clenched fists safely at my sides, resisting the urge.

"Why'd you let him touch you?"

"I didn't. I asked him to move back and he refused.
That's when you arrived." I rubbed at my mouth with my
fingers, fast running out of patience. "We're just going
around in circles here. Maybe we should talk about this
later when you've had a chance to calm down."

Hands shaking, I turned toward the door.

"You're leaving? Fucking perfect." He threw himself
back onto the bed. Laughter wholly lacking in humor
came out of his mouth. "So much for us sticking together."

"What? No. I don't want to fight with you, David. I'm
going downstairs before we start saying things we don't
mean. That's all."

"Go," he said, his voice harsh. "I fucking knew you
would."

"God," I growled, turning back to face him. The desire

to scream and shout at him, to try to make some sense of this, boiled over inside of me. "Are you even listening to me? Are you hearing me at all? I'm not leaving you. Where is this coming from?"

He didn't answer, just stared at me, eyes accusing. It made no sense.

I almost tripped getting back to him, my feet fumbling. Landing on my face would be perfect. It was exactly where this was heading. I didn't even understand what we were fighting about anymore, if I ever had.

"Who are you comparing me to here?" I asked, every bit as angry as him now. "Because I am not her."

He kept right on glaring at me.

"Well?"

His lips stayed shut and my frustration and fury sky-rocketed. I wanted to grab him and shake him apart. Make him admit to something, anything. Make him tell me what the hell was really going on.

I crawled onto the bed, getting in his face. "David, talk to me!"

Nothing.

Fine.

I pushed back with trembling legs and tried to clamber off the mattress. He grabbed at my arms, trying to hold on. And like fuck he was. I pushed back hard. All brawling limbs, we tumbled off the bed and rolled onto the floor. His back hit the hardwood floor. Immediately, he rolled us again, putting me on the bottom. My blood pounded behind my ears. I kicked and pushed and wres-tled him with all the hurt he'd inspired. Before he could get his bearings I rolled us again, regaining the uppermost position. He couldn't stop me, the bastard. Escape was im-minent.

But it didn't happen.

David grabbed my face in both hands and mashed his lips to mine, kissing the stuffing out of me. I opened my

mouth and his tongue slipped in. The kiss was rough and
wet. Breathing was an issue. We both had anger manage-
ment problems and neither of us entirely refrained from
biting. With his bruised mouth, he definitely had the most
to lose. It wasn't long before the metallic taste of blood
hit my tongue.

He pulled back with a hiss, fresh blood on his swollen
top lip. "Fuck."

He grabbed my hands. I didn't make it easy on him,
struggling for all I was worth. But he was stronger. He
pinned them to the floor above my head with relative ease.
The press of his hard-on between my legs felt exquisite,
insane. And the more I bucked against him, the better it
got. Adrenaline had already been pouring through me,
amping me up. The need to have him sat just below the
surface, prickling my skin, making me hyperaware of
everything.

So this was angry sex. I couldn't bring myself to hurt
him, not really. But there were other ways to assert myself in this situation. He came back to my mouth and I
nipped him again in warning.

A mad smile appeared on his face. It probably matched
my own. We were both panting, fighting for air. Both as
stubborn as hell. Without another word, he released my
wrists and drew back. Quickly, he grabbed my waist and
turned me over, pulling me up onto my elbows and knees.
Arranging me how he wanted me. Rough hands tore at
the button and zip on my jeans. He yanked down my
denim and my crazily overpriced thong, body poised over
mine.

His hands smoothed over my ass. Teeth dragged over
the sensitive skin of one cheek, just above the tattoo of
his name. A hand slipped beneath to cup my sex. The
press of his fingers against me had me seeing stars. When
they started stroking me, working me higher, I couldn't
hold back my moan. He nipped me on the rump, a sharp

sting of sensation. Then he pressed kisses up my spine. Stubble from his chin scratched my shoulder.

The lack of words, the absolute silence apart from our heavy breathing made it more. It made it different.

One finger slid inside me. Not nearly enough, damn it. He slid in a second finger, stretching me a little. Once, twice he slowly pumped them into me. I pushed back against his hand, needing more. Next came the sound of the bedside drawer sliding open as he searched for a condom. His fingers slid out of me and the loss was excruciating. I heard his zipper being lowered, the rustle of clothes, and the crinkle of a condom wrapper. Then his cock pressed against me, rubbing over my opening. He pushed in slow and steady, filling me up until there was nothing left that wasn't me and him. For a moment he stopped, letting me adjust.

But not for long.

Hands gripped my hips and he began to move. Each thrust was a little faster and harder than the last. Labored breathing and the slap of skin against skin swallowed the silence. The scent of sex hung heavy in the air. I pushed back against him, meeting him thrust for thrust, spurring him on. It was nothing like the sweet and slow of this morning. Neither of us was tender. My jeans shackled me at the knees, making me slip forward a little with each thrust. His fingers dug into my hips, holding me in place. He stroked over something inside me and I gave a startled gasp. Again and again he concentrated on that spot, making me mindless. I felt superheated. Like fire burned through me. Sweat dripped off my skin. I hung my head, closed my eyes, and held onto the floor with all my might. My voice called out without my consent, saying his name. Damn it. My body wasn't my own. I came hard, awash with sensation. My back bowed, every muscle drawn tight.

David pounded into me, hands slipping over my slick

skin. He came a moment later in silence, holding himself deep. His face rested against my back, arms wrapped around my body, which was lucky. I'd lost all traction. Slowly I slid to the floor. If he hadn't been holding me I'd have face-planted. I doubt I'd have even cared.

In silence, he picked me up and carried me into the bathroom, sat me on the sink. Without fuss he dealt with the condom, started running a bath, holding a hand beneath the faucet to check the temperature. He undressed me like I was a child, pulling off my sneakers and socks, my jeans and panties. He tugged off my shirt and unclipped my bra. His own clothes were ripped off with far less care. I felt curiously naked with him now, the way he was treating me. Being so careful with me despite my biting and big-boned unwieldiness. He treated me like I was precious. Like I was a china doll. One he could apparently have rough sex with upon occasion. Once more, he checked the water, then he picked me up again and into the bath we went.

I huddled against him, my skin cooling off fast. My teeth chattered. He held me tighter, resting his cheek against the top of my head.

"I'm sorry if I was too rough," he said finally. "I didn't mean it, accusing you of shit like that. I just . . . . fuck. I'm sorry."

"Rough wasn't a problem, but the trust issue . . . we're going to need to talk about it sometime." I rested my head against his shoulder, stared up into his troubled eyes.

His chin jerked as he gave me a tight nod.

"But right now, I'd like to talk about Vegas."

The arms around me tensed. "What about Vegas?"

I stared back at him, still trying to think everything through. Not wanting to get this wrong, whatever this was.

Marriage, that's what it was.

Shit.

"We've covered a lot of ground in the last twenty-four hours," I said.

"Yeah, I guess we have."

I held up my hand, my sparkly ring. The size of the diamond didn't matter. That David had put it on me was what made it important. "We talked about lots of things. We slept together, and we made promises to each other, important ones."

"You regretting any of it?"

My hand slid around the back of his neck. "No. Absolutely not. But if you woke up tomorrow, and you'd somehow forgotten all of this. If it was all gone for you, like it had never happened, I would be furious at you."

His forehead wrinkled.

"I'd hate you for forgetting all this when it's meant everything to me."

He licked his lips and turned off the tap with a foot. Without the water gushing out, the room quieted instantly.

"Yeah," he said. "I was angry."

"I'm not going to let you down like that again."

Beneath me his chest rose and fell heavily. "Okay."

"I know it takes time to learn to trust someone. But in the meantime, I need you to at least give me the benefit of the doubt."

"I know." Wary blue eyes watched me.

I sat up and reached for the washcloth on the edge of the bath. "Let me clean you up a little."

A dark lump sat on his jaw. Blood lingered beneath his nose and near his mouth. He was a mess. A big red mark was on his ribs.

"You should see a doctor," I said.

"Nothing's broken."

Carefully, I wiped the blood from the side of his mouth and beneath his nose. Seeing him in pain was horrible. Knowing I was the cause made my stomach twist and turn. "Tell me if I press too hard."

"You're fine."

"I'm sorry you got hurt. In the bar tonight, and in Vegas. I didn't mean for that to happen."

His eyes softened and his hands slid over me. "I want you to come back to LA with me. I want you with me. I know school will start back eventually and we're gonna have to work something out. But whatever happens, I don't want us apart."

"We're not going to be."

"Promise?"

"Promise."

CHAPTER THIRTEEN

Morning light woke me. I rolled over and stretched, working out the kinks. David lay on his back beside me, fast asleep. He had an arm flung over his face, covering his eyes. With him there, everything was right with my world. But also, everything was on show. He'd kicked off the sheet sometime during the night. So the morning wood thing was true. There you go. Lauren had been right on that count.

Waking up beside him with my wedding ring back on my finger had me grinning like a loon. Of course waking up beside a bare-naked David would have made just about anybody smile. Between my legs felt a little sore from last night's efforts, but nothing too bad. Nothing sufficient to distract me from the view that was my husband.

I shuffled down the bed a bit, checking him out at my leisure for once. He didn't have much of a belly button. It was basically a small indent followed by a fine trail of dark hair leading down across his flat stomach directly to it. And it was hard, thick, and long.

"It" being his penis, of course.

Gah. No, that didn't sound right.

His cock. Yeah, much better.

We'd sat in the warm bath for a while last night at his insistence, soaking. We'd just talked. It had been lovely. There'd been no mention of the woman who'd obviously cheated on him and/or left him at some time in his past. But I'd felt her presence lurking. Time would kick her out the back door, I was sure of it.

He smelled faintly of soap, a little musky, perhaps. Warm wasn't something I'd ever registered as having a smell before, but that's what David smelled of. Warmth, like he was liquid sunshine or something. Heat and comfort and home.

I quickly checked his face. His eyes were still closed beneath the length of his arm, thank goodness. His chest rose and fell in a steady rhythm. I really didn't need him catching me sniffing at his crotch, no matter how poetic my thoughts. That would be embarrassment on a scale I'd prefer not to experience.

The skin looked super smooth despite the veins, and the head stood out distinctly. He was uncircumcised. Curiosity got the better of me, or maybe it already had. With all of his front half at my disposal, look where I'd wound up. I gently laid the palm of my hand atop him. The skin was soft and warm. Carefully, I wrapped my fingers around him. His cock twitched and I jerked back, startled.

David burst out laughing, loud and long.

Bastard.

Embarrassment was a dam that had burst wide open inside of me. Heat flashed up my neck.

"I'm sorry," he said, reaching for me with his hand. "But you should have seen your face."

"It's not funny."

"Baby, you wouldn't believe how fucking funny it was." He wrapped his fingers around my wrist, dragging me up and onto him. "Come here. Aw, the tips of your ears are all pink."

"No, they're not," I mumbled, lying across his chest.

He stroked my back, still sniggering. "Don't let this scar you for life, though, hey? I like you touching me."

I huffed noncommittally.

"You know, if you play with my dick, things will always happen. I guarantee it."

"I know that." The crook of his neck was handy for burying my hot face in, so I took full advantage. "I just got a surprise."

"You sure did." He squeezed me tight, then slid a hand down to cup my bottom. "How are you feeling?"

"Okay."

"Yeah?"

"A little sore," I admitted. "A lot happy. Though that was before you callously mocked me."

"Poor baby. Let me see," he said, rolling me over onto the mattress until he was on top.

"What?"

He sat up between my legs with a hand holding my knees open. With a practiced eye he checked me over. "You don't look too swollen. Probably just a bit sore inside, yeah?"

"Probably." I tried to pull my legs up, to close them. Because I heartily doubted having him look at me there in that way helped the color of my ear tips.

"I have to be more careful with you."

"I'm fine. Not that breakable, honestly."

"Mm."

"Takes more than a round of rough sex on the hardwood floor to worry me."

"That so? Stay still for me," he said, shuffling back to lie down at the end of the mattress.

This situated him distinctly between my legs, face-to-face with my girl bits, guaranteeing I wouldn't be going anywhere. I'd heard good things about this, things that made my embarrassment levels redundant. Plus, I was curious.

He brushed his lips against my sex, the warmth of his breath making me shiver. My stomach muscles spasmed in anticipation.

His gaze met mine over the top of my torso. "Okay?"

I gave him a jerky nod, impatient.

"Put the other pillow behind your head too," he instructed. "I want you to be able to watch."

My husband had the best ideas. I did as asked, settling in to watch though my legs were aquiver. He kissed the inside of my thighs, first one, then the other. Everything in me focused on the sensations emanating from there. My world was a small perfect place. Nothing existed outside our bed.

His eyes closed but mine stayed open. He kissed his way over the lips of my sex and then traced the divide with the tip of his tongue. That worked. Warmth suffused me inside. Hands wrapped around the underneath of my thighs, fingers rubbing small circles into my skin. His lips never left my sex. It was exactly as if he was kissing me there. Mouth open wide and tongue stroking, making me writhe. The grip on my thighs tightened, holding me to him. Even the brush of his hair and the prickle of his stubble against me were thrilling things. I don't know when I stopped watching. My eyes shut of their own accord as the pleasure took over. It was amazing. I didn't want it to end. But the pressure inside me built until I couldn't contain it any longer. I came with a shout, my body drawn tight from top to toe. Every part of me tingled. He didn't pull back until I lay perfectly still, concentrating on just breathing.

"Am I forgiven for laughing at you?" he asked, crawling up the bed to plant a kiss on my shoulder.

"Sure."

"How about the rough sex on the hardwood floor? Am I forgiven for that too?"

"Mmhmm."

The mattress shifted beneath me as he hovered above. His wet mouth lingered over the curve of my breast, the line of my collarbone.

"I really liked that," I said, my voice low and lazy. Gradually I opened my eyes.

"Fuck drunk suits you, Evelyn." A hand smoothed over my hip, and he smiled down at me. "I'll eat you out whenever you like. You only have to ask."

I smiled back at him. And the smile may have twitched a little at the edges. Talking about this kind of thing was still new to me.

"Tell me you liked me licking your gorgeous pussy."

"I said I liked it."

"You're embarrassed." David's brows drew together. There was mischief in his eyes. "You can talk rough sex on hardwood floors but not cunnilingus, hey? Say 'pussy.'"

I rolled my eyes. "Pussy."

"Again. Not as in 'cat.'"

"I'm not saying it as in 'cat.' Pussy. Pussy, pussy, pussy. Pussy not as in 'cat.' Happy?" I laughed, moving a hand to slide down his chest, heading for his groin. "Can I do something for you now?"

He stopped my hand, brought it to his mouth and kissed it. "I'm going to wait till tonight when we can make love again, if you're feeling okay."

"We're making love tonight, Mr. Smooth?"

"Sure." He smirked, climbing off the bed. "We'll make love again and then we'll fuck again. I think we should put some serious time into exploring the differences. It'll be fun."

"Okay," I quickly agreed. I wasn't stupid.

"That's my girl." He held a hand out for me, eyes intent.

"You are so damn pretty. You know, I'm never going to be able to wait until tonight."

"No?"

"Nope. Look at you lying all naked on my bed. I've never seen anything I've liked more." He shook his head, mouth rueful as his eyes traveled over my body. My husband was incredibly good for my ego. But he made me feel humble at the same time, grateful. "I was a fucking idiot to suggest waiting," he said, taking a step back and crooking his finger at me. "And you know how I hate being away from you. Come help me in the shower? It'll give you some good hands-on experience."

I crawled off the bed after him. "That so?"

"Oh, yeah. And you know how seriously I take you and your education."

"You suck," said Lauren, her voice echoing down the line. Pam had warned me some parts of the coast could be iffy with cell coverage.

"I'm not saying I don't still love you," she said. "But, you know . . ."

"I know. I'm sorry," I said, settling into the corner of the lounge. The menfolk were busy downstairs making music. Pam had gone running errands in town. I had calls to make. Boxes to unpack. Dreams of blissful wedlock to work up to insane, impossible proportions inside my head.

"Never mind. Update me," she demanded.

"Well, we're still married. In a good way this time."

Lauren screamed in my ear. It took her a good couple of minutes to calm down. "Oh, my God, I was hoping something would work out. He's so fucking hot."

"Yes, indeed he is. But he's more than that. He's wonderful."

"Keep going."

"I mean, really wonderful."

She huffed out a laugh. "You already used 'wonderful.'

Try a new word, Cinderella. Give my inner fangirl something to work with here."

"Don't crush on my husband. That's not cool."

"You're six years too late with that warning. I was crushing on David Ferris long before you put a ring on him in Vegas."

"Actually, he doesn't have a ring."

"No? You should fix that."

"Hmm." I stared out the window at the ocean. Out in the distance a bird drifted in lazy circles high up in the sky. "We're at his place in Monterey. It's beautiful here."

"You left LA?"

"LA was not so great. What with the groupies and lawyers and business managers and everything, it was pretty shitty."

"Details, babe. Gimme."

I drew my knees up to my chest and fidgeted with the seam of my jeans, feeling conflicted. Discussing our personal details behind David's back didn't sit well with me. Not even with Lauren. Things had changed. Most noticeably, our marriage had changed. But there were still some things I could share. "The people there were like something from another planet. I did not fit in. Though you would have liked seeing the parties they threw. All the glamorous people packed into this mansion. It was impressive."

"You're making me insanely jealous. Who was there?"

I gave her a couple of names as she oohed and aahed.

"But I don't miss LA. Things are so good now, out here, Lauren. We've put the annulment on hold. We're going to see how things go."

"That's so romantic. Tell me you've jumped that fine-looking man's bones, please. Don't make me cry."

"Lauren." I sighed.

"Yes or no?"

I hesitated, and she got screamy at me, rather predictably. "YES OR NO?"

"Yes. All right? Yes."

This time, her shriek definitely did my eardrums permanent damage. All I could hear was ringing. When it ended, someone was mumbling in the background. Someone male.

"Who was that?" I asked.

"No one. Just a friend."

"A friend-friend or a friend?"

"Just a friend. Hang on, changing rooms. And we were talking about you, partner of David Ferris, world-famous lead guitarist for Stage Dive."

"A friend that I know?" I asked, curiosity now fully aroused.

"You are aware of the picture of your ass making the rounds, aren't you?"

Cue the squirming. "Uh, yeah. I am."

"Bummer. Haha! But seriously, you look good. Mine wouldn't have looked half as nice. Bet you're glad you walked to campus last semester instead of driving all the time like lazy ol' me. That sure was some night you had in Vegas, missy."

"Let's talk about your friend instead of my butt. Or Vegas."

"Or we could talk about your sex life. Because we've been talking about mine for a couple of years now, but we haven't much been able to talk about yours, girlfriend," she said in a glee-filled singsong voice.

"Evvie! Want a soda?" Mal shouted as he sailed past on his way to the kitchen, having emerged from below.

"Yes, please."

"Who is that?" asked Lauren.

"The drummer. They're doing some work in the studio downstairs."

Lauren gasped. "The whole band is there?"

"No, just Mal and another friend of David's."

"Malcolm is there? He's really hot, but a total man slut," she supplied helpfully. "You should see the number of women he gets photographed with."

"Here you go, child bride." Mal passed me an icy-cold bottle, the top already removed.

"Thanks, Mal," I said.

He winked and wandered off again.

"None of my business," I told Lauren.

She clucked her tongue. "You haven't been on the Internet to find anything out about them, have you? You're flying totally blind in this situation."

"It feels wrong checking up on them behind their backs."

"Naïveté is only sexy up to a point, chica."

"It's not naïveté, chica. It's respecting their personal lives."

"Which you're now a part of."

"Privacy matters. Why should they trust me if I'm stalking them online?"

"You and your excuses." Lauren sighed. "So you don't know that the band started touring when David was only sixteen? They got a gig supporting a band through Asia and have pretty much stayed on the road or in the recording studio from then onward. Hell of a life, huh?"

"Yeah. He said he's ready to slow down."

"I'm not surprised. Rumors about the band breaking up are everywhere. Do try and stop that from happening if you can, please. And get your husbo to get his shit into gear and hurry up and write a new album. I'm counting on you."

"No problem," I said, not sharing that David was writing me songs. That was private. For now, at least. The list of things I didn't feel I could share with Lauren was growing exponentially.

"I wanted you to crush that boy's heart so we could have another album like *San Pedro*. But I can tell you're going to be difficult about that."

"Your powers of perception are uncanny."

She chuckled. "You know there's a song about the Monterey house on that album?"

"There is?"

"Oh, yeah. That's the famous 'House of Sand.' Epic love song. David's high school sweetheart cheated on him while he was touring in Europe at age twenty-one. He'd bought that house for them to live in."

"Stop, Lauren. This is . . . shit, this is personal." My heart and mind raced. "This house?"

"Yeah. They'd been together for years. David was gutted. Then some bitch he slept with sold her story to the tabloids. Also, his mother left when he was twelve. Expect there to be some issues all around where women are concerned."

"No, Lauren, stop. I'm serious," I said, nearly strangling the phone. "He'll tell me things like that when he's ready. This doesn't feel right."

"It's just being prepared. I don't see what the problem is."

"Lauren."

"Okay. No more. You did need to know those tidbits, though, seriously. Events like that leave a permanent scar."

She had a point. The information did explain his accusations regarding my leaving and the strength of his reactions to that. Two of the most important women in his world had deserted him. Though finding out this way about his history still felt wrong. When he trusted me enough to tell me, he would. But I hadn't had enough of a chance yet to earn that sort of trust from him. Personal information didn't just roll off the tongue at the first meeting. How horrible to have it all set out there on the Internet just waiting for people to look it up and mull it over for their entertainment. So much for privacy. Little wonder he'd been worried about my talking to the press.

I took a sip of the soda, then rested the cold bottle against my cheek. "I really want this to work."

"I know you do. I can hear it in your voice when you talk about him—you're in love with him."

My spine snapped to attention. "What? No. That's crazy talk. Not yet, at least. It's only been a couple of days. Do I sound in love? Really?"

"Time is irrelevant where the heart is concerned."

"Maybe," I said, concerned.

"Listen, Jimmy has been dating Liv Andrews. If you meet her, I definitely want an autograph. Loved her last film."

"Jimmy is not the greatest. That could get uncomfortable."

She huffed. "Fine. But you are in love."

"Hush now."

"What? I think it's nice."

Mutterings from Lauren's mysterious friend interrupted my rising fear.

"I've got to go," she said. "Keep in touch, okay? Call me."

"I will."

"Bye."

I said "bye," but she was already gone.

CHAPTER FOURTEEN

"You're frowning." David walked up behind me slowly. His head cocked to the side, making his dark hair fall over the side of his face. He tucked it behind an ear and moved closer. "Why are you doing that, hmm?"

I'd been putting together dinner. I'd found pizza crusts in the freezer, so I took them out to defrost and started cutting up toppings and grating cheese, while worrying about what Lauren had told me, of course. The house didn't seem so welcoming anymore. Armed with the knowledge that it had been bought with another woman in mind, my feelings toward the place had shifted. I was back to feeling like an interloper. Horrible but true. Insecurities sucked.

"Gimme." From behind me he snagged my wrist and brought my hand to his mouth, sucking a smear of tomato paste from my finger. "Mm. Yum."

My stomach squeezed tight in response. God, his mouth on me this morning. His plans for us tonight. It all felt like a dream, a crazy beautiful dream that I didn't want to wake from. Nor did I need to. All would be well. We'd work things out. We were married again now, committed. He snaked an arm around me and pressed himself against my back, leaving no room between us for doubt.

"How are things going downstairs?" I asked.

"Real good. We've got four songs shaping up nicely. Sorry we ran a bit over," he said, planting a kiss on the side of my neck, chasing the last of the bad thoughts far away. "But now it's our time."

"Good."

"Making pizza?"

"Yeah."

"Can I help?" he asked, still nuzzling the side of my neck. The stubble on his jaw scratched lightly at my skin, feeling strange and wonderful all at once. He made me shivery. Right up until he stopped. "You're putting broccoli on it?"

"I like vegetables on pizza."

"Zucchini too. Huh." His voice sounded slightly incredulous and he perched his chin on my shoulder. "How about that?"

"And bacon, sausage, mushrooms, peppers, tomatoes, and three different types of cheeses." I pointed the chopping knife at my excellent collection of ingredients. "Wait till you taste them. They're going to be the best pizzas ever."

"Course they are. Here, I'll put them together." He turned me to face him, rearing back when my chopping knife accidentally waved at him. His hands fastened onto my hips and he lifted me up onto the kitchen island. "Keep me company."

"Sure thing."

From the fridge he took a beer for him and a soda for me, since I was still avoiding alcohol. Tyler's and Mal's voices drifted through from the lounge room.

"We working again tomorrow?" Tyler called out.

"Sorry, man. We gotta head back to LA," said David, washing his hands at the sink. He had great hands, long, strong fingers. "Give me a couple of days to sort shit out down there then we'll be up again."

Tyler stuck his head around the corner, giving me a wave. "Sounds good. The new stuff is coming together well. Bringing Ben and Jimmy back with you next time?"

David's brow wrinkled, his eyes not so happy. "Yeah, I'll see what they're up to."

"Cool. Pammy's outside, so I gotta run. It's date night."

"Have fun." I waved back.

Tyler grinned. "Always do."

Chuckling quietly, Mal ambled in. "Date night, seriously . . . what the fuck is that about? Old people are the weirdest. Dude, you can't put broccoli on pizza."

"Yeah, you can." David kept busy, scattering peppers around the little trees of broccoli.

"No," said Mal. "That's just not right."

"Shut up. Ev wants broccoli on the pizza, then that's what she gets."

Ice-cold lovely sweet soda slid down my throat, feeling all sorts of good. "Don't stress, Mal. Vegetables are your friend."

"You lie, child bride." His mouth stretched wide in disgust and he retrieved a bottle of juice from the fridge. "Never mind. I'll just pick it off."

"No, you're going out," said David. "Me and Ev are having date night too."

"What? You're fucking kidding me. Where am I supposed to go?"

David just shrugged and scattered pepperoni atop his steadily growing creations.

"Oh, come on. Evvie, you'll stand up for me, won't you?" Mal gave me the most pitiful face in all of existence. It was sadness blended with misery with a touch of forlorn on top. He even bent over and laid his head on my knee. "If I stay in town they'll know we're here."

"You've got your car," said David.

"We're in the middle of nowhere," Mal complained.

"Don't let him throw me out into the wild. I'll get eaten by fucking bears or something."

"I'm not sure they have bears around here," I said.

"Cut the shit, Mal," said David. "And get your head off my wife's leg."

With a growl, Mal straightened. "Your wife is my friend. She's not going to let you do this to me!"

"That so?" David looked at me and his face fell. "Fuck, baby. No. You cannot be falling for this shit. It's only one night."

I winced. "Maybe we could go up to our room. Or he could just stay downstairs or something."

David shoved his hands through his hair. The bruise on his poor cheek, I needed to kiss it better. His forehead did that James Dean wrinkling thing as he studied his friend. "Jesus. Stop making that pathetic face at her. Have some dignity."

He cuffed the back of Mal's head, making his long blond hair fly in his face. Skipping back, Mal retreated beyond the line of fire. "All right, I'll stay downstairs. I'll even eat your shitty broccoli pizza."

"David." I grabbed his T-shirt and tugged him toward me. And he came, abandoning his pursuit of Mal.

"This is supposed to be our time," he said.

"I know. It will be."

"Yes!" hissed Mal, getting gone while he was ahead. "I'll be downstairs. Yell when dinner's ready."

"He's got a girl in every city," said David, scowling after him. "No way was he sleeping in his car. You've been played."

"Maybe. But I would have worried about him." I tucked his dark hair behind his ears, then trailed my hands down to the back of his neck, drawing him closer. The studs in his ears were all small, silver. A skull, an X, and a super-tiny winking diamond. He pressed his earlobe between his thumb and a finger, blocking my view.

"Something wrong?" he asked.

"I was just looking at your earrings. Do they mean anything special?"

"Nope." He gave me a quick peck on the cheek. "Why were you frowning earlier?" He picked up a handful of mushrooms and started adding them to the pizzas. "You're doing it again now."

Crap. I kicked my heels, turned all the excuses over inside my head. I had no idea how he'd react to my knowing the things Lauren had told me. What would he think if I asked about them? Starting a fight did not appeal. But lying didn't either. Withholding was lying, deep down where it mattered. I knew that.

"I talked to my friend Lauren today."

"Mmhmm."

I pushed my hands down between my legs and squeezed them tight, delaying. "She's a really big fan."

"Yeah, you said." He gave me a smile. "Am I allowed to meet her, or is she off-limits like your dad?"

"You can meet my dad if you want."

"I want. We'll take a trip to Miami sometime soon and I'll introduce you to mine, okay?"

"I'd like that." I took a deep breath, let it out. "David, Lauren told me some things. And I don't want to keep secrets from you. But I don't know how happy you're going to be about these things that she told me."

He turned his head, narrowed his eyes. "Things?"

"About you."

"Ah. I see." He picked up two handfuls of grated cheese and sprinkled them across the pizzas. "So you hadn't looked me up on Wikipedia or some shit?"

"No," I said, horrified at the thought.

He grunted. "It's no big deal. What do you want to know, Ev?"

I didn't know what to say. So I picked up my soda and downed about half of it in one go. Bad idea—it didn't help.

Instead, it gave me a mild case of brain freeze, stinging above the bridge of my nose.

"Go on. Ask me whatever you want," he said. He wasn't happy. The angry monobrow from drawing his eyebrows together clued me in to that. I didn't think I'd ever met anyone with such an expressive face as David. Or maybe he just fascinated me full stop.

"All right. What's your favorite color?"

He scoffed. "That's not one of the things your friend told you about."

"You said I could ask whatever I wanted, and I want to know what your favorite color is."

"Black. And I know it's not really a color. I did miss a lot of school, but I was there that day." His tongue played behind his cheek. "What's yours?"

"Blue." I watched as he opened the gargantuan oven door. The pizza trays clattered against the racks. "What's your favorite song?"

"We're covering all the basics, huh?"

"We are married. I thought it would be nice. We sort of skipped a lot of the getting-to-know-you stuff."

"All right." The side of his mouth kicked up and he gave me a look that said he was onto my game of avoidance. The faint smile set the world to rights.

"I got a lot of favorite music," he said. " 'Four Sticks' by Led Zeppelin, that's up there. Yours is 'Need You Now' by Lady Antebellum, as sung by an Elvis impersonator. Sadly."

"Come on, I was under the influence. That's not fair."

"But it is true."

"Maybe." I still wished I could remember it. "Favorite book?"

"I like graphic novels. Stuff like *Hellblazer*, *Preacher*."

I took another mouthful of soda, trying to think up a genius question. Only all the blatantly obvious ones appeared inside my head. I sucked at dating. It was probably just as well that we'd skipped that part.

"Wait," he said. "What's yours?"

"*Jane Eyre*. How about your favorite movie?"

"*Evil Dead 2*. Yours?"

"*Walk the Line*."

"The one about the Man in Black? Nice. Okay." He clapped his hands together and rubbed them. "My turn. Tell me something terrible. Something you did that you've never confessed to another living soul."

"Ooh, good one." Scary, but good. Why couldn't I have thought of a question like that?

He grinned around the top of his bottle of beer, well pleased with himself.

"Let me think . . ."

"There's a time limit."

I screwed up my face at him. "There is not a time limit."

"There is," he said. "Because you can't try and think up something half-assed to tell me. You've gotta give me the first worst thing that comes into your head that you don't want anyone else ever knowing about. This is about honesty."

"Fine." I sniffed. "I kissed a girl named Amanda Harper when I was fifteen."

His chin rose. "You did?"

"Yes."

He sidled closer, eyes curious. "Did you like it?"

"No. Not really. I mean, it was okay." I gripped the edge of the bench, hunching forward. "She was the school lesbian and I wanted to see if I was one too."

"There was just the one lesbian at your school?"

"Oh, I suspected quite a few people, but only she was open about it. She gave herself the title."

"Good for her." His hands settled on my knees and

pushed them apart, making room for him. "Why did you think you were a lesbian?"

"To be accurate, I was hoping I was bi," I said. "More options. Because, honestly, the guys at school were . . ."

"They were what?" He gripped my butt and pulled me across the bench, bringing me closer. No way did I resist.

"They didn't really interest me, I guess."

"But kissing your lesbian friend Amanda didn't do it for you either?" he asked.

"No."

He clicked his tongue. "Damn. That's a sad story. You're cheating, by the way."

"What? How?"

"You were meant to tell me something terrible." His smile left a mile way behind. "Telling me you tongue-kissed a girl isn't even remotely terrible."

"I never said there was tongue."

"Was there?"

"A little. The briefest of touches, maybe. But then I got weirded out and stopped it."

He took another swig of beer. "Your ear tips are doing the pink thing again."

"I bet they are." I laughed and ducked my head. "I didn't cheat. I never told anyone about that kiss. I was going to take it to my grave. You should feel honored by my trust in you."

"Yeah, but telling me something I'm likely to find a huge turn-on is cheating. You were meant to tell me something terrible. The rules were clear. Go again and give me something bad this time."

"It's a huge turn-on, huh?"

"Next time I hit the shower I'm definitely using that story."

I bit my tongue and looked away. Memories from this morning of David soaping up my hands and then putting them on him assailed my mind. The thought of him masturbating to my brief bout of teen sexual experimentation . . . "honored" wasn't quite the right word. But I couldn't say I wasn't pleased by the notion. "Well, remember to make me older. Fifteen is a bit skeevy."

"You only kissed her."

"You'll leave it at that in your head? You'll respect accuracy and legalities, and not take it any further between Amanda and me?"

"Fine, I'll make you older. And wildly fucking curious." He pulled me closer, using the hands-on-my-butt method again, and I put my arms around him.

"Now, go again, and do it right this time."

"Yeah, yeah."

He gave the side of my neck a lingering kiss. "You weren't lying about Amanda, were you?"

"No."

"Good. I like that story. You should tell it to me often. Now go again."

I ummed and ahhed, procrastinating my little heart out. David rested his forehead against mine with a heavy sigh. "Just fucking tell me something."

"I can't think of anything."

"Bullshit."

"I can't," I whined. Not anything I wanted to share, anyway.

"Tell me."

I groaned and bumped my forehead against his ever so lightly. "David, come on, you're the last person I want to make myself look bad in front of."

He drew back, inspecting me down the length of his nose. "You're worried about what I think of you?"

"Of course I am."

"You're honest and good, baby. Nothing you might have done is gonna be that bad."

"But honest isn't always good," I said, trying to explain.

"I've opened my mouth plenty of times when I shouldn't have. Given people my opinion when I should have kept quiet. I react first and think later. Look at what happened in Vegas, between us. I didn't ask any of the right questions that morning. I'm always going to regret that."

"Vegas was a pretty extreme situation." His hand rubbed my back, reassuring me. "You got nothing to worry about."

"You asked me how I felt when you had that groupie hanging off you in LA. I dealt with it then. But the fact is, if that happened now and some woman tried to come on to you, I'd probably get stabby. I'm not always going to react well to the rock star hoopla that surrounds you. What happens then?"

He made a noise in his throat. "I dunno, I finally have to realize that you're human? That you fuck up sometimes just like everybody else?"

I didn't answer.

"We'll both screw up, Ev. That's a given. We just gotta be patient with each other." He put a finger beneath my chin, raising it up so he could kiss me. "Now tell me about what Lauren told you today."

I stared at him, caught and cornered. The contents of my stomach curdled for real. I had to tell him. There would be no getting around it. How he reacted was beyond my control. "She told me that your first girlfriend cheated on you."

He blinked. "Yeah. That happened. We'd been together a long time, but . . . I was always either recording or on the road," he said. "We'd been touring Europe for eight, nine months when it happened. Touring fucks up a lot of couples. The groupies and the whole lifestyle can really screw with you. Being left behind all the time is probably no picnic either."

I bet it wasn't. "When do you tour next?"

He shook his head. "There're none booked. Won't be until we get this new record down, and that hasn't been going so well until now."

"Okay. How does this work? I mean, do you believe what happens on the road, stays on the road?" I asked. The boundaries of our relationship had never really been established. Exactly what did our marriage mean? He wanted us to stick together, but I had school to consider, my job, my life. Maybe the good wives just dumped it all and went with the band. Or maybe wives weren't even invited. I didn't have a clue.

"You asking me if I'm planning on cheating on you?"

"I'm asking how we fit into each other's lives."

"Right." He pinched his lips between his thumb and finger. "Well, I think not fucking around on each other would be a good start. Let's just make that a rule for us, okay? As for the band and stuff, I guess we take it as it comes."

"Agreed."

Without a word he stepped back from me, crossing over to the staircase. "Mal?"

"What?"

"Close the door down there and lock it," David yelled. "Don't you come up here under any circumstances. Not till I tell you it's okay. Understood?"

There was a pause, then Mal yelled back, "What if there's a fire?"

"Burn."

"Fuck you." The door downstairs slammed shut.

"Lock it!"

Mal's reply was muffled, but the pissy tone carried just fine. These two were more akin to actual brothers than David and his biological sibling. Jimmy was a jerk and just one of the very good reasons we should never return to LA. Sadly, hiding out in Monterey wasn't a viable long-term solution.

School, band, family, friends, blah blah blah.

David reached for the back of his T-shirt and dragged it off over his head. "Rule number two, if I take my shirt off you have to take off yours. The shirt-off rule now applies to these sorts of conversations. I know we need to talk about stuff. But there's no reason we can't make it easier."

"This'll make it easier?" Highly doubtful. All that smooth, hot skin just waiting for my touch, and my fingers itching to do so. Keeping my tongue inside my mouth while his flat stomach and six-pack were revealed tested my moral fortitude no end. All that beautiful inked skin on display, driving any attempt at a coherent thought straight out of my mind. Good God, the man had some power over me. But wait up, we were married. Morally, I was obliged to ogle my husband. It would be unnatural and wrong to do otherwise.

"Get it off," he said, tipping his chin at my offending items of clothing.

The staircase sat calm and quiet. No signs of life.

"He ain't coming up here. I promise." David's hands gripped the bottom of my T-shirt and carefully pulled it off over my head, rescuing my ponytail when it got caught.

When he reached for my bra, I pressed my forearms to my chest, holding it in place. "Why don't I keep the bra, just in case . . ."

"It's against the rules. You really wanna go breaking rules already? That's not like you."

"David."

"Evelyn." The bra's band relaxed as he undid the clasp. "I need to see your bare breasts, baby. You have no idea how much I fucking love them. Let it go."

"Why do you get to make all the rules?"

"I only made that one. Oh, no—two. We have the no-cheating rule as well." He tugged at my bra and I eased my grip, letting him take it. No way was I moving my arms, though.

"Go on, you make some rules," he said, running his fingers over my arms, making every little hair stand on end.

"Are you just trying to distract me from the conversation with the no-clothes thing?"

"Absolutely not. Now make a rule."

My hands stayed tucked beneath my chin, arms covering all the essentials, just in case. "No lies. Not about anything."

"Done."

I nodded, relieved. We could do this marriage thing. I knew it in my head, my heart. We were going to be okay. "I trust you."

He stopped, stared. "Thanks. That's big."

I waited, but he said no more.

"Do you trust me?" I asked, filling the silence. The minute the words left my lips I wanted them back. If I had to demand his faith and affection, it didn't mean a damn thing. Worse than that, it did damage. I could feel it, a sudden jagged wound between us. One that I'd made. Of all the stupid times for me to get impatient! I wished it was the middle of winter so I could go stick my head in a snowdrift.

His gaze wandered away, over my shoulder. There was my answer right there. Honesty had already shown me who was boss. How about that? I suddenly felt cold, and though it had nothing to do with losing my shirt, I really wanted to put it back on.

"I'm getting there, Ev. Just . . . give me time." Frustration lined his face. He pressed his lips together till they whitened. Then he looked me in the eye. Whatever he saw didn't help matters. "Shit."

"It's okay, really," I said, willing it to be true.

"You lying to me?"

"No. No. We'll be fine."

In lieu of an answer, he kissed me.

You couldn't beat a well-timed distraction. Heat rushed back into me. His regret and my hurt both took a backseat when I placed my hands on top of his. With fingers meshed, I moved our combined hands to cover my breasts. We both groaned. The heat of his palms felt sublime. The chill of disappointment couldn't combat it. Our chemistry won out every time. I had to believe more feelings would follow. My shoulders pushed forward, pressing me harder into his hands as if gravity had shifted toward him. But also, I wanted his mouth. Hell, I wanted to crawl around inside him and read his mind. I wanted everything. Each dark corner of him. Every stray thought.

Our lips met again and he groaned, hands kneading my breasts. His tongue slipped into my mouth, and that fast and easy I ached for him. Needed him. My insides squeezed tight and my legs wrapped around him, holding on. Let him try and get away now. I'd fight tooth and nail to keep him. Thumbs stroked over my nipples, teasing me. My hands slid up his arms, curved over his shoulders, holding steady. Hot kisses trailed over my face, my jaw, the side of my neck. Half naked or not, I don't think I'd have cared if my high school marching band paraded through the room. They could bring baton twirlers and all. Only this mattered.

No wonder people took sex so seriously, or not seriously enough at all. Sex addled your wits and stole your body. It was like being lost and found all at once. Frankly, it was a little frightening.

"We will be fine," he said, teasing my earlobe with his teeth. Rubbing his hardness against me. God bless whoever had thought to put a seam right there in jeans. Lights danced before my eyes. Did it feel as good for him? I wanted it to be the best and I wanted him to be right about us being fine.

"Sweet baby, just need time," he said, his warm breath skating over my skin.

"Because of her," I said, needing it to be out there in the open. No secrets.

"Yeah," he said, his voice faint. "Because of her."

The truth bit.

"Evelyn, there's just you and me in this. I swear." He returned to my mouth and kissed me as if I was delicate, giving me only the briefest taste of him. An awareness of warmth, the firmness of his lips.

"Wait," I said, making my legs give up their grip on him.

He blinked dark, hazy eyes at me.

"Move back. I want to hop down."

"You do?" His lovely mouth turned down at the edges. The front of his jeans was in a state of obvious distress. I'd done that to him. A victory lap around the kitchen counter would probably be taking it too far, but still, it felt good. That knowledge sat well within me. She didn't do that to him these days. I did.

I shuffled off the edge of the counter and he grabbed my hips, easing my descent to the floor. Just as well. My legs were liquid. He stared down at me, his brow wrinkled.

"There's something I want to do," I explained, fingers shaking from nerves and excitement. First I wrangled with the button of his jeans before moving on to the straining zipper.

His hands gripped my wrists. "Hey. Wait."

I hesitated, wanting to hear what he had to say. Surely he wouldn't try to tell me he didn't want this. Every guy liked this, or so I'd been told. He looked perplexed, as if I was a piece that refused to fit the puzzle. I honestly didn't know if he meant to stop me or hurry me onward.

"Is there a problem?" I asked, when he didn't speak.

Slowly he removed his hands from my wrists, setting me free. He held them up like I'd pointed a gun at him. "This is what you want?"

"Yes. David, why is this a big deal? Don't you want my mouth on you?"

A soft smile curved his lips. "You have no idea how much I want that. But this is another first for you, isn't it?"

I nodded, fingers fiddling with the waistband of his jeans, but going no further.

"That's why it's a big deal. I want all your firsts to be perfect. Even this. And I'm pretty fucking worked up here just at the thought of you sucking me."

"Oh."

"I've been thinking about you all damn day. I kept fucking things up, couldn't concentrate for shit. Amazing we got anything done." He pushed his fingers through his long hair, pulling it back from his face. His hands stayed on top of his head, stretching out his lean, muscular torso. The bruise on his ribs from the bar fight last night was a dark gray smudge, marring perfection. I leaned in, kissing it. His gaze never left me because my bare breasts were still most definitely a part of me. My eyes, my mouth, my breasts: he couldn't seem to decide what fascinated him the most.

Carefully, I lowered the zipper over his erection. No underwear. At least I didn't jump this time when his hard-on made its sudden appearance. With two hands I pushed down his jeans, freeing his cock. It stood tall and proud. Just like this morning, I pressed my hand against the underside, feeling the heat of the silken skin. Funny, the idea of the male appendage had never particularly moved me before. But now I felt moved, as my clenched thighs attested.

Moved and more than a little proprietary.

"You're mine," I whispered, my thumb rubbing around the edge of the head, feeling out the ridge and the dip in the middle. Learning him.

"Yeah."

The sweet spot sat below that little tuck. Over the years, I'd read enough magazines and listened to enough of Lauren's tales of sexcapades to know as much. She did love her details. I made a mental note to thank her, take her out to dinner somewhere nice.

I moved my hand around so that I gripped him and massaged the area with the pad of my thumb, waiting to see what happened. Much easier to see what was going on without the soap bubbles in the way. It didn't take long. Especially not once I tightened my hold on him a little and pumped slightly. His stomach muscles flinched and danced, the same as they had this morning in the shower. My fingers moved the soft, smooth skin, massaging the hard flesh beneath, pumping once, twice. A bead of milky fluid leaked from the small slit in the top.

"That means you're fucking killing me," my husband supplied helpfully, his voice guttural. "Just in case you were wondering."

I grinned.

He swore.

"I swear it gets bigger every time I see it."

His smile was lopsided. "You inspire me."

I stroked him again and his chest heaved. "Evelyn. Please."

Time to put him out of his misery. I knelt, the floor uncomfortably hard beneath me. If you were going to kneel in front of someone, some minor discomfort seemed an obvious part of the territory. It all added to the atmosphere, the experience. The musky scent of him was stronger later in the day. I took his cock in hand and nuzzled his hip bone, breathing him in deep.

He still watched. I checked to be sure. Hell, his eyes were huge and dark and focused solely on me. Beside him, his hands gripped the counter as if he expected a tremor to hit at any time, knuckles white.

When I took him into my mouth, he moaned. My inexperience and his size prevented me from taking him too deep. He didn't seem to mind. The salty taste of his skin and the bitterness of that liquid, the warm scent of him and the feel of his hardness merged into one unique experience. Pleasing David was a brilliant thing.

He groaned and his hips jerked, pushing him farther into my mouth. My throat tightened in surprise and I gagged slightly. His hand flew to my hair, patting, soothing. "Fuck, baby. Sorry."

I resumed my ministrations, rubbing my tongue against him, drawing on him. Figuring out the best way to fit him into my mouth. Doing everything I could to make him tremble and cuss. What a glorious thing giving head was. His hand tightened in my hair, pulling some, and I loved it. All of it. Anything with the ability to reduce my world-weary husband to a stammering mess while giving him such pleasure deserved a serious time investment. His hips shifted restlessly and his cock jerked against my tongue, filling my mouth with that salty, bitter taste faster than I could swallow.

So it was messy. Never mind. My jaw hurt a little. Big deal. And I could have done with a glass of water. But his reaction . . .

David dropped to his knees and gathered me up in his arms, all the better to squish me against him. My ribs creaked, and his dug into me over and over as he fought for breath. I pressed my face against his shoulder and waited till he'd calmed down some to seek my acclaim.

"Was it okay?" I asked, reasonably certain of a favorable response. Which is always the best time to ask, in my opinion.

He grunted.

That was it? I sat there feeling rather proud of myself and he gave me a grunt. No, I needed more validation than that. I both wanted and deserved it. "Are you sure?"

He sat back on his heels and stared at me. Then he

looked around, searching for something. The T-shirt he'd left forgotten on the floor. And then he wiped beneath my chin, cleaning me up. Nice.

"There's some on your shoulder too." I pointed at the unfortunate spillage I'd obviously transferred onto him. He wiped it up as well.

"Sex can get messy," he said.

"Yes, it can."

"You on the pill?"

"You can't get pregnant that way, David."

The side of his mouth twitched. "Cute. Are you on the pill?"

"No, but I have the birth control thing implanted in my arm because my periods are erratic so—" His mouth slammed over the top of mine, kissing me hard and deep. Shutting me up really effectively. A hand cradled the back of my head as he took me down to the floor, stretching out on top of me. The cold, hard flooring beneath my bare back barely registered. It didn't matter so long as he kissed me. My hands clung to his shoulders, fingers sliding over slick skin.

"I care about your periods, Ev. Honest to fuck I do." He kissed my cheeks, my forehead.

"Thanks."

"But right now I wanna know how you feel about us going bare?"

"You mean more than losing the shirts, I take it?"

"I mean fucking without a condom." His hands framed my face as he stared down at me, eyes that intense shade of blue. "I'm clean. I've been tested. I don't do drugs and I always used protection, ever since I broke up with her. But it's your call."

The mention of "her" cooled me a bit, but not much or for long. Impossible with David sprawled all over me and the scent of sex so heavy in the air. Plus pizza. But mostly

David. He made my mouth water, forget about the food. Thinking wasn't easy given the situation. I'd said I trusted him and I did.

"Baby, just think about it," he said. "There's no rush. Okay?"

"No, I think we should."

"Are you certain?"

I nodded.

He exhaled a deep breath and kissed me again.

"I fucking love your mouth." With the top of a finger he traced my lips, still swollen from what we'd been up to.

"You did like it? It was okay?"

"It was perfect. Nothing you do could be wrong. I almost lose it just knowing it's you. You could accidentally bite me and I'd probably think it was fucking hot." He gave a rough laugh, then hastened to add, "But don't do that."

"No." I arched my neck and pressed my lips to his, kissing him sweet and slow. Showing him what he meant to me. We were still rolling around on the kitchen floor when the buzzer on the oven screeched, startling us apart. Then the phone rang.

"Shit."

"I'll get the pizza," I said, wriggling out from beneath him.

"I'll grab the phone. No one should even have this damn number."

An oven mitt sat waiting on the counter and I slipped it over my hand. Hot air and the rich scent of melted cheese wafted out when I opened the oven door. My stomach rumbled. So maybe I was hungry after all. The pizzas were a touch burnt around the edges. Nothing too bad, though. The tips of my broccoli were toasted golden brown. We could concentrate on the middle. I transferred the pizzas onto the cool stovetop and turned off the heat.

David talked quietly in the background. He stood in

front of the bank of windows, legs spread wide and shoulders set like he was bracing himself for an attack. Relaxed, happy people didn't strike that pose. Outside the sun was setting. The violet and gray of evening cast shadows on his skin.

"Yeah, yeah, Adrian. I know," he said.

Trepidation tightened me one muscle at a time. God, please, not now. We were doing so well. Couldn't they stay away just a little longer?

"What time's the flight?" he asked.

"Fuck," came next.

"No, we'll be there. Relax. Yeah, bye."

He turned to face me, phone dangling from his hand. "There's some stuff going on in LA that Mal and I need to be there for. Adrian's sending a chopper for us. We all need to get ready."

My smile strained my face, I could feel it. "Okay."

"Sorry we're getting cut short here. We'll come back soon, yeah?"

"Absolutely. It's fine."

That was a lie, because we were going back to LA.

CHAPTER FIFTEEN

David's knee jiggled all the way back to LA. When I put my hand on his leg, he took to toying with my wedding ring instead, turning it around on my finger. Seemed we were both fidgeters, given the right circumstances.

I'd never been in a helicopter before. The view was spectacular, but it was loud and uncomfortable—I could see why people preferred planes. A chain of lights, from streetlights to houses to the blazing high-rise towers in LA, lit the way. Everything about the situation had changed, but I was the same bundle of nervous energy in need of sleep that I had been leaving Portland not so many days back. Mal had thrown himself into the corner, closed his eyes, and gone to sleep. Nothing fazed him. Of course, there was no reason this should. He was part of the band, welded into David's life.

We landed a little before four in the morning, having left sometime after midnight. Bodyguard Sam stood waiting at the helicopter pad with a business face on.

"Mrs. Ferris. Gentlemen." He ushered us into a big black SUV waiting nearby.

"Straight back home, thanks, Sam," David said. His home, not mine. LA had no happy memories for me.

Then we were ensconced in luxury, locked away behind dark windows. I sank back against the soft seating, closing my eyes. It kind of amazed me I could be so damn tired and worried all at once.

Back at the mansion, Martha waited, leaning against the front door, wrapped up in some expensive-looking red shawl. His PA gave me all the bad feelings. But I was determined to fit in this time. David and I were together. Screw her, she'd have to adapt. Her dark hair shone, flowing over her shoulders, not a strand out of place. No doubt I looked like someone who'd been awake for over twenty hours.

Sam opened the SUV door and offered me a hand. I could feel Martha's eyes zero in on the way David slung an arm around me, keeping me close. Her face hardened to stone. The look she gave me was poison. Whatever her issues, I was too damn tired to deal with them.

"Martie," Mal crowed, running up the steps to slip an arm around her waist. "Help me find breakfast, O gorgeous one."

"You know where the kitchen is, Mal."

The curt dismissal didn't stop Mal from sweeping her off with him. Martha's first few steps faltered, but then she strutted once more, ever on show. Mal had cleared the way. I could have kissed his feet.

David said nothing as we made our way up the stairs to the second floor, our footsteps echoing in the quiet. When I went to turn toward the white room, the one I'd stayed in last time, he steered me right instead. At a set of double doors we stopped and he fished a key out of his pocket. I gave him a curious look.

"So I have trust issues." He unlocked the door.

Inside, the room was simple, lacking the antiques and flashy décor of the rest of the house. A huge bed made up with dark gray linens. A comfortable sofa to match. Lots of guitars. An open wardrobe, full of clothes. Mostly, there was empty space. Room for him to breathe, I think.

This room felt different from the rest of the house, less showy, calmer.

"It's okay, you can look around." His hand slid down to the base of my spine, resting just above the curve of my ass. "It's our room now," he said.

God, I hoped he didn't want to live here permanently. I mean, I did have school to go back to eventually. We hadn't yet gotten around to discussing where we'd live. But the thought of Martha, Jimmy, and Adrian being around all the time sent me into a panic. Shit. I couldn't afford to think like that. Negativity would swallow me whole. What was important was being with David. Sticking together and making it work.

How horrible, being forced to live in the lap of luxury with my wonderful husband. Poor me. I needed a good slap and a cup of coffee. Or twelve hours' sleep. Either would work wonders.

He drew the curtains, blocking out the dawn's early light. "You look beat. Come lie down with me?"

"That's, umm . . . yeah, good idea. I'll just use the bathroom."

"Okay." David started stripping, dumping his leather jacket on the lounge chair, pulling off his T-shirt. The normal hoorah of my hormones was sorely missing in action. Drowned out by the nerves. I fled into the bathroom, needing a minute to pull myself together. I closed the door and switched on the lights. The room blazed to life, blinding me. Spots flickered before my eyes. I stabbed switches at random until finally it dimmed to a soft glow. Much better.

A giant white tub that looked like a bowl, gray stone walls, and clear glass partitions. Simply put, it was opulent. One day I'd probably become inured to all this, but I hoped not. Taking it for granted would be terrible.

A shower would soothe me. Sitting in the giant soup bowl would have been nice. But I didn't totally trust myself to get into it without falling on my butt and breaking something. Not in the overtired, wound-up state I was in.

No, a long, hot shower would be perfect.

I stepped out of my flats and undid the zip on my jeans, getting undressed in record time. The shower could have fit me and ten close friends. Steaming hot water poured out from overhead and I stepped into it, grateful. It pounded down in the best way possible, making my muscles more pliable in minutes, relaxing me. I loved this shower. This shower and I needed to spend quality time together, often. Apart from David, and occasionally Mal, this shower was the best damn thing in the whole house.

David's arms slipped around me from behind, drawing me back against him. I hadn't even heard him come in.

"Hi." I leaned back against him, lifting my arms to thread them around his neck. "I think I'm in love with your shower."

"You're cheating on me with the shower? Damn, Evelyn. That's harsh." He picked up a bar of soap and started washing me, rubbing it over my belly, my breasts, softly between my legs. Once the soapsuds had reached critical mass, he helped the warm water chase the bubbles away. His big hands slid over my skin, bringing it to life and returning my hormones to me tenfold. One strong arm wrapped around my waist. The fingers of his other hand, however, lingered atop my sex, stroking lightly.

"I know you're worried about being here. But you don't need to be. Everything'll be fine." His lips brushed against my ear as the magic he was working on me grew. I could feel myself turning liquid hot like the water. My thighs trembled. I widened my stance, giving him more room.

"I—I know."

"It's you and me against the world."

I couldn't have kept the smile off my face if I tried.

"My lovely wife. Let's go this way." With careful steps he turned us, so that his back was to the water. I braced my hands on the glass wall. The tip of his finger teased between the lips of my sex, coaxing me open. God, he was good at this. "Your pussy is the sweetest fucking thing I've ever seen."

My insides fluttered with delight. "Whatever I did to deserve you, I need to do it much more often."

He chuckled, his mouth fixing to the side of my neck and sucking, making me groan. I swear the room spun. Or that might have been my blood rushing about. For certain, my hips bucked of their own volition. But he didn't let me go far. The hard length of him pressed against my butt and my lower back. My sex clenched unhappily, aching for more.

"David."

"Hmm?"

I tried to turn, but his splayed hand against my middle stopped me. "Let me."

"Let you what? What do you want, baby? Tell me and it's yours."

"I just want you."

"You've got me. I'm all over you. Feel." He pressed himself hard against me, holding me tight.

"But—"

"Now, let's see what happens when I strum your clit."

Feather-light strokes worked me higher and higher, all centered around that one magic spot. No great surprise he could play me to perfection. He'd already proved it several times over. And the way he rubbed himself against me drove me out of my mind. My body knew exactly what it wanted and it wasn't his damn clever fingers. I wanted to feel that connection with him again.

"Wait," I said, my voice high and needy.

"What, baby?"

"I want you inside of me."

He eased a finger into me, massaging an area behind my clit that made me see stars. Still, it was wrong, wildly insufficient. Not a bit funny. It would be a tragedy to have to kill him, but he was really pushing it.

"David. Please."

"No good?"

"I want you."

"And I want you. I'm crazy about you."

"But—"

"How about I get you off with a showerhead? Wouldn't that be nice?"

I actually stamped my foot, despite my wobbling knees. "No."

At which point my husband cracked up laughing and I hated him.

"I thought you were in love with the shower." He tittered away, highly amused with himself and all but begging for death.

Tears of frustration actually welled in my eyes. "No."

"You sure? I'm pretty certain I remember hearing you say it."

"David, for fuck's sake, I'm in love with you."

He stilled completely. Even the finger embedded within me stopped moving. There was only the sound of the water falling. You'd think those words would have lost their power. Weren't we already married? Hadn't we decided to stay married? Invoking the *l*-word should have lost its mystical punch, given our crazy situation. But it hadn't.

Everything changed.

Strong hands turned me and lifted me, leaving my feet dangling precariously in the air. It took me a second to figure out where I was and what had happened. I wrapped my legs and arms around him for safekeeping, holding on tight. His face . . . I'd never seen such a fierce, determined expression. It went well beyond lust and closer toward being what I needed from him.

His hands gripped my rear, taking my weight and

holding me to him. Slowly, steadily, he lowered me onto him. There was none of the pain this time to rob me of pleasure. Nothing to distract me from the feel of him filling me. It was such a strange, wonderful sensation, having him inside of me. I squirmed, trying to get more comfortable. Instantly, his fingers dug into my butt cheeks.

"Fuck," he groaned.

"What?"

"Just . . . just stay still for a minute."

I scrunched up my nose, concentrated on catching my breath. This sex stuff was tricky. Also, I wanted to memorize every moment of this perfect experience. I didn't want to forget a thing.

He balanced my back against the shower wall and pushed more fully into me. A startled sound burst out of my mouth. Most closely it resembled "argh."

"Easy," he murmured. "You okay?"

I felt really full. Stretched. And it might have felt good. It was hard to tell. I needed him to do something so I could figure out where this new sensation was taking me. "Are you going to move now?"

"If you're okay now."

"I'm okay."

He did move then, watching my face all the while. The slide out lit me up inside in a lovely rush, but the thrust back in got my immediate attention. Whoa. Good or bad, I still couldn't quite tell. I needed more. He gave it to me, his pelvis shifting against me, keeping the warmth and tension building. My blood felt fever hot, surging through me, burning beneath my skin. I fit my mouth to his, wanting more. Wanting it all. The wet of his mouth and the skill of his tongue. All of him. No one kissed like David. As though kissing me beat breathing, eating, sleeping, or anything else he might have otherwise planned to do with the rest of his life.

My back bumped hard against the glass wall and our teeth clinked together. He broke the kiss with a wary look, but he never stopped moving. Harder, faster, he rocked into me. It just got better and better. We needed to do this all the time. Constantly. Nothing else mattered when it was like this between us. Every worry disappeared.

It was so damn good. He was all that I needed.

Then he hit upon some spot inside of me and my whole body seized up, nerves tingling and running riot. My muscles squeezed him tight, and he thrust in deep several times in rapid succession. The world blacked out, or I closed my eyes. The pressure inside me shattered into a million amazing pieces. It went on and on. My mind left the stratosphere, I was sure of it. Everything sparkled. If it felt anything like that for David, I don't know how he stayed on his feet. But he did. He stood strong and whole with me clutched tight against him like he'd never let me go.

Eventually, about a decade later, he did set me down. His hands hovered by my waist, just in case. Once my limbs proved trustworthy, he turned me to face the water. With a gentle hand, he cleaned me between my legs. I didn't get what he was up to at first and tried to back away. Touching anything there right then didn't seem a smart idea.

"It's okay," he said, drawing me back into the spray of water. "Trust me."

I stood still, flinching out of instinct. He took nothing but care. The whole world seemed weird, everything too close and yet buffered at the same time. Weariness and the best orgasm of my life had undone me.

Next he reached over and turned off the water, stepped out, and grabbed two towels. One he tied around his waist, the other he patted me dry with.

"That was good, right?" I asked as he dried off my hair, tending to me. My body still shook and quivered. It seemed like a good sign. My world had been torn apart and remade into some sparkly surreal love-fest thing. If he said it was only okay, I might hit him.

"That was fucking incredible," he corrected, throwing my towel onto the bathroom counter.

Even my grin quivered. I saw it in the mirror. "Yes. It was."

"Us together, always is."

Hand in hand we walked back into the bedroom. Being naked in front of him didn't feel weird for once. There was no hesitation. He discarded his towel and we climbed onto his giant-size bed, gravitating naturally toward the middle and each other. We both lay on our sides, face-to-face. I could slip into a coma, I was so worn out. Such a pity to have to close my eyes when he lay right there in front of me. My husband.

"You swore at me," he said, eyes amused.

"Did I?"

His hand sat atop of my thigh, his thumb sliding back and forth over my hip bone. "Gonna pretend you don't remember what you said? Really?"

"No. I remember." Though I hadn't meant to say it, neither the cuss word nor the declaration of love. But I had. Big-girl-panties time. "I said I was in love with you."

"Mm. People say stuff during sex. It happens."

He was giving me an out, but I couldn't take it. I wouldn't take it, no matter how tempting. I wasn't about to diminish the moment like that.

"I am in love with you," I said, feeling awkward. The same as when I'd said I trusted him, he was going to leave me hanging here too. I knew it.

His gaze lingered on my face, patient and kind. It hurt. Something inside me felt brittle and he brought it straight to the fore. Love made spelunking look sensible. BASE jumping and wrestling bears couldn't be far behind. But it was much, much too late to worry. The words were already out there. If love was for fools, then so be it. At least I'd be an honest one.

He stroked my face with the back of his fingers. "That was a beautiful thing to say."

"David, it's okay—"

"You're so fucking important to me," he said, stopping me short. "I want you to know that."

"Thank you." Ouch, not exactly the words I wanted to hear after I admitted I loved him.

Rising up on one elbow, he brought his lips to mine, kissing me silly. Stroking my tongue with his and taking me over. It left no room for worry.

"I need you again," he whispered, kneeling between my legs.

This time we did make love. There was no other word for it. He rocked into me at his own pace, pressing his cheek against mine, scratching me with his stubble. His voice went on and on, whispering secrets in my ear. How no one had ever been this right for him. How he wanted to stay just like this as long as we could. Sweat dripped off his body, running over my skin before soaking into the bedsheet. He made himself a permanent part of me. It was bliss. Sweet, tender, and slow. Maddeningly slow near the end.

It felt like it went on for forever. I wish it had.

CHAPTER SIXTEEN

Adrian went ballistic over the bruises on David's face. He didn't seem too pleased to see me again, either. There was a brief flash of shark's teeth before I was hustled into a corner of the big dressing room out of harm's way. Security stood outside, letting only those invited into the inner sanctum.

The show was in a ballroom at one of the big, fancy hotels in town. Lots of twinkling chandeliers and red satin, big round tables crammed full of stars and the pretty-people posses that accompanied them. Luckily, I'd worn a blue dress, the only one that remotely covered everything, and a pair of the mile-high shoes Martha had ordered. Kaetrin, Bikini Girl, David's old friend, had been on the other side of the room, wearing a red frock and a scowl. She was going to get wrinkles if she kept that up. Happily, she got bored with pouting at me after a while and wandered away. I didn't blame her for being mad. If I'd lost David, I'd be pissed too. Women hovered near David, hoping for his attention. I could have high-fived someone over the way he ignored them.

There was no sign of Jimmy. Mal sat with a stunning Asian girl on one knee and a busty blond on the other, much too busy to talk to me. I still hadn't met the fourth member of the band, Ben.

"Hey," David said, exchanging my untouched glass of Cristal for a bottle of water. "Thought you might prefer this. Everything okay?"

"Thank you. Yes. Everything's great."

Wonderful man, he knew I still hadn't recovered enough from Vegas to risk the taste of alcohol. He nodded and passed the glass of champagne off to a waiter. Then he started slipping out of his leather jacket. Other people might put on tuxedos, but David stuck to his jeans and boots. His one concession to the occasion was a black button-down shirt. "Do me a favor and put this on."

"You don't like my dress?"

"Sure I do. But the air-conditioning's a bit cold in here," he said, wrapping the jacket around my shoulders.

"No, it's not."

He gave me a lopsided grin that would have melted the hardest of hearts. Mine didn't stand a chance. With an arm either side of my head, he leaned in, blocking out the rest of the room and everyone in it.

"Trust me, you're finding it a bit cool." His gaze fell to my chest and understanding dawned on me. The dress was made from some light, gauzy fabric. Gorgeous, but not so subtle in certain ways. And obviously my bra wasn't helping at all.

"Oh," I said.

"Mm. And I'm over there, trying to talk business with Adrian, but I can't. I'm totally fucking distracted because I love your rack."

"Excellent." I put an arm over my chest as subtly as possible.

"They're so pretty and they fill my hands just right. It's like we were made for one another, you know?"

"David." I grinned like the horny, lovesick fool I was.

"Sometimes there's this almost-smile on your face. And I wonder what you're thinking, standing over here watching everything."

"Nothing in particular, just taking it all in. Looking forward to seeing you play."

"Are you, now?"

"Of course I am. I can't wait."

He kissed me lightly on the lips. "After I'm finished we'll get out of here, yeah? Head off somewhere, just you and me. We can do whatever you feel like. Go for a drive or get something to eat, maybe."

"Just us?"

"Absolutely. Whatever you want."

"It all sounds good."

His gaze dipped back to my chest. "You're still a little cold. I could warm you up. Where do you stand on me copping a feel in public?"

"That's a no." I turned my face to take a sip of the water. Arctic air or no, I needed cooling down.

"Yeah, that's what I thought. Come on. With great breasts come great responsibility." He took my hand and led me through the crowd of party people as I laughed. He didn't stop for anyone.

There was a small room attached to the back with a rack of garment bags and some makeup scattered around. Mirrors on the walls, a big bouquet of flowers, and a sofa that was very much occupied. Jimmy sat there in another dapper suit, legs spread with a woman kneeling between them. Her face was in his lap, head bobbing. No prizes for guessing what they were up to. The red of her dress clued me in to her identity, though I could have lived a long and happy life never knowing. Kaetrin's dark hair was wrapped tight around Jimmy's fist. In his other hand he held a bottle of whiskey. Two neat white lines of powder sat on the coffee table along with a small silver straw.

Holy crap. So this was the rock 'n' roll lifestyle. Suddenly my palms felt sweaty. But this wasn't what David was into. This wasn't him. I knew that.

"Ev," Jimmy said in a husky voice, a sleazy, slow smile spreading across his face. "Looking good, darlin'."

I snapped my mouth shut.

"Come on." David's hands clutched my shoulders, turning me away from the scene. He was livid, his mouth a bitter line.

"What, not going to say hi to Kaetrin, Dave? That's a bit harsh. Thought you two were good friends."

"Fuck off, Jimmy."

Behind us Jimmy groaned long and loud as the show on the couch reached its obvious conclusion. David slammed the door shut. The party continued on, music pumping out of the sound system, glasses clinking, and lots of loud conversation. We were out of there, but David stared off into the middle distance, oblivious of everything, it seemed. His face was lined with tension.

"David?"

"Five minutes," yelled Adrian, clapping his hands high in the air. "Showtime. Let's go."

David's eyelids blinked rapidly, as if he was waking up in the middle of a bad dream.

The atmosphere in the room was suddenly charged with excitement. The crowd cheered and Jimmy staggered on out with Kaetrin in tow. More cheering and shouts of encouragement for the band to take to the stage, along with some knowing laughter over Jimmy and the girl's reappearance.

"Let's do this!" shouted Jimmy, shaking hands and clapping people on the back as he moved through the room. "Come on, Davie."

My husband's shoulders hiked up. "Martha."

The woman sauntered over, her face a careful mask. "What can I do for you?"

"Look after Ev while I'm onstage."

"Sure."

"Look, I've got to go but I'll be right back," he said to me.

"Of course. Go."

With a final kiss to my forehead, he went, shoulders hunched in protectively. I had the maddest impulse to go after him. To stop him. To do something. Mal joined him at the door and slung an arm around his neck. David didn't look back. The bulk of the people followed them. I stood alone, watching the exodus. He'd been right, the room was cold. I clutched his jacket around me tighter, letting the scent of him soothe me. Everything was fine. If I kept telling myself that, sooner or later it would become true. Even the bits I didn't understand would work out. I had to have faith. And damn it, I did have faith. But my smile was long gone.

Martha watched me, her immaculate expression never altering.

After a moment, her red lips parted. "I've known David a very long time."

"That's nice," I said, refusing to be cowed by her cool gaze.

"Yes. He's enormously talented and driven. It makes him intense about things, passionate."

I said nothing.

"Sometimes he gets carried away. It doesn't mean anything." Martha stared at my ring. With an elegant motion she tucked her dark hair back behind her ear. Above a beautifully set cluster of dark red stones sat a single, small, winking diamond. Little more than a chip, it didn't really seem to fit Martha's expensive veneer. "When you're ready, I'll show you where you can watch the show from."

The sensation of spiraling that had started when David walked away from me became stronger. Beside me, Martha waited patiently, not saying a word, for which I was grateful. She'd said more than enough already. Only the clutter of red stones hung from her other ear. Paranoia wasn't pretty. Could this be the mate to the diamond earring David wore? No. That made no sense.

Lots of people wore tiny diamond solitaire earrings. Even millionaires.

I pushed my water aside, forcing a smile. "Shall we go?"

Watching the show was amazing. Martha took me to a spot to the side of the stage, behind the curtains, but it still felt like I was right in the thick of things. And things were loud and thrilling. Music thrummed through my chest, making my heart race. The music was a great distraction from my worries about the earring. David and I needed to talk. I'd been all for waiting until he felt comfortable enough to tell me things, but my questions were getting out of hand. I didn't want to be second-guessing him in this way. We needed honesty.

With a guitar in his hands, David was a god. Little wonder people worshiped him. His hands moved over the strings of his electric guitar with absolute precision, his concentration total. The muscles flexing in his forearms made his tattoos come to life. I stood in awe of him, mouth agape. There were other people onstage too, but David held me spellbound. I'd only seen the private side of him, who he was when he was with me. This seemed to be almost another entity. A stranger. My husband had taken a backseat to the performer. The rock star. It was actually a little daunting. But in that moment, his passion made perfect sense to me. His talent was such a gift.

They played five songs, then it was announced another big-name artist would take to the stage. All four of the band members exited by the other side. Martha had disappeared. Hard to be upset about that, despite backstage being a maze of hallways and dressing rooms. The woman was a monster. I was better off alone.

I made my way back on my own, taking tiny, delicate steps because my stupid shoes were killing me. Blisters lined my toes where the strap cut across, rubbing away at my skin. Didn't matter, my joy would not be dimmed. The memory of the music stayed with me. The way David had looked all caught up in the performance, both exciting and unknown. Talk about a rush.

I smiled and swore, quietly, ignoring my poor feet and wending my way through the mix of roadies, sound technicians, makeup artists, and general hangers-on.

"Child bride." Mal smacked a noisy kiss on my cheek. "I'm heading to a club. You guys coming or taking off back to your love nest?"

"I don't know. Just let me find David. That was amazing, by the way. You guys were brilliant."

"Glad you liked it. Don't tell David I carried the show, though. He's so precious about that sort of thing."

"My lips are sealed."

He laughed. "He's better with you, you know? Artistic types have a bad habit of disappearing up their own asses. He's smiled more in the last few days with you than I've seen him do in the last five years put together. You're good for him."

"Really?"

Mal grinned. "Really. You tell him I'm going to Charlotte's. See you there later, maybe."

"Okay."

Mal took off and I made my way toward the band's dressing room through the even bigger and better crush of people assembled. Inside the dressing room, however, things were quiet. Jimmy and Adrian had stood huddled out in the hallway, deep in conversation as I passed on by. Definitely not stopping. Sam and a second security person nodded to me as I passed.

The door to the back room where Jimmy had been busy earlier stood partly open. David's voice carried to me, clear as day, despite the noise outside. It was like I was becoming tuned in to him on some cosmic level. Scary but exhilarating at the same time. I couldn't wait to get out of here with him and do whatever. Go meet Mal or take off on our own. I didn't mind, so long as we were together.

I just wanted to be with him.

The sound of Martha's raised voice from within the same room decreased my happy.

"Don't," someone said from behind me, halting me at the door.

I turned to face the fourth member of the band: Ben. I remembered him now from some show Lauren had made me sit through years ago. He played bass, and he made Sam the bodyguard look like a cute, fluffy kitten. Short dark hair and the neck of a bull. Attractive in a strange, serial-killer kind of way. Though it might have just been the way he looked at me, eyes dead serious and jaw rigid. Another one on drugs, perhaps. To me, he felt nothing but bad.

"Let them sort it out," he said, voice low. His gaze darted to the partially open doorway. "You don't know what they were like when they were together."

"What?" I edged back a bit and he noticed, taking a step to the side to get closer to the door. Trying to maneuver me to the outer.

Ben just looked at me, his thick arm barring the way. "Mal said you're nice and I'm sure you are. But she's my sister. David and her have always been crazy about each other, ever since we were kids."

"I don't understand." I flinched, my head shaking.

"I know."

"Move, Ben."

"I'm sorry. Can't do that."

Fact was, he didn't need to. I held his gaze, making sure I had his full attention. Then I balanced my weight on one of my hooker heels, using the other to kick the door open. Since it had never been fully closed, it swung inward with ease.

David stood with his back partially turned toward us. Martha's hands were in his hair, holding him to her. Their mouths were mushed together. It was a hard, ugly kiss. Or maybe that was just the way it looked from the outside.

I didn't feel anything. Seeing that should have been big, but it wasn't. It made me small and it shut me down inside. If anything, it felt almost oddly inevitable. The pieces had all been there. I'd been so stupid, trying not to see this. Thinking everything would be fine.

A noise escaped my throat and David broke away from her. He looked over his shoulder at me.

"Ev," he said, face drawn and eyes bright.

My heart must have given up. Blood wasn't flowing. How bizarre. My hands and feet were ice-cold. I shook my head. I had nothing. I took a step back, and he flung out a hand to me.

"Don't," he said.

"David." Martha gave him a hazardous smile. No other word for it. Her hand stroked over his arm as if she could sink her nails into him at any time. I guessed she could.

David came toward me. I took several hasty steps back, stumbling in my heels. He stopped and stared at me like I was a stranger.

"Baby, this is nothing," he said. He reached for me again. I held my arms tight to my chest, guarding myself from harm. Too late.

"It was her? She's the high school sweetheart?"

The familiar old muscle in his jaw went pop. "That was a long time ago. It doesn't matter."

"Jesus, David."

"It has nothing to do with us."

The more he spoke, the colder I felt. I did my best to ignore Ben and Martha hovering in the background.

David swore. "Come on, we're getting out of here."

I shook my head slowly. He grabbed my arms, stopping me from retreating any farther. "What the fuck are you doing, Evelyn?"

"What are *you* doing, David? What have you done?"

"Nothing," he said, teeth gritted. "I haven't done a damn thing. You said you trusted me."

"Why do you both still wear the earrings if it's nothing?"

His hand flew to his ear, covering the offending items. "It's not like that."

"Why does she still work for you?"

"You said you trusted me," he repeated.

"Why keep the house in Monterey all these years?"

"No," he said and then stopped.

I stared at him, incredulous. "No? That's it? That's not enough. Was I supposed to just not see all this? Ignore it?"

"You don't understand."

"Then explain it to me," I pleaded. His eyes looked right through me. I might as well not have spoken. My questions went unanswered, same as they ever had. "You can't do it, can you?"

I took another step back and his face hardened to fury. His hands fisted at his sides. "Don't you dare fucking leave me. You promised!"

I didn't know him at all. I stared at him, transfixed, letting his anger wash over me. It couldn't hope to pierce the hurt. Not a chance.

"You walk out of here and it's over. Don't you fucking think of coming back."

"Okay."

"I mean it. You'll be nothing to me."

Behind David, Ben's mouth opened but nothing came out. Just as well. Even numb had its limits.

"Evelyn!" David snarled.

I slipped off the stupid shoes and went barefoot for my

grand exit. Might as well be comfortable. Normally I'd never wear heels like that. There was nothing wrong with normal. I was long overdue for a huge heaping dose of it. I'd wrap myself in normal like it was cotton wool, protecting me from everything. I had the café to get back to, school to start thinking about. I had a life waiting.

A door slammed shut behind me. Something thumped against it on the other side. The sound of shouting was muted.

Outside the dressing room door, Jimmy and Adrian were still deep in conversation. By which I mean Adrian spoke and Jimmy stared at the ceiling, grinning like a lunatic. I doubted a rocket ship could have reached Jimmy just then, he looked that high.

"Excuse me," I said, butting in.

Adrian turned and frowned, the flash of bright teeth coming a moment too late. "Evelyn. Honey, I'm just in the middle of something here—"

"I'd like to go back to Portland now."

"You would? Okay." He rubbed his hands together. Ah, I'd pleased him. His smile was huge, genuine for once and glaringly bright. Headlights had nothing on him. He'd apparently been holding back previously.

"Sam!" he yelled.

The bodyguard appeared, weaving through the crowd with ease. "Mrs. Ferris."

"Miss Thomas," Adrian corrected. "Would you mind seeing her safely returned to her home, thanks, Sam?"

The polite professional expression didn't falter for a second. "Yes, sir. Of course."

"Excellent."

Jimmy started laughing, big belly laughs that shook his whole body. Then he started cackling, the noise vaguely reminiscent of the Wicked Witch of the West in *The Wizard of Oz*. If she'd been on crack or cocaine or whatever Jimmy had been digging into, of course.

These people, they made no sense.

I didn't belong here. I'd never belonged here.

"This way." Sam pressed a hand lightly to the small of my back, which was sufficient to get me moving. Time to go home, wake up from the too-good-to-be-true dream that had twisted into this warped nightmare.

The laughter got louder and louder, ringing in my ears, until suddenly it cut off. I turned in time to watch Jimmy slump to the ground, his slick suit a mess. One woman gasped. Another chuckled and rolled her eyes.

"Fuck's sake," growled Adrian, kneeling beside the un-conscious man. He slapped at his face. "Jimmy. Jimmy!"

More burly bodyguards appeared, crowding around the fallen singer, blocking him from view.

"Not again," Adrian ranted. "Get the doctor in here. Goddamn it, Jimmy."

"Mrs. Ferris?" asked Sam.

"Is he all right?"

Sam scowled at the scene. "He's probably just passed out. It's been happening a lot lately. Shall we go?"

"Get me out of here, Sam. Please."

I was back in Portland before the sun rose. I didn't cry on the trip. It was as if my brain had diagnosed the emergency and cauterized my emotions. I felt numb, as if Sam could swerve the car into the oncoming traffic and I wouldn't utter a peep. I was done, frozen solid. We went via the mansion so Sam could collect my bag before heading to the airport. He put me on the jet and we flew to Portland. He got me off the jet and drove me home.

Sam insisted on carrying my bag, just like he'd insisted on calling me by my married name. The man did the best subtle, concerned sidelong glance I'd ever seen. Never said much, though, which I appreciated immensely.

I sleepwalked my sorry self up the stairs to the apartment Lauren and I shared. Home was a garlic-scented hallway courtesy of Mrs. Lucia downstairs, constantly cooking. Peeling green wallpaper and worn wooden floorboards, scuffed and stained. Lucky I'd put the Converses on, or my feet would have been full of splinters. This floor was nothing like the gloss and gleam of David's house. You could see yourself in that sucker.

Shit. I didn't want to think of him. All of those memories belonged in a box buried in the back of my mind. Never again would they see the light of day.

My key still fit the lock. It comforted me. I might as well have been missing for years instead of days. It hadn't even been a week. I'd left early Thursday morning and now it was Tuesday. Less than six short days. That was insane. Everything felt different. I pushed open the door, being quiet because of the early hour. Lauren would be asleep. Or she might not be. I heard laughing.

She might, in fact, be spread out over our small breakfast table, giggling as some guy stuffed his head beneath one of the old oversized T-shirts she slept in. He buried his face in her cleavage and tickled her. Lauren squirmed, making all sorts of happy noises. Thankfully the guy's pants were still on, whoever he was. They were really into it, didn't notice our entry at all.

Sam stared at the far wall, avoiding the scene. Poor guy, the things he must have witnessed over the years.

"Hi," I said. "Um, Lauren?"

Lauren screeched and rolled, twisting the guy up in her shirt as he fought to get free. If she accidentally strangled him, at least he'd go happy, given the view.

"Ev," she panted. "You're back."

The guy finally liberated his face.

"Nathan?" I asked, stupefied. I cocked my head just to be sure, narrowed my eyes.

"Hi." My brother raised one hand while pulling down Lauren's shirt with the other. "How are you?"

"Fine, yeah," I said. "Sam, this is my friend Lauren and my brother, Nate. Guys, this is Sam."

Sam did his polite nod and set down my bag. "Can I do anything else for you, Mrs. Ferris?"

"No, Sam. Thank you for seeing me home."

"You're very welcome." He looked to the door then back at me, a small wrinkle between his brows, I couldn't be certain, but I think it was as close as Sam got to an actual frown. His facial expressions seemed limited. Restrained was probably a better word. He reached out and gave me a stiff pat on the back. Then he left, closing the door behind him.

My eyes heated, threatening tears. I blinked like crazy, holding it in. His kindness nearly cracked the numb, damn it. I couldn't afford that yet.

"So, you two?" I asked.

"We're together. Yes," said Lauren, reaching behind her. Nate took her hand and held on tight. They actually looked good together. Though, seriously, how much stranger could things get? My world had changed. It felt different, though the small apartment looked the same. Things were pretty much where I'd left them. Lauren's collection of demented porcelain cats still sat on a shelf collecting dust. Our cheap or secondhand furniture and turquoise blue walls hadn't altered. Though I might never use the table again, considering what I'd seen. Lord knew what else they'd been up to on there.

I flexed my fingers, willing some life back into my limbs. "I thought you two hated each other?"

"We did," confirmed Lauren. "But, you know . . . now we don't. It's a surprisingly uncomplicated story, actually. It just kind of happened while you were away."

"Wow."

"Nice dress," said Lauren, looking me over.

"Thanks."

"Valentino?"

I smoothed the blue fabric over my stomach. "I don't know."

"That's a statement, matching it with the sneakers," Lauren said. Then she gave Nate a look. They apparently already had the silent communication thing down because he tippy-toed off toward her bedroom. Interesting . . .

My best friend and my brother. And she'd never said a word. But then, there were plenty of things I hadn't told her either. Maybe we were past the age of sharing every last little detail of our lives. How sad.

Loneliness and a healthy dose of self-pity cooled me right off and I wrapped my arms around myself.

Lauren came over and pried one of my hands loose. "Hon, what happened?"

I shook my head, warding off questions. "I can't. Not yet."

She joined me leaning against the wall. "I have ice cream."

"What kind?"

"Triple choc. I was thinking of torturing your brother with it later in a sexually explicit manner."

There went my vague interest in ice cream. I scrubbed my face with my hands. "Lauren, if you love me, you'll never say anything like that to me ever again."

"Sorry."

I almost smiled. My mouth definitely came close to it but faltered at the last. "Nate makes you happy, doesn't he?"

"Yeah, he really does. It just feels like . . . I don't know, it's like we're in tune or something. Ever since the night he picked me up from your folks' place we've pretty much been together. It feels right. He's not angry like he used to be in high school. He's given up his man-slut ways. He's calmed down and grown up. Shit, out of the two of us, he's the sensible one." She mock pouted. "But our days of sharing every last detail about our lives really are over, aren't they?"

"I guess they are."

"Ah, well. We'll always have middle school."

"Yeah." I managed a smile.

"Hon, I'm sorry things went bad. I mean, that's obviously why you're back looking like shit in that absolutely exquisite dress." She eyed up my gown with great lust.

"You can have it." Hell, she could have all of the other stuff as well. I never wanted to touch any of it ever again. His jacket I'd left with Sam, the ring stuffed into a pocket. Sam would take care of it. See that it got back to him. My hand seemed bare without it, lighter. Lighter and freer should have gone together, but they didn't. Inside me sat a great weight. I'd been dragging my sorry ass around for hours now. Onto the plane. Off the plane. Into the car. Up the stairs. Neither time nor distance had helped so far.

"I want to hug you but you're giving off that don't-touch-me vibe," she said, propping her hands on her slim hips. "Tell me what to do."

"Sorry." The smile I gave her was twisted and awful. I could feel it. "Later?"

"How much later? Because frankly, you look like you need it bad."

I couldn't stop the tears this time. They just started flowing, and once they started, they wouldn't stop. I wiped at them uselessly, then just gave up and covered my face with my hands. "Fuck."

Lauren threw her arms around me, held me tight. "Let it go."

I did.

CHAPTER SEVENTEEN

Twenty-eight days later . . .

The woman was taking forever to order. Her eyes kept shifting between me and the menu as she leaned across the counter. I knew that look. I dreaded that look. I loved being in the café, with the aroma of coffee beans and the soothing blend of music and chatter. I loved the camaraderie we had going on behind the counter and the fact that the work kept my hands and brain busy. Weirdly enough, being a barista relaxed me. I was good at it. With my studies a constant struggle, I reveled in that fact. If everything ever hit the wall, I'd always have coffee to fall back on. It was the modern-day Portland equivalent of typing. The city ran on coffee beans and cafés. Coffee and beer were in our blood.

Lately, however, some customers had been a pain in the ass to deal with.

"You seem really familiar," she started, much as they all did. "Weren't you all over the Internet a while back? Something to do with David Ferris?"

At least I didn't flinch at his name anymore. And it had been days since I'd felt the urge to actually vomit. Definitely not pregnant, just getting annulled.

After the first few days of hiding in bed, crying my

eyes out, I took every shift the café would give me to keep busy. I couldn't mourn him forever. Pity my heart remained unconvinced. He was in my dreams every night when I closed my eyes. I had to chase him out of my mind a thousand times a day.

By the time I surfaced, the few lingering paparazzi had cleared off back to LA. Apparently Jimmy had gone into rehab. Lauren switched channels every time I walked in, but I couldn't help but catch enough news to know what was going on. It seemed Stage Dive were being talked about everywhere. Someone had even asked me to sign a picture of David striding into the treatment facility, head hanging down and hands stuffed in his pockets. He'd looked so alone. Several times, I'd almost called him. Just to ask if he was okay. Just to hear his voice. How stupid was that? And what if I rang and Martha answered?

At any rate, Jimmy's meltdown was much more interesting than me. I barely rated a mention on the news these days.

But people, customers, they drove me nuts. Outside of work, I'd become a complete shut-in. That had its own issues on account of my brother basically living with us now. People in love were sickening. It was a proven medical fact. Customers with speculation shining bright in their beady little eyes weren't much better.

"You're mistaken," I told the nosy woman.

She gave me a coy look. "I don't think so."

Ten bucks said she was working her way up to asking me for his autograph. This would make the eighth attempt to obtain one today. Some of them wanted to take me home for intimate relations because, you know, rock star's ex. My vagina clearly had to be something special. I sometimes wondered if they thought there was a little plaque on my inner thigh saying David Ferris had been there.

This chick, however, wasn't checking me out. No, she wanted an autograph.

"Look," she said, speculation turning to wheedling. "I wouldn't ask, it's just that I'm such a huge fan of his."

"I can't help you, sorry. We're actually about to close. So would you like to order something before that happens?" I asked, pleasant smile firmly in place. Sam would have been proud of that smile, as fake as it was. But with my eyes I told the woman the truth. That I was all used up and I honestly had no fucks left to give. Especially when it came to David Ferris.

"Can you at least tell me if the band is really breaking up? Come on. Everyone's saying an announcement's going to be made any day now."

"I don't know anything about it. Would you like to order something, or not?"

Further denial generally led to either anger or tears. She chose anger. A good choice, because tears annoyed the living hell out of me. I was sick of them, both on myself and others. Despite it being common knowledge that I'd been dumped, they still figured I had connections. Or so they hoped.

She did a fake little laugh. "There's no need to be a bitch about it. Would letting me know what's happening really have killed you?"

"Leave," said my lovely manager, Ruby. "Right now. Get out."

The woman switched to incredulous, mouth open wide. "What?"

"Amanda, call the cops." Ruby stood tall beside me.

"On it, boss." Amanda snapped open her cell and punched in the numbers, leveling the woman with her evil eye. Amanda, having moved on from being my high school's sole lesbian, was studying drama. These confrontations were her favorite part of the day. They might have sapped my strength, but Amanda sucked all of her power from them. A dark, malevolent force, to be sure, but it was all hers and she reveled in it. "Yes, we've got a fake blonde with a bad tan giving us trouble, Officer. I'm pretty certain I saw her at a frat party doing some serious underage drinking last week. I don't want to say what happened after that but the footage is available on YouTube for your viewing pleasure if you're over eighteen."

"No wonder he dropped you. I saw the picture, your ass is wide as fucking Texas," the woman sneered, and then sped out of the café.

"Do you really have to stir them up?" I asked.

Amanda clucked her tongue. "Please. She started it."

I'd heard worse than what she'd said. Way worse. Several times now I'd had to change my e-mail address to stop the hate mail from flooding in. I had closed my Facebook account early on.

Still, I checked my butt to be sure. It was a close call, but I was pretty sure Texas was, in fact, wider.

"As far as I can tell you're living on a diet of breath mints and lattes. Your ass is not a concern." Amanda had long since forgiven me for the bad kiss back in high school, bless her. I was beyond lucky to have the friends I did. I really don't know how I'd have made it through the last month without them.

"I eat."

"Really? Whose jeans are those?"

I started cleaning the coffee machine because it really was getting on closing time. That, and for reasons of subject avoidance. Fact was, getting cheated on and lied to by rock 'n' roll's favorite son did make for quite the diet. Definitely not one I'd recommend. My sleep was shot to shit and I was tired all the time. I was depression's bitch. Inside and out, I didn't feel like me. The time I'd spent with David, the way it had changed things, was a constant agitation, an itch I couldn't scratch. Partly because I lacked the power but also because I lacked the will. You could sing "I Will Survive" only so many times before the urge to throttle yourself took over.

"Lauren doesn't wear these. Said they were the wrong shade of dark wash and that the placement of the back pockets made her look hippy. Apparently pocket placement matters."

"And you started wearing that skinny cow's clothes when?"

"Don't call her that."

Amanda rolled her eyes. "Please, she takes it as a compliment."

True. "Well, I think the jeans are nice. Are you wiping down the tables, or would you like me to?"

Amanda just sighed. "Jo and I want to thank you for helping us move last weekend. So we're taking you out tonight. Drinking and dancing ahoy!"

"Oh." Alcohol and I already had a bad reputation. "I don't know."

"I do."

"I had plans to—"

"No you don't. This is why I left it to the last minute to tell you. I knew you'd try to make excuses." Amanda's dark eyes brooked no nonsense. "Ruby, I'm taking our girl out for a night on the town."

"Good idea," Ruby called out from the kitchen. "Get her out of here. I'll clean up."

My practiced pleasant smile fell off my face. "But—"

"It's the sad eyes," said Ruby, confiscating my cleaning cloth. "I can't bear them any longer. Please go out and have some fun."

"Am I that much of a killjoy?" I asked, suddenly worried. I honestly thought I'd been putting on a good front. Their faces told me otherwise.

"No. You're a normal twenty-one-year-old going through a breakup. You need to get back out there and reclaim your life." Ruby was in her early thirties and soon to be wed. "Trust me. I know best. Go."

"Or," said Amanda, waggling a finger at me, "you could sit at home watching *Walk the Line* for the eight hundredth time while listening to your brother and best friend going hard at it in the room next door."

When she put it like that . . . "Let's go."

"I want to be bi," I announced, because it was important. A girl had to have goals. I pushed back my chair and rose to my feet. "Let's dance. I love this song."

"You love any song that's not by the band who shall not be named." Amanda laughed, following me through the crowd. Her girlfriend, Jo, just shook her head, clinging to her hand. Vodka was doubtless as bad an idea as tequila, but I did feel somewhat unwound, looser. It was good to get out, and on an empty stomach three drinks went a long way, clearly. I did suspect Amanda had made at least one of them a double. It felt great to dance and laugh and let loose. Out of all of the getting-over-a-breakup tactics I'd attempted, keeping busy worked best. But going out dancing and drinking all dressed up shouldn't be mocked.

I tucked my hair behind my ears because my ponytail had started falling apart again. Perfect metaphor for my life. Nothing worked right since I'd gotten back from LA. Nothing lasted. Love was a lie, and rock 'n' roll sucked. Blah blah blah. Time for another drink.

And I'd been in the middle of making an important point.

"I'm serious," I said. "I'm going bi. It's my new plan."

"I think that's a great plan," yelled Jo, moving next to me. Jo also worked at the café, which was how the two had met. She had long blue hair that was the envy of all.

Amanda rolled her eyes at me. "You're not bi. Babe, don't encourage her."

Jo grinned, totally unrepentant. "Last week she wanted

to be gay. Before that she talked monasteries. I think this is a constructive step toward her forgiving every penis-possessing human and moving on with her life."

"I am moving on with my life," I said.

"Which is why you two have been talking about him for the past four hours?" Amanda grinned, throwing her arms around Jo's shoulders.

"We weren't talking about him. We were insulting him. How do you say 'useless stinking sheep fornicator' in German again?" I asked, leaning in to be heard over the music. "That was my favorite."

Jo and Amanda got busy close dancing and I let them go, unperturbed. Because I wasn't afraid of being alone. I was action-packed, full of single-girl power. Fuck David Ferris. Fuck him good and hard.

The music all blended into one long time-bending beat, and so long as I kept moving it was all perfect. Sweat slicked my neck and I popped another button on my dress, widening the neckline. I ignored the other people dancing around me. I shut my eyes, staying safe in my own little world. The alcohol had given me a nice buzz.

For some reason, the hands sliding over my hips didn't bother me, even though they were uninvited. They went no farther, made no demands on me. Their owner danced behind me, keeping a small safe distance between us. It was nice. Maybe the music had hypnotized me. Or maybe I had been lonely, because I didn't fight it. Instead I relaxed against him. For all of the next song we stayed like that, melded together, moving. The beat slowed down and I raised my arms, linking my hands behind his neck. After a month of avoiding almost all human contact, my body woke. The short, soft hair at the back of his neck brushed over my fingers. Smooth, warm skin beneath.

God, it was so nice. I hadn't realized how touch starved I was.

I leaned my head back against him and he whispered

something softly. Too soft for me to hear. The bristles on his cheek and jaw lightly prickled the side of my face. Hands slid over my ribs, up my arms. Calloused fingers lightly stroked the sensitive underside of my arms. His body was solid behind me, strong, but he kept his touch light, restrained. I wasn't in the market for a rebound. My heart was too bruised for that, my mind too wary I couldn't bring myself to move away from him, however. It felt too good there.

"Evelyn," he said, his lips teasing my ear.

My breath caught, my eyelids shot open. I turned to find David staring back at me. The long hair was gone. It was still longish on top but cut short at the sides. He could probably do a neat Elvis pompadour if the fancy took him. A short, dark beard covered his lower face.

"Y-you're here," I stuttered out. My tongue felt thick and useless inside my dry mouth. Christ, it was really him. Here in Portland. In the flesh.

"Yeah." His blue eyes burned. He didn't say anything else. Music kept playing, people kept moving. The world only stopped turning for me.

"Why?"

"Ev?" Amanda put a hand to my arm and I jumped, the spell broken. She gave David a quick glance, and then her face screwed up in distaste. "What the fuck is he doing here?"

"It's okay," I said.

Her gaze moved between David and me. She didn't really seem convinced. Fair enough.

"Amanda. Please." I squeezed her fingers, nodded. After a moment she turned back to Jo, who stared at David with open disbelief. And a healthy dose of star-struck. His new look made for a brilliant disguise. Unless you knew who you were looking for, of course.

I pushed through the crowd, getting the hell out of there. I knew he'd follow. Of course he would. It was no

accident he was there, though I had no damn idea how
he'd found me. I needed to get away from the heat and the
noise so I could think straight. Down the back hallway
past the men's and women's toilets. There, that was what
I wanted. A big black door opened onto a back alleyway.
Open night air. A few brave stars twinkled high overhead. Otherwise it was dark back here, damp from earlier
summer rain. It was horrible and dirty and hateful. An
ideal setting.

I might have been feeling a bit dramatic.

The door slammed shut behind David. He faced me,
hands on hips. He opened his mouth to start talking and
no, not happening. I snapped.

"Why are you here, David?"

"We need to talk."

"No, we don't."

He rubbed at his mouth. "Please. There're things I have
to tell you."

"Too late."

Looking at him revived the pain. As if I had wounds
lingering just beneath the skin, waiting to resurface. I
couldn't help staring at him, however. Parts of me were
desperate for the sight of him, the sound of him. My head
and heart were a wreck. David didn't appear so great himself. He looked tired. There were shadows beneath his
eyes and he seemed a little pale, even in this crappy lighting. The earrings were missing, all of them gone. Not that
I cared.

He rocked back on his heels, eyes watching me desperately. "Jimmy went into rehab and there were other
things going on I had to deal with. We had to do therapy
together as part of his treatment. That's why I couldn't
come right away."

"I'm sorry to hear about Jimmy."

He nodded. "Thanks. He's doing a lot better."

"Good. That's good."

Another nod. "Ev, about Martha—"

"Whoa." I held up a hand, backing up. "Don't."

His mouth turned down at the edges. "We have to talk."

"Do we?"

"Yes."

"Because now you've decided you're ready? Fuck you, David. It's been a month. Twenty-eight days without a word. I'm sorry about your brother, but no."

"I wanted to make sure I was coming after you for the right reasons."

"I don't even know what that means."

"Ev—"

"No." I shook my head, hurt and fury pushing me hard. So I pushed at him even harder, sending him back a step. He hit the wall and I had nowhere else to go with him. But that didn't stop me.

I went to push at him again and he grabbed my hands. "Calm down."

"No!"

His hands encircled my wrists. He gritted his teeth, grinding his molars together. I heard it. Impressive that he didn't crack anything. "No what? No to talking now? What? What do you mean?"

"I mean no to everything and anything to do with you." My words echoed through the narrow alleyway, up the sides of the buildings until they emptied out into the uncaring night sky. "We're finished, remember? You're fucking done with me. I'm nothing to you. You said so yourself."

"I was wrong. Goddamn it, Ev. Calm down. Listen to me."

"Let me go."

"I'm sorry. But it's not what you think."

Out of options, I got in his face. "You don't get to come here now. You lied to me. You cheated on me."

"Baby—"

"Don't you dare call me that," I yelled.

"I'm sorry." His gaze roamed my face, searching for sense, maybe. He was shit out of luck. "I'm sorry."

"Stop."

"I'm sorry. I'm sorry." Over and over he said, chanting the most worthless words in all of time and space. I had to stop it. Shut him up before he drove me insane. I smashed my mouth to his, halting the useless litany. He groaned and kissed me back hard, bruising my lips, hurting me. But then I hurt him too. The pain helped. I pushed my tongue into his mouth, taking what was supposed to be mine. In that moment I hated him and I loved him. There didn't seem to be any difference.

My hands were freed and I wound them around his neck. He turned us, setting my back to the rough brick wall. His touch burned through my skin and bones. It all happened so fast, there wasn't time to wonder about the wisdom of it. He pushed up my dress and tore at my panties. They didn't stand a chance. The cool of the night air and the heat of his palms smoothed over my thighs.

"I missed you so fucking much," he groaned.

"David."

He lowered his zipper and pushed down the front of his jeans. Then he lifted my leg, bringing it up to his hip. My hands dragged at his neck. I think I was trying to climb him. There wasn't much thought going into it. Just the drive to get as close to him as physically possible. He nipped at my lips, taking my mouth in another hard kiss. His cock pushed against me, easing into me. The feel of him filling me made my head spin. The slight ache as he stretched me. His other hand slid around beneath my butt, then he lifted me up, pushing in all the way, making me moan. I wrapped my legs around him and held on tight. He pounded himself into me with nil finesse. Rough suited both our moods. My fingernails clawed at his neck, my heels drumming his ass. His teeth pressed hard into the side of my neck. The pain was perfect.

"Harder," I panted.

"Fuck yes."

The rough brickwork abraded my back, pulling at the fabric of my dress. The hard drive of his cock took my breath away. I clung on tight, trying to savor the feel of him, the tension building inside me. It was all too much and still not enough. The thought that this could be our last time, a brutally angry joining like this . . . I wanted to cry but I didn't have the tears. His fingers dug into my ass cheeks, marking my flesh. The pressure inside me grew higher and higher. He changed his angle slightly, hitting my clit, and I came hard, my arms wrapped around his head, my cheek pressed against his. His beard brushed against up my face. My whole body shuddered and shook.

"Evelyn," he snarled, grinding himself into me, emptying himself inside me.

Every muscle in my body went liquid. It was all I could do to hang on to him.

"It's fine, baby." His mouth pressed against my damp face. "It'll be okay, I promise. I'll fix it."

"P-put me down."

His shoulders rose and fell on a harsh breath, and carefully he did so. Quickly I pulled down the skirt of my dress, set myself to rights. Like that was even possible. This situation was out of control. Without fuss he pulled up his jeans, made himself presentable. I looked everywhere but at him. An alleyway. Holy hell.

"Are you all right?" His fingers brushed over my face, tucked back my hair. Until I put a hand to his chest, forcing him back a step. Well, not forcing him. He chose to give me my space.

"I . . . um." I licked my lips and tried again. "I need to go home."

"Come on, I'll get us a cab."

"No. I'm sorry. I know I started this. But . . ." I shook my head.

David hung his.

"That was good-bye."

"Like fuck it was. Don't you even try to tell me that." His finger slid beneath my chin, making me look at him. "We are not finished, you hear me? Not even fucking remotely. New plan. I'm not leaving Portland until we've talked this out. I promise you that."

"Not tonight."

"No. Not tonight. Tomorrow, then?"

I opened my mouth but nothing came out. I had no idea what I wanted to say. My fingernails dug into my sides through my dress. What I wanted these days was a mystery even to me. To stop hurting would be nice. To remove all memory of him from my head and heart. To get my breathing back under control.

"Tomorrow," he repeated.

"I don't know." Now I felt tired, facing him. I could have slept for a year. My shoulders slumped and my brain stalled.

He just stared at me, eyes intense. "Okay."

Where that left us, I had no idea. But I nodded as if something had been decided.

"Good," he said, taking a deep breath.

My muscles still trembled. Semen slid down the inside of my leg. Shit. We'd had the talk, but things had been different back then.

"David, you practiced safe sex, right, the last month?"

"You have nothing to worry about."

"Good."

He took a step toward me. "As far as I'm concerned we're still married. So no, Evelyn, I haven't been fucking around on you."

I had nothing. My knees wavered. Probably due to the recent action they'd seen. Relief over him not taking to the groupies with a vengeance after our split couldn't be part of it, surely. I didn't even want to think about Martha, that tentacle-wielding sea monster from the deep.

Sex was so messy. Love was far and away worse.

One of us had to go. He made no move, so I left, hightailing it back toward the club to find Amanda and Jo. I needed new panties and a heart transplant. I needed to go home. He followed me, opening the door. The heavy bass of the music boomed out into the night.

I rushed into the ladies' room and locked myself into a stall to clean up. When I came out to wash my hands, looking in the mirror was hard. The harsh fluorescent lighting did me no favors. My long blond hair hung around my face a knotted mess thanks to David's hands. My eyes were wide and wounded. I looked terrified, but of what I didn't want to say. Also, there was the mother of all hickeys forming on my neck. Hell.

A couple of girls came in, giggling and casting longing looks back over their shoulders. Before the door swung shut, I caught a glance of David leaning against the wall opposite, waiting, staring at his boots. The girls' excited chatter was jarringly loud. But they made no mention of his name. David's disguise was holding up. Arms wrapped around myself, I went out to meet him.

"Ready to go?" he asked, pushing off from the wall.

"Yeah."

We made our way back through the club, dodging dancers and drunks, searching for Amanda and Jo. They were on the edge of the dance floor, talking. Amanda had her cranky face on.

She took me in and a brow arched. "Are you fucking kidding me?"

"Thanks for asking me out, guys. But I'm going to head home," I said, ignoring the pointed look.

"With him?" She jerked her chin at David, who lurked at my shoulder.

Jo stepped forward, wrapping me up in her arms. "Ignore her. You do what's right for you."

"Thanks."

Amanda rolled her eyes and followed suit, pulling me in for a hug. "He hurt you so bad."

"I know." My eyes welled with tears. Highly unhelpful. "Thanks for asking me out."

I'd bet all the money I had Amanda was roasting David over my shoulder with her eyes. I almost felt bad for him. Almost.

We left the club as one of his songs came over the speakers. There were numerous cries of "Divers!" Jimmy's voice purred out the lyrics, "Damn I hate these last days of love, cherry lips and long good-byes . . ."

David ducked his head and we rushed out. Outside in the open air, the song was no more than the faraway thumping of bass and drums. I kept sneaking sidelong glances, checking he was really there and not some figment of my imagination. So many times I'd dreamed he'd come to me. And every time I'd woken up alone, my face wet with tears. Now he was here and I couldn't risk it. If he broke me again, I wasn't convinced I'd manage to get back up a second time. My heart might not make it. So I did my best to keep my mouth and my mind shut.

It was still relatively early and there weren't many people milling about outside. I held out my hand to the passing traffic and a cab cruised to a stop soon after. David held the door open for me. I climbed in without a word.

"I'm seeing you home." He slid in after me and I scurried across the seat in surprise.

"You don't need—"

"I do. Okay. I do need to do that much, so just . . ."

"All right."

"Where to?" The cabdriver asked, giving us an uninterested look in the rearview mirror. Another feuding couple in his backseat. I'm sure he saw at least a dozen a night.

David rattled off my address without blinking. The taxi pulled out into the flow of traffic. He could have gotten my address from Sam, and as for the rest . . .

"Lauren," I sighed, sinking back against the seat. "Of course, that's how you knew where to find me."

He winced. "I talked to Lauren earlier. Listen, don't be mad at her. She took a lot of convincing."

"Right."

"I'm serious. She ripped me a new one for messing things up with you, yelled at me for half an hour. Please don't be mad at her."

I gritted my teeth and stared out the window. Until his fingers slid over mine. I snatched back my hand.

"You'll let me inside you but you won't let me hold your hand?" he whispered, his face sad in the dim glow of the passing cars and streetlights.

It was on the tip of my mouth to say that it had been an accident. That what had happened between us was wrong. But I couldn't do it. I knew how much it would hurt him. We stared at each other as my mouth hung open, my brain useless.

"I missed you so fucking much," he said. "You have no idea."

"Don't."

His lips shut but he didn't look away. I sat there caught by his gaze. He looked so different with his long hair gone, with the short beard. Familiar but unknown. It wasn't a long trip home, though it seemed to take forever. The cab stopped outside the old block of flats, and the driver gave us an impatient look over his shoulder.

I pushed open the car door, ready to be gone but hesitating just the same. My foot hovered in thin air above the curb. "I honestly didn't think I'd ever see you again."

"Hey," he said, his arm stretching out across the back of the seat. His fingers reached toward me but fell short of making contact. "You're going to see me again. Tomorrow."

I didn't know what to say.

"Tomorrow," he repeated, voice determined.

"I don't know if it'll make any difference."

He lifted his chin, inhaling sharply. "I know I fucked us up, but I'm going to fix it. Just don't make up your mind yet, all right? Give me that much."

I gave him a brief nod and hurried inside on unsteady legs. Once I'd locked myself inside, the cab pulled away, its taillights fading to black through the frosted glass of the downstairs door.

What the hell was I supposed to do now?

CHAPTER EIGHTEEN

I was running late for work. Rushing about like a mad thing trying to get ready. I ran into the bathroom, jumped in the shower. Gave my face a good scrub to get rid of the remnants of last night's makeup. Gruesome, crusty stuff. It would serve me right if I got the pimple from hell. Last night had all been some bizarre dream. But this was real life. Work and school and friends. My plans for the future. Those were the things that were important. And if I just kept telling myself that, everything would be fine and dandy. Someday.

Ruby didn't much mind what we wore at work beyond the official café T-shirt. Her roots were strongly alternative. She'd planned to be a poet but wound up inheriting her aunt's coffee shop in the Pearl District. Urban development had upped property prices and Ruby became quite the well-to-do businesswoman. Now she wrote her poetry on the walls in the café. I don't think you could find a better boss. But late was still late. Not good.

I'd stayed up worrying about what had happened with David in that alleyway. Reliving the moment where he told me he considered us still married. Sleep would have been far more beneficial. Pity my brain wouldn't switch off.

I pulled on a black pencil skirt, the official café T-shirt, and a pair of flats. Done. Nothing was going to help the bruises beneath my eyes. People had pretty much gotten used to them on me lately. It took about half a stick of concealer to cover the bruise on my neck.

I roared out of the bathroom in a cloud of steam, just in time to see Lauren waltz out of the kitchen, broad smile on her face. "You're late for work."

"That I am."

I looped my handbag over my shoulder, grabbed my keys off the table, and got going. There wasn't time for this. Not now. Quite possibly not ever. I couldn't imagine her ever having a good enough reason for siding with David. Over the last month she'd spent many nights by my side, letting me talk myself hoarse about him when I needed to. Because eventually, it all had to come out. Daily I told her that I didn't deserve her, and she'd smack a kiss on my cheek. Why betray me now? I thumped down the stairs with extra oomph.

"Ev, wait." Lauren ran after me as I stormed down the front steps.

I turned on her, house keys held before me like a weapon. "You told him where I was."

"What was I supposed to do?"

"Oh, I don't know. Not tell him? You knew I didn't want to see him." I looked her over, noticing all sorts of things I didn't want to. "Full hair and makeup at this hour? Really, Lauren? Were you expecting him to be here, perhaps?"

Her chin dipped as she had the good grace to look embarrassed at last. "I'm sorry. You're right, I got carried away. But he's here to make amends. I thought you might at least want to hear what he has to say."

I shook my head, fury bubbling away inside me. "Not your call."

"You've been miserable. What was I supposed to do?"

She threw her arms sky-high. "He said that he'd come to make things right with you. I believe him."

"Of course you do. He's David Ferris, your very own teen idol."

"No. If he wasn't here to kiss your feet I'd have killed him. No matter who he is, he hurt you." She seemed sincere, her mouth pinched and eyes huge. "I'm sorry about dressing up this morning. It won't happen again."

"You look great. But you're wasting your time. He's not going to be here. That isn't going to happen."

"No? So who gave you that monster on your neck?"

I didn't even need to answer that. Damn it. The sun beat down overhead, warming up the day.

"If there's a chance you think he might be the one," she said, making my stomach twist. "If you think you two can sort this out somehow . . . He's the only one that ever got to you. The way you talk about him . . ."

"We were only together a few days."

"You really think that matters?"

"Yes. No. I don't know," I flailed. It wasn't pretty. "We never made sense, Lauren. Not from day one."

"Gah," she said, making a strangled noise to accompany it. "This is about your fucking plan, isn't it? Let me clue you in on something. You don't have to make sense. You just have to want to be together and be willing to do whatever it takes to make that happen. It's amazingly simple. That's love, Ev, putting each other first. Not worrying about if you fit into some fucktard plan that your dad brainwashed you into believing was what you wanted out of life."

"It's not about the plan." I scrubbed at my face with my hands, holding back tears of frustration and fear. "He broke me. It feels like he broke me. Why would anyone willingly take that chance again?"

Lauren looked at me, her own eyes bright. "I know he hurt you. So punish the bastard, keep him waiting. The fucker, he deserves it. But if you love him, then think about hearing what he has to say."

Maybe I was coming down with a cold, tight chest and itchy eyes. Having your heart broken should come with some positives, some perspective to balance out the bad. I should have been wiser, tougher, but I didn't feel it just then. I jangled my house keys. Ruby was going to kill me. I'd have to forgo my usual walk and catch a streetcar to have even a hope in hell of not getting my Texas-size ass fired. "I have to go."

Lauren nodded, face set. "You know, I love you so much more than I ever loved him. Without question."

I snorted. "Thanks."

"But has it occurred to you that you wouldn't be this upset if you didn't still love him at least a little bit?"

"I don't like you making sense at this hour of the morning. Stop it."

She took a step back, giving me a smile. "You were always there talking sense at me when I needed it. So I'm not going to stop nagging you just because you don't like what you're hearing. Deal with it."

"I love you, Lauren."

"I know, you Thomas kids are crazy for me. Why, just last night, your brother did this thing . . ."

I fled from the sound of her evil laughter.

Work was fine. Two guys came in to ask me to a frat party that was coming up. I'd never received such invites pre-David. I therefore declined them post-David. If I was indeed post-David. Who knew? Various people tried for autographs or information, and I sold them coffee and cake instead. We closed up at dusk.

All day I'd been on edge, wondering if he'd put in an appearance. Tomorrow was today, but I hadn't seen any sign of him. Maybe he'd changed his mind. Mine changed from one minute to the next. My promise to him not to decide yet was safe and sound.

We were just locking up when Ruby jabbed me in the ribs with her elbow. Probably a bit harder than she meant to because I'm pretty sure I sustained a kidney injury.

"He's really here," she hissed, nodding at David who did indeed lurk nearby, waiting. He was here, just like he'd said he'd be. Nervous excitement bubbled up inside of me. With a ball cap on and the beard, he blended well. Especially with the haircut. My heart sobbed a little at the loss of his long dark hair. But I'd never admit to it. Amanda had told Ruby about his reappearance last night. Given the lack of paparazzi and screaming fans in the vicinity, it must still be a secret from the rest of the city.

I stared at him, unsure how to feel. Last night at the club had been surreal. Here and now, this was me living my normal life. Seeing him in it, I didn't know how I felt. Discombobulated was a good word.

"Do you want to meet him?" I asked.

"No, I'm reserving judgment. I think actually meeting him might render me partial. He's very attractive, isn't he?" Ruby gave him a slow look over, lingering on his jeans-clad legs longer than necessary. She had a thing for men's thighs. Soccer players sent her into a frenzy. Odd for a poet, but then I'd found no one ever really fit a certain type. Everyone had their quirks.

Ruby continued looking him over like he was meat at market. "Maybe don't divorce him."

"You sound very impartial. See you later."

Her hand hooked my arm. "Wait. If you stay with him will you still work for me?"

"Yes. I'll even try to be on time more often. Night, Ruby."

He stood on the sidewalk, hands stuffed into the pockets of his jeans. Seeing him felt similar to standing at a cliff's edge. The little voice in the back of my head whispered damn the consequences, you know you can probably fly. If you can't, imagine the thrill of the fall. Reason, on the other hand, screamed bloody murder at me.

At what point exactly could you decide you were going insane?

"Evelyn."

Everything stopped. If he ever figured out what it did to me when he said my name like that, I was done for. God, I'd missed him. It'd been like having a piece of me missing. But now that he was back, I didn't know how we fit together anymore. I didn't even know if we could.

"Hi," I said.

"You look tired," he said, mouth turning downward. "I mean, you look good, of course. But . . ."

"It's fine." I studied the sidewalk, took a deep breath. "It was a busy day."

"So this is where you work?"

"Yeah."

Ruby's café sat quiet and empty. Fairy lights twinkled in the windows alongside a host of flyers taped to the glass advertising this and that. Streetlights flickered on around us.

"Looks nice. Listen, we don't have to talk right now," he said. "I just wanna walk you home."

I crossed my arms over my chest. "You don't have to do that."

"It's not like it's a chore. Let me walk you home, Ev. Please."

I nodded and after a moment started a hesitant stride down the city street. David fell into step beside me. What to talk about? Every topic seemed loaded. An open pit full of sharp stakes lay waiting around every corner. He kept shooting me wary sidelong glances. Opening his mouth and then shutting it. Apparently the situation sucked for both of us. I couldn't bring myself to talk about LA. Last night seemed safer territory. Wait. No, it wasn't. Bringing up alley sex was never going to pass for smart.

"How was your day?" he asked. "Apart from busy."

Why couldn't I have thought of something innocuous like that?

"Ah, fine. A couple of girls came in with stuff for you to sign. Some guys wanted me to give you a demo tape of their garage-reggae-blues band. One of the big-name jocks from school came in just to give me his number. He thinks we could have fun sometime," I babbled, trying to lighten the mood.

His face became thunderous, dark brows drawn tight together. "Shit. That been happening often?"

And I was an idiot to have opened my mouth. "It's no big deal, David. I told him I was busy and he went away."

"So he fucking should." He tipped his chin, giving me a long look. "You trying to make me jealous?"

"No, my mouth just ran away without my head. Sorry. Things are complicated enough."

"I am jealous."

I stared at him in surprise. I don't know why. He'd made it clear last night he was here for me. But the knowledge that maybe I wasn't alone out on the lovelorn precipice, thinking of throwing myself off . . . there was a lot of comfort in that.

"Come on," he said, resuming the walking. At the corner we stopped, waiting for the traffic to clear.

"I might get Sam up here to keep an eye on you," he said. "I don't want people bothering you at work."

"As much as I like Sam, he can stay where he is. Normal people don't take bodyguards to work."

His forehead scrunched up, but he said nothing. We crossed the road, continuing on. A streetcar rumbled past, all lit up. I preferred walking, getting in some outside time after being shut inside all day. Plus, Portland's beautiful: cafés and breweries and a weird heart. Take that, LA.

"So what did you do today?" I asked, proving myself a total winner in the creative conversation stakes.

"Just had a look around town, checking things out. I don't get to play the tourist too often. We're going left here," he said, turning me off the normal path toward home.

"Where are we going?"

"Just bear with me. I need to pick something up." He escorted me into a pizza place I went to occasionally with Lauren. "Pizza's the only thing I know you definitely eat. They were willing to stick on every fucking vegetable I could think of, so I hope you'll like it."

The place was only about a quarter full due to the early hour. Bare brick walls and black tables. A jukebox blared out something by the Beatles. I stood in the doorway, hesitant to go farther with him. The man nodded to David and fetched an order from the warmer behind him. David thanked him and headed back toward me.

"You didn't have to do that." I stepped back out onto the street, giving the pizza box suspicious glances.

"It's just pizza, Ev," he said. "Relax. You don't even have to ask me to share it with you if you don't want. Which way is it to your place from here?"

"Left."

We walked another block in silence with David carrying the pizza box up high on one hand.

"Stop frowning," he said. "When I picked you up last night you were lighter than in Monterey. You've lost weight."

I shrugged. Not going there. Definitely not remembering him lifting me and my legs going around him and how badly I'd missed him and the sound of his voice as he—

"Yeah, well, I liked you the way you were," he said. "I love your curves. So I came up with another plan. You're getting pizza with fifteen cheeses on it until you've got them back."

"My first instinct here is to say something snarky about how my body is no longer any of your business."

"Lucky you thought twice about saying that, huh? Especially since you let me back into your body last night." He met my scowl with one of his own. "Look, I just don't want you losing weight and getting sick, especially not on my account. It's that simple. Forget the rest and stop giving the pizza dirty looks or you'll hurt its feelings."

"You're not the boss of me," I muttered.

He barked out a laugh. "You feel better for saying that?"

"Yes."

I gave him a wary smile. Having him beside me again felt too easy. I shouldn't get comfortable, who knew when it would once again blow up in my face? But the truth was, I wanted him there so bad it hurt.

"Ba—" He cleared his throat and tried again, without the sentiment that would have earned him an automatic smackdown. "Friend. Are we friends again?"

"I don't know."

He shook his head. "We're friends. Ev, you're sad, you're tired, and you've lost weight, and I fucking hate that I'm the cause of it. I'm going to make this right with you one step at a time. Just . . . give me a little room to maneuver here. I promise I won't step on your toes too badly."

"I don't trust you anymore, David."

His teasing smile fell. "I know you don't. And when you're ready we're gonna talk about that."

I swallowed hard against the lump in my throat.

"When you're ready," he reiterated. "Come on. Let's get you home so you can eat this while it's still hot."

We walked the rest of the way home in silence. I think it was companionable. David gave me occasional small smiles. They seemed genuine.

He tramped up the stairs behind me, not really bothering to look around. I'd forgotten he'd been here last night when he got my whereabouts from Lauren. I unlocked the door and took a peek inside, still scarred from catching Lauren and my brother on the couch last week. Living with them wasn't going to work long term. I think everyone was getting to the point of needing their own space.

The last month, though, had been beneficial for Nate and me. It had given us a chance to talk. We were closer than we'd ever been. He loved his job at the mechanic shop. He was happy and settled. Lauren was right, he'd changed. My brother had figured out what he wanted and where he belonged. Now if I could just get my shit together and do the same.

Rock music played softly and Nate and Lauren danced in the middle of the room. An impromptu thing, obviously, given my brother's still-greasy work clothes. Lauren didn't seem to care, holding on to him tight, staring into his eyes.

I cleared my throat to announce our arrival and stepped into the room.

Nate looked over and gave me a welcoming smile. But then he saw David. Blood suffused his face and his eyes changed. The temperature in the room seemed to rocket.

"Nate," I said, making a grab for him as he charged David.

"Shit." Lauren ran after him. "No!"

Nate's fist connected with David's face. The pizza went flying. David stumbled back, blood gushing from his nose.

"You fucking asshole," my brother yelled.

I jumped on Nate's back, trying to wrestle him back. Lauren grabbed at his arm. David did nothing. He covered his bloody face but made no move to protect himself from further damage.

"I'm going to fucking kill you for hurting her," Nate roared.

David just looked at him, eyes accepting.

"Stop, Nate!" My feet dragged at the floor, my arms wrapped around my brother's windpipe.

"You want him here?" Nate asked me, incredulous. "Are you fucking serious?" Then he looked at Lauren tugging at his arm. "What are you doing?"

"This is between them, Nate."

"What? No! You saw what he did to her. What she's been like for the last month."

"You need to calm down. She doesn't want this." Lauren's hands patted over his face. "Please, babe. This isn't you."

Slowly, Nate pulled back. His shoulders dropped back to normal levels, his muscles relaxing. I gave up my choke hold on him, not that it had done much good. My brother did the raging bull thing scarily well. Blood leaked out from between David's fingers, dripped onto the floor. "Crap. Come on." I grabbed his arm and led him into our bathroom.

He leaned over the sink, swearing quietly but profusely. I bundled up some toilet paper and handed it to him. He stuffed it beneath his bloody nostrils.

"Is it broken?"

"I dunno." His voice was muffled, thick.

"I'm so sorry."

"S'okay." From his back jeans pocket came a ringing noise.

"I'll get it." Carefully, I extracted his phone. The name flashing on screen stopped me cold. The universe had to be playing a prank. Surely. Except it wasn't. It was just the same old heartbreak playing out all over again inside of me. I could already feel the ice-cold numbness spreading through my veins.

"It's her." I held the phone out to him.

Above the ball of bloody toilet paper his nose looked wounded but intact. Violence wasn't going to help. No matter the anger working through me, winding me up just then.

His gaze jumped from the screen to me. "Ev."

"You should go. I want you to go."

"I haven't talked to Martha since that night. I've had nothing to do with her."

I shook my head, out of words. The phone rang shrilly, the noise piercing my eardrums. It echoed on and on inside the small bathroom. It vibrated in my hand and my whole body trembled. "Take it before I break it."

Bloodstained fingers took it from my hand.

"You gotta let me explain," he said. "I promise, she's gone."

"Then why is she calling you?"

"I don't know and I'm not answering. I haven't spoken to her once since I fired her. You gotta believe me."

"But I don't. I mean, how can I?"

He blinked pained eyes at me. We just stared at one another as realization dawned. This wasn't going to work. This had never been going to work. He was always secrets and lies, and I was always on the outside looking in. Nothing had changed. My heart was breaking all over again. Surprising, really, that there was enough of it left to worry over.

"Just go," I said, my stupid eyes welling up.

Without another word, he walked out.

CHAPTER NINETEEN

David and I didn't speak after that. But every afternoon after work he was there, waiting across the street. He'd be watching me from beneath the brim of his baseball cap. All ready to stalk me home safely. It pissed me off, but in no way did I feel threatened. I'd ignored him for three days as he trailed me. Today was day number four. He'd traded his usual black jeans for blue, boots for sneakers. Even from a distance, his upper lip and nose looked bruised. The paparazzi were still missing in action, though today someone had asked me if he was in town. His days of moving around Portland unknown were probably coming to an end. I wondered if he knew.

When I didn't just ignore him as per my usual modus operandi, he took a step forward. Then stopped. A truck passed between us among a steady stream of city traffic. This was crazy. Why was he still here? Why hadn't he just gone back to Martha? Moving on was impossible with him here.

Decision half made, I rushed across during the next break in traffic, meeting him on the opposite sidewalk.

"Hi," I said, not fussing with the strap on my bag at all, "What are you doing here, David?"

He stuffed his hands in his pockets, looked around. "I'm walking you home. Same as I do every day."

"This is your life now?"

"Guess so."

"Huh," I said, summing up the situation perfectly. "Why don't you go back to LA?"

Blue eyes watched me warily and he didn't answer at first. "My wife lives in Portland."

My heart stuttered. The simplicity of the statement and the sincerity in his eyes caught me off guard. I wasn't nearly as immune to him as I should have been. "We can't keep doing this."

He studied the street, not me, his shoulders hunched over. "Will you walk with me, Ev?"

I nodded. We walked. Neither of us rushed, instead strolling past shop fronts and restaurants, peering into bars just getting going for the evening. I had a bad feeling that once we stopped walking we'd have to start talking, so dawdling suited me fine. Summer nights meant there were a fair number of people around.

An Irish bar sat on a street corner about halfway home. Music blared out, some old song by the White Stripes. Hands still stuffed into his pockets, David gestured toward the bar with an elbow. "Wanna get a drink?"

It took me a moment to find my voice. "Sure."

He led me straight to a table at the back, away from the growing crowd of after-work drinkers. He ordered two pints of Guinness. Once they arrived, we sat in silence, sipping. After a moment, David took off his cap and set it on the table. Shit, his poor face. I could see it more clearly now, and he looked like he had two black eyes.

We sat there staring at one another in some bizarre sort of standoff. Neither of us spoke. The way he looked at me, like he'd been hurt too, like he was hurting . . . I couldn't take it. Waiting to drag this whole sorry mess of a relationship out into the light wasn't helping either of us. Time for a new plan. We'd clear the air, then get on with our respective lives. No more hurt and heartache. "You wanted to tell me about her?" I prompted, sitting up straighter, preparing myself for the worst.

"Yeah. Martha and I were together a long time. You probably already know, she was the one who cheated on me. The one we talked about."

I nodded.

"We started the band when I was fourteen, Mal and Jimmy and me. Ben joined a year later and she'd hang around too. They were like family," he said, brow puckered. "They are family. Even when things went bad I couldn't just turn my back on her . . ."

"You kissed her."

He sighed. "No, she kissed me. Martha and I are finished."

"I'm guessing she doesn't know that, since she's still calling you and all."

"She's moved to New York, no longer working for the band. I don't know what the phone call was about. I didn't return it."

I nodded, only slightly appeased. Our problems weren't that clear-cut. "Does your heart understand you're finished with her? I guess I mean your head, don't I? The heart's just another muscle, really. Silly to say it decides anything."

"Martha and I are finished. We have been for a long time. I promise."

"Even if that's true, doesn't that just make me the consolation prize? Your attempt at a normal life?"

"Ev, no. That's not the way it is."

"Are you sure about that?" I asked, disbelief thick in my voice. I picked up my beer, gulping down the bitter dark ale and creamy foam. Something to calm the nerves. "I was getting over you," I said, my voice a pitiful, small thing. My shoulders were right back where they belonged, way down. "A month. I didn't really give up on you until day seven, though. Then I knew you weren't coming. I knew it was over then. Because if I'd been so important to you, you'd have said something by then, right? I mean, you knew I was in love with you. So you'd have put me out of my misery by then, wouldn't you?"

He said nothing.

"You're all secrets and lies, David. I asked you about the earring, remember?"

He nodded.

"You lied."

"Yeah. I'm sorry."

"Did you do that before or after our honesty rule? I can't remember. It was definitely after the cheating rule, though, right?" Talking was a mistake. All of the jagged thoughts and emotions he inspired caught up with me too fast.

He didn't deign to reply.

"What's the story behind the earrings, anyway?"

"I brought them with my first paycheck after the record company signed us."

"Wow. And you both wore them all this time. Even after she cheated on you and everything."

"It was Jimmy," he said. "She cheated on me with Jimmy."

Holy shit, his own brother. So many things fell into place with that piece of information. "That's why you got so upset about finding him and that groupie together. And when you saw Jimmy talking to me at that party."

"Yeah. It was all a long time ago, but . . . Jimmy flew back for an appearance on a TV show. We were in the middle of a big tour, playing Spain at the time. The second album had just hit the top ten. We were finally really pulling in the crowds."

"So you forgave them to keep the band together?"

"No. Not exactly. I just got on with things. Even back then Jimmy was drinking too much. He'd changed." He licked his lips, studied the table. "I'm sorry about that night. More fucking sorry than I can say. What you walked in on . . . I know how it must have looked. And I hated myself for lying to you about the earring, for still wearing it in Monterey."

He flicked at his ear in annoyance. There was a visible wound there with shiny, pink, nearly healed skin around it. It didn't look like a fading earring hole at all.

"What did you do there?" I asked.

"Cut across it with a knife." He shrugged. "An earring hole takes years to grow over. Made a new cut when you left so it could heal properly."

"Oh."

"I waited to come talk to you because I needed some time. You walking out on me after you'd promised you wouldn't . . . that was hard to take."

"I didn't have any choice."

He leaned toward me, his eyes hard. "You had a choice."

"I'd just seen my husband kissing another woman. And then you refused to even discuss it with me. You just started yelling at me about leaving. Again." My hands gripped the edge of the table so tight I could feel my fingernails pressing into the wood. "What the fuck should I have done, David? Tell me. Because I've played that scene over in my head so many times and it always works out the same way, with you slamming the door shut behind me."

"Shit." He slumped back in his seat. "You knew you leaving was a problem for me. You should have stuck with me, given me a chance to calm down. We worked it out in Monterey after that bar fight. We could have done it again."

"Rough sex doesn't fix everything. Sometimes you actually have to talk."

"I tried to talk to you the other night at that club. Wasn't what was on your mind."

I could feel my face heat up. It just pissed me off even more.

"Fuck. Look," he said, rubbing at the back of his neck. "The thing is, I needed to get us straight in my head, okay? I needed to figure out if us being together was the right thing. Honestly, Ev, I didn't want to hurt you again."

A month he'd left me to stew in my misery. It was on the tip of my tongue to give him a flippant thank-you. Or even to flip him off. But this was too serious.

"You got us straight in your head? That's great. I wish I could get us straight in my head." I stopped babbling long enough to drink more beer. My throat was giving sandpaper serious competition.

He held himself perfectly still, watching me crash and burn with an eerie calm.

"So, I'm kind of beat." I looked everywhere but at him. "Does that cover everything you wanted to talk about?"

"No."

"No? There's more?" Please, God, don't let there be more.

"Yeah."

"Have at it." Time to drink.

"I love you."

I spat beer across the table, all over our combined hands. "Shit."

"I'll get some napkins," he said, releasing my hand and rising out of his chair. A moment later he was back. I sat there like a useless doll while he cleaned my arm and then the table, trembling was all I was good for. Carefully, he pulled back my seat, helped me to my feet, and ushered me out of the bar. The hum of traffic and rush of city air cleared my senses. I had room to think out on the street.

Immediately my feet got moving. They knew what was up. My boots stomped across the pavement, putting serious distance between me and there. Getting the hell away from him and what he'd said. David stayed right on my heels, however.

We stopped at a street corner and I punched the button, waiting for the Walk light. "Don't say that again."

"Is it such a surprise, really? Why the fuck else would I be doing this, huh? Of course I love you."

"Don't." I turned on him, face furious.

His lips formed a tight line. "All right. I won't say that again. For now. But we should talk some more."

I growled, gnashed my teeth.

"Ev."

Crap. Negotiation wasn't my strong suit. Not with him. I wanted him gone. Or at least I was pretty certain I wanted him gone. Gone so I could resume my mourning for him and us and everything we might have been. Gone so I didn't have to think about the fact that he now thought he loved me. What utter emotional bullshit. My tear ducts went crazy right on cue. I took huge deep breaths trying to get myself back under control.

"Later, not today," he said, in an affable, reasonable voice. I didn't trust it or him at all.

"Fine."

I strode another block with him hanging at my side until again a red light stopped us cold, leaving room for conversation. He had better not speak. At least not until I got my shit together and figured all this out. I straightened my pencil skirt, tucked back my hair, fidgeted. The light took forever. Since when did Portland turn against me? This wasn't fair.

"We're not finished," he said. It sounded like both a threat and a promise.

* * *

The first text arrived at midnight while I was lying on my bed, reading. Or trying to read. Because trying to sleep had been a bust. School started back soon, but I was finding it hard to raise my usual enthusiasm for my studies. I had the worst feeling that the seed of doubt David had planted regarding my career choices had taken root inside my brain. I liked architecture, but I didn't love it. Did that matter? Sadly, I had no answers. Lots of excuses—some bullshit and some valid—but no answers.

David would probably say I could do whatever the fuck I wanted to. I knew all too well what my father would say. It wouldn't be pretty.

I'd been avoiding seeing my parents since I got back. Easy enough to do considering I'd hung up on the lecture my father had attempted to give me the second day after my return. Relations had been frosty since then. The real surprise was that I wasn't surprised. They had never encouraged anything that didn't directly support the plan. There was a reason I'd never returned their calls when I was in Monterey. Because I couldn't tell them the things they wanted to hear anymore, it had seemed safer to stay mute.

Nathan had been running interference with the folks, which I appreciated, but my time was up. We'd all been summoned to dinner tomorrow night. I figured the text was my mother ensuring I wasn't going to try and weasel out of it. Sometimes she sat up late watching old black-and-white movies when her sleeping pills didn't kick in.

I was wrong.

> David: She surprised me when she kissed me.
> That's why I didn't stop her right away. But I
> didn't want it.

I stared at my cell, frowning.

David: You there?

Me: Yeah.

David: I need to know if you believe me about
Martha.

Did I? I took a breath, searched deep. There was frustration, plenty of confusion, but my anger had apparently burned itself out at long last. Because I didn't doubt he'd told me the truth.

Me: I believe you.

David: Thank you. I keep thinking of more. Will you
listen?

Me: Yes.

David: My folks got married because of Jimmy.
Mom left when I was 12. She drank. Jimmy's
been paying her to keep quiet. She's been
hustling him for years.

Me: Holy hell!

David: Yeah. I got lawyers onto it now.

Me: Glad to hear it.

David: We retired Dad to Florida. I told him about
you. He wants to meet.

Me: Really? I don't know what to say . . .

David: Can I come up?

Me: You're here??

I didn't wait for a reply. Forget my pajama shorts and ragged old T-shirt, washed so many times its original color was a faded memory. He'd just have to take me as he found me. I unlocked the front door of our apartment and padded down the stairs on bare feet, my cell still in my hand. Sure enough, a tall shadow loomed through the frosted glass of the building's front door. I pushed it open to find him sitting on the step. Outside, the night was still, peaceful. A fancy silver SUV was pulled up at the curb.

"Hey," he said, a finger busy on the screen of his cell. Mine beeped again.

David: Wanted to say good night.

"Okay," I said, looking up from the screen. "Come in."

The side of his mouth lifted and he looked up at me. I met his gaze, refusing to feel self-conscious. He didn't seem put off by my slacker bedtime style. If anything, his smile increased, his eyes warming. "You about to go to bed?"

"I was just reading. Couldn't sleep."

"Is your brother here?" He stood and followed me back up the stairs, his sneakers loud on the old wooden floors. I half expected Mrs. Lucia from downstairs to come out and yell. It was a hobby of hers.

"No," I said, closing the door behind us. "He and Lauren went out."

He looked around the apartment with interest. As usual he took up all the space. I don't know how he did that. It was like a magician's trick. He was somehow so much bigger than he actually seemed. And the man didn't seem small to begin with. In no rush at all, his gaze wandered around the room, taking in bright turquoise walls (Lauren's doing) and the shelves of neatly stacked books (my doing).

"Is this yours?" he asked, poking his head into my bedroom.

"Ah, yes. It's a bit of a mess right now, though." I squeezed past him and started speed-cleaning, picking up the books and other assorted debris scattered across the floor. I should have asked him to give me five minutes before coming up. My mother would be horrified. Since returning from LA I'd let my world descend into chaos. It suited my frazzled state of mind. Didn't mean David needed to see it. I needed to make a plan to clean up my act and actually stick to it this time.

"I used to be organized," I said, flailing, my fallback position for everything lately.

"It doesn't matter."

"This won't take a minute."

"Ev," he said, catching hold of my wrist in much the same manner that his gaze caught me. "I don't care. I just need to talk to you."

A sudden horrible thought entered my mind. "Are you leaving?" I asked, today's dirty work shirt clutched in my suddenly shaking hand.

His grip tightened around my wrist. "You want me to leave?"

"No. I mean, are you leaving Portland? Is that why you're here, to say good-bye?"

"No."

"Oh." The pincer grip my ribs had gotten on my heart and lungs eased back a little. "Okay."

"Where did that come from?" When I didn't answer, he tugged me gently toward him. "Hey."

I took a reluctant step in his direction, dropping the dirty laundry. He pressed for more, sitting on my bed and pulling me down alongside him. I sort of stumbled my butt onto the double mattress as opposed to doing it with any grace. Story of my life. Object achieved, he gave up his grip on me. My hands clenched the edge of the bed.

"So, you got a weird look on your face and then you asked me if I was leaving," he said, blue eyes concerned. "Care to explain?"

"You haven't turned up at midnight before. I guess I wondered if there was more to it than just dropping by."

"I drove by your apartment and I saw your light was on. Figured I'd send you a text, see what mood you were in after our talk today." He rubbed at his bearded chin

with the palm of his hand. "Plus, like I said, I keep thinking of stuff I need to tell you."

"You drive by my apartment often?"

He gave me a wry smile. "Only a couple of times. It's
my way of saying good night to you."

"How did you know which window was mine?"

"Ah, well, that time I talked to Lauren when I first came
to town? She had the light on in the other room. Figured
this one must be yours." He didn't look at me, choosing
instead to check out the photos of me and my friends on
the walls. "You mad that I've been around?"

"No," I answered honestly. "I think I might be running
out of mad."

"You are?"

"Yeah."

He let out a slow breath and stared back at me, saying
nothing. Dark bruises lingered beneath his eyes, though
his swollen nose had gone back to normal size.

"I really am sorry Nate hit you."

"If I was your brother, I'd have done the exact same
fucking thing." He braced his elbows on his knees but
kept his face turned toward me.

"Would you?"

"Without question."

Males and their penchant for beating on things, it knew
no end.

The silence dragged out. It wasn't uncomfortable, exactly. At least we weren't fighting or rehashing our breakup
one more time. Being broken and angry got old.

"Can we just hang out?" I asked.

"Absolutely. Lemme see this." He picked up my iPhone
and started flicking through the music files. "Where are
the earbuds?"

I hopped up and retrieved them from among the crap
on my desk. David plugged them in, then handed me an
earbud. I sat at his side, curious what he'd choose out of

my music. When the rocking, jumpy beat of "Jackson" by Johnny Cash and June Carter started, I looked at him in amusement. He smirked and mouthed the lyrics. We had indeed gotten married in a fever.

"You making fun of me?" I asked.

Light danced in his eyes. "I'm making fun of us."

"Fair enough."

"What else have you got here?"

Cash and Carter finished and he continued his search for songs. I watched his face, waiting for a reaction to my musical tastes. All I got was a smothered yawn.

"They're not that bad," I protested.

"Sorry. Big day."

"David, if you're tired, we don't have to—"

"No. I'm fine. But do you mind if I lie down?"

David on my bed. Well, he was already on my bed but . . . "Sure."

He gave me a cagey look but started tugging off his sneakers. "You just being polite?"

"No, it's fine. And, I mean, legally the bed is still half yours," I joked, pulling out the earbud before his movements did it for me. "So, what did you do today?"

"Been working on the new album and sorting out some stuff." Hands behind his head, he stretched out across my bed. "You lying down too? We can't share the music if you don't."

I crawled on and lay down next to him, wriggling around a bit, making myself comfortable. It was, after all, my bed. And he would be the only male who'd ever lain on it. The slight scent of his soap came to me, clean and warm and David. All too well, I remembered. For once, hurt didn't seem to come attached to the memory. I poked around inside my head, double-checking. When I'd said I was out of mad, it had apparently been nothing more than the truth. We had our issues, but him cheating on me wasn't one of them. I knew that now and it meant a lot.

"Here." He handed me back the earbud and started playing with my cell again.

"How's Jimmy?" I rolled onto my side, needing to see him. The strong line of his nose and jaw was in profile, the curve of his lips. How many times had I kissed him? Not nearly enough to last me if it never happened again.

"He's doing a lot better. Seems to have really gotten himself right. I think he's going to be okay."

"That's great news."

"At least he comes by his problems honestly," he said, his tone turning bitter. "Our mother is a fucking disaster from what I hear. But then, she always was. She used to take us to the park because she needed to score. She'd turn up to school plays and parent-teacher nights high as a kite."

I kept my mouth shut, letting him get it out. The best thing I could do for him was to be there and listen. The pain and anger in his voice were heartbreaking. My parents had their overbearing issues, certainly, but nothing like this. David's childhood had been terrible. If I could have bitch-slapped his mother right then for putting that pain in his voice, I would have. Twice over.

"Dad ignored her using for years. He could. He was a long-haul truck driver, away most of the time. Jimmy and me were the ones that had to put up with her shit. The number of times we'd come home to find her babbling all sorts of stuff or passed out on the couch. There'd be no food in the house 'cause she'd spent the grocery money on pills. Then one day we came home from school and she and the TV were gone. That was it." He stared up at nothing, his face drawn. "She didn't even leave a note. Now she's back and she's been hurting Jimmy. It drives me nuts."

"That must have been hard for you," I said. "Hearing about her from Jimmy."

One of his shoulders did a little lift. "He shouldn't have

had to deal with her on his own. Said he wanted to protect me. Seems my big brother isn't a completely selfish prick."

"Thank you for texting me."

"S'okay. What do you feel like listening to?" The sudden change in topic told me he didn't want to talk about his family anymore. He yawned again, his jaw cracking. "Sorry."

"The Saint Johns."

He nodded, flicking through to find the only song I had of theirs. The strum of the guitar started softly, filling my head. He put the cell on his chest and his eyelids drifted down. A man and a woman took turns singing about their head and their heart. Throughout it, his face remained calm, relaxed. I started to wonder if he'd fallen asleep. But when the song finished, he turned to look at me.

"Nice. A bit sad," he said.

"You don't think they'll be together in the end?"

He rolled onto his side too. There was no more than a hand's width between us. With a curious look, he handed me the cell. "Play me another song you like."

I scrolled through the screens, trying to decide what to play for him. "I forgot to tell you, someone was in saying she'd seen you today. Your anonymity might be about to run out."

He sighed. "Bound to happen sooner or later. They'll just have to get used to me being around."

"You're really not leaving?" I tried to keep my voice light, but it didn't work.

"No. I'm really not." He looked at me and I just knew he saw everything. All of my fears and dreams and the hopes I did my best to keep hidden, even from myself. But I couldn't hide from him if I tried. "Okay?"

"Okay," I said.

"You asked me if you were my attempt at normal. I need you to understand, that's not it at all. Being with you, the way I feel about you, it does ground me. But that's because it makes me question fucking everything. It makes me want to make things better. Makes me want to be better. I can't hide from shit or make excuses when it comes to you, because that won't work. Neither of us is happy when things are that way, and I want you to be happy . . ." His forehead furrowed and his dark brows drew tight. "Do you understand?"

"I think so," I whispered, feeling so much for him right then I didn't know which way was up.

He yawned again, his jaw cracking. "Sorry. Fuck, I'm beat. You mind if I close my eyes for five minutes?"

"No."

He did so. "Play me another song?"

"On it."

I played him "Revelator" by Gillian Welch, the longest, most soothing song I could find. I'd guess he fell asleep about halfway through. His features relaxed and his breathing deepened. Carefully, I pulled out the earbuds and put the cell away. I switched on the bedside lamp and turned off the main one, shut the door so Lauren and Nate's eventual return didn't wake him. Then I lay back down and just stared at him. I don't know for how long. The compulsion to stroke his face or trace his tattoos made my fingers itch, but I didn't want to wake him. He obviously needed the sleep.

When I woke up in the morning, he was gone. Disappointment was a bitter taste. I'd just had the best night's sleep I'd had in weeks, devoid of the usual tense and angsty dreams I seemed to specialize in of late. When had he left? I rolled onto my back and something crinkled, complaining loudly. With a hand, I fished out a piece of paper. It had obviously been torn from one of my notepads. The message was brief but beautiful:

I'm still not leaving Portland.

CHAPTER TWENTY

I think I'd have preferred to find Genghis Khan staring back at me from across the café counter than Martha. I don't know—a Mongol horde versus Martha, tough call. Both were horrible in their own unique ways.

The lunchtime crowd had eased to a few determined patrons, settling in for the afternoon with their lattes and friands. It had been a busy day and Ruby had been distracted, messing up orders. Not like her usual self at all. I'd sat her at a corner table with a pot of tea for a while. Then we'd gotten busy again. When I'd asked what was wrong, she'd just waved me away. Eventually, I'd corner her.

And now here was Martha.

"We need to talk," she said. Her dark hair was tied back and her makeup minimal. There was none of the LA flashiness to her now. If anything, she seemed somber, subdued. Still just a touch smarmy, but hey, this was Martha, after all. And what the hell was she doing here?

"Ruby, is it okay if I take my break?" Jo was out back stocking shelves. She'd just come back from her break, making me due for mine. Ruby nodded, giving Martha a covert evil eye. No matter what was going on with her, Ruby was good people. She recognized a man-stealing sea monster when she saw one.

Martha headed back outside with her nose in the air, and I followed. The usual flow of city traffic cruised by. Overhead, the sky was clear blue, a perfect summer's day. I'd have felt more comfortable if nature had been about to dump a bucketload of rain on top of her perfect head, but it was not to be.

After a brief inspection of the surface, Martha perched on the edge of a bench. "Jimmy called me."

I sat down a little way away from her.

"Apparently he has to apologize to people as part of his rehab process." Perfectly manicured nails tapped at the wooden seat. "It wasn't much of an apology, actually. He told me I needed to come to Portland and clean up the shit I'd caused between you and David."

She stared determinedly ahead. "Things aren't great between Ben and him. I love my brother. I don't want him on the outs with Dave because of me."

"What do you expect me to do here, Martha?"

"I don't expect you to do anything for me. I just want you to listen." She ducked her chin, shut her eyes for a second. "I always figured I could get him back whenever I wanted. After he'd had a few years to calm down, of course. He never got to screw around, we were each other's first. So I just bided my time, let him sow all the wild oats. I was his one true love, right, no matter what I'd done? He was still out there playing those songs about me night after night, wearing our earring even after all those years . . ."

Traffic roared past, people chatted, but Martha and I were apart from it. I wasn't sure I wanted to hear this, but I soaked up every word anyway, desperate to understand.

"Turns out artists can be very sentimental." Her laughter sounded self-mocking. "It doesn't necessarily mean anything." She turned to me, eyes hard, hateful. "I think I was just a habit for him back then. He never gave up a damn thing for me. He sure as hell never moved cities to fit in with what I wanted."

"What do you mean?"

"He's got the album written, Ev. Apparently the new songs are brilliant. The best he's ever done. There's no reason he couldn't be in whatever studio he wanted putting it together, doing what he loves. Instead he's here, recording in some setup a few streets over. Because being close to you means more to him." She rocked forward, her smile harsh. "He's sold the Monterey house, bought a place here. I waited years for him to come back, to have time for me. For you he reorganizes everything in the blink of a fucking eye."

"I didn't know," I said, stunned.

"The band is all here. They're recording at a place called the Bent Basement."

"I've heard of it."

"If you're stupid enough to let him go, then you deserve to be miserable for a very long time." The woman looked at me like she had firsthand experience with that situation. She stood, brushed off her hands. "That's me done."

Martha walked away. She disappeared among the crowds of midafternoon shoppers like she'd never been.

David was recording in Portland. He'd said he was working on the new album. I hadn't imagined that meant actually recording here. Let alone buying a place.

Holy shit.

I stood and moved in the opposite direction from the one Martha had taken. First I walked, trying to figure out what I was doing, giving my brain a chance to catch up with me. Then I gave it up as a lost cause and ran, dodging pedestrians and café tables, parked cars and whatever. Faster and faster my Doc Martens boots carried me. I found the Bent Basement two blocks over, situated down a flight of stairs, between a microbrewery and an upmarket dress shop. I slapped my hands against the wood, pushed it open. The unassuming green door was unlocked. Speakers carried the strains of an almighty electric guitar solo through the dark-painted rooms. Sam sat on a sofa, reading a magazine. For once his standard black suit was missing, and he wore slacks and a short-sleeved Hawaiian shirt.

"Mrs. Ferris." He smiled.

"Hi, Sam," I panted, trying to catch my breath. "You look very cool."

He winked at me. "Mr. Ferris is in one of the sound booths at the moment, but if you go through that door there you'll be able to observe."

"Thanks, Sam. Good to see you again."

The thick door led to the soundboard setup. A man I didn't know sat behind it with headphones on. This setup left the small studio at Monterey in the dust. Through the window I could see David playing, his eyes closed, enmeshed with the music. He too wore headphones.

"Hey," Jimmy said quietly. I hadn't realized the rest of them were behind me, lounging, waiting to take their turn.

"Hi, Jimmy."

He gave me a strained smile. His suit was gone. So were the pinprick eyes. "It's good to see you here."

"Thanks." I didn't know what the etiquette was regarding rehab. Should I ask after his health, or sweep the situation under the rug? "And thank you for calling Martha."

"She came to talk to you, huh? Good. I'm glad." He slid his hands into the pockets of his black jeans. "Least I could do. I'm sorry about our previous meetings, Ev. I was . . . not where I should have been. I hope we can move on from that."

Off the drugs, the similarities between him and David were more pronounced. But his blue eyes and his smile didn't do to me the things David's did. No one else's ever could. Not in five years, not in fifty. For the first time in a long time, I could accept that. I was good with it, even. The epiphanies seemed to be coming thick and fast today.

Jimmy waited patiently for me to come back from

wherever I was and say something. When I didn't, he continued on. "I've never had a sister-in-law before."

"I've never had a brother-in-law."

"No? We're useful for all sorts of shit. Just you wait and see."

I smiled and he smiled back at me, far more relaxed this time.

Ben sat on the corner of a black leather lounge, talking with Mal. Mal tipped his chin at me, and I did the same back. All Ben gave me was a worried look. He was still every bit as big and imposing, but he seemed more afraid of me than I was of him today. I nodded hello to him and he returned it, with a tight smile. After talking to Martha, I could understand a little better where he'd been coming from that night. We'd never be besties, but there would be peace for David's sake.

The guitar solo cut off. I turned back to see David watching me, pulling off his headphones. Then he lifted his guitar strap off over his head and headed for the connecting door.

"Hey," he said, coming toward me. "Everything okay?"

"Yes. Can we talk?"

"Sure." He ushered me back into the booth. "Won't be long, Jack."

The man at the board nodded and fiddled with some buttons, turning off the microphones, I assume. He didn't seem overly irritated with the interruption. Instruments and microphones were everywhere. The place was organized chaos. We stood in the corner, out of view of the rest.

"Martha came to see me," I said once he'd closed the door. He stood tall in front of me, blocking out everything else. I rested my back against the wall and looked up at him, still trying to catch my breath. My heart had been calming down after the sprint. Had been. But now he was here and he was so damn close. I put my hands behind my back before they started grabbing at him.

David did the wrinkly brow thing. "Martha?"

"It's okay," I rushed on. "Well, you know, she was her usual self. But we talked."

"About what?"

"You two, mostly. She gave me some things to think about. Are you busy tonight?"

His eyes widened slightly. "No. Would you like to do something?"

"Yeah." I nodded. "I missed you this morning when I woke up, when I realized you'd gone. I've missed you a lot, the last month. I don't think I ever told you that."

He exhaled hard. "No . . . no, you haven't. I missed you too. I'm sorry I couldn't stay this morning."

"Another time."

"Definitely." He took a step closer till the toes of his boots touched mine. No one had ever been more welcome in my personal space. "I'd promised we'd start here early or I would have been there when you woke."

"You didn't tell me about the band recording here."

"We've had other things to deal with. I thought it could wait."

"Right. That makes sense." I stared at the wall beside me, trying to get my thoughts in order. After a whole lot of slow and painful, everything seemed to be happening at once.

". . . About tonight, Ev?"

"Oh, I'm going to dinner at my parents'."

"Am I invited?"

"Yes," I said. "Yes, you are."

"Okay. Great."

"Did you actually buy a house here?"

"A three-bedroom condo a couple of blocks up. I figured it was close to your work and not too far from your school . . . you know, just in case." He studied my face. "Would you like to see it?"

"Wow." I changed the subject to buy some time. "Uh, Jimmy's looking well."

He smiled and put his hands either side of my head, closing the distance between us. "Yeah. He's doing good. Relocating up here is working out well for pretty much everyone. Seems I wasn't the only one ready for a break from all the fuckwittery in LA. Our playing's sharper than it's been in years. We're focusing on the important stuff again."

"That's great."

"Now, what did Martha say to you, baby?"

The endearment came accompanied by the warm old familiar feeling. I almost swayed, I was so grateful. "Well, we talked about you."

"I get that."

"I guess I'm still making sense of everything."

He nodded slowly, leaning in until our noses almost brushed. The perfect intimacy of it, the faint feel of his breath against my face. My need to get close to him had never disappeared. No matter how I'd tried to shut it down. Love and heartbreak made you breathtakingly stupid, desperate, even. The things you'd try to tell yourself to make it through, hoping one day you'd believe it.

"All right," he said. "Anything I can help you with?"

"No. I just wanted to check you were really here, I think."

"I'm here."

"Yes."

"That's not changing, Evelyn."

"No. I think I get that now. I guess I can be a little slow sometimes picking up on these things. I just wasn't sure, you know, with everything that's happened. But I still love you." Apparently I was back to blurting crap out whenever it occurred to me. With David, though, it was okay. I was safe. "I do."

"I know, baby. The question is, when are you going to come back to me?"

"It's really big, you know? It hurt so much when it fell apart last time."

He nodded sadly. "You left me. I think that's about the worst fucking thing I've ever experienced."

"I had to go, but also . . . part of it was me wanting to hurt you like you'd hurt me, I think." I needed to hold his hand again, but I didn't feel like I could. "I don't want to be vindictive like that, not with you, not ever again."

"I said some horrible shit to you that night. Both of us were hurting. We're just going to have to forgive each other and let it go."

"You didn't write a song about it, did you?"

He looked away.

"No! David," I said, aghast. "You can't. That was such a terrible night."

"On a scale of one to ten, how pissed would you be exactly?"

"Where one is divorce?"

He moved his lower body closer, placing his feet between mine. There was no more than a hair's breadth between us. I'd never catch my breath at this rate. Never.

"No," he said, his voice soft. "You don't even remember us getting married, so divorce or annulment or what-the-fuck-ever is not on. It never was. I just told the lawyers to keep looking busy for the last month while I figured things out. Did I forget to mention that?"

"Yeah, you did." I couldn't help but smile at that. "So what's one?"

"One is now. It's this, us living apart and being fucking miserable without each other."

"That is pretty horrible."

"It is," he agreed.

"Is the song a headliner, or are you just going to shove

it in somewhere and hope no one notices? It's just a B-side or something, right? Unlisted and hidden at the end?"

"Let's pretend we'd been talking about making one of the songs the name of the album."

"One of them? How much of this brilliant album I've been hearing about is going to be about us?"

"I love you."

"David." I tried to maintain the mock angry, but it didn't work. I didn't have the strength for it.

"Can you trust me?" He asked, his face suddenly serious. "I need you to trust me again. About more than just the songs. Seeing that worry in your eyes all the time is fucking killing me."

"I know." I frowned, knitting my fingers together behind my back. "I'm getting there. And I'll learn to deal with the songs. Really. Music is a big part of who you are, and it's a huge compliment that you feel that strongly for me. I was mostly just teasing."

"I know. And they're not all about us splitting up."

"No?"

"No."

"That's good. I'm glad."

"Mm."

I licked my lips and his eyes tracked the movement. I waited for him to close the distance between us and kiss me. But he didn't and I didn't either. For some reason, it wasn't right to rush this. It should be perfect. Everything between us settled. No people waiting in the next room. Us being this close together, however, hearing the low rumble of his voice, I could have stayed there all day. But Ruby would be wondering what the hell had happened to me. I also had a small errand to run before I returned.

"I'd better get back to work," I said.

"Right." He drew back, slowly. "What time would you like me to pick you up tonight?"

"Ah, seven?"

"Sounds good." A shadow passed over his face. "Do you think your parents will like me?"

I took a deep breath and let it go. "I don't know. It doesn't matter. I like you."

"You do?"

I nodded.

The light in his eyes was like the sun rising. My knees trembled and my heart quaked. It was powerful and beautiful and perfect.

"That's all that matters, then," he said.

CHAPTER TWENTY-ONE

My parents hadn't liked him. For the better part of the meal they'd ignored David's presence. Every time they blatantly passed him over, I'd opened my mouth to object and David's foot would nudge mine beneath the table. He'd given me a small shake of the head. I'd sat and steamed, my anger growing by the moment. Things had long since moved beyond awkward, though Lauren had done her best to cover the silences.

David, for his part, had gone all out, wearing a gray button-down shirt with the sleeves secured to his wrists. It covered the bulk of his tattoos. Black jeans and plain black boots completed his meet-the-parents wardrobe. Considering he'd refused to dress up for a ballroom full of Hollywood royalty, I was impressed. He'd even poofed up his hair into a vaguely James Dean do. On most men I would not have liked it. David was not most men. Frankly, he looked gosh-almighty awesome, even with the fading bruises beneath his eyes. And the gracious manner with which he dealt with my parents' abysmal behavior only reinforced my belief in him. My pride that he'd chosen to be with me. But back to the dinner conversation.

Lauren was giving a detailed synopsis of her plans for

classes for the upcoming semester. My dad nodded and listened intently, asking all the appropriate questions. Nate's falling for her was beyond my parents' wildest dreams. She'd been a de facto part of the family for a long time now. They couldn't have been more delighted. But more than that, she seemed to make them take a look at their son anew, noticing the changes in him. When Lauren talked about Nate's work and his responsibilities, they listened.

Meanwhile, David was only on the other side of the table, but I missed him. There was so much to talk about that I didn't know where to start. And hadn't we already talked over the bulk of it? So what was the problem? I had the strangest sensation that something was wrong, something was slipping away from me. David had moved to Portland. All would be well. But it wasn't. Classes started back soon. The threat of the plan still hung over my head because I allowed it to.

"Ev? Is something wrong?" Dad sat at one end of the table, his face drawn with concern.

"No, Dad," I said, my smile full of gritted teeth. There'd been no mention of my hanging up on him. I suspected it had been chalked up to brokenhearted girl rage or something similar.

Dad frowned, first at me and then at David. "My daughter goes back to school next week."

"Ah, yes," said David. "She did mention that, Mr. Thomas."

My father studied David from over the top of his glasses. "Her studies are very important."

A cold kind of panic gripped me as the horror unrolled right before my eyes. "Dad. Stop."

"Yes, Mr. Thomas," said David. "I have no intention of interrupting them."

"Good." Dad steepled his hands in front of him, settling in to give a lecture. "But the fact is, young women imagining themselves in love have a terrible tendency to not think."

"Dad—"

My dad held up a hand to stop me. "Ever since she was a little girl, she's planned to become an architect."

"Okay. No."

"What if you go on tour, David?" my father asked, continuing despite my commotion. "As you inevitably will. Do you expect her to drop everything and just follow you?"

"That would be up to your daughter, sir. But I don't plan on doing anything to make her have to choose between me and school. Whatever she wants to do, she's got my support."

"She wants to be an architect," Dad said, his tone absolute. "This relationship has already cost her dearly. She had an important internship canceled when all of this nonsense happened. It's set her back considerably."

I pushed back, rising from my chair. "That's enough."

Dad gave me the same glare he'd first dealt David, hostile and unwelcome. He looked at me like he no longer recognized me.

"I won't have you throwing away your future for him," he thundered.

"Him?" I asked, horrified at his tone. Anger had been pooling inside of me all night, filling me up. No wonder I'd barely touched my dinner. "The person you've both been unconscionably rude to for the past hour? David is the last person who would expect me to throw away anything that mattered to me."

"If he cared for you, he would walk away. Look at the damage he's done." A vein bulged on the side of my father's forehead as he stood too. Everyone else watched in stunned silence. It could be said I'd gone the bulk of my life backing down. But those had all been about things that didn't matter, not really. This was different.

"You're wrong."

"You're out of control," my father snarled, pointing his finger at me.

"No," I said to my father. Then I turned and said what I should have said a long time ago to my husband. "No, I'm not. What I am is the luckiest fucking girl in the entire world."

A smile lit David's eyes. He sucked in his bottom lip, trying to keep the happy contained in the face of my parents' fury.

"I am," I said, tearing up and not even minding for once.

He pushed back his chair and rose to his feet, facing me across the table. The promise of unconditional love and support in his eyes was all the answer I needed. And in that one perfect moment, I knew everything was fine. We were fine. We always would be if we stuck together. There wasn't a single doubt inside of me. In silence, he walked around the table and stood at my side.

The look on my parents' faces . . . whoa. They always said it was best to rip the Band-Aid off all at once, though, get it over and done with. So I did.

"I don't want to be an architect." The relief in finally saying it was staggering. I'm almost certain my knees knocked. There'd be no backing down, however. David took my hand in his, gave it a squeeze.

My father just blinked at me. "You don't mean that."

"I'm afraid I do. It was your dream, Dad. Not mine. I should never have gone along with this. That was my mistake and I'm sorry."

"What will you do?" asked my mother, her voice rising. "Make coffee?"

"Yes."

"That's ridiculous. All that money we spent—" Mom's eyes flashed in anger.

"I'll pay it back."

"This is insane," Dad said, his face going pale. "This is about him."

"No. This is about me, actually. David just made me start questioning what I really wanted. He made me want to be a better person. Lying about this, trying to fit in with your plan for so long . . . I was wrong to do that."

My father glared at me. "I think you should leave now, Evelyn. Think this over carefully. We'll talk about it later."

I guessed we would, but it wouldn't change anything. My good-girl status had well and truly taken a dive.

"You forgot to tell her that whatever she decides, you still love her." Nathan got to his feet, pulling out Lauren's chair for her. He faced my father with his jaw set. "We'd better go too."

"She knows that." Face screwed up in confusion, Dad stood at the head of the table.

Nate grunted. "No, she doesn't. Why do you think she fell into line for so many years?"

Mom knotted her hands.

"That's ridiculous," sputtered Dad.

"No, he's right," I said. "But I guess everyone has to grow up sometime."

Dad's eyes turned even colder. "Being an adult is not about turning your back on your responsibilities."

"Following in your footsteps is not my responsibility," I said, refusing to back down. The days of my doing that were gone. "I can't be you. I'm sorry I wasted so many years and so much of your money figuring that out."

"We only want what's best for you," said Mom, voice thick with emotion.

"I know you do. But that's for me to decide now." I turned back to my husband, keeping a firm hold on his hand. "And my husband isn't going anywhere. You need to accept that."

Nate walked around the table, gave Mom a kiss. "Thanks for dinner."

"One day," she said, looking between the both of us, "when you have your own children, then you'll understand how hard it is."

Her words pretty much wrapped things up. My dad just kept shaking his head and huffing out breaths. I felt guilty for disappointing them. But not bad enough to return to my former ways. I'd finally reached an age where I understood that my parents were people too. They weren't perfect or omnipotent. They were every bit as fallible as me. It was my job to judge what was right.

I picked up my handbag. It was time to go.

David nodded to both my parents and escorted me out. A sleek new silver Lexus Hybrid sat waiting by the curb. It wasn't a big SUV like the ones Sam and the other bodyguards used. This one came in a more user-friendly size. Behind us, Nate and Lauren climbed into his car. Nothing much was said. Mom and Dad stood in the house's open doorway, dark silhouettes from the light behind them. David opened the door for me and I climbed into the passenger seat.

"I'm sorry about my father. Are you upset?" I asked.

"No." He shut my door and walked around to the driver's side.

"No? That's it?"

He shrugged. "He's your dad. Of course he's going to be concerned."

"I thought you might have been running for the hills by now with all the drama."

He flicked on the indicator and pulled out onto the road. "Did you really?"

"No. Sorry, that was a stupid thing to say." I watched my old neighborhood passing by, the park I'd played in and the path I'd taken to school. "So I'm a college dropout."

He gave me curious glance. "How does that feel?"

"God, I don't know." I shook my hands, rubbed them

together. "Tingly. My toes and hands feel tingly. I don't know what I'm doing."

"Do you know what you want to do?"

"No. Not really."

"But you know what you don't want to do?"

"Yes," I answered definitely.

"Then there's your starting point."

A full moon hung heavy in the sky. The stars twinkled on. And I'd just upended my entire existence. Again. "You're now officially married to a college dropout who makes coffee for a living. Does that bother you?"

With a sigh, David flicked on the indicator and pulled over in front of a neat row of suburban houses. He picked up one of my hands, pressing it gently between both of his. "If I wanted to quit the band, would that bother you?"

"Of course not. That's your decision."

"If I wanted to give all the money away, what would you say?"

I shrugged. "You made the money, it's your choice. I guess you'd have to come live with me then. And I'm telling you now, the apartment we'd have on my salary alone would be small. Minuscule. Just so you know."

"But you'd still take me in?"

"Without question." I covered one of his hands with my own, needing to borrow a bit of his strength just then. "Thank you for being there tonight."

Little creases lined his perfect dark blue eyes. "I didn't even say anything."

"You didn't have to."

"You called me your husband."

I nodded, my heart stuck in my throat.

"I didn't kiss you at the studio today because it felt like there was still too much up in the air between us. It didn't feel right. But I want to kiss you now."

"Please," I said.

He leaned into me and I met him halfway. His mouth covered mine, lips warm and firm and familiar. The only ones I wanted or needed. His hands cupped my face, holding me to him. The kiss was so sweet and perfect. It was a promise, one that wouldn't be broken this time. We'd both learned from our mistakes and we'd keep learning all our lives. That was marriage.

His fingers eased into my hair and I stroked my tongue against his. The taste of him was as necessary to me as air. The feel of his hands on me was the promise of everything to come. What started out as an affirmation turned into more at light speed. The groan that came out of him. Holy hell. I wanted to hear that noise for the rest of my life. My hands dragged at his shirt, trying to pull him closer. We had some serious time to make up for.

"We have to stop," he whispered.

"We do?" I asked, in between panting breaths.

"Sadly." He chuckled, nudged the tip of my nose with his. "Soon, my luckiest fucking girl in the world. Soon. Did you really have to throw the 'fucking' in there?"

"I really did."

"Your parents looked about ready to have kittens."

"I'm so sorry about the way they treated you." I ran my fingers over the spiky short dark hair on the side of his head, feeling the bristles.

"I can deal."

"You shouldn't have to. You won't have to. I'm not sitting by and—"

He shut down my rant by kissing me. Of course, it worked. His tongue played over my teeth, teasing me. I undid my seat belt and crawled into his lap, needing to get closer. Nobody kissed like David. His hands slipped beneath my top, molding to the curves of my breasts. Thumbs stroked my nipples. The poor things were so damn hard it hurt. Talking of which, I could feel David's erection pressing into my hip. We kept our lips locked until a car full of kids went by, horn blaring. Apparently our makeout session was somewhat visible from the street despite the fogged-up windows. Classy.

"Soon," he promised, his breathing harsh against my neck. "Fuck, it's good to get you alone. That was intense. But I'm proud of you for standing up for yourself. You did good."

"Thank you. You think we'll understand when we have kids, like my mom said?"

He looked up at me, his beautiful face and serious eyes so wonderfully familiar I could cry.

"We've never talked about kids," he said. "Do you want them?"

"One day. Do you?"

"One day, yeah. After we've had a few years' worth of alone time."

"Sounds good," I said. "You going to show me this condo of yours?"

"Of ours. Absolutely."

"I think you're going to need to take your hands out of my top if you're planning on driving us there."

"Mm. Pity." He gave my breasts a final squeeze before slipping his hands free of my clothing. "And you're going to have to hop back into your seat."

"Okeydokey."

His hands wrapped around my hips, helping me climb back over to my side of the vehicle. I refastened my seat belt while he took a deep breath. With a wince he adjusted himself, obviously trying to get more comfortable. "You're a terror."

"Me? What did I do?"

"You know what you did," he grouched, pulling back out onto the road.

"I don't know what you're talking about."

"Don't you give me that," he said, giving me a narrow-eyed look. "You did it in Vegas and then you did it in

Monterey and LA too. Now you're doing it in Portland. I can't take you anywhere."

"Are you talking about the state of your fly? Because I'm not the one in control of your reactions to me, buddy. You are."

He barked out a laugh. "I've never been in control of my reactions to you. Not once."

"Is that why you married me? Because you were helpless against me?"

"You make me tremble in fear, rest assured." The smile he gave me made me tremble, and fear had nothing to do with it. "But I married you, Evelyn, because you made sense to me. We make sense. We're a whole lot better together than apart. You notice that?"

"Yeah, I really did."

"Good." His fingers stroked over my cheekbone. "We need to get home. Now."

I'm pretty sure he broke several speed limits on the drive. The condo was only a couple of blocks back from Ruby's café. It was located in a big old brown-brick building with Art Deco stonework surrounding the glass double doors. David punched in a code and led me into a white marble lobby. A statue of what looked like driftwood stood tall in the corner. Security cameras hid in the ceiling corners. He didn't give me time to look, rushing me through. I practically had to run to keep up with him.

"Come on," he said, tugging on my hand, drawing me into the elevator.

"This is all very impressive."

He pushed the button for the top floor. "Wait till you see our place. You're moving in with me now, right?"

"Right."

"Ah, we've got some visitors at the moment, by the way. Just while we record the album and all that. A few more weeks, probably." The elevator doors slid open and we stepped into the hall. At which point David took my handbag from me. Then he bent and set his shoulder to my stomach, lifting me high. "Here we are."

"Hey," I squeaked.

"I got you. Time to get carried over the threshold again."

"David, I'm wearing a skirt." It nearly went to my knees, but still. I'd rather not flash his guests and band members if I could avoid it.

"I know you are. Have I thanked you for that yet? I really appreciate having that easy access." His black boots thumped along the marble flooring. I took the opportunity to grope his ass because I was allowed to. My life was fucking fantastic like that.

"You're not wearing any underwear," I informed him.

"That so?"

A hand felt up my rear. Over my clothing, thankfully.

"You are," he said, voice low and growly in the best way possible. "Which ones you wearing, baby? Boy shorts by the feel."

"I don't think you've seen these."

"Yeah, well we're gonna change that real soon. Trust me."

"I do."

I heard the sound of a door opening, and the marble beneath me turned to a glossy, black-painted wooden floor. The walls were a pristine white. And I could hear male voices, laughing and trash-talking nearby. Music played in the background, Nine Inch Nails, I think. Nate had been playing his music at the apartment and they were a favorite of his. Of course the condo looked amazing. There were dark wooden dining room chairs and green couches. Plenty of space. Guitar cases were strewn about the place. From what I could see, it looked beautiful and lived in. It looked like a home.

Our home.

"You kidnapped a girl. That's awesome but illegal, Davie. You're probably going to have to give her back."

My hair was lifted and Mal appeared, crouched beside me. "Hey there, child bride. Where's my hello kiss?"

"Leave my wife alone, you dickwad." David lifted one booted foot and negligently pushed him aside. "Go get your own."

"Why the fuck would I want to get married? That's for crazy folk like you two fine people. And while I applaud your insanity, no goddamn way am I following in your footsteps."

"Who the fuck would have him?" Jimmy's smoother voice moved up alongside me. "Hey, Ev."

"Hi, Jimmy." I took a hand off the seat of my husband's jeans and waved at him. "David, do I have to stay upside down?"

"Ah, right. It's date night," my husband announced.

"Got it," Mal said. "Come on, Jimmy. We'll go find Benny-boy. He was going to that Japanese place for a bite."

"Right." Jimmy's sneakers headed for the door. "Later, guys."

"Bye!" I gave him another wave.

"Night, Evvie." Mal left too, and the door slammed shut behind them.

"Alone at last." David sighed and started moving again, down a long hallway. With me still over his shoulder. "You like the place?"

"What I can see of it is lovely."

"That's good. I'll show you the rest later. First things first, I really need to get into those panties of yours."

"I don't think they'd fit you." I giggled. He slapped me on the ass. White-hot lightning, though it was more of a shock than anything. "Christ, David."

"Just warming you up, funny girl." He turned into the last room at the end of the hallway, kicked the door shut. My handbag was thrown into a chair. Without a word of warning, he upended me onto a king-size bed. My body bounced on the mattress. The blood was rushing around in my head, making it spin. I pushed my hair out of my face and rose up onto my elbows.

"Don't move," he said, voice guttural.

He stood at the end of the bed, undressing. The most amazing sight in existence. I could watch him do this always. He reached back and pulled off his shirt and I knew bone deep I wasn't the luckiest fucking girl in the world. I was the luckiest fucking girl in the entire universe. That was the truth. Not just because he was beyond beautiful and I was the only one that got to see him do this, but the way he watched me through hooded eyes the entire time. Lust was there, but also a whole lot of love.

"You have no idea how often I've imagined you lying on that bed in the last week." He pulled off his boots and socks, tossing them aside. "How many times I nearly called you in the last month."

"Why didn't you?"

"Why didn't you?" he asked, undoing the top button on his jeans.

"Let's not do that again."

"No. Never." He crawled onto the bed, smoothing his hands down my calf muscles. My shoes went flying and his fingers slipped beneath my skirt, easing it up, higher and higher. Without breaking eye contact, he dragged down my boy shorts. He obviously wasn't interested in checking out my panties after all. The man had priorities. "Tell me you love me."

"I love you."

"Again."

"I love you."

"I missed the taste of you so fucking much." Big hands parted my legs, exposing me to his gaze. "I might just spend a few days with my head between your legs, all right?"

Oh, God. He rubbed his beard against my inner thigh, making my skin prickle with awareness. I couldn't speak if I tried.

"Say it again."

I swallowed hard, trying to get myself back under control.

"I'm waiting."

"I l-love you," I stuttered, my voice sounded barely there, breathy. My pelvis almost shot off the bed at the first touch of his mouth. Every bit of me was wound tight and trembling.

"Keep going." His tongue parted the lips of my sex, sliding between before delving within. The sweet, firm feel of his mouth and the ticklish sensation of his beard.

"I love you."

Strong hands slid beneath my ass, holding me to his mouth. "More."

I groaned out something. It must have been enough. He didn't stop or speak again. David attacked me. There was nothing easy about it. His mouth worked me hard, driving me sky-high in a matter of moments. The knot inside me tightened and grew as his tongue laved me. Electricity streaked up my spine. I don't know when I started shaking. But the strength went out of me and my back hit the mattress once again. I fisted my hands in his hair, fingers gripping at the short, gelled strands.

It was almost too much. I didn't know if I needed to get closer or get away. Either way, his hands held me to him. Every muscle in me tensed and my mouth opened on a soundless cry. Fireworks filled my mind. I came and came.

When my heart eased up on the hammering, I opened my eyes. David knelt between my legs. His jeans had been pushed down and his erection grazed his flat stomach. Dark blue eyes stared down at me.

"I can't wait."

"No. Don't." I tightened my legs around his hips. One of his hands remained beneath my ass, holding me high. With the other, he guided himself into me. He didn't rush. We were both still at least half dressed, him on the bottom and me on the top. There was no time to waste. We were too needy to wait and do this skin to skin. Next time

He entered me so slowly I couldn't breathe. The only thing that mattered was feeling. And God, the feel of him thick and hard pushing inside of me. The perspiration on his bare chest gleamed in the low lighting. The muscles in his shoulders stood out in stark relief as he began to move.

"Mine," he said.

I could only nod.

He looked down on me, watching my breasts jiggle beneath my top with each thrust. Fingers gripped my hips hard. Mine clutched at the bedding, trying to find purchase so I could push back against him. His expression was wild, mouth swollen and wet. Only this was real, me and him together. Everything else could come and go. I'd found what was worth fighting for.

"I love you."

"C'mere." He picked me up off the mattress, holding me tight again him. My legs were braced around his waist, muscles burning from how hard I'd been holding on. I wound my arms around his neck as he sat me on his cock.

"I love you too." His hands slid beneath the back of my top. We moved harshly together. Our furious breaths mingled into one. Sweat slicked both our skins, the fabric of my shirt sticking to me. The heat gathered low inside me again. It didn't take long in this position. Not with the way he ground himself against me. His mouth sucked at the section of skin where my neck met my body, and I shuddered in his arms, coming again. The noises he made and the way he said my name . . . I never wanted to forget. Not a moment of it.

Eventually, he laid us both back on the bed. I wasn't willing to let him go, so he covered my body with his. The weight of him pressing me down into the bed, the feel of his mouth on the side of my face. We should never move. In the best-case scenario, we'd just stay like this forever.

But actually, I did have something I had to do.

"I need my bag," I said, squirming beneath him.

"What for?" He rose up on his elbows.

"I have to do something."

"What could be more important than this?"

"Roll over," I said, already urging him in that direction.

"All right. But this had better be good." He relaxed and let me roll him. I scampered across the mattress, trying to tug my skirt back down at the same time. David must have liked what he saw, because he came after me with snapping teeth.

"Get back here, wife," he ordered.

"Give me a second."

"My name looks good on your ass," he said. "The tattoo has healed very nicely."

"Well, thank you." I finally got off the mattress and set my pencil skirt to rights. In the month we'd been apart, I'd ignored my ink. But now, I was glad it was there.

"That skirt's coming off."

"Just wait."

"And that top. We have a lot more making up to do."

"Yes, in a minute. I've missed my topless cuddles."

He'd dumped my bag on a blue velvet wing-back chair by the door. Whoever had decorated the condo had done a hell of a job. It was beautiful. But I'd check it out later. Right now I had something important to do.

"I bought you a present today, after we talked at the studio."

"Did you, now?"

I nodded, searching my bag for the treasure. Bingo. The fancy little box was right where I'd left it. With it hidden in my hand, I walked back to him, a wide smile on my face. "Yes, I did."

"What have you got in your hand?" He climbed off the bed. Unlike me, he stripped off his jeans My husband stood before me naked and perfectly disheveled. He looked at me like I was everything. As long as I lived, I knew I wouldn't want anyone else.

"Evelyn?"

For some reason I felt suddenly shy, awkward. Any money, the tips of my ears glowed bright pink.

"Give me your left hand." I reached for his hand and he gave it to me. Carefully I slid on the thick platinum band I'd blown my savings on that afternoon, working it past his big knuckle. Perfect. I'd walk all winter and freeze my ass off, happily. David meant more to me than replacing my crappy old car. Given the money I now owed my parents, the timing wasn't brilliant. But this was more important.

Except the ring covered half of the second-to-last *E* on his *Live Free* tattoo. Shit, I hadn't thought of that. He probably wasn't going to want to wear it.

"Thank you."

My gaze darted to his face, trying to judge his sincerity. "You like it?"

"I fucking love it."

"Really? Because I forgot about your ink, but—"

He shut me up by kissing me. I kind of liked his new habit of doing that. His tongue stroked into my mouth and my eyes slid shut, every worry forgotten. He kissed me until not a single doubt remained as to how taken with his ring he was. Fingers fussed with the buttons on my top, slipping it off my shoulders. Next the band on my bra loosened.

"I love my ring," he said, his lips traveling over my jaw and down my neck. My bra straps slid down my arms and my breasts were free. Next he started in on my skirt, wrestling with the zip and pushing it down over my hips. He didn't stop until I was every bit as bare as him. "I'm never taking it off."

"I'm glad you like it."

"I do. And I need to get you naked right now and show you how much I like it. But then I'll give you back your ring. I promise."

"No rush," I murmured, arching my neck to give him better access. "We've got forever."

CHAPTER TWENTY-TWO

We'd planned to meet Amanda, Jo, and a few other friends at one of the local bars the next night. My insides were in a permanent state of upheaval. Excited and nervous and a hundred other emotions I couldn't begin to process. But not doubtful. Never that. I'd talked to Ruby about continuing on with the extra shifts at the café and she'd been delighted. It turned out her distraction the previous day had been on account of her finding out she was pregnant. My dropping out of college couldn't come at a better time as far as she was concerned. Eventually I'd go back to school. I liked the idea of teaching, maybe. I don't know. There was time.

The bar was one of the smaller ones, not far from our new home. A four-piece rock band on the small corner stage played grunge classics interspersed with a few new songs. Jo waved us over to a table out of the way. Meeting David was obviously big for her. Puppies jumped less.

"David. It's so great," she said over and over. That was about it. If she started to hump his leg, I was stepping in.

Amanda, on the other hand, needed to turn that frown upside down. At least, unlike my parents', her protest was silent. I appreciated her concern, but she'd just have to get used to David being around.

David ordered drinks for us and settled into a seat pulled up beside me. The music was really too loud for conversation. Soon afterward, Nate and Lauren arrived. A fragile peace had emerged between my brother and my husband, for which I was profoundly grateful.

David shuffled closer. "I wanna ask you something."

"What?"

He slipped a hand around my waist, drawing me closer. I did the job better by simply planting myself in his lap. With a warm smile, his arms wound around me, holding me tight. "Hey."

"Hey," I said. "What did you want to ask me?"

"I was wondering . . . would you like to hear one of the songs I wrote for you?"

"Really? I'd love to."

"Excellent," he said, his hand smoothing over the back of my simple black dress. Worn because it was his favorite color, of course. Also, I'd strongly suspected the V-neck would appeal to him. Tonight, I was all about pleasing my husband. There'd no doubt be times in the future when we needed to kick each other's asses, but not tonight. We were here to celebrate.

Lauren led Nate out onto the dance floor and Amanda and Jo followed, abandoning us to our private talk. I honest to God had the best brother and friends in the whole wide world. All of them had taken the news of the plan going boom with calm faces. They had hugged me, and not one word of doubt over my sudden change in direction had been voiced. When Lauren recounted her version of how David stood beside me at dinner, I'd caught Amanda giving him a nod of approval. It gave me great hope.

I'd even called my mother earlier. The conversation had been brief, but I was glad I had. We were still family.

David had eventually given me my ring back the night before. Turned out his list of things to do to me was long.

He fed me ice cream in bed for breakfast while the sun rose. Best night ever.

It felt right having the ring back on my hand. The weight and fit of it were perfect. As promised, his own had stayed put. He'd been proudly showing it to his brother when I'd stumbled out in search of coffee at midday. Once I'd been caffeinated, David and Jimmy had moved me into the condo. Mal and Ben had been busy at the studio. Nate and Lauren had helped move me too, once David and Jimmy finished signing everything Divers-related she could find. Despite her protestations that she'd miss me, I think she was also looking forward to having the apartment for her and Nate alone. They were good together.

"I've got something else I want to ask you too," he said.

"The answer is yes to everything and anything with you."

"Good, because I want you to come work for me as my assistant. When you're not working at the café, I mean." His hand rubbed down my back. "'Cause I know you wanna do that."

"David . . ."

"Or you could just let me pay the college money back to your parents so that's not hanging over your head."

"No," I said, my voice determined. "Thank you. But I need to do that. And I think my parents are going to need to see me doing that."

"That's what I figured you'd say. But that's a lot of money for you to make, baby. If you take a second job we're never going to see each other."

"You're right. But do you think that's a wise idea, us working together?"

"Yeah," he told me, blue eyes serious. "You like organizing and that's what I need. It's a real job and I want you for it. If we find it starts to interfere with us, then we'll make a new plan. But I think mostly it'll just mean we spend more time together and have sex at work."

I laughed. "You promising to sexually harass me, Mr. Ferris?"

"Absolutely, Mrs. Ferris."

I kissed him soundly on the cheek. "Thank you for thinking of it. I'd love to work for you."

"If you decide to go back to college, then I'll get Adrian to find me a replacement. Not a big deal." He pulled me in against his chest. "But in the meantime, we're good."

"Best plan ever."

"Why, thank you. Coming from you, that means a lot."

David's gaze wandered over to the bar where Mal, Jimmy, and Ben were hanging out, keeping a low profile. I hadn't known they were joining us tonight. Jimmy had been steering clear of clubs and bars. "About time they got here," he murmured.

Next David turned to the band, rocking out in the corner. They were just in the process of winding up a solid rendition of a Pearl Jam classic.

"Wait here." David rose, taking me with him. He placed me back on the chair and signaled to his bandmates. Then he made his way toward the stage. His tall figure moved through the crowd with ease and the guys fell in behind him. En masse, they were pretty damn impressive. No matter how low-key they were trying to be. But I got the distinct feeling they were about to make their presence known. Once the band finished the song, David called the singer over. Holy shit. This was it. I bounced in my chair from excitement.

They talked for a moment, then the singer brought the guitarist into it. Sure enough, the man gave his six-string over to David's waiting hands. I could see the look of surprise on both their faces as David's identity finally sank in. Jimmy gave the singer a nod and stepped up onto the platform. Behind him, Mal was already high-fiving the drummer and stealing his sticks. Even grim Ben smiled as he accepted the bass guitar from its original owner. The

Divers took to the stage. Few in the bar seemed to realize quite what was going on yet.

"Hi. Sorry to interrupt, folks. My name's David Ferris and I'd like to play a song for my wife, Evelyn. Hope you don't mind."

Stunned silence broke out into thunderous applause. David stared at me across the sea of people as everyone swamped the dance floor to get closer.

"She's a Portland girl. So I guess that makes us in-laws. Be gentle with me, yeah?"

The crowd went batshit crazy in response. His hands moved over the strings, making the sweetest mix of rock and country music possible. Then he started to sing. Jimmy joined him for the chorus, their voices melding beautifully.

I thought I could let you go
I thought that you could leave and know
The time we took would fade
But I'm colder than the bed where we lay

You let go if you like, I'll hold on
Say no all you want, I'm not done
Baby, I promise you

Did you think I'd let you go?
That's never happening and now you know
Take your time, I'll wait
Regretting every last thing I said

The song was simple, sweet, and perfect. And the noise when they finished was deafening. People shouted and stamped their feet. It sounded like the roof was coming down on us. Security helped David and the guys move through the crush of people. More had arrived as they performed, alerted to the show by texts and calls and each and every sort of social media. A tidal wave of fans swamped them as they pressed through. A hand wrapped around my arm. I looked up to find Sam beside me with a grin on his face. We got our asses out of there pronto.

Sam and the security men cleared a path for us to the door and the waiting limousine outside. They were well prepared. We all bundled into the back of the limo. Immediately, David pulled me onto his lap. "Sam's going to make sure your friends are okay."

"Thank you. I think Portland knows you're here now."

"Yeah, I think you're right."

"Davie, you are a fucking show pony," Mal said, shaking his head. "I knew you were going to pull something like this. Guitarists are such a bunch of posers. If you had an ounce of sense, young lady, you'd have married a drummer."

I laughed and wiped the tears from my face.

"Why the fuck is she crying, what did you say to her?" David pulled me in closer. Outside people banged on the windows as the car slowly started moving forward.

"Are you okay?"

"I told her the truth, that she should have married a drummer. Impromptu fucking performances!" said Mal.

"Shut up."

"Like you've never gone all out to impress a girl," scoffed Ben.

"What happened in Tokyo?" asked Jimmy, reclining in the corner. "Remind me again about, ah . . . what was her name?"

"Oh shit, yeah. The chick from the restaurant," said Ben. "How much did they charge you for the damages, again?"

"I don't even know what you're talking about. Davie said to shut up," shouted Mal above the pair's raucous laughter. "Have some respect for his touching moment with Evelyn, you assholes."

"Ignore them." David cupped my face in the palm of his hand. "Why were you crying, hmm?"

"Because this is ten. If one was us being miserable and apart, then ten is your song. It's beautiful."

"You really liked it? 'Cause I can take it if you didn't, you don't have—"

I grabbed his face and kissed him, ignoring the noise and heckling around us. And I didn't stop kissing him until my lips were numb and swollen and so were his.

"Baby." He smiled, wiping away the last of my tears. "You say the best fucking things."

Play

For Hugh. Always and ever and all the rest.

ACKNOWLEDGMENTS

Any lyrics come courtesy of Soviet X-Ray Record Club. You can learn more about the band here: www.sovietxray-recordclub.com.

Many thanks to my awesome agent, Amy Tannenbaum; my beyond wonderful editor, Rose Hilliard at St. Martin's Press; Cate, Haylee, Danielle, and everyone at Macmillan Australia (you rock); everyone at Macmillan UK; and to Joel, Mark, and Tara at Momentum. Also, thank you to Chas and everyone at Rockstar PR and Literary Services for all your hard work.

Big thanks to my beta and crit queens: Jo (you're not quite as bad as I make you out to be, mostly), Sali Benbow-Powers, Kendall Ryan, and Hang Le. The time you spend and care you invest in giving me your honest opinion is always appreciated.

Thanks to my friends, Joanna Wylde, Kim Karr, Katy Evans, Kim Jones, and Renee Carlino for being the wealth of sanity and support that they are.

Thank you to all the bloggers and readers, especially to Dear Author, Jen and Gitte from Totally Booked, Aestas, Natasha is a Book Junkie, Maryse, The Rock Stars of Romance, Smut Book Club, Shh Mom's Reading, Up All

Night Book Blog, Smexy Books, The Book Pushers, Twinsie Talk, Book Chatter Cath, Katrina, Dawn, Under the Covers, Kaetrin, Amber, Angie, Lori, and all of my Groupie Girls. Without a doubt I've forgotten important people who have been kind and supportive. My apologies and thank you very much. I wish I could give you all your own rock star for Christmas.

CHAPTER ONE

Something was wrong. I knew it the moment I walked in the door. With one hand I flicked on the light, dumping my purse onto the couch with the other. After the dimly lit hallway, the sudden glare was dazzling. Little lights flashed before my eyes. When they cleared all I saw were spaces . . . spaces where, just this morning, things had been.

Like the couch.

My purse hit the floor and everything came tumbling out, tampons, loose coins, pens and makeup. A stick of deodorant rolled into the corner. The now empty corner since both the TV and its cabinet were gone. My thrift-store retro table and chairs remained, same with my overflowing bookcase. But the bulk of the room lay bare.

"Skye?"

No answer.

"What the hell?" A stupid question, what had happened here was obvious. Across from me, my roommate's door stood wide open. Nothing but darkness and dust bunnies in there. No point in denying it.

Skye had bailed on me.

My shoulders slumped as the weight of two months' worth of back rent, food and utilities came crushing down upon me. Even my throat closed tight. So this is what it felt like to have a friend fuck you over. I could barely breathe.

"Anne, can I borrow your velvet coat? I promise I'll . . ." Lauren, my neighbor from the apartment next door, strode in (knocking never had been her style). Then, like me, she stopped dead. "Where's your couch?"

I took a deep breath and let it out slow. It didn't help. "I guess Skye took it."

"Skye's gone?"

My mouth opened, but really, what was there to say?

"She's gone and you didn't know she was leaving?" Lauren cocked her head, making her mass of long dark hair swing to and fro. I'd always envied her that hair. Mine was strawberry blond and fine. Anything past shoulder length and it hung limp like I'd stuck my head in a bucket of grease. It's why I didn't tend to let it grow longer than jaw length.

Not that hair mattered.

Making rent mattered.

Having food to eat mattered.

Hair styles? Not so much.

My eyes burned, betrayal stung like a bitch. Skye and I had been friends for years. I'd trusted her. We'd trash-talked boys and shared secrets, cried on each other's shoulders. It just didn't make sense.

Except it did.

It so very painfully did.

"No." My voice sounded strange. I swallowed hard, clearing my throat. "No, I didn't know she was leaving."

"Weird. You two always seemed to get along great."

"Yeah."

"Why would she take off like that?"

"She owed me money," I admitted, kneeling to collect the contents of my purse. Not to pray to God. I'd given up on him a long time ago.

Lauren gasped. "You're joking. That fucking bitch!"

"Babe, we're running late." Nate, my other next-door neighbor, filled the doorway, eyes impatient. He was a tall well-built guy with an edge. Normally, I envied Lauren her boyfriend. Right then the glory of Nate was lost on me. I was so fucked.

"What's going on?" he asked, looking around. "Hey, Anne."

"Hi, Nate."

"Where's your shit?"

Lauren threw her hands in the air. "Skye took her shit!"

"No," I corrected. "Skye took *her* shit. But she took *my* money."

"How much money?" Nate asked, displeasure dropping his voice by about an octave.

"Enough," I said. "I've been covering for her since she lost her job."

"Damn," muttered Nate.

"Yeah." Seriously, *yeah*.

I picked up my purse and flipped it open. Sixty-five dollars and one lone shiny quarter. How had I let it get this far? My pay check from the bookshop was gone and my credit card maxed. Lizzy had needed help yesterday paying for textbooks and no way would I turn her down. Getting my sister through college came first.

This morning I'd told Skye we needed to talk. All day I'd felt crappy about it, my stomach churning. Because the truth was, the sum total of my talk involved telling her that she needed to ask her parents, or her fancy ass new boyfriend, for a loan to pay me back. I couldn't keep the both of us housed and fed any longer while she searched for a new job. So she also needed to talk to one of them about a place to stay. Yes, I was kicking her to the curb. The guilt had weighed in my stomach like a stone.

Ironic really.

What were the chances of her feeling any remorse for screwing me over? Not likely.

I finished retrieving the contents of my handbag and zipped it up tight. "Ah, yeah, Lauren, the coat's in my closet. At least I hope it is. Help yourself."

Rent was due in eight days. Maybe I could work a miracle. There were sure to be some cash-savvy twenty-three-year-olds with savings in the bank out there. At least one of them must need a place to stay? I'd been doing fine before this. But there'd always been something my sister or I needed more than future financial stability. Books, clothes, a night on the town, all those little treats that made living worthwhile. We'd sacrificed enough already. Yet here I was, broke and on my knees.

Guess I should have prioritized better. Hindsight sucked.

Worst-case scenario, I could probably get away with sleeping on the floor of Lizzy's dorm room if we were super sly. God knows our mom didn't have the cash. Asking her for help was out. If I sold my great-aunt's pearls it might help toward the deposit on another apartment, a smaller one that I could afford on my own.

I'd fix this somehow. Of course, I would. Fixing shit was my specialty.

And if I ever saw Skye again I was going to fucking kill her.

"What'll you do?" asked Nate, lounging against the door frame.

I rose to my feet, dusting off the knees of my black pants. "I'll work something out."

Nate gave me a look and I returned it as calmly as I could. The next thing to come out of his mouth had better not be pity. My day had been crappy enough. With great determination, I gave him a smile. "So, where are you guys off to?"

"Party at David and Ev's," Lauren answered from inside my room. "You should come with us."

Ev, Nate's sister and Lauren's former roomie, had married David Ferris, premier rock god and lead guitarist for the band Stage Dive, a few months ago. Long story. I was still trying to get my head around it, frankly. One minute, she'd been the nice blond girl next door who went to the same college as Lizzy and made killer coffee at Ruby's Café. The next, our apartment block had been surrounded by paparazzi. Skye had given interviews on the front step— not that she'd known anything. I'd snuck out the back.

Mostly, my relationship with Ev had involved saying hi when we'd passed on the stairs, back when she used to live here, and with me hitting Ruby's Café every morning for a big-ass coffee on my way to work. We'd always been friendly. But I wouldn't say we were friends exactly. Given Lauren's penchant for borrowing my clothes, I knew her much better.

"She should come, right, Nate?"

Nate grunted his affirmation. Either that or his disinterest. With him it was kind of hard to tell.

"That's okay," I demurred. Debris lined the walls where the couch and cabinet had stood; all of the collected crap Skye had left behind. "I had a new book to read, but I should probably get busy cleaning. Guess we hadn't dusted under the furniture for a while. At least I won't have much to move when the time comes."

"Come with us."

"Lauren, I wasn't invited," I said.

"Neither are we half the time," said Nate.

"They love us! Of course they want us there." Lauren reemerged from my room and gave her boyfriend the stink eye. She looked better in the black vintage jacket than I ever would, a fact that I chose not to secretly hate her for. If that didn't earn me points into heaven then nothing would. Maybe I'd give it to her as a good-bye present before I left.

"Come on, Anne," she said. "Ev won't mind."

"Good to go?" Nate jiggled his car keys impatiently.

Hanging with rock stars didn't seem the appropriate response to learning you'd soon be out on the street. Maybe one day when I was at my sparkling, buffed-up best I could strut on by and say hi. That day was not today. Mostly I felt tired, defeated. Given I'd been feeling that way since I turned sixteen, it wasn't the strongest of excuses. Lauren didn't need to know that, however.

"Thanks, guys," I said. "But I only just got home."

"Um, honey, your home kind of sucks ass right now," said Lauren, taking in my dust bunnies and lack of décor with a sweeping glance. "Besides, it's Friday night. Who sits at home on a Friday night? You wearing your work gear or jumping into jeans? I'd suggest the jeans."

"Lauren . . ."

"Don't."

"But—"

"No." Lauren grasped my shoulders and looked me in the eye. "You have been fucked over by a friend. I have no words to tell you how furious that makes me. You're coming with us. Hide in a corner all night if you want. But you're not sitting here alone dwelling on that thieving ho. You know I never did like her."

Stupidly, I did. Or had. Whatever.

"Didn't I say that, Nate?"

Nate shrugged and jangled his keys some more.

"Go. Get ready." Lauren gave me a push in the general direction of my bedroom.

In my current situation, this might be my only opportunity to meet David Ferris. Ev still showed up here now and then, but I'd never seen him, despite occasionally "hanging out" on the steps just in case. He wasn't my absolute favorite out of the four members of Stage Dive. That honor was reserved for the drummer, Mal Ericson. A few years ago, I'd crushed on him something hard. But still . . . *the* David Ferris. For the chance to meet even just one of them, I had to go. A few years ago, I'd had a bit of a thing for the band. Nothing to do with their being buff rock gods. No, I was a musical purist.

"Alright, give me ten minutes." It was the absolute minimum time frame within which I could mentally, if not physically, prepare myself to face the rich and famous. Fortunately, my care factor was now dangerously close to fuck-it levels. Tonight would probably be the best time to meet Mr. Ferris. I might actually manage to keep my cool and not be an awestruck waste of space.

"Five minutes," said Nate. "The game will be starting."

"Would you relax?" asked Lauren.

"No." The man made a snapping sound and Lauren giggled. I didn't look back. I didn't want to know. The walls here were disgustingly thin so Lauren and Nate's nocturnal mating habits weren't much of a secret. Happily I was usually at work during the day. Those hours were a mystery to me, and not one that I pondered.

Oh, alright. Occasionally I pondered because I hadn't gotten anything non-self-induced in a while. Also, apparently I had some repressed voyeuristic tendencies in need of addressing.

Was I really up to a night of watching couples rubbing against one another?

I could call Reece, though he'd said he had a date tonight. Of course, he always had a date. Reece was perfect in every way apart from his man-whore tendencies. My best guy friend liked to spread his love around, to put it mildly. He seemed to be on a conjugal-related first-name basis with the better part of the straight Portland female population aged eighteen to forty-eight. Everyone except me, basically.

Which was fine.

There was nothing wrong with just being friends. Though someday I truly believed we'd make a great couple. He was just so easy to be around. With everything we had in common, we could go the distance. In the meantime, I was content to wait, do my own thing. Not that lately I'd been doing anything or anyone, but you get what I mean.

Reece would listen to me whine about Skye. He'd probably even cancel his date, come over, and keep me company while I moped. He would, however, definitely say "I told you so." When he'd found out I'd been covering for her, he hadn't been happy. He'd outright accused her of using me. Turned out he'd been 110 percent right on that score.

The wound, however, was too raw to be prodded and poked. So . . . no Reece. In all likelihood, Lizzy would give me the exact same ass kicking Reece had. Neither had been a fan of the save Skye plan. Decision made. I'd go to the party and have fun before my world turned to shit.

Excellent. I could do this.

CHAPTER TWO

I couldn't do this.

David and Ev lived in a luxury condo in the Pearl District. The place was sprawling, taking up half the top floor of a beautiful old brown brick building. It must have been surreal for Ev, going from our poky, drafty, thin-walled building to this sort of splendor. It must have been awesome. The old apartment building sat on the edge of downtown, close to the university, but David and Ev lived smack-dab in the middle of the very cool and expensive Pearl District.

Happily, Ev seemed delighted to see me. One potentially awkward moment negated. Mr. Ev, the rock star, gave me a chin tip in greeting while I did my best not to stare. I itched to ask him to sign something. My forehead would do.

"Help yourself to anything in the kitchen," said Ev. "There are plenty of drinks and pizza should be here soon."

"Thanks."

"You live next to Lauren and Nate?" asked David, speaking for the first time. Good lord, his dark hair and sculpted face were breathtaking. People shouldn't be so greedy; was it not enough that he was insanely talented?

"Yes," I said. "I used to be Ev's neighbor and I'm a regular at Ruby's Café."

"Every morning without fail," said Ev with a wink. "Double shot skinny latte with a hit of caramel coming right up."

David nodded and seemed to relax. He slipped an arm around his wife's waist and she grinned up at him. Love looked good on her. I hoped they lasted.

I'd loved, really loved, four people in my lifetime. They weren't all romantic love, of course. But I'd trusted my heart to all of them. Three had failed me. So I figured there was a twenty-five percent chance for success.

When David and Ev started sucking face, I took it as my cue to go explore.

I grabbed a beer from the kitchen (state of the art and beyond fancy) and faced the big living room with renewed determination. I could totally do this. Socializing and me were about to be best buds. A couple dozen people were scattered around the place. A huge flat screen blared out the game and Nate sat dead center in front of it, enraptured. There were a few faces amongst the crowd that I recognized; most belonged to people I'd never dare approach. I took a sip of beer to wet my parched throat. Being the odd one out at a party is a unique sort of torture. Given today's events, I lacked the courage to start a conversation. With my talent for picking who to trust, I'd probably ask the only axe murderer in the room for his sign.

Lauren gestured to me to join her right when my cell starting buzzing in my back jeans pocket. My butt cheek vibrated, giving me a thrill. I waved to Lauren and pulled out my cell, walking quickly out onto the balcony to escape the noise and chatter. Reece's name flashed on the screen as I shut the balcony doors.

"Hey," I said, smiling.

"Date canceled on me."

"That's a shame."

"What are you up to?"

Wind whipped up my hair, making me shiver. Typical weather for Portland at this time of year—October could definitely get cold, wet, dark, and miserable. I huddled down deeper into my blue woolen jacket. "I'm at a party. You're going to have to entertain yourself. Sorry."

"A party? What party?" he asked, the interest in his voice moving up a notch.

"One I wasn't exactly invited to, so I can't extend the offer to you."

"Damn." He yawned. "Never mind. Might get an' early night for a change."

"Good idea." I wandered over to the railing. Cars rushed by on the street below. The Pearl District was a mecca of bars, cafés, and general coolness. Plenty of people were out and about braving the weather. All around me, the city lights broke up the darkness and the wind howled. It was lovely in a moody, existential-crisis sort of way. No matter the weather, I loved Portland. It was so different from back home in southern California, something I appreciated immensely. Here the houses were built for snow and ice instead of sunshine. The culture was weirder, more lenient in ways. Or maybe I just had a hard time remembering any of the good regarding my hometown. I'd escaped. That was all that mattered.

"I should go be social, Reece."

"You sound off. What's up?"

Groan. "Let's talk tomorrow at work."

"Let's talk now."

"Later, Reece. I need to put on my happy face and go make Lauren proud."

"Anne, cut the shit. What's going on?"

I screwed up my face and took another sip of beer

before answering. We'd been working together for almost two years now. Apparently, plenty of time for him to figure out my tells. "Skye's gone."

"Good. About time. She pay you back?"

I let my silence do the talking.

"Fuuuuck. Anne. Seriously."

"I know."

"What did I tell you?" he snarled. "Didn't I say—"

"Reece, don't go there. Please. At the time, I thought it was the right thing to do. She was a friend and she needed help. I couldn't just—"

"Yeah, you could. She was fucking using you!"

I took a deep breath and let it out slowly. "Yes, Skye was fucking using me. You were right, I was wrong."

He mumbled a long string of expletives while I waited mostly patiently. No wonder I hadn't wanted to have this conversation. There'd never be a good way to spin such a shitty tale. Frustration boiled up inside of me, warming me against the cold.

"How much do you need?" he asked, voice resigned.

"What? No. I'm not borrowing money off you, Reece. Getting further into debt is not the answer." Besides, business owner or not, I wasn't sure he had it to spare. Reece wasn't any better at saving than I was. I knew this because of the designer gear he wore to work on a daily basis. Apparently being Portland's resident Mr. Lover-Lover required one hell of a wardrobe. To be fair, he wore it extremely well.

He sighed. "You know, for someone who's always helping others, you're shit at accepting help yourself."

"I'll figure something out."

Another pained sigh. I leaned over the railing and hung my head, letting the cold, wet wind batter my face. It felt nice, offsetting the tension headache threatening to start up behind my forehead. "I'm going to hang up now,

Reece. They have beer and pizza here. I'm pretty sure if I try hard enough I can find my happy place."

"You're going to lose the apartment, aren't you?"

"It's likely I'll have to move, yes."

"Stay with me. You can crash on my sofa."

"That's sweet of you." I tried to laugh, but the noise that came out was more of a strangled cough. My situation sucked too much for humor. Me sleeping on Reece's couch while he went hard at it in the next room with some stranger. No. Not happening. As it was, I felt small and stupid for letting Skye play me. Bearing witness to Reece's oh-so-active sex life would be too much.

"Thanks, Reece. But I'm pretty sure you've done unspeakable things to many, many people on that couch. I'm not sure anyone could sleep there."

"You think it's haunted by the ghosts of coitus past?"

"It wouldn't surprise me."

He snorted. "My gross sofa is there if you need it, okay?"

"Thank you. I mean that."

"Call me if you need anything."

"Bye, Reece."

"Oh, hey, Anne?"

"Yeah?"

"Can you work Sunday? Tara's had something come up. I told her you'd cover for her."

"I spend Sundays with Lizzy," I said carefully. "You know that."

Reece's answer was silence.

I could actually feel the guilt slinking up on me. "What if I do a different shift for her? Is it something she can move?"

"Ah, look, never mind. I'll deal with it."

"Sorry."

"No problem. Talk to you later."

And he hung up on me.

I put away my cell, took another mouthful of beer, and stared out at the city. Dark clouds drifted across the crescent moon. The air seemed colder now, making my bones ache like I was an old woman. I needed to drink more. That would solve everything, for tonight at least. My beer, however, was almost finished and I hesitated to head back inside.

Ugh.

Enough of this.

Once the drink was done, my lonely-girl pity party was up. I'd quit lurking in the shadows, pull my head out of my ass, and go back inside. This was an opportunity not to be missed, like I hadn't wished a million times or more to cross paths with someone from the band. I'd already met David Ferris. So there, wishes could come true. I should put in a request for bigger boobs, a smaller ass, and better choice in friends while I was at it.

And money enough to pay for my sister's college education and to keep a roof over my head, of course.

"Want another?" a deep voice asked, startling me. My chin jerked up, eyes wide. I'd thought I was alone but a guy sat slouched in the corner. Wavy, shoulder-length blond hair shone dully but the rest of him remained in shadow.

Whoa.

No. It couldn't be him.

I mean it could be, of course. But it couldn't be, surely.

Whoever he was, he had to have heard my half of the phone conversation, which was more than enough to mark me out as being one of the great idiots of our time. There was the clink and hiss of a beer being opened then he held it out to me. Light from inside reflected off the perspiration on the bottle, making it gleam.

"Thanks." I stepped closer, close enough to make him out even with the low lighting, and reached for the beer.

Holy shit. It was him, Malcolm Ericson.

The pinnacle moment of my life was officially upon me. So I might have had one or two photos of Stage Dive on my bedroom wall when I was a teenager. Fine, maybe there were three. Or twelve. Whatever. The point is there was one poster of the whole band. At least, the photographer probably thought it was of the whole band. Jimmy was out in front, his face contorted as he screamed into the microphone. To his right, half shrouded in shadow and smoke, was David, smoldering over his guitar. And to the left, toward the front of the stage, stood the bulk that was Ben, playing his bass.

But they didn't matter. Not really.

Because behind them all, there he was with the lights shining up through his drum kit. Naked from the waist up and dripping sweat, the picture had caught him mid-strike. His right arm cut across his body, his focus on his target, the cymbal he was about to strike. To smash.

He played with abandon and he looked like a god.

How many times after a day of looking after my mother and sister, working hard and doing the good, responsible thing, had I lay on my bed and looked at that photo. And now here he was.

Our fingers grazed in the way that's pretty much inevitable during such a hand over. No way could he have failed to miss the trembling in mine. Thankfully, he didn't comment. I scurried back to my place by the edge, leaning casually with a beer in hand. Cool people leaned. They looked relaxed.

He chuckled softly, letting me know I wasn't fooling anybody. Then he sat forward, resting his elbows on his knees. His face came fully into the light and I was caught, captivated. My mind blanked.

No question about it. It really was most definitely without a doubt him.

The man had hooker lips, I shit you not. High cheekbones and one of those notches in his chin. I'd never understood the appeal of those things before. Now I got it. But it was him as a whole that blew my mind. The parts meant nothing without the amused gleam in his eye and the hint of a smirk. God, I hated people who smirked. Apparently, I also wanted to lick them all over because my mouth started watering.

"I'm Mal," he said.

"I—I know," I stuttered.

His smirk heightened. "I know you know."

Huh. I kept my mouth shut.

"Sounds like someone had a bad day."

Nope, I still had nothing. A brain-dead stare was the best I could do.

Why was he out here in the dark? From all reports, the man was the life of the party. Yet here he was, drinking alone, hiding like me. Slowly, he stretched, rising out of his seat. Thank you, Lord. He'd go back inside and I'd be off the hook. I wouldn't have to try and make conversation. Fortunate, given my sudden bout of starstruck stupidity.

Only he didn't leave.

Instead, he walked toward me, his lean, muscular frame moving with careless grace. He had maybe five, six inches on me height wise. Enough to intimidate if it was his purpose. Muscular arms put the sleeves of his shirt to the test. Drummer's arms. They were certainly nice as body parts went, covered in ink and bulging in all the right ways. I bet they felt good, too.

And I was so obviously checking him out someone should slap me.

If I kept this up, I would slap me. Hard.

"What's your name?" he asked, joining me at the railing. God, even his voice felt good. The little hairs on the back of my neck stood on end with delight.

"My name?"

He stood close enough that our elbows bumped. His bare elbow, since he wore only jeans, a pair of Chucks, and a fitted "Queens of the Stone Age" T-shirt. Mal Ericson had touched me. I'd never wash again.

"Yeeeah, your name," he drawled. "The point of me telling you my name, even when you already knew it, was so you'd give me yours. That's how these things go."

"You knew I knew?"

"The crazy eyes kinda gave it away."

"Oh."

A moment later, he groaned. "Never mind, this is taking too long. I'll just make one up for you."

"Anne."

"Anne, what?"

"Anne Rollins."

A brilliant grin lit his face. "Anne Rollins. See, that wasn't so tough."

I gritted my teeth and tried to smile. Most likely I resembled a lunatic. One that had spent way too much time imagining him naked. Good god, the shame.

Gently, he tapped his bottle of beer against mine. "Cheers, Anne. Nice to meet you."

I took another sip, hoping it would calm the shaking. The booze wasn't hitting me hard enough fast enough to deal with this. Maybe I should move on to something stronger. One's first intimate conversation with a rock star should probably be conducted over hard liquor. Ev was definitely on to something with her tequila-fueled antics in Vegas. And look how well it had worked out for her.

"What brings you here tonight, Anne?"

"I came with Nate and Lauren. They brought me. They're my neighbors. They live next door."

He nodded. "You're friends with Ev?"

"Yeah, I, well . . . I've always been friendly with her. I wouldn't want to presume . . . I mean, I don't know that I'd say we were close friends, exactly, but—"

"Yes or no, Anne?"

"Yes," I answered, then snapped my mouth shut against another outbreak of verbal diarrhea.

"Yeah, Ev's good people. Davie was lucky to find her." He stared off at the city lights in silence. The amusement fell from his face and a frown creased his brow. He seemed sad, a little lost, maybe. For certain, his much-vaunted party-rocker personality was nowhere in evidence. I should know better. People had painted Ev to be the next Yoko Ono, riding on David's coattails, sucking him dry of fame and fortune. I didn't have to be her BFF to know it couldn't be further from the truth. Chances were, whoever Mal was had little to do with the nonsense flowing freely on the Internet.

But more important, how badly had I embarrassed myself?

"I didn't really get a crazy look in my eyes, did I?" I asked, dreading the answer.

"Yeah, you did."

Crap.

"So you're a friend of Ev's? I mean, you're not in the music business or anything?" he asked, focusing on me once more. His face had cleared, his mood shifting. I couldn't keep up. With the flats of his palms he beat out a swift rhythm on the balcony railing.

"No. I work in a bookshop a few blocks from here."

"Okay." He gazed down at me, apparently pleased with my answer. "So what was that phone call about?"

"Nothing."

"No?" He stepped closer. "What happened to your nose?"

Immediately my hand flew up to block his view of my face. It was only a small bump, but still. "My sister broke it when we were little."

"Don't cover it. I think it's cute."

"Great." I lowered my arm. He'd already seen the flaw, so what was the use?

"Why'd she break it?"

"She got mad one day and threw a toy truck at me."

"Not how. Why?"

I smothered a sigh. "She wanted a kitten and I'm allergic to cats."

"You couldn't get a puppy instead?"

"I wanted to but Mom said no. My sister still blamed me."

He scowled. "So you never had any pets growing up?"

I shook my head.

"That's fucking terrible. Every kid should get to have a pet." He appeared sincerely outraged on my behalf.

"Yeah, well, time's past and I'm kind of over it now." I frowned and swallowed some more beer. Everything told me I was going to need it. This conversation was just plain weird.

He stood, watching me with his faint smile. Just that easily I was riveted once again. My lips curled into some sort of vaguely hopeful idiotic half grin of their own accord.

Mal.

Mal Ericson.

Damn, he was beautiful. My long-dormant hormones broke into a dance of joy. Something was definitely going on in my pants. Something that hadn't happened in a very long time.

"There go the crazy eyes again," he whispered.

"Shit." I shut my eyes tight. Lizzy walking in on me and my boyfriend seven years ago had been pretty damn embarrassing, especially given that she then ran and told mom. Not that mom had been coherent enough to care. This, however, topped it.

"Your cheeks have gone all rosy. Are you thinking rude thoughts about me, Anne?"

"No."

"Liar," he taunted in a soft voice. "You're totally thinking of me with no pants on."

I totally was.

"That's just gross, dude. A massive invasion of my privacy." He leaned in closer, his breath warming my ear. "Whatever you're imagining, it's bigger."

"I'm not imagining anything."

"I'm serious. It's basically a monster. I cannot control it."

"Malcolm—"

"You're pretty much going to need a whip and chair to tame it, Anne."

"Stop it."

"That okay with you?"

I covered my hot face with my hands. Not giggling. Not even a little, because grown women didn't do that shit. What was I, sixteen?

Inside the condo, Nate started shouting. The sound was only slightly muted by the sliding glass doors. My eyelids flew open as he hurled abuse at the TV, arms waving madly. Lauren laughed and my brain came back on line, sending all sorts of emergency signals throughout my body. Like I didn't already realize I needed to get the hell out of there before I humiliated myself further. Good one, frontal lobe. At least I could think if I didn't look at Mal directly.

This was a brilliant and timely discovery.

And it worked right up until he leaned over, getting in my face, making my lungs feel like they were about to explode.

"You have a little gap between your two front teeth," he informed me, eyes narrowed in perusal. "You know that?"

"Yes."

He studied me like I was an alien species, a curiosity that had been dumped on his doorstep. His gaze slid down my body. It wasn't as if he could possibly see anything what with me wearing a coat, jeans, and boots. But that knowledge didn't help at all. His lazy, appreciative grin made my knees knock. It took about forever for his gaze to return to my face.

Damn, he was good. I'd been professionally sullied without a single item of clothing removed.

"Your eyes are a pleasing shade of . . . Is that blue?" he asked. "It's hard to tell in this light."

I cleared my throat. "Yep, blue. Will you please not do that?"

"What?" he asked, sounding vaguely aggrieved. "What am I doing?"

"You're staring at me and making me feel all uptight. I don't like it."

"You stared at me first. Besides, you were wired long before you came out here. If I had to guess, I'd say you're uptight in general. But don't worry, I'm here to help. Go on; tell Uncle Mal all your troubles."

"Wow, that's really kind of you. But I'm good."

He shuffled closer and I shuffled back. Pity there was nowhere for me to go. "What were you talking about on the phone before, Anne?"

"Oh, you know . . . personal stuff. I don't really want to discuss it."

"You were saying your friend ripped you off and you're going to lose your place, right?"

"Right." I slumped, my heart hurting. Fucking Skye. I wasn't a pleaser, but I did look after the people I loved. Stupid me, I thought that's what you did. When mom got sick, I'd stepped up, done what needed doing. There'd been no other choice. The state of my finances right now, however, would suggest it had become a bit of a bad habit. "Yeah. That about sums it up."

His eyes widened in sudden alarm. "Shit. Don't cry. I'm not Davie. I don't know how to deal with that."

"Shut up, I'm not going to cry." I blinked furiously,

turning my face away. "I told you I didn't want to talk about it."

"Didn't think you'd burst into tears. Christ."

My beer was empty; time to go. Besides, I needed to escape before my watery eyes betrayed me. And Mal had to have better things to do with his time than talking to me. Teasing me. This had been the most excruciatingly awkward and awesome conversation in my entire life. For a while there, I'd forgotten all about my problems.

He'd made me smile.

"So." I thrust my hand out for shaking, wanting that final contact, needing to touch him properly just once. He'd been on my bedroom wall back home for years. I'd end meeting him on a high if it killed me. "It's been lovely to meet you."

"Are you trying to get rid of me?" he asked, laughing.

"No, I—"

"Stop looking over my shoulder, Anne. Look me in the face," he ordered.

"I am!"

"Are you scared you're going to make crazy eyes at me again?"

"Yes, probably." I clicked my tongue, exasperated. "Do you normally taunt your fans like this?"

"No. I never realized it could be this much fun."

My hand hung in the air between us. I was about to retract it when he grabbed hold. I stared him in the face, determined not to lose it this time. The problem with Mal Ericson was that he was physically flawless. Not a single imperfection marred him, big or small. If he kept riding my ass, though, I'd fix that for him.

"What's that look mean?" he asked, leaning in. "What are you thinking now?"

My stomach swooped and all thoughts of violence were pushed aside. "Nothing."

"Hmm. You're not a very good liar."

I tried to pull my hand from his grasp. Instead, he held it firmly.

"One last quick question. This shit with your friend, that sort of thing happen often?"

"What?"

"'Cause when you were on the phone, talking with your other friend, it sounded like it did." He loomed over me, blocking out the night sky. "It sounded like it was a problem for you, people using you."

"We don't need to talk about this." I twisted my hand, trying to get free. Even with the sweaty palms it was an impossible task.

"Did you notice how your friend asked for a favor even knowing you were all sad faced about this other friend ripping you off? How do you feel about that?"

I yanked on my arm, but he held fast. Seriously, how strong was this bastard?

"Because I think that was kind of a low move. Between you and me, I don't think you have very good friends, Anne."

"Hey. I have great friends."

"Are you fucking kidding me? They rip you off and expect shit from you when you're down. Seriously, dude. Only assholes would do that."

"Mal—"

"But what's worse is that you're letting them. I don't get that."

"I'm not letting them do anything."

"Yes, you are," he said, voice rising in volume. "You so are."

"Good god, do you have a mute switch?"

"It's appalling! I'm officially appalled," he yelled, clueing the whole damn neighborhood in on my life. "This must end! I will stand for it no longer. Do you hear me, Portland?"

"Let me go," I said through gritted teeth.

"You, Miss Rollins, are a doormat."

"I am not a doormat," I growled, everything in me rebelling at the idea. Either that or running in fear of it. I was so worked up it was hard to tell.

He rolled his eyes. "C'mon, you know you are. It's right there on your face."

I shook my head, beyond words.

"So, I've given this absolutely no thought and decided that you need boundaries, Anne. Boundaries. Are. Your. Friends." Each word was punctuated with his finger tapping the tip of my nose. "Do you hear me? Is this getting through?"

Which is about when I snapped and started screaming. "You want boundaries? How about getting the hell out of my face! How's that for a boundary, huh? None of this is any of your damn business, you obnoxious dickhead."

He opened his mouth to reply but I charged on regardless.

"You don't know a damn thing about me. And you think you can get in my face and tear my psyche apart for fun? No. Fuck you, buddy. Fuck you hard."

Everything went quiet, even the music inside. The most horrible silence reigned supreme. People were watching us through the glass with curious faces. Lauren's mouth was a perfect O.

"Shit," I muttered.

"Anne?"

What had I done? Lauren had invited me to this nice party and I'd just gone psycho on one of the guests. It was time to wither and die, I could feel it. "Please let my hand go."

"Anne, look at me."

Never.

"C'mon, gimme your eyes."

Slowly, wearily, I turned back to him. The slowest of

smiles curled his perfect lips. "That was fucking awesome. I'm so proud of you right now."

"You're insane."

"Nooo."

"Yes. You really are."

"You're just thinking that now. But give it some time. Think about what I said."

I just shook my head in silence.

"It was great to meet you, Anne. We'll talk again real soon," he said, pressing a kiss to the back of my hand before releasing it. There was a light in his eyes, one I didn't want to decipher. One I certainly didn't trust. "I promise."

CHAPTER THREE

I'd only just wandered back inside when David Ferris appeared at my elbow, probably to throw me out. Yelling at rock stars had to be severely frowned upon at such events.

"Hey." David spoke to me but his gaze stayed on the other side of the room where Lauren and Ev were huddled together. A possible problem, since Lauren talked with her hands. Every few seconds Ev got whacked in the arm. She didn't seem to mind, however.

"Hi."

"Having fun?" he asked.

"Um, sure."

He nodded, his demeanor as cool and detached as earlier.

"Great," I whispered.

The two beers and bizarre confrontation had left me a little light-headed. Maybe drinking wasn't such a good idea after all. Especially if I had to keep talking to important people and actually making sense as opposed to yelling abuse at them. Music was pumping once again, people mingling and chatting their hearts out. No one even really gave me a second glance. I could only hope that picking random strangers' lives apart was Mal's thing and they'd seen it all before. "You talked to him?" he asked.

"Him? Mal?"

"Yeah."

"Ah, yes. I did." I'd thought everyone had heard.

"Hmm." Across the room, Ev burst out laughing. An answering smile tugged at his lips. "You argue about something?"

"No, nothing really," I stumbled. "Just nothing."

David turned to me and his forehead creased, the smile long gone. For a long time he just looked at me.

"Never mind." He slinked away, leaving me boggled.

Was I not supposed to have talked to Mal? He'd talked to me first. I might have started the staring, but he'd definitely kicked off the conversation. And the yelling, for that matter. Not my fault I'd interacted with one of the most famous drummers on the planet. But a memory of Mal looking out over the city came back to me. The frown he'd had on his face before he'd gotten busy poking fun at me once more. The way he'd bounced between moods. And now with David checking up on him . . .

Curiouser and curiouser.

If cash and conquests were everything, then Mal had it covered. I'd seen a picture of his beautiful beach house down in L.A. Photos of him covered in scantily clad women were the norm. Money didn't buy happiness. I knew that. Given my current situation, though, the knowledge wouldn't quite stick. Plus the man had fame, worldwide adoration, and an awesome job involving lots of travel. How dare he not be deliriously, ridiculously happy! What was his problem?

Good question.

"That's a big frown." Lauren hooked her arm with mine, drawing me further into the party. "You okay?"

"Fine."

"I heard you and Mal fighting."

"I'm assuming pretty much everyone did." I winced. "Sorry about that."

She laughed. "Please, Mal lives to get a reaction."

"He certainly got one from me."

"Let me guess, that was your friend, Reecy, calling earlier?" Her voice dripped with disdain. Lauren and I started spending time together when Ev got married and moved out. Often on weekends Nate would wind up needing to work. Lauren had a low boredom threshold for her own company. So we'd grab a coffee or go see a movie. It was good. Especially since Skye had taken to avoiding me the past few months. It had been on the pretext of spending time with her new boyfriend but now I had to wonder.

I hated doubting everything that'd happened. The feeling of losing all trust. It was skin crawling and noxious.

"Reece's date bailed on him," I said. "Did Ev say something about pizza? I'm starving."

"One day, you're going to stop being that boy's backup plan."

My spine straightened. "We're just friends, Lauren."

She steered me into the kitchen. A vast array of pizza boxes had been spread across the marble benchtop.

"Please," she huffed. "He's a cunt tease. He knows you like him and plays on it."

"No, he doesn't. I repeat, just friends." I'd only recently finished embarrassing myself in front of Malcolm Ericson. Thoughts regarding my possible foolish behavior around Reece Lewis could wait for another time.

Or never. Never would also be fine.

"You could do better if you bothered to," she said.

I made some vague noise. Hopefully it was enough to end this topic of conversation. Then my stomach rumbled loudly. Yum, melted cheese. Earlier, I'd been so worried about the talk with Skye, I'd skipped lunch. With two beers sloshing around inside my belly, food was long overdue. Though the toppings laid out weren't what I expected. "Is that artichoke and spinach?"

"Probably." Lauren shook her head and shoved a piping-hot piece of ham and pineapple at me, taking the time to set it on a napkin first. "Here, try this one. Evelyn hasn't wrecked it with any of her vegetable nonsense. I love her, I do. But the girl has the strangest taste in pizza toppings of anyone I've ever met. It's unnatural."

I bit into it immediately, scalding my tongue and the roof of my mouth. One day I'd learn to wait until it cooled down. Not today, but one day.

Out in the living room, the music suddenly jumped in volume by about a billion decibels. My ears started ringing. The walls shuddered. Black Rebel Motorcycle Club thundered through the condo. Someone else managed to be louder. "Par-tay!"

Lauren smiled and leaned in closer to be heard. "Mal's decided to join in!" she shouted. "Now the fun begins."

Ben Nicholson, Stage Dive's bull-necked bass player arrived, blowing my mind just a bit more. He and Mal started pouring shots. I stuck to my mostly full beer. Holding it gave my hands something to do. What followed was pretty much everything I'd ever expected from a rock star party. Well, there weren't really drugs or groupies so much. But plenty of pretty people getting drunk and lots of noise. It was a bit like the college parties Lizzy talked me into attending now and then. Only instead of cheap beer in red Solo cups, they passed around bottles of CÎROC and Patrón. Most everyone's clothes were top-of-the-line designer goodies and we were sitting in a million-dollar condo instead of some crappy student apartment.

So, actually, it was nothing like the parties I went to with Lizzy. Forget I said that.

Lauren, Ev, and I had danced and chatted earlier. It'd been fun. For certain, Lauren had done me a favor dragging me out tonight. I'd had a hell of a lot better time than I ever would have sitting at home all by my lonesome. Mal had gone off with David and Ben to another room for a while. Not that I'd been keeping an eye out for him.

For a while I'd hung out in the kitchen, talking to a sound technician by the name of Dean. Apparently he worked with someone called Tyler, who'd been with the band for forever and was basically a family friend. Dean was nice, intelligent, with cool black hair and a piercing through his lip. Yes, he was sort of hot. He asked me back to his hotel room, and it was tempting. But all of my current stresses were running on a loop in the back of my mind. It would basically take a Sex God to make me unwind right now.

I bid Dean good night at the kitchen door.

Then Mal and the guys returned and the music got turned way up again. As inevitably happened, everyone had started pairing up. David and Ev disappeared. No one commented. Lauren sat on Nate's lap in the corner of the couch, their hands all over each other. I stifled a yawn. It'd been a blast, but it was nearing three in the morning. I was running out of steam. We'd probably be leaving soon.

I hoped we'd be leaving soon. In a few hours I had to rise and shine. The shining part might be problematic with the way Mal's words were beating around inside my brain. Overly trusting and broke? Yes. Doormat, my ass.

"Benny boy," hollered Mal. He was dancing on top of the coffee table with a long-legged brunette. The girl seemed hell-bent on wrapping herself around him, strangler-vine style. Somehow he managed to keep her at a polite distance. Well, almost.

"Yo," replied Ben in a very manly manner.

"You met my girl, Anne?" Mal nodded to where I sat perched on the end of a couch. I froze. For hours he'd been otherwise occupied. I'd thought he'd forgotten about me entirely.

"You got a girl?" asked Ben.

"Yeah. Isn't she cute?"

I got a brief looking over from Ben, followed by a chin tip. It seemed eerily similar to the one I'd gotten from David. Maybe this was the equivalent of a rock star's secret handshake.

"We were talking earlier outside. We're moving in together," Mal informed him. The brunette in his arms scowled. He didn't even notice. But more important, what the hell was he talking about? "It's serious, man. Real serious. She's got a few issues with her friends going on. It's a fucking mess. Anyway, she really needs me with her right now for support and shit, you know?"

My hands quietly throttled the poor innocent bottle of beer.

"You doing the Dave and Ev thing?" asked Ben.

"Abso-fucking-lutely. I'm settling down. I'm a changed man. True love and all that."

"Right. This should be interesting," said Ben. "How long you think it'll last?"

"Mine and Anne's lustful passion will be eternal, Benny boy. Just you wait and see."

Ben's eyebrow arched. "You willing to bet on this?"

"Name your price, punk!"

"Five large says you can't make it till we go on tour."

"Fuck that. Make it worth my time. Twenty."

Ben guffawed. "Easiest twenty grand I'll ever make."

"You're moving in with me?" I asked, interrupting all the male bravado and talk of money. I wasn't even touching upon my supposed friend issues.

"Yes, pumpkin," said Mal, his face deadly serious. "I am moving in with you."

I cringed at the horrid nickname but chose to focus on the real concern for now. "When did we talk about this exactly?"

"Actually, you might have left by then. But it doesn't change the facts." He turned back to Ben. "Perfect timing with Mom coming to town. She's going to love her. Mom always wanted me to find a nice girl and settle down and shit."

"Thought you didn't like Portland," commented Ben.

"I don't like Portland. But I like Anne." He gave me a wink. "Besides, Davie's not moving back to L.A. anytime soon. Even Jimmy's been talking about relocating, maybe buying the place next door."

"Has he?"

"Yeah. You met his new babysitter?"

"Nah, not yet. What happened to the old one, the big black dude?"

"Ha, no. He's long gone. There's been several since him. New girl started a while back." Mal chuckled. The sound was distinctly evil. "If Jimmy doesn't want someone around, he has ways of making their life fucking intolerable."

"Sh-i-i-t. Tell me later."

Mal chuckled some more. "Anyways, things are tight between me and Anne. I may as well stay."

The brunette turned her glare up to high beam. My look was probably more confused. Maybe he meant another Anne. One that had a clue what the hell he was talking about.

"Your girl doesn't mind watching some chick crawling all over you?" Ben gave me a raised brow. "I need a girlfriend like that."

"Ah, fuck. Good point. Honestly, this whole monogamy thing. It takes so much getting used to, man." Mal set the distinctly cranky brunette away from him, the muscles in his arms flexing. He deposited her gently back down onto the floor. "Apologies. I'm sure you're very nice and all but my heart beats only for Anne."

The brunette threw a withering glance my way, flicked her hair, and turned to leave. Ignoring her huffing, Ben

caught the girl around the waist, pulling her onto his lap.
The girl's transfer of affections took all of a millisecond.
To be fair, Ben was a big burly guy. Few would say no.

Mal threw himself at my feet. I scuttled back in my
chair in surprise.

"Forgive me, Anne! I didn't mean to stray."

"It's fine." I didn't know exactly how much he'd had to
drink. A truckload would probably be a good guess.

"Guess what, pumpkin?" Mal jumped onto the couch
beside me, towering over me on his knees. "You don't
make crazy eyes at Ben."

I needed to shoot him at least twice. Once for calling
me pumpkin and then again for embarrassing me every
damn chance he got. Instead, I studied my beer with great
intensity.

"She makes crazy eyes at you?" asked Ben.

"Oh, yeah. Anne?" A finger slid beneath my chin and
gently lifted, forcing me to face him.

Mal stared at me and I stared back despite my best intentions. His face gentled. None of the drunken amusement remained. He just looked at me and all that stuff
about seeing someone's soul began to make sense. It was
terrifying. I could almost feel a connection between us.
Like there was something I could reach out and grab
hold of.

It couldn't be real.

But for one perfect moment, it was just me and him.
We were in our own little bubble and nothing or no one
else existed. It was strangely peaceful.

"There we go," he said, not taking his eyes off me.
"She doesn't do it for you or Davie though. Only I get the
crazy eyes. Because I'm special."

Ben said something. I didn't hear what. Then Mal
looked away and the moment was gone. The spell was
broken. "It's sweet, really. She can't live without me."

"Obviously." Ben laughed.

My jaw clenched. Fuck Mal Ericson and his games very much.

"I haven't met your lead singer, Jimmy, yet," I said, finally finding my fight. It was either words or fists. Given the way he just exposed me to ridicule, I was good with either. "Maybe he's the real favorite and you're just the runner-up. Did you think of that?"

His mouth fell open. "You did not just say that to me."

I didn't answer. Let's see how he enjoyed being teased.

"Anne, are you trying to make me jealous? You wouldn't like me when I'm jealous!" The drunken lunatic roared and started pounding on his chest like King Kong or the Hulk or whatever the hell he was trying to be. "Take it back."

"No."

"Don't toy with me, Anne. Take it back or I'll make you."

I screwed up my face, incredulous. And he said *I* was crazy. Or crazy eyed. Whatever.

The madman shrugged. "Okay, pumpkin. Don't say I didn't warn you."

Without further ado, he launched himself at me. I screeched in alarm. The noise was awesome. My beer bottle went flying across the floor.

It could be said I'm somewhat ticklish. Sure as shit, I hated being tickled. His fingers were dancing and digging in turn, hitting all my sensitive spots, damn it. It was like someone had given him a map to my body. I was panting and squirming, trying to get away from him.

"Boundaries, you bastard," I hissed.

His answering laugh was no less than wicked.

Then I started to slip off the couch.

To be fair, he did try to break my fall and he used himself to do so. Hands grabbed hold of me, turning as opposed to torturing. We fell in a tangle of limbs, me landing flat on top of him. Mal grunted as the back of his head bounced off the hardwood floor.

Ouch; that had to hurt.

Despite the knock, his arms remained tight, holding me to him. The man felt good, better than I'd ever imagined. And you had to know I'd done some serious imagining, even out there on the balcony. The playful light disappeared from his eyes and every inch of him tensed. He stared up at me, unblinking, his mouth slightly open. I got the distinct feeling he was waiting to see what I'd do next. If I'd take things further. Mostly, I concentrated on breathing. Then he looked at my lips.

Breathing was out.

He couldn't want me to kiss him. Surely this was just another game. Except it wasn't, not entirely. I could feel him hardening against my thigh. Things low inside of me tightened in response. I hadn't been this wound up in ages.

Fuck it, I was going for it. I had to know how his lips felt. In that moment, not kissing him was out of the question.

"Malcolm, no!" Ev stared down at us sprawled on the floor, her face a picture of dismay. "Let her go. Not my friends. You promised."

All trace of sexual tension melted away as embarrassment filled me to overflowing. Everyone was laughing. Well, everyone except for David and Ev. Sadly, they'd chosen that moment to rejoin the party.

"Your friend and I are meant to be together. Suck it up." He gave me a squeeze. "You know, I thought you at least would recognize true love when you saw it. I'm very disappointed in you right now, Evelyn."

"Let her go."

"Davie, control your wife, she's making a scene."

Distracted, Mal's hold on me loosened and I managed to scurry off of him. Lucky for him, my knee didn't land in his groin.

"You're the one rolling around on the floor, dude," said David.

"Not. My. Friends." Ev repeated through gritted teeth.

"Your shirt is on inside out, child bride," said Mal, the side of his mouth kicking up. "What have you been doing?"

Ears turning pink, Evelyn crossed her arms over her chest. Her husband did a bad job of hiding a smile. "None of your fucking business what we've been doing," he said in a gruff voice.

"You two disgust me." Mal climbed to his feet then grabbed hold of my hand, hauling me upright. "You okay?" he asked.

"Yeah. You?"

He gave me a goofy grin and rubbed at the back of his skull. "My head would probably hurt if I could feel it."

There was my answer. He was plastered. I was entertainment. Any romantic notions were strictly mine. The story of my life, really.

Finally the laughter quieted down. We were still the focus of every eye in the room, however.

"Malcolm, is that your beer on the floor?" asked Ev, pointing at the mess my fallen bottle had made.

Before I could open my mouth to apologize, Mal was there.

"Yes. Yes, it is. But do not despair. I've got this." He ripped off his T-shirt and knelt, mopping up the spill. There was a whole lot of hard flesh and bronzed skin right there. A truly impressive amount. His back was covered in ink, an intricate scene of a bird taking flight, the opening wings spanning across the breadth of his shoulders. A sigh rippled around the room at the sight of him half naked on his knees. It wasn't just me making the noise, I swear. Though yes, I definitely contributed heartily.

"Christ, Mal," said Lauren. "Put some clothes on before you start a riot."

The man just looked up and grinned.

"And I think that's our cue to leave." Lauren pushed herself off Nate's lap. "It's been fun. But we've got work tomorrow, unlike you musical slackers."

"You're taking my Anne?" Mal asked. His lips turned down at the edges. He climbed to his feet, leaving his sodden shirt on the ground. "You can't take my Anne. I need her for stuff . . . private stuff, in my room."

"Another time." Lauren patted him on the back.

"Stay and play with me, Anne."

"No," repeated Ev.

"Night, Mal," I said. I couldn't tell if he was serious or not. But no way, come morning, would I be scraping myself out of his bed and doing the walk of shame down my friend's hallway.

Nuh-uh.

"Anne, pumpkin, don't leave me," he wailed.

"Run. Go." Ev ushered me toward the door. "He's impossible when he gets like this. You'd swear he didn't get enough hugs as a child."

"Good to see you again, Ev," I said.

She pulled me in for a quick kiss on the cheek. "You too."

"I need sexual healing," Mal continued behind us. He then did a new dance. This one consisted of rhythmic pelvic thrusting while his hand swung through the air, mimicking spanking someone's ass. The "Oh yeah" and "harder baby" only made it better. If ever a vagina was going to sit up and take notice, this would surely do it. The man had all the moves.

"You need some fucking impulse control and coffee.

That's what you need." David's forehead crinkled. He pushed Mal back with a hand, bringing his porno dance performance to a halt. "Better yet, when was the last time you actually slept?"

"I'll sleep with Anne."

"No, you won't."

"Yes, I will." He raised a hand high. "For I am Malcolm, Lord of the Sex!"

With a muttered oath, David went nose to nose with him. Immediately Ben stood, sending the brunette sliding onto the floor. Poor girl, she wasn't having the best night.

"You heard Ev," said David, getting in his face. "Not her friend. That's not cool."

Mal's eyes hardened. "You cock-blocking me, Davie?"

"You bet I am."

"That's not okay, bro."

Ben slung an arm over Mal's shoulders, ruffled his hair. "Come find another toy."

"I am not a child." Mal pouted.

"How about her?" Ben pointed to a sleek blond who smiled and preened in response. "I bet she'd like to meet you."

"Ooh, she's shiny."

"Why don't you go ask her what her name is?" suggested Ben, patting him on the back.

"Do I need to know her name?"

"I've heard it helps."

"Maybe for you," Mal scoffed. "I just call out my own name during sex."

Laughter broke out across the room. Even the corner of David's mouth started twitching.

But when it came to women, Mal was clearly a whore. I'd seen more than enough to confirm it. David and Ev had done me a favor, warning him off. Jealousy didn't hit me in the gut when he leered at the other woman. Something else did. I don't know what it was, but it was definitely something else.

Weirdest night of my life. Hands down, this was the absolute winner.

Wait till I told Skye about it when I got home. She'd laugh her ass off. Shit, no she wouldn't. Mal's antics had momentarily made me forget all about her. Surprisingly enough, as annoying as he'd been, he kept making me smile.

The man himself apparently remembered me again then. I stood ensconced between Evelyn and Lauren as if I needed protecting. Maybe I did. All I know is, when he looked at me my mind went far, far away.

What was it about bad boys? Someone needed to invent a cure.

My lust object gave me a wink. "See you later, crazy eyes."

CHAPTER FOUR

"The skank unfriended me too," said Reece, staring at the shop's computer, sitting on the front sales counter. Facebook sat open on the screen in all its blue brilliance.

"Bitch," I muttered.

Skye had a new name and it wasn't nice. Much deserved, but not nice.

Between Reece and I, we'd called everyone who might have known where she'd gone. Lucky it'd been a quiet morning so far. We'd had no luck with our search. People either didn't know or weren't saying. Everyone sounded sorry. But no one could, or would, help. Some days, humanity sucked.

"I think we should stop," I said.

"What? Why?"

"Think about it. Realistically, what would I even do if I found her?" I crossed my arms and leaned my hip against the counter. The pose was all the better for holding my shit together. "Slapping her silly is illegal. As nice as it would be to rip her a new one, it won't get me my money back. There's no point going to the police because it's just her word against mine. I'm screwed."

"There's the defeatist attitude I've come to know and love."

"Shuddup." I smiled.

Reece smiled back at me, little lines appearing at the corners of his eyes behind his cool-guy thick-rimmed black glasses. A dimple popped in his cheek. He had an awesome smile. No matter how many times I'd seen it, I'd never quite become inured. Though, upon reflection, it didn't make me stupid like Mal's cocky grin.

Huh, interesting.

There was, however, a lot to be said for not being reduced to brain-dead hormonal mush by a man. Reece and I were solid. Though, for some reason, the usual rush I got from being around him was missing. Still, I barely knew Mal. Reece was real. Mal was just a dream on my teenage bedroom wall.

And since when did I compare Reece's smile to anyone's?

"What was the party you went to?" Reece asked, scratching his head in his usual adorable manner. His dark hair flopped over his forehead and I just knew we'd make great babies together one day. Marriage would never be in the cards, not for me. The institution meant so little. But there was a lot to be achieved just by living in sin, by being a life partner.

Reece would make a great life partner.

When Lauren had hinted at my having a thing for Reece last night, she might have known what she was talking about.

Ah, Reece.

I'd worked at Lewis's bookshop since moving to Portland two years ago. Lizzy had asked me to come out for a while, to help her settle in. Obviously, I was still here. I liked being close to my sister and Portland was a cool city. I liked my job and the friends I'd made. Everything was better here.

"Lauren invited me to drinks at Ev's," I said.

Reece's chin retreated in what appeared to be

amazement. "The girl that married the dude from Stage Dive?"

"That's the one."

"And you didn't invite me? Damn, A. I like a couple of their songs. That *San Pedro* album wasn't bad. Their new stuff is shit, though, gotta say."

"I love the new album. 'Over Me' is a great song."

He snickered, the corner of his mouth lifting. "It's a song about someone doing your friend."

"I choose to ignore that aspect."

An elderly woman in tie-dye wandered in, heading straight for the self-help/philosophy section. Two teenagers started making out next to the new cookbook display. Sweet, but this was hardly the place for it. When a hand wandered too far south I cleared my throat, loudly. "Keep it above the waist, boys."

The bell above the door jangled crazily as they bolted from the shop at light speed. One turned on the most amazing blush. I almost felt bad for him. Guess he'd wanted that grope something fierce.

Reece chuckled. Well, he might. He picked up regularly within these four walls. A habit he'd hopefully grow out of one day soon. "Calm down. They weren't hurting anyone."

"There's a time and a place."

The little bell above the door dinged again as about the last person I expected strolled on in. Evelyn entered with a cup of coffee in hand and a hesitant smile on her face. Despite only working a couple of blocks away, I don't think she'd ever been in the shop before. For certain, she'd never delivered coffee to me. If that was what was about to happen.

I stared in surprise.

Reece perked up. Then he spotted her humongous wedding engagement ring combo and perked back down again. Coming in from across the river, he didn't go past Ruby's Café like I did. Ev was unknown to him.

"We missed you this morning," she said, sliding the tall cardboard cup of coffee onto the counter in front of me. "You didn't stop by for your regular. Figured I'd bring it to you."

"You're wonderful. I woke up late for some reason."

"Fancy that." She smiled.

I took a sip of the superhot brew. Perfect. It was fucking perfect. Evelyn was basically the patron saint of the coffee bean. What I'd do in a few weeks when she left to go on tour with the band, I had no idea.

Cry, most likely.

Ev's long blond hair was tied back in a braid. Like me, she wore head-to-toe black. Only she wore a pencil skirt while I'd gone for skinny jeans. "Ruby's Café" was plastered across her bounty of boobs while "Lewis's Independent Book Store" was written over my more sedate mounds. Apart from the chunk of ice on her finger she could have been any other local girl. Why she kept working as a barista when she'd married a millionaire I had no idea and it wasn't my place to ask.

I turned to introduce her to Reece but he'd taken the opportunity to disappear out back, all interest in Ev gone as soon as he saw the ring.

"I also wanted to apologize for last night," she said, resting her arms on the counter.

"What for?"

"The part where Mal tackled you onto the floor, mostly. Unless there's something else I missed I should also be apologizing for?"

"No." I waved her words away, smiling. No need to bring up my shouting abuse at her guest earlier in the evening. "That was fine. He was just playing."

"Yeah. He's kind of like a puppy on steroids. Doesn't

know his own strength." She looked around the shop, face open, curious. "This place is great. Why haven't I been in here before?"

"Time, probably. When you weren't working you were studying. Now you're married."

"True." She beamed. "It was good to see you last night, Anne. I'm glad to hear Mal didn't do any permanent damage."

"No, I'm fine. And thank you very much for the coffee. I seriously needed it. I don't know how you handle getting up so early after the late nights."

She lifted a shoulder in a half shrug. "Things wound down pretty much straight after you left. Ben and Mal went out, taking everyone with them. David and I crashed. We don't do the party thing often. If we did I'd be ruined this morning."

"Ah."

"Sooo, David said you were talking to Mal out on the balcony for a while. . . ." Which was about when her coffee-bearing visit started to make sense.

"Yeah, I was," I said. "And then David asked me if he'd said anything. I still don't know what that was about."

Ev's lips pressed tight. "Mm."

"He sent you to ask me about it," I guessed. Correctly, if the flash of guilt in her eyes was any indicator.

"You deserved coffee, anyway. But yes, he did ask if I would mind talking to you."

"Okay." I licked my lips, buying some time to get my thoughts in order. Out of sight my foot fidgeted, doing its best to wear a hole in the carpet. "Honestly, we didn't talk about much, nothing particularly personal or private. Just some nonsense about my ex-roommate."

"Lauren mentioned." Pity filled Ev's eyes.

I shrugged. "Yeah, never mind. I'll figure it out. But really, Mal and I didn't talk much about himself. Mostly, he just teased me."

"He does that." For a moment longer, she looked at me. Trying to gauge the truth, I guess. She was clearly pretty worried about Mal, but the fact was we didn't know one another well enough for this sort of heart-to-heart. It felt awkward, stilted.

"Thanks for letting me know," she said at last. "Mal's been acting strange since he came up a week ago. Manic . . . more so than usual. Then other times he just stares into space. We've tried talking to him, but he says nothing's wrong."

"I'm sorry."

"We don't know if he's depressed or on drugs or what. And after having Jimmy go through rehab so recently . . ." She gave me a small, sad smile. "I'd appreciate you not mentioning this to anyone."

"Of course."

"Anyway, I'm done for the day. I'd better get going. David will be wondering where I am. It was good to see you."

"You too."

"Come over again soon, okay?" She backed toward the door, waving good-bye. The request seemed genuine. It soothed my heart. After the horror of Skye I could do with some real friends.

"I will. Thanks again for the caffeine."

She gave me the rock-star chin tip and then she was gone.

Reece wandered back out, his own cup of coffee in hand. "Your friend go?"

I snapped back to reality, dragging my mind away from the six-foot something conundrum that was Mal. My mind liked lingering on him far too much. He'd apparently become my new go-to thought despite all of the other things happening in my life. "Yeah, she had to get back to work."

"You're frowning. Still worrying about the bitch?"

I nodded the lie. Though it wasn't exactly a lie. I worried

about everything. Mal had been wrong. Uptight wasn't my thing, worry was, and right now I was worrying about him. I shook off my frown, drank some more coffee. "Why don't we do some work today, boss?"

"This is why you should be in charge." Reece sighed dramatically. He had an impressive business degree behind him while I'd only barely finished high school, but most days it seemed I was the one with the work ethic. When mom went through her darkest time after Dad left, I couldn't just leave her on her own. The day I came home to find her lining up codeine and sleeping pills on her bedside table convinced me of that. So I was "homeschooled." Child Protection Services came around once and we put on a good enough show.

I made damn sure Lizzy turned up to classes at the local high school Monday to Friday, however.

Reece lifted a box of new stock onto the counter so we could start pricing it out. "Tell me more about last night."

"Ah, I got to meet a couple of the band members. That was cool."

"You got to talk to them?" Reece's expression was rapt. Usually shop talk revolved around his innuendos and escapades due to my life being boring. His language, not mine. I'm pretty sure you don't need to be balling every female in the downtown Portland area to make conversation. Perhaps that was why we'd never gotten together. Our hobbies differed so wildly.

My thoughts were remarkably bitter and twisted today.

Where had I left my happy face? Most likely it still lay on my doorstep, where it had fallen some sixteen hours ago. Malcolm Ericson had briefly resuscitated my joy before he'd started in on my supposed failings. Still, just thinking about him made me feel lighter.

How strange.

Lizzy hadn't texted me back yet. Not a surprise. Her

college lifestyle kept her pretty busy. She could also be crap at remembering to charge her cell. I didn't doubt my sister would be there for me, though. Her and her dorm-room floor. I'd left a message for my landlord and received no response from him either. Fat chance he'd give me an extension on the rent. Even if I found a new roommate in record time, I still couldn't come up with my half of the money.

Time to admit defeat whether Reece liked it or not. Time to move on.

Said friend waved his hand in my face. "Anne, fill me in. You get to talk to them or not?"

"Sorry. Yes, I talked to Mal, the drummer."

"About?"

There was the question on everyone's lips.

"Not much, it was only briefly. He was busy. There were lots of people there." For some reason, I was loath to admit to more. Actually, for several reasons. Talking to Reece about another man would be weird. Also, I'd clearly blown the night out of proportion when it came to Mal Ericson. There'd been no connection. No one had looked into anyone else's soul. My fevered imagination had obviously been working overtime last night. So I rushed right on. "David seemed nice. Ben was there too, but I didn't really get to speak to him."

"You're totally dropping names right now." He chuckled.

I gave him a friendly smack in the ribs. "You asked. It's not name dropping if you asked."

"Okay, okay, I believe you. Don't beat me up. So can you get me into the next party there?"

"I doubt I'll be going to another party there, Reece. It was a pure fluke I wound up there last night."

"What use are you?" he joked.

The elderly tie-dyed woman shuffled toward the counter with a copy of *The Alchemist* in hand.

"That's a great book. I think you'll really like it." I rang up her purchase and handed it over for her to put in her reusable bag. Was there anything more wonderful than sending someone home with a book you loved? No, there was not.

I turned to Reece, who was straightening up some credit card receipts. "So you want to hang out tonight?" I asked. "If you're not doing anything. Maybe I'll try to perfect my martini."

"Hmm, I'm kind of leaving my calendar open tonight. There's a girl I'm waiting to hear from."

Of course there was.

"Buuut," he strung out the word. "If she doesn't call me, how about I come over for a martini?"

My heart sank a little bit. Stupid heart. I put on a fake smile. "Sure, Reece, it's not like I have anything better to do than wait around for you all night."

"Exactly," he said, and I couldn't tell if he was joking or not. At that moment, I wondered what exactly I had been chasing and why. Answer: a dream, because I was an idiot. Maybe Mal had a point about my usability. I'd covered for mom for so many years, perhaps the habit had stuck.

He was fiddling with his phone now, a goofy half smile on his face. "She wants to meet up," he said. "So . . . I have a huge favor. Could you close up tonight? Since you're not doing anything?"

"I should really say no. Shit, Reece. I'm not a total loser. I do have some boundaries." No matter what Malcolm Ericson said.

"Please. I'm sorry. You're right, I shouldn't have asked that. And I respect your boundaries, I do. I'm an ass and you're a name-dropping celebrity party animal. Forgive me?" He didn't look sorry, just vaguely desperate. But whatever, this was Reece. The man had offered me his couch last night as an emergency home.

And let's face facts. He was right; I didn't have any grand plans outside of reading.

"Alright," I said, resentment burning deep down in my soul. It soon gave way to sadness. Probably, I should buy chocolate or alcohol on my way home. A truly wise use of the extra money made from the extra hours. Chocolate martini, here I come.

"Thanks. I owe you."

"No worries. Not like I have anything going on."

It wasn't as if I'd be seeing Mal ever again.

CHAPTER FIVE

Something was wrong. Again. This time, I knew it before I walked in the door.

Work had picked up in the afternoon. There'd been no more time for worry, or bitter and twisted thoughts. Definitely a good thing. Now, I was ten types of tired. Two hours of sleep and stressing over money had done me in. The icy cold wind I'd walked in after getting off the MAX had frozen my neck and the tip of my nose. Any chocolate- and booze-fetching plan had flown straight out the window. I wanted a bath and bed. That was my entire plan for the night and it was a beautiful thing.

In a daze, I slid my key into the lock, which was when the door flew in—it wasn't even latched. Balance shot to shit, I fell, face planting in the middle of a hot, hard, sweaty chest.

I oomphed.

He grunted.

Strong hands grabbed me about the waist, holding me steady. A good thing, I really needed a hand right then or my ass might've met the floor. Perhaps I'd entered the wrong apartment. My mind had been elsewhere, worlds away from reality. Another apartment would certainly explain the delicious warm body I was up against.

Since when did sweat smell so good?

It was all I could do not to rub my face in, breathing deep. A sniff or two shouldn't be going too far. Discreetly done, of course.

"Anne. Dude." The chest vibrated beneath my cheek. "Welcome home!"

I knew that voice. I did. But what the hell was it doing in my apartment? Stunned, I blinked up at a familiar beautiful face. "Mal?"

"'Course it's me." He laughed. "You on drugs or something? You shouldn't do drugs. They're not good for you."

"I'm not doing drugs." Though drugs might have gone a ways toward explaining what I was seeing. Because what I was seeing was surreal. "You're here."

No doubt about it. He definitely was. I would know because my hands were still all over his hot, half-naked body. My hormones sidetracked any thoughts about their removal. I couldn't blame them.

"I know," he said. "Isn't it great?"

"Yeah. Wow."

He nodded.

I stared. How the hell did he get in? The door had been locked when I left.

"Work good?" he asked.

"Fine. Thank you."

He smiled down at me. "I was expecting you hours ago."

"Yeah, I had to close up and some people came in at the last minute. Mal, why are you here in my apartment without a shirt on? How did that happen?"

"It got hot moving shit." He rolled his neck, stretching out the muscles. "You're only on the second floor, but the stairs start to add up, you know? Nate and Lauren helped out for a bit, then they had to go. Anyway, not like you care, right? No dress code I need to know about?"

I still stared. Words came out of his mouth but they continued to make no sense. Nothing about this did.

His eyes narrowed on me. "Hang on, I've got my shirt off and everything and you're not giving me crazy eyes. What's with that?"

"Ah, I guess I'm too surprised at seeing you here."

His brows descended, as did the corners of his gorgeous lips. The man looked seriously sad. "Been looking forward to it all day."

"Sorry."

"Never mind. Come on, check it out." He pulled me into the apartment, my apartment, slamming the door shut behind me. Not answering the important question about his presence even a little. But what was truly upsetting was the way he separated my hands from his body. They wept silently. Either that or I was sweating. Most likely the latter. He had the weirdest effect on me.

"Ta-da," he sang, waving a hand about in a grand gesture, presenting my small living room to me.

"Wow."

"Awesome, right?"

"Yeah?"

"Yeah! I knew you'd love this."

I stared some more. Then I rubbed my eyes because they were starting to hurt. It was probably from all the bulging but I couldn't be sure.

What the hell was happening here?

"You moved in with me somehow." There could be no other reason for an entire drum kit appearing in the corner, let alone all the other stuff. The Twilight Zone had officially been entered. "You . . . huh. How about that."

He grimaced and rocked back on the heels of his Chucks. "I know what you're gonna say, it's sooner than I thought too. But Davie threw me out today so I figured, why wait?"

I just blinked, the rest of me being too frozen to respond.

"Okay. Long story short, I accidentally saw Ev naked." He held up his hands, protesting his innocence. "It was only side boob, I swear. No nipple or anything like that. But you know what he's like with her, the fucking drama queen. He completely lost his shit."

I nodded. I didn't actually have a clue, but it seemed a response was required.

"Exactly. As if it's my fault. It was in the fucking kitchen! I just wanted something to eat and there they are, dry humping against the wall. I didn't even know she'd gotten home from work. As if I want to see that. It's like walking in on your folks. Well, except Ev actually has great tits." His guilty gaze slid to my face. "Alright, there might have been a flash of nipple but I swear it's not like I went out of my way to see it. Not my fault she was topless. Anyway, Davie went ballistic."

"He did?"

"Oh yeah. Huge. Harsh words were said. We may have even wrestled slightly. But I forgive him. Love makes you psycho, right?"

"Right." There was a sentiment I could wholeheartedly get behind. When my first boyfriend broke up with me at sixteen, my tiny little world had been rocked. And look at my mom. She'd lost her shit completely when dad left.

"Mm."

"So you moved in with me?" I said, ever so slowly piecing the story together.

Mal shrugged. "Well, hell yeah!"

"No, I mean, you actually moved in with me. Here. Into my apartment. Um, how did you get in again, just out of interest?"

"Is this going to be an issue?" he asked with a long, winded sigh. "Anne, come on. We talked about this last night. If you were gonna have a problem with me moving in, that was the time to bring it up, not now."

"I thought you were joking."

"Dude, that's offensive. Why would I joke about important stuff like that?"

"Because you were drunk?"

"I get some of my best ideas under the influence."

"I didn't even think you'd remember."

"Again, offended," he said. "I'm not some fifteen-year-old. I know what I can handle."

"Sorry." I don't quite know why I was the one apologizing. But never mind. My legs felt weak. I perched on the edge of the nearest couch. It was incredibly comfortable, though it did little for my sudden light-headedness.

Mal Ericson.

Living with me.

He did indeed look serious as evidenced by the little indent between his brows from frowning back at me. Ever so subtly I kicked myself, to check I was awake and not dreaming. Crap, it hurt. Pain radiated from my ankle-bone, making me wince. Yep, wide awake. Also, the heel on my Docs packed a punch.

"You're looking at me weird again," he said.

"Am I?"

He rolled his eyes. "Women. Honest, I swear, it was a hint of nipple and no more. I meant no disrespect to Evvie."

I leaned down, surreptitiously rubbing my brand-new bruise. "I believe you."

"Good. Can you please stop bringing it up?"

I opened my mouth to tell him I hadn't. But it seemed safer to keep the thought to myself. Who knew what tangent it would launch him into next? Mal Ericson was a hard man to keep up with.

"Shit, you don't like the couch do you?" he asked. "That's what the look is about."

"The couch?"

"Man." Mal hung his head, hands on his slim hips. "I

called Ev to ask what color you'd want but she started
asking questions and then she started yelling and it was
just a fucking mess. I can't be standing in some furniture
shop arguing on the phone with some chick, you know?
I've gotta reputation to consider. So I tried calling Lauren 'cause I figured she might have a spare key to your
place—which she did."

"Lauren let you in?"

"Yeah. And she said to definitely get that one, said
you'd go nuts for it."

"No, it's . . . um, it's really nice." I ran my palm over
the velvet fabric. It felt divine, super soft. No way did I
want to know what it must have cost.

"Really?" He looked at me from beneath his brows,
mouth tight with concern. Still, the green and hazel of
his eyes was crystal clear. He seemed almost childlike
somehow, vulnerable. "You're sure you like it?"

I couldn't tear my gaze away from him to give the
item of furniture a proper perusal. No doubt, however, it
looked every bit as good as it felt. "It's beautiful, Mal."

"Phew." His sudden grin lit my world.

I smiled back so hard my face hurt. "Look, I'm not
saying no to you moving in. I guess I'm still trying to get
my head around the concept. But why do you want to live
with me?"

"I like you," he said simply.

"You barely know me."

"You're a friend of Ev's and Lauren's. We talked. I tackled you. We rolled around on the floor together. It was a
real bonding experience."

I blinked.

"More? Seriously?"

"Please."

"You know, I've never lived with a female before. Well,
not since my mom and sisters, and they don't count.
Gimme a minute, this is way harder than it looks." He

threw himself into the black leather wingback chair across from me. Very cool chair. No match for the man sitting in it, but still, nice chair. I waited as he made various pained expressions, finally pinching the bridge of his nose. "You seem like a nice girl, you know?"

I didn't know whether to laugh or cry. Laughter seemed safer. "Thanks."

"Hang on," he groaned. "I'm not used to having to talk women into shit, either. Usually, they're just happy to go along with whatever."

And I did not blame them one bit. But I was reasonably certain there lay the path to ruin. I'd be trailing around behind him like a lovelorn puppy in no time. Not good.

His fingers tapped out a beat on the rolled wooden chair arms. He was a restless soul, was Malcolm Ericson. Never still. You could see how all of his energy made him such a great drummer. "You know, it was fun hanging out with you last night. I enjoyed it. Cool that you weren't being psycho or getting in anyone's face. Despite you being so into me that you get all crazy eyed, I kinda find you strangely soothing to be around right now."

A shadow passed over his face, there and gone in an instant. If not for Ev's visit I might have convinced myself I'd imagined it. But no. Something was definitely up with this man.

"You don't bug me with a lot of questions. Well, you didn't last night." He reclined in the chair like a king, resting his ankle on his knee. The energy or tension running through him kept his fingers jittering, endlessly tapping. "Let's look at it this way. You need money, right?"

I hesitated, but it was the truth. We both knew it. "Right."

"I need something too."

My eyes narrowed. If he started yelling about sexual healing again I'd throw him out, cool furniture, drum kit, and all. Or I'd lick him all over. With my current confusion and stress levels, chances were fifty/fifty. An opportunity to throw myself at him might just be too good to miss. After all, how many more chances would I get? My luck had to run out eventually.

"And I think you'll suit my needs to perfection," he continued.

"Your needs?"

One side of his mouth hitched higher (forty/sixty). "Every man has needs, young Anne. How old are you, by the way?"

"Twenty-three. I'm aware everyone has needs. But Mal, I'm *not* going to meet yours." My nose went high. Sweet baby Jesus, I so badly wanted to meet his needs, but not when he gave me that smug grin. A girl had to have her pride.

"Sure you are." He laughed softly, evilly, seeing right through me (twenty/eighty). "You're dying to meet my needs. You can't look away from my luscious half-naked body. The minute I opened the door you were pawing at me. It was like you were in heat or something."

Fuck.

I squeezed my eyes shut for a moment, blocking him out in an attempt to regain my wits. If only my heart would stop slipping into cardiac arrest at the sight and sound of him. It would make things so much easier. "No, Mal. I lost my balance when you opened the door on me. Finding you here has actually come as a bit of a surprise. I'm not used to people just moving themselves in with me without some serious discussion up front."

When I opened my eyes, he was silently watching me. Judging me.

"And I wasn't pawing at you."

The too-calm expression on his face spoke volumes. He didn't believe me, not even a little. "Hey, now, don't be embarrassed."

I wasn't a clueless virgin. My V-card had been stamped

with my first and last long-term boyfriend at age sixteen. Since coming to Portland, I'd indulged in the odd date. Why wouldn't I? I was young and free. I enjoyed sex. Thoughts of mounting a half-naked man on a wingback chair? Not so much.

I was out of control. No way could I let him know this, however.

"It's okay, pumpkin. I don't mind you pawing at me. If that's how you feel the need to express your affection, that's cool."

"Mal." This was going from bad to worse. I don't even know why I started laughing. "Please stop talking. I need a minute. Consider this a boundary."

His eyes lit with delight. "Hey, you've been thinking about what I said. That's great. I respect your boundary, Anne."

"Then why are you still talking?"

"Right. Sorry."

I tried to find my calm. Why had I never made time for yoga? Deep breathing exercises would have been so useful.

When I opened my eyes, Mal smiled back at me serenely. The arrogant jerk. So confident. So hot. And so damn shirtless. What was with that? It was fall in Portland, cool weather, raining on and off. Normal people wore clothes this time of year.

"Can you put a shirt on?"

He scratched at his chin. "Mm, no. That's my boundary, sorry. I like your sexy looks too much to get dressed."

Crap, was I making crazy eyes?

"You're perfect," he muttered, smirk firmly in place.

Damn it, I was.

"What do you think my needs are, Anne?"

"I'm aware you're talking about sex, Mal. That's kind of obvious. But why, out of all the women at your disposal, would you choose me? That I don't understand. And why you would move yourself in with me, I don't really get that either. You could have gone to a hotel or rented a place of your own much nicer than here."

"Noooo." He slumped back in the seat, laying his meshed fingers on his flat belly. "I'm not talking about sex. I like to think you and I are above all of that messy, physical stuff, despite your infatuation with me. What I need is a girlfriend . . . well, a pretend girlfriend, and you, Anne Rollins, are perfect."

"Fuck, what?"

He burst out laughing.

"You're joking," I said, relieved. Well, mad and relieved. Were rock stars so bored these days they had to resort to such extremes for entertainment?

"No, I'm not joking. Your reaction was funny, is all." Long fingers brushed back his blond hair, pulling it off his face. "This is serious, a business transaction, and it's gotta be kept on the down low. I've paid your rent. I got you furniture to replace what that asshole friend of yours took. In return, I want you to play my girlfriend for a while."

My jaw gave way to gravity. "You're not serious."

"Why do you never believe anything I say? Anne, I am very serious."

"Why me?"

He sighed and stared at the ceiling long and hard. "I dunno, the way you helped your friend out, even if she didn't do right by you."

"Mal, that doesn't make me a good person. It makes me an idiot." Given how things had gone down it was nothing less than the cold, hard truth. "You basically said as much yourself last night. I let her use me."

Mal bared his teeth. "Hey, I never said you were an idiot and I don't want to hear you talking like that again. There's another boundary, right there."

"O-kay, relax."

"I am perfectly relaxed. Look, we've all got our

problems, Anne. I never said you were perfect." He paused, scratched his chin. "Oh, no wait. I did say that. Well, I didn't mean it exactly like . . . not that you're not great and everything but . . . yeah, let's move this on."

"No. Come on, rock star. How did you mean it?" I asked, suppressing a giggle. It was just him. I couldn't help it, the man was hilarious.

He waved away the question. "No, we've moved on. Out of interest, did it even occur to you to hit Ev up for the money you needed last night?"

I reared back in surprise. "What? No."

"She'd have given it to you. Fuck knows her and Davie have got it."

"It's not her problem."

He gave me another smug look.

"That proves nothing. And if you've chosen me for my ethics then am I really the best person to be lying to your friends and family, Mal?"

"Pumpkin . . . we're not going to be hurting anyone. We're just going to be helping each other out, that's all."

"You said I was a hopeless liar."

"You'll be fine." He waved my protests away.

I just sat there and reeled. Was this really something we could pull off?

"Trust me."

"Why do you need a pretend girlfriend?"

"Because I do."

"Mal."

He rolled his eyes, face tensing. "Because it's none of your business why, okay? I've paid up your rent. Your sweet ass will not be evicted. In return, all I ask is that you gaze adoringly at me around other people. You do that anyway; what's the big deal here?"

"So you're not going to tell me?"

"Have you had your hearing tested lately? Let's just say I have a good reason, a personal reason, and leave it at that. Honestly, you're as bad as Davie and Ev. 'What's wrong, Mal?' 'Are you okay, Mal?' Well, I was until everyone asked me a thousand fucking times." He pushed to his feet and started pacing the room. Given the length of his legs, he didn't get very far. Three steps forward, three steps back. After a couple of laps he stopped, stared out the window at the street below.

"Why does everyone insist on being heavy all the fucking time? Life's too short for all this oversharing. You're here. I'm here. We can help each other out and have a good time while we're at it. That's all that matters." He spun on his heel to face me, arms out wide. "Life's a song, Anne. Let's play."

My life hadn't been much of a song . . . at least, not up until this point.

Neither of us spoke for a moment. Expectation and impatience oozed from him. I did indeed have a bad feeling I was being played again. However, not maliciously this time. Mal didn't seem like he'd harm a fly. But he might accidentally trample one.

From the outside, it seemed a good deal. I really did need the money. I also liked being around him. He was about a bazillion times more fun than I'd ever known. Whatever happened, this was bound to be a hell of a ride. And if I knew he would leave, up front, there'd be no risk of getting overly attached. I'd just enjoy the time I had with him and then say good-bye. This could very well be fantastic.

"Alright," I said at last. "You have pulled my ass out of the fire. Thanks for that. But I'm still not completely convinced about this girlfriend plan. I guess we'll see how it goes."

He clapped his hands in glee. "You won't regret this. I won't mess with your life. Much."

"Much?"

"And you know I'm a fucking delight to have around.

People don't always get that about me. Plus, I'll open jars and lift heavy shit. I hear those are issues for women." He bounced around the room. Good god, this man had energy to spare like he snorted sugar. "So, what should we do tonight? Wanna order some food? What do you feel like?"

I slumped back in the chair, tired from just watching him. "Mal, I don't have money for that, but you go ahead."

"Would you stop worrying about money? That's why I'm here. Everything's fine. Now what do you feel like?"

"Whatever you want is great."

"That is so the correct answer. We are going to be the best fake couple ever, pumpkin."

"Please don't call me that."

"Puuuumpkin," he drawled, eyebrows waggling. "It's a great nickname. Your hair is kinda that color and we're a couple now. Couples always have dumb-ass names for each other. C'mon, you think up one for me."

"I'll get right to work on that."

"Cool. Then we'll have touching time." He rubbed his hands together. "Actually, never mind, we can do that later in bed."

My mind scrambled for purchase. "Bed? Touching time? Is that a euphemism? I thought we weren't having sex. You said we were just pretending."

"Geez, relax. We're not having sex, we're just sleeping together. The whole plan will totally collapse if we start having sex. What I need is a respectable long-term-looking relationship. We start fucking and you'll be all 'Oh Mal, I never dreamed such ecstasy was possible. I cannot live without you! Fuck me, Mal. Pleeeeease.' " His knees buckled until he fell flat onto the floor. It was an impressive performance. The man knew how to bat his eyelashes.

I giggled like a vapid schoolgirl. A noise that pretty much made me want to shoot myself on principle.

"And then everything will go all psycho Fatal Attraction. Trust me, I've seen it happen and it's not pretty. So let's keep it strictly above the belt. Get your mind out of the gutter, Anne."

"You're that good, huh?"

He leveled me with a look. "Miss Rollins, you have no idea."

"You know, I honestly can't decide if your ego is repulsive or just impressive."

"You want me to lie to you instead?"

"Mal, I can barely tell when you're being serious as it is."

He rolled onto his hands and knees, then crawled over to me, eyes full of mischief. "If I'm talking to you, I'm serious. Now, we'll have to kiss in public, obviously. And what if we're out to dinner and I stick my tongue in your ear and you get all weirded out? People might start to wonder. So we need to practice the touching thing."

"Your tongue? Really? I don't know . . ."

"Lucky for you, I'm here and I do." He stood and picked up a cell phone, his finger flicking over the screen. "We need to make sure we look tight. Lauren's been over fucking constantly. We can't risk separate bedrooms. Do you know she doesn't even knock, just bursts on in like she owns the place? Some people, no manners."

I was too overwhelmed to point out the irony in that statement.

"Yes, but we could lock the door," I suggested, growing slightly palm-sweaty desperate again. Though, to be honest, I'd never really stopped.

Me sleeping with Mal? No. Not a good idea. Him bouncing around my apartment half naked was enough. Touching in the dark would do me in for sure. I'd attack him despite my best intentions. Given we'd be living together for the foreseeable future, pushing for more would be a freaking disaster.

"We can't just lock the door," he said. "Lauren went and got another key made. You need better security, pumpkin."

"Very true."

"Hey, you don't snore do you?"

I gave him my very best withering glare.

"Just asking." He backed away, still playing with his phone. "And I'll make sure I keep any hookups on the down low, okay? I won't embarrass you with any of that."

"Thanks." I shouldn't have been surprised. But I was. Stupid, stupid me. "Were you just setting this up last night? Was that what it was all about?"

"Well, yeah."

I opened my eyes wide. Painfully wide. I took a deep breath in through my nose. It didn't matter really. My pride had taken a hit, but I had a roof over my head for the foreseeable future. Time to suck it up.

This sleeping-together thing wouldn't work. It couldn't. The fact that I was buzzing with tension just from the thought of it confirmed as much. But me playing his girlfriend part? I owed it to him to try. It could even be fun. Serious fun. And god knew I was overdue for some of that in my life.

I sat up straight, took a deep breath. "Okay, I'm agreeing to everything but the touching time."

He opened his mouth to protest but I plowed on before he could get a word out. "And tomorrow we put a sliding lock on the door to keep Lauren out and you start sleeping in the spare room. These are my conditions."

"Look at you, all assertive. I like it. Though really, I'd prefer it if you thought of me as being beyond boundaries."

"I'm serious, Mal. Take it or leave it. I just got out of one clusterfuck of a roommate situation. I won't fall straight into another."

Mal crossed his arms and looked down the length of his nose at me. At first, I thought he would argue. Some evil subversive part of me might have even hoped he would, at least on the sleeping front. But he didn't.

"Very well, I accept your terms. Tell you what," he said slowly. "Why don't I hit the couch tonight?"

My shoulders dropped in what was most likely relief. "That would be great. Thanks."

"No problem." He gave me a vaguely amused look. "Whatever works for you, Anne."

"Great. I'm going to go have a bath."

"Have fun."

"Yeah."

The bathroom door was locked shut behind me in record time. I sat on the edge of the big old battered clawfoot tub, blood rushing loud behind my ears. My mind was a blur. I'd just talked my way out of sleeping with a rock star. What had I done?

Disappointment made my insides ache.

But this was the right move. I needed to remember how into Reece I was. He was a far safer crush option. One day, he and I had a chance of actually working out.

Once all of the noise in my head faded, I looked at myself in the mirror. My hair hung flat around my face. My eyes were wide and wild. Within the space of twenty-four hours I'd been turned upside down. I might not be sleeping with one, but I most certainly now lived with a rock star. Didn't see that one coming.

"What the hell have you gotten yourself into?" I asked the girl in the mirror.

She had nothing but a dazed, surprised smile to offer. Clearly she was a sucker for Mal's particular brand of crazy. Thank goodness I was more mature.

I pulled my work T-shirt off over my head and started in on the laces of my boots. The sudden banging on the door almost made me fall off my perch. I put a hand to the floor and pushed myself upright before I fell face forward.

"Anne?"

"Yeah?" I sat back up and crossed my arms over my

black bra, covering things up even though he couldn't possibly see.

"I forgot to say thanks. For letting me live here with you and agreeing to be my girlfriend. I really appreciate it."

"Well, thank you for paying my rent and for the furniture and everything."

"That was nothing. I would've done that anyway. Didn't like seeing you sad last night."

"Really?" My throat tightened and I stared at the door, amazed. That was huge. I really didn't know what to say. He barely knew me and yet he would have come to my rescue? Mal Ericson might be a bad boy, but he was also a good man.

One that I liked very much.

"Yeah. 'Course. It's going to be fun, Anne," he said, his voice close to the door. "You wait and see."

"Okay."

He sounded like he needed me to believe him. Funny thing was, I did.

CHAPTER SIX

I started getting Mal's texts just before lunch.

Mal: Awake
Anne: Morning

Mal: Going for a run with Jim
Anne: Have fun!

Mal: Back from run having lunch
Anne: K

Mal: Where's cleaning stuff?
Anne: To clean what?
Mal: Pizza exploded in microwave
Anne: Spray bottle under sink

Mal: When you home?
Anne: 5:30
Mal: Bored
Anne: Sorry
Mal: What you doing?
Anne: Working right now. Gotta go. Talk later.

Mal: Your taste in music sucks

Anne: Thanks

Mal: Seriously, we need to talk it's that bad.
Everything apart from Stage Dive needs to go.

Anne: Wait. What are you doing?

Mal: Fixing it

Anne: Mal, WTH are you doing?

Mal: Making you new playlists with decent shit.
Relax

Anne: K Thanks

Mal: Bored again

Mal: Ben's coming over to play Halo

Anne: Great! But you don't have to tell me
everything you do, Mal.

Mal: Davie says communication's important

Mal: When are you on the rag? Davie said to find
out if you want cupcakes or ice cream

Anne: I want to not talk about this ever

Mal: Bored. Ben's late

Mal: Let's get a dog

Anne: Apartment has no pets rule

Mal: Nice green lace bra

Anne: Get out of my drawers, Mal.

Mal: Matching panties?

Anne: GET OUT NOW.

Mal: :)

Mal: Sext me

Mal: Come on it'll be funny

Mal: Plz?

> Mal: High level of unhealthy codependency traits exhibited by both parties relationship possibly bordering on toxic
>
> Anne: WTF?
>
> Mal: Did magazine quiz. We need help. Especially you
>
> Anne: . . .
>
> Mal: Booking us couples counseling. Tues 4:15 alright?
>
> Anne: We are not going to counseling.
>
> Mal: What's wrong? Don't you love me anymore?
>
> Anne: Turning phone off now.

"Problem?" asked Reece, moseying on up and looking over my shoulder.

"No. Sorry." I shoved my cell into my back pocket. "I'm working, I swear."

"Sure you are." He winked. Being friends with the boss did pay off sometimes. "Do anything interesting last night?"

Had I ever. Mal seemed hell-bent on driving me crazy today, but last night had been fantastic. We'd had a floor picnic with some of the best tapas I'd tasted in a long time, washed down with Spanish beer. He'd told me hilarious stories about big-name musicians. Lots of tawdry sexploits and insane backstage demands, Mal knew about them all. He made for awesome company.

I wasn't ready to explain Mal to Reece, however. Looking at Reece, I might never be ready. Where would I begin? Even if I could keep a straight face, he knew me well enough to know I didn't jump into relationships. Not in this way. Luckily, Reece's attention had already slipped away. I shouldn't have worried. His gaze rested on a young woman browsing in the True Crime section. You'd have thought he'd have enough sense to turn away when she picked up a book on female serial killers, but no.

"I didn't get up to anything much last night," I lied, feeling zero guilt.

He did a half nod, probably not even listening. "I'll just go see if she needs help."

"Okeydokey." I pulled my cell out, switched it back on. As soon as the screen flashed to life I started one finger typing, a smile already on my face.

Anne: Ben arrive yet?
Mal: He's here. How you doing? Home soon?
Anne: Soon.

Ben was lazed on the love seat, hands busy on the game controls, when I walked in the door. There was lots of blood and guts happening on the TV screen. The novelty of walking in to find famous people hanging in my apartment would probably never fade. I sincerely hoped it wouldn't. Disappointingly, Mal was nowhere in sight. I'd been rushing through tasks, eager to see him all afternoon. Lizzy had called me and it'd almost killed me not telling her about him. But I honestly didn't know how to plausibly explain his sudden appearance in my life. She'd been furious about the shit with Skye. I hadn't been able to muster much anger about it, funnily enough. Good things were happening. That was all in the past.

Now I was finally home, my heart banging around inside my chest, and I felt inexcusably shy. Hesitant almost. Forget it, this was my apartment. My home. And he had chosen to live here, with me, for whatever reason. Back straight and boobs out, what little there was of them.

"Hey, Anne," he said.

"Hi, Ben. Is Mal around?" My ability to play it cool was improving. I hardly stuttered at all.

"In the kitchen."

"Thanks." I dashed past him, trying not to mess with his on-screen killing spree.

Mal was staring out the small kitchen window, his cell to his ear. "What aren't you telling me?"

A pause.

"Yeah, okay. What'd he say?"

Another pause.

"No. Just lay it out for me. C'mon."

The break was longer this time. After a while, he grabbed hold of the edge of the counter, gripping it so hard his knuckles turned white. Obviously, this was a private moment, but I couldn't walk away. The pain in his voice and the lines of his body were acute. He was hurting.

"That can't be right. What about if we—"

He listened in silence. Back out in the living room, the boom of explosions and the rattle of gunfire continued on.

"Okay. Thanks for letting me know." He pressed end on the call and threw his cell aside. Both hands now gripped the edge of the counter, squeezing so hard it creaked.

"Mal?"

The whites of his eyes were huge, rimmed with red. What the hell was going on?

"Anne. Hey. Didn't hear you come in."

"Are you okay?"

He breathed in hard, shook his head. "Yeah! Slept like shit. Then the run with Jimmy wore me out. But all good. Aren't you cute, worrying about me? That's very girl-friendish."

"Ha." I smiled. He didn't smile back.

"Let's, ah . . . You say hi to Ben already?"

"Yes, I did."

His hands grasped my shoulders, turning me and marching me back out into the living room. "You really need to greet your guests properly, pumpkin. You don't want him thinking you're rude."

"Mal, I—"

"Ben. Look, my awesome girlfriend came home."

"Hi, Mal's awesome girlfriend." Ben didn't take his eyes off the screen. "This place is a bit smaller than your L.A. pad, dude. You gonna stay here or buy bigger?"

"Anne's been talking about getting a dog, so I'm thinking we'll trade up eventually."

Ben nodded.

I didn't bother to correct Mal. Really the best way to handle him was to simply roll with it. Plus, this current mood of his concerned me.

"Time to beat drums," Mal announced, rubbing his hands together, then shaking his arms. He still wasn't smiling. The manic energy was clearly back despite his claim of being tired.

This time, Ben did take his eyes off the screen. "Thought we were getting dinner and hanging out with Miss Awesome here."

"Need to burn off some energy. Anne understands, don't you, pumpkin?"

I pushed my disappointment aside and nodded. A man had to do what a man had to do. I just wish I knew what was going on. Whatever the phone call had been about, it wasn't good news. It also wasn't my business, I know.

"She's very supportive of my career. Always has been. In many ways, she is my inspiration."

"You only met her two days ago." Ben turned off the game, throwing the control aside.

"And I've done some of my best work in that time."

"Whatever. So that's what you wanna do, go play some music?" Eyes narrowed, Ben watched Mal bopping up and down beside me.

"That's what I said. Keep up, Benny boy." He curled his hands into fists. "Let's go."

"'Kay." Ben's sharp gaze turned to me like he expected

me to have answers. I shrugged. As he'd pointed out, I'd only known Mal for forty-eight hours.

No, I didn't know what was going on with him, but damned if I wasn't going to find out.

CHAPTER SEVEN

Someone was yelling. A male someone. Then another voice joined in, the noise carrying through my bedroom wall. I bolted upright, bewildered but wide awake. Five-fifteen glowed green on the little alarm clock beside my bed.

Damn, it was early.

Due to Mal's nocturnal habits, I hadn't gotten the best night's sleep. When he'd eventually returned just after eleven, he'd been dripping with sweat. I'd crashed earlier in the evening and had been half asleep, dragging my sorry ass out to check if he needed anything. He'd said he'd be crashing soon, so I'd gone back to bed. But for hours I'd lain there, listening to him moving around the apartment. He'd watched TV, talked on the phone, and hummed for hours. Actually, I didn't mind the humming. It was kind of nice. Though humming death metal was more of an art form than you'd imagine. I'd finally fallen asleep to something by Metallica. Good lord, had my dreams been weird.

But why couldn't Mal sleep?

The shouting escalated. I crawled off my bed and bolted for the door, flannel pajamas, bed hair, and all. Out in the living room, Mal's back was to me, barring the front door.

He wore only a pair of black boxer briefs. Not that I was complaining because good god, the man's ass. I almost lost my tongue. To the floor or my throat, I'm not sure which. Both were strong contenders.

"Even if you are a friend of pumpkin's this is not a suitable hour to visit," Mal hissed.

"Who the fuck are you and why are you calling Anne *pumpkin*?" That was Reece and he sounded distinctly enraged. Like, rampaging enraged.

My boss and I weren't an item, though. We were just friends. So a semi-naked man answering my door at odd hours of the morning was actually none of his damn business.

"Morning," I said, standing tall.

Mal gave me a brief cranky look over his shoulder. As nice as the couch was, I'd probably be in a bad mood if I'd slept on it too. Maybe that was why he'd stayed up so late. He'd ordered another bed for the spare room, but for some reason it had yet to arrive. Tonight, I'd ask if he wanted to share with me. Just as friends.

His shoulders were distractingly large with his hands on his hips. I was no lightweight, but if he was willing to stand with his arms out, I'd give climbing him a try. Years back, before all the shit with mom, I'd been different, braver. Something about Mal reminded me of the adrenaline-junkie tomboy I'd been. I missed that girl. She'd been fun.

"You woke her, asswipe." For once, Mal didn't sound the least bit light and easy as he gave Reece hell. "Do you have any idea how stressful shit's been for her lately? Plus she had to work late last night."

And as relaxed as Reece was about work, that comment was not good. "Mal, it's okay. This is my friend and *my boss*, Reece."

"Reece?" He sneered. "This is who you were talking to on your phone at the party?"

"Yes."

"Huh. Figured it was a chick."

"Guess again." Reece pushed his way past the mostly naked drummer to shove a box of donuts into my arms. Voodoo Donuts. My saliva glands kicked into overdrive despite the early hour and manly standoff.

To be fair, partly also because of it, yes.

"What the fuck is going on, A? Who is this asshole?"

"Reece, not cool."

His bloodshot eyes blazed angrily, his dark hair sticking out. The scent of stale perfume lingered around him like a miasma. I'd also question his sobriety because his movements seemed a bit off. Here was a man who had not yet been to bed.

At least, not his own bed.

"A?" asked Mal, crossing his arms over his chest. He turned and winked at me. "You call her 'A'? What, saying her whole name's too much of a commitment for you?"

I barked out a laugh. Then attempted to turn it into a cough. Reece didn't look convinced, but I didn't care. Relief made me weak in the knees. My Mal was back, cracking jokes and smiling. A real smile this time, not the harsh manic parody from the night before.

It was amazing. I could actually see Reece's hackles rising. Mal might have had a good half a head on him, but violence was not out of the question. Meanwhile, Mal just looked amused. The depth to which he didn't give a fuck was actually a large part of his charm. I'd never met anyone like him.

Not to say he wouldn't throw down with Reece. I had no doubt the man could handle himself.

"Why don't I make coffee?" I took a hesitant step toward the tiny kitchen, hoping someone would follow. Either one of them would do. Neither made a move so I stayed put.

Reece's brows drew tight together. "Even for a hookup you can do a hell of a lot better."

"What?" Not only was it an extraordinarily rude thing to say, it wasn't even remotely true.

"You heard me."

"Shit, Reece, how can you even . . ." I stared at Mal, frowned, and cocked my head. So much skin. I looked and looked until I hit the dusting of dark blond hair leading down from his belly button, heading straight for No-Anne Land. He had a treasure trail. A map to hidden delights. The donut box trembled in my hands.

I could and should avert my eyes. But I didn't.

"Anne?" Reece demanded angrily, dragging me out of my porny daydreams.

"Um . . ." Yes, such was my genius statement.

"There's the crazy eyes," said Mal in a low, rough voice. "Looks like my pumpkin is ready for round six of the sexin'."

Oh. Crap. He didn't.

Reece's forehead furrowed, his fingers curling into fists.

Alright, so he did.

I crushed the box of donuts against my chest. "That's a really sweet offer, Mal."

"Pumpkin, if you're still walking straight, my work here is clearly not done. Hell, we haven't even gotten around to breaking in the new couch yet." He turned to Reece, enjoying himself way too much if the light in his eyes was any indicator. "She's worried we'd stain the material. Like I wouldn't just buy her another, right? Women."

No answer from Reece apart from the white lines around his mouth.

Mal exhaled hard. "Next time let's stick to leather. Wipe clean is so much easier and it won't chafe your soft skin nearly as much as you think, Anne. Not if we—"

"Enough," I barked, feeling the cardboard box cave in.

"Too much sex talk in front of friends?"

I nodded.

"Sorry," said Mal. "Real sorry. My bad."

So much hostility in such a confined space. And there was no question, Reece was genuinely jealous. He was all puffed up and radiating fury. His gaze shifted between Mal and me, mouth fierce.

You have to understand, before now, I hadn't been entirely certain Reece even realized I was female. Yet here he was, edging toward me as if I was territory to be protected. Something Mal didn't intend to allow if his side-stepping maneuver meant anything. It was like some strange animalistic caveman dance, the two of them slowly hemming me in. Amusing in a way.

The first male to pee on me, however, would pay with his balls.

"Thinks I'm a hook-up," scoffed Mal with a side look. "Set him straight, pumpkin."

At those words, Reece's nostrils flared. I stood, pinned to the spot. My heart beat so hard, I'm certain ribs were bruised in the process. Wild bed hair or not, this moment was glorious. I wanted it up on YouTube for all time. (Okay, maybe I didn't want it on YouTube. But you get what I mean.)

I cleared my throat and steeled my spine. Today, I stood about ten times taller. "Reece, Mal and I are seeing each other."

"We're living together," Mal corrected.

"Right. That too. I've been meaning to tell you. Mal and I are living very happily together since the day before yesterday."

"Mal?" My boss froze. "Mal Ericson, the drummer?"

"Yep."

Reece's reddened eyes blazed even brighter. Nothing more was said.

"Now that we've got that straightened out, I'm gonna hit the shower," Mal announced. "Give you two kids a chance to talk."

"Thanks," I said.

"No problem." His hand smacked into my ass, making me jump. Then, fingers lazily scratching at stubble, he sauntered into the bathroom. My butt cheek stung. I made a mental note to kill him later, once we were alone. Kill him or screw him, whatevs. My hormones were so confused.

The second the door clicked shut Reece grabbed my arm and hustled me into the tiny kitchen. Dawn had yet to make an appearance. Light from the living room shone weakly on his surly face. His black-rimmed glasses were askew, adding to his whole thoroughly ruffled appearance. I probably should've been jealous. But for once I actually wasn't.

"What the hell is this, Anne? You said you met him, that's all. Fuck, I thought he looked familiar . . ."

"It came as something of a surprise to me as well. But it's great, right?" The boy had bed head and it wasn't from sleeping. No way was he coming into my home and giving me shit over finding me similarly (allegedly) occupied.

"Great," he replied flatly.

"He's a really nice guy when you get to know him."

"Sure."

"He makes me smile, you know? Doesn't take me for granted," I said, going in for the kill. So I had some early morning bloodlust going on. It wasn't like he didn't deserve it for being rude to Mal. I might not like most of the women he had hanging around at various times, but I sure as hell never insulted them. "And I'd appreciate it if you didn't talk to him like that again."

Reece's mouth fell open. "Anne, the way he spoke to me—"

"You're going to go with he started it? Seriously? You don't knock on my door at this hour and call the person that answers it an asshole, Reece. That's not cool."

"Sorry." He gave my battered old fridge a foul look.

"What's happening here? You've never cared about me dating before. Not that I've done much of it recently."

"Nothing. I just wasn't expecting . . ."

I waited, but he didn't finish the sentence. Maybe the subject was best left alone. "Would you like some coffee?"

"No, I'm heading home."

"Okay. Well, thanks for the donuts." I sat the broken box on the counter.

"No problem." He just stared at me, his eyes a mixture of mad and sad. I didn't really know what to do with that. Anger still gripped me.

"Reece . . ."

"It's fine."

"I don't want this affecting our friendship."

His shoulders pushed back. "No. Of course it won't."

"Good." I don't know what came over me, but I had to hug him. He was feeling down, I wanted to fix it. Mom had never been into the touchy-feely stuff and I'd inherited the talent, or lack of one. Accordingly, my arms were stiff, awkward. I patted him once on the back and then got the hell out of there before he could react. A surprise attack, if you will.

"How did your date go last night?" I asked.

"It was nothing special. What were you up to?"

"Mal ordered dinner. Just a quiet night in." As soon as I mentioned Mal's name, Reece's face turned grumpy. It'd have been easier to empathize with him if he hadn't reeked of sex and behaved like an entitled jerk.

"I'm going to go," he said. "I'll see you later."

"Later."

I was still standing there staring after him long after

the front door slammed shut. Deep down inside, I was neither angry nor sad. Just a little shocked perhaps to find Reece cared about me in that way after all. How it would affect things, I had no idea.

When Mal reemerged it was with his long hair slicked back. The blond was much darker when wet and the angles of his face were displayed to perfection. He'd put on a pair of jeans and a soft-looking, worn old AC/DC T-shirt. But his feet were bare. His long toes were lightly dusted with hairs. Neat, square nails.

"Coffee?" I asked, already pouring him a cup. It gave me a solid excuse to look away from his apparently fascinating toes. What was it about bare feet?

"Yeah, thanks. Your little hipster friend gone already?"

I set his cup on the counter and he started piling in sugar from the canister. One, two, three heaping spoonfuls. All his energy had to come from somewhere, I guess.

"Reece left a while back," I confirmed, picking through the chunks of donut. Delicious.

"Hard not to think less of you there."

"Why?"

Mal took a sip of coffee, eyeing me over the rim. "You like the douche. You like him a lot."

I filled my mouth with food. Such a great excuse for not answering. If I chewed really slowly it could kill the entire conversation.

"Even with you giving me crazy eyes, I could tell," he unfortunately continued. "You're just lucky I'm not the jealous type."

I choked down the mother load of food in my mouth. "Is that why you started up with the sex adventure stories?"

He laughed, low and mocking. But who he was laughing at exactly, I couldn't tell.

"Mal?"

"He shows up here, fresh from a night out drinking and

fucking, fully expecting to find you waiting with open arms . . . I didn't like it."

"We're just friends."

He looked away, licked his lips. "Anne."

The disappointment in his voice stung. I wanted to make excuses. Roll out the old standards. I wanted to protect myself. But I didn't even know what I was protecting myself from. Mal hadn't attacked me. His quiet reproof slipped past my guard in a way Lauren's lectures and demands never could.

"Thing is, you're both straight," he said. "Men and women as friends doesn't really work. One person's always into the other. Fact of life."

"Yes, I like him," I admitted. "I have for a while now. He, ah . . . he doesn't see me that way."

"Maybe. Maybe not. He sure as fuck didn't like finding me here." Mal set down his cup and leaned against the corner of the faded gray kitchen counter, arms braced on either side. His damp hair slid forward, shielding his face. "Were you planning on using me to make him jealous?"

"Manipulating him and being an asshat to you? No, I hadn't planned on doing that. But thank you for asking."

"No skin off my nose." He shrugged. "And he's a douche who deserves what he gets. Turning up here, acting like you owe him something."

I wrapped my arms around myself. "I'm sorry he was rude to you. I had a word with him. That won't happen again."

He snorted out a laugh. "You don't have to protect me, Anne. I'm not that delicate."

"Beside the point." I took a sip of coffee.

"You know, I can live with you using me to get at him. Hell, we're already using each other, right?"

Something in the way he said it stopped me. If only he wasn't hiding behind his hair, I could see him better, gauge where this was going.

"No reason why we can't milk this baby for all it's worth," he said.

"You'd do that for me?"

He half smiled. "If that's what you want. Pushing asswipe's buttons is too easy but I'm willing to make the effort. Hell, this body was born to make mortal men jealous."

I smiled back at him, cautiously. Not committing to anything. This situation called for serious thought. The temptation to leap was huge.

"I do think he's right about one thing. You can do better." Green eyes stared me down. There was amusement there, as always. He seemed to be daring me, pushing me to see what happened. I really wanted to push back.

"But whatever," he said, rolling his shoulders back in some sort of overdeveloped shrug. "Your call. After all, you've known this guy for how long?"

"Two years."

"Two years you've been into him and never done a thing about it? You must have your reasons, right?"

"Right," I said, sounding not the least bit believable.

He laughed and right then, I disliked him just a little. I'd never openly admitted my thing for Reece to anyone and here was Mal, ever so sweetly rubbing my face in it. Problem was, the status quo with Reece was infinitely preferable to anything I'd had since I was sixteen. If he settled down with someone else, my heart wouldn't be broken. But who knew, we might get together one day.

Why act when doing so little was serving me so well?

The big blond guy mocked me with his eyes, smirk in place. He knew. I don't know how he knew, but he definitely did. Man, I hated being a foregone conclusion, especially to him. Hated it with the passion of a thousand fiery hells.

"Alright," I said. "Let's do it."

He stopped laughing.

"I'm serious. I want to make Reece jealous. If you're still willing to help me, of course."

"Said I would not a minute ago. Didn't think you'd actually go for it, but . . ." He picked up his cup of coffee and drained it. "This should be interesting. Exactly how much do you know about being a heartbreaker?"

"I need to be a heartbreaker?" Across the other side of the living room, the bathroom door stood wide open. A wet towel sat forgotten in the middle of the floor. Mal's boxer briefs lay abandoned alongside.

I needed to do some cleaning today.

"Problem?" he asked.

"No."

Funny, when Skye had lived here, I'd usually wound up doing the bulk of the tidying for her too. It hadn't occurred to me at the time. A leftover habit from running a household early, most likely.

"What is it, Anne?"

"Your towel and dirty clothes are on the bathroom floor." I pointed to them, just in case he'd forgotten where the bathroom was.

"Random change of topic." Mal sidled up next to me, standing closer than he needed to. "But you're right. They are indeed decorating the floor and doing a lovely job too."

He said no more.

The dirty laundry lay there, taunting me. And I'm pretty sure that Mal in his silence did the same. Either that or I was a neurotic mess. It was a close call.

"Whatcha gonna do about it, pumpkin?" he asked in a quiet voice.

"I really don't like you calling me that."

He made a dismissive noise in his throat.

I sighed. This was one war I'd likely never win. If taking over the care of a thirteen-year-old had taught me anything, it was to pick my battles.

"That's not my problem," I said.

"No?"

"You need to tidy up after yourself," I said firmly.

"That a boundary I'm hearing there?"

I stood taller. "Yes, it is. I'm not your mommy. You need to pick up your shit, Mal."

He grinned. "I'll get right on that."

"Thanks." I smiled back at him, feeling lighter already. "What was that about being a heartbreaker?"

"You're going to smash me in two, after showing the jerkwad what a momentous girlfriend you make, of course."

I'd only ever been on the receiving end of heartbreak. But fuck that too. Bad habits could be broken. "I can do that."

Mal looked away.

"I can."

"Not doubting you, pumpkin. Not doubting you at all."

CHAPTER EIGHT

Lauren barged in a bit before six in the evening. Or she tried to. The door rattled. Next came the swearing and banging.

"Anne! What's wrong with your door?"

I undid the new sliding bolt and she thundered into the room.

"Your door's broken," she said, her brow creased.

"No, Mal had a new lock put on it. He was worried about security."

A bald, muscular man had appeared after Mal disappeared off to band practice. Apparently, rock stars outsourced household chores to the head of their security team. This guy had the new sliding bolt installed in no time. He was eerily efficient and uberpolite. The whole experience had weirded me out a little.

"Hey, wow. You look great." I said, taking in her slick dress and hairdo. A beautiful white orchid sat behind her ear. "What are you all dressed up for? Where are you off to?"

"What, this old thing?" She smoothed a hand over the slinky caramel-colored silk dress. "Thanks. And can I just take a moment to say, awesome job landing Malcolm Ericson. He probably doesn't deserve you, but go you."

"Uh, thanks."

"When he told me the story, I couldn't believe it. Love at first sight. That's beautiful." Shit, her eyes actually misted up. "I think you'll be wonderful together. And why aren't you dressed, by the way?"

"Huh?"

Right then, Mal strode out of the second bedroom in a black three-piece suit. Since when had wearing a vest looked so fucking hot? My lungs shrunk a size. Either that or the oxygen in the room had been mixed wrong. He was beyond slick with his hair tucked back behind his ears, the angular line of his jaw perfectly smooth. I'd barely gotten used to him half naked and now he was throwing Armani at me. I never stood a chance. Prostrating myself at his feet was the obvious reaction to such a heavenly sight. How I managed to remain upright I have no idea.

Forget Bond and his ilk. I'd take a drummer in a suit any day of the week.

With a low wolf whistle, Lauren looked him over. "Malcolm. Who's a pretty boy?"

"Only pumpkin is allowed to objectify me," he said, straightening his cuffs. French cuffs with cufflinks.

"Fuck me," I muttered, then smacked a hand over my mouth because crap, my mouth. It was an idiot determined to make an ass out of me.

"Anytime." He winked. The liar.

"Your pumpkin needs to get ready," said Lauren, ignoring our carrying on.

He looked me over and frowned. "Anne, Davie wants everyone dressed up. You can't go in jeans and a T-shirt."

"What are you talking about?"

"The party. Pumpkin, c'mon. We don't have time to mess around."

I shook my head, clueless. "Okay, you two. I have no idea what you're talking about. Will someone please clue me in?"

"I told you about this."

"Like you told me about you moving in here?"

"You didn't tell her you were moving in with her?" asked Lauren, voice low and deadly.

"It was a surprise," he said, recovering quickly. "A great big beautiful romantic gesture because I knew how much my Anne wanted me with her. She was just too shy to say so. Look at her! The woman practically worships the ground I walk on. And you heard her, demanding I sexually service her at all hours of the day. I can't do that shit from afar, you know?"

Lauren raised a brow. "You told me she okayed it and had forgotten to give you a key, Mal."

"Which was basically the truth." He threw his hands out wide. "C'mon, ladies, we don't have time for this."

"Anne, I'm so sorry," said Lauren.

"It's fine. I'm happy he's here." And though a tempting idea, throwing something at him right now wouldn't actually help. I took a deep breath and tried to keep calm. "Let's get back to the 'What the hell is going on here' question. We're meant to go to something formal tonight, I take it?"

"I told you." He pulled out his phone, flicked through a few screens then shoved it in front of my face. "I'm a fucking great boyfriend, see?"

The message on screen read: *AMEX ON TABLE. DRESS UP TONIGHT.* My name, however, was nowhere in sight. Sure enough, over on the dining room table a black credit card sat waiting. I'd figured he'd just forgotten the thing. Him leaving it for me to go on a spending spree had never crossed my mind.

"It says you sent this to someone called Angie," I said tightly. "Not me, Mal."

"I did?" He glared at the phone. "Shit. Sorry."

"Who's Angie?" asked Lauren.

"Fucked if I know, but apparently she's still looking for

the card." He laughed. "As if I'd give it to just anyone. Right, sorry. Anyway, Anne, can you throw something on? We gotta go."

"Where?"

"Out."

I scowled at him and didn't move an inch. "Try again."

"It's a thing at David and Ev's, a wedding anniversary party. Not that it's even been a year, but whatever. Davie put lots of effort into it and asked us all to dress up. I'm sorry I screwed up telling you." He fell to his knees, hands clasped to his chest. "Please? I'm sorry. I'm really fucking sorry. See, look, I'm on my knees, Anne. I'm groveling just for you."

"Okay. I'll go. Next time, please make sure I get the message."

"I will. Thank you. Thank you so much," he gushed. "You're the best, pumpkin."

There was only one really good dress in my wardrobe. A vintage black lace dress from the fifties. I'd bought it for my twenty-first birthday two years ago. I liked to believe I'd just stepped off the set of *Mad Men* in it. Luckily, my hair wasn't looking too bad hanging loose. Some concealer, mascara, and lip gloss were about as primed as I could get in less than five minutes. One of these days I'd have time to go all out getting ready to meet the members of Stage Dive. Just not today.

Out in the living room, the pair of them bickered.

"I can't believe you accidentally messaged some stray instead of your girlfriend," said Lauren.

"Does my girlfriend seem bothered? No. So remind me again, what business is it of yours, hmm?"

"If you hurt her, Ev and I are going to take turns disemboweling you with a shovel. Be warned."

A gruesome mental image, but I had to smile. It felt good to have friends watching my back.

Mal scoffed. "You can't disembowel someone with a shovel."

"Sure you can. It's just messier."

He grunted.

"Anyway, why are you in the spare bedroom? She sick of you already?"

"Gotta put my shit somewhere, Anne's closet is packed. You girls, no idea about sharing."

I shut the bedroom door and started shrugging out of my jeans, pulling off my shirt. Next came the panties. The neckline on the dress was wide and strapless bras always dug into my sides. There were few torture devices more horrible than a strapless bra. It wasn't like my breasts were big. The girl in the mirror looked good and happily, the dress still fit just fine. No way could I do up the zipper on the back however. I slid my feet into my super-high black heels saved for special occasions and headed on out, trying to hold my dress together.

"Lauren, would you mind—"

"That's my job now." Mal smiled and stepped behind me. "Cool dress. Classy."

"Thanks."

Mal leaned in closer, his breath warming my neck as he slowly did up the back. I immediately broke out into goose bumps.

"I never noticed how long your neck is. It's very nice."

"Mm."

"And you have sweet little ears."

"Um, thanks."

"No bra?" he asked, his voice casual.

"No. With this dress, I can't . . . We don't actually need to discuss this right now."

The tips of his fingers trailed up my spine, ahead of the zipper. I got shivery, the English language leaving my mind.

"That's going to be a hell of a distraction, pumpkin," he breathed. "Trying to look down the front of your dress all night."

The look he gave me made me quiver in strange places. This was the problem; my inability to tell if he was serious or not. The whole scene was about establishing ourselves as a couple for Lauren's benefit, right? It just didn't feel like it for some reason. It felt personal. With Mal touching me, I kind of forgot Lauren was even in the room. She was, however, most definitely present.

Lauren groaned, loudly. "Oh good god, my ears are bleeding."

He made me feverish without even trying. I needed to guard my reactions and keep it together. It was the only way this would work.

"Thank you," I said, as my dress finished tightening around my chest and settled into place.

"My pleasure."

I expected him to move back. He didn't. If anything, he got closer. The warm male scent of him, the iron-hard feel, all of it got closer and closer. I tried to bend away from him in an effort to preserve what remained of my sanity, but he just followed. Overwhelming didn't cover it.

"Guys." Lauren was tapping her foot. "Whatever you're doing, stop it."

"Ignore her. She's just jealous of our love." Mal's arm came around my middle, holding me to him. The press of his hardening cock against my rear could not be mistaken. I know we were supposed to be playing the couple, but was rubbing his penis against me really necessary? Me liking it was beside the point. Don't even go there.

"Yes, Malcolm, I'm jealous of your love. That's it." Lauren shook her head slowly. "Come on, let's get moving. Nate will be waiting and he doesn't wait well."

"We better go," I said.

"Yeah." His voice was soft and dreamy, and spoke of good, hard times in bed. Then he shook his head, gave me his usual grin. "Pumpkin, stop rubbing your ass against me. We gotta go! I don't have time to do you now. Prioritize, woman."

Sometimes the temptation to hit him was so huge.

Twice the crowd had gathered at David and Ev's condo tonight. They varied in age from young teens to elderly, from conservative to edgy. All of them primped to perfection. Every inch of David and Ev's condo had been decorated, also. White candles of every size sat in clusters around the room. Vases filled with bright bouquets were on every available flat surface. The ring of fine crystal and the popping of champagne corks battled classic rock for supremacy. Tonight's vibe leaned heavily toward the romantic.

There was a buzz in the air, one of expectation. It was exciting.

Mal kept a tight hold on my hand, his big, warm fingers encasing mine. I took my cues from him, staying close to his side. Whenever some sexy siren tried to approach him he basically shoved me at them with a "Meet my girlfriend, Anne." I'd almost tripped the first few times he'd used me as a human shield, but I was getting the hang of it now. With the last one I'd just held up a hand and said "He's with me." She'd taken it with relatively good grace.

"I thought that one was going to hit me," I said, watching the disappointed girl stalk off into the crowd. "Being your girlfriend is dangerous."

"What can I say? I'm a magnificent specimen of manhood. Of course they all want me. But I do appreciate you protecting my honor."

"I should hope so." I smiled.

"Come and meet Jimmy. This'll give you a thrill." He

wound his way through the crowd, drawing me along behind him. "'Scuse us. Move please. Move."

Jimmy Ferris stood beside the mantel like a painter had
positioned him there. The man was living art. Dark hair
brushed back, blue eyes bright. He was a lot like his brother,
David, long and lean, but smoother and harder. More
intense if it was possible. Maybe meeting Ev had chilled
David out. Jimmy certainly lacked the lost-in-love eyes.

The dark looks he gave the woman at his side were far
less than friendly. She kept her nose high in the air and ignored him. I'm not sure I could have maintained her pose
of complete indifference so well. Jimmy Ferris had a lot of
presence. There'd been all sorts of rumors going around
about what he'd been up to since rehab. Given the size of
him, I'd say lifting weights featured heavily. Ben was a big
guy in general, heading on into lumberjack territory. But
Jimmy appeared to have been working at it, hard.

"Jimbo," said Mal, making room for me beside him.
"This is my girlfriend, Anne. Anne, this is Jim."

Yep, Jimmy gave me the same chin tip as the others. It
was a secret handshake. So I gave him one back. He
smiled, but only just. It was a fleeting thing.

Mal leaned down in front of me, getting in my face.
"Nope. No crazy eyes. Your theory is bullshit, pumpkin.
They're only for me."

"It's lovely to meet you, Jimmy," I said, pushing my
pretend partner out of the way.

"She still doing the eyes thing?" asked Jimmy.

Rock stars gossiped. There you go.

"Lust has no expiration date, Jimbo. And hello, Lena.
You look very nice." Mal offered his free hand to the
woman at Jimmy's side. The arctic chill of her manner
turned equatorial in an instant. How strange.

"Mal. How are you?" The woman gave his fingers
a brief squeeze, before offering her hand to me to shake.

Brown hair fell past her shoulders and funky red plastic-rimmed glasses sat on her nose. "And this must be Anne. Great to meet you. Mal's told me so much about you."

"He has?" I shook her hand, returning her smile.

"At band practice today, you were all he could talk about," she said.

"She's the love of my life," sighed Mal, throwing an arm around my shoulders.

"See? You're the love of his life." Lena gave me a charmed smile. Apparently it was only Jimmy she detested.

"This week," said Jimmy.

With a small sigh, Lena half turned her head toward him. That was all it took.

Jimmy gave me a strained smile. "Sorry. That was a shitty thing to say."

"Pumpkin, Lena is what we in the industry call 'a babysitter'," said Mal. "If you're an unmitigated fucking asshole who doesn't know how to behave, you get a gorgeous girl like Lena to follow you around, making sure you're not a PR disaster for the record company."

"I said I was sorry." Jimmy stared out across the room, doing the same crinkly forehead thing his brother did. It kind of reminded me of James Dean.

"Hey." Ben appeared on my free side, staring down at me from his lofty height. There was more chin tipping. All of the band members wore matching black suits, but Jimmy had lost the vest and added a thin black tie. Ben wore the tie but had ditched the vest and jacket and the sleeves of his white shirt were rolled up his strong arms. Both limbs were liberally inked. Tattoos and suits made for a damn good combination.

The quality of the eye candy tonight was off the scale. Mal still had them all beat, of course.

"Pumpkin, guess what?"

"What?"

Before I knew what was happening I'd been dipped back over his arm. The entire room had turned upside down. Fuck, was the front of my dress gaping? I slapped my hand down over my collarbone, just in case.

"Shit, Mal! Up."

He immediately righted me. Blood rushed about inside my head and the room spun. Beside us, Ben and Lena laughed. I think Jimmy was busy doing his bored-stare thing. It was hard to see with my head still spinning. I'm pretty sure people were watching. If I heard an upside-down girl shouting obscenities, I'd probably take a look.

"No one saw anything," Mal said, reading my mind. "You okay?"

I nodded. "Fine."

His thumbs rubbed circles into my hip bones through the fabric of my dress. He held his face close to mine. "Sorry, pumpkin. I didn't think."

"It's okay."

He squinted down at me. "Is it really okay or are you just saying it's okay and you're going to bust my balls about it later?"

I thought about it for a moment to be sure. "No. But don't do it again or I'll hurt you."

"Got it. No more throwing you around."

"Thank you."

"I won't embarrass you again, Anne. Promise."

"I'd appreciate that."

"See," he said, his smile huge. "Our communication skills as a couple are fucking excellent. We're working out great!"

"Yeah, we are," I said, my heart elated. It was strange, we'd only known each other a few days but I trusted him. I liked him and I was really grateful to spend this time with him. After the disaster with Skye, I needed Malcolm

Ericson in my life right now. Hell, after the last seven years I needed him. He brought out the sun.

"Yeah," he whispered.

And then he kissed me and ruined everything.

CHAPTER NINE

It wasn't a soft kiss. No passing brush of the lips or token peck of affection would do for Mal. Hell no, of course not. It was an amnesia-inducing drug of a kiss. No memory of another remained. Chemical bliss. I'd obviously never been really and truly kissed before because this . . . he covered my mouth with his and owned me. His tongue slipped over my teeth and his hands slid into my hair. In response, I grabbed two fistfuls of his vest. It might have started out being in surprise or anger. But it turned into a safety measure fast. My knees went weak.

The man kissed me stupid.

His tongue rubbed at mine, encouraging me to play. It might not have been the smart thing to do, but I couldn't hold back. I moaned into his mouth and kissed him hard. Every bit as hard as he was kissing me. My thighs tensed and my toes curled. Every hair on my body stood on end. His hold on me tightened, as if he couldn't let go. I, on the other hand, was basically clawing my way through his three-piece suit. The need to get closer was huge. Nothing else mattered.

All around us applause broke out, which was fair enough. A kiss this awesome deserved a standing ovation. Fireworks wouldn't be overkill. The string quartet seemed a little odd, however. Surely a crazed drum solo would be more in keeping, something primal to match the demented beat of my heart.

"Guys," Ben hissed, nudging us with an elbow. "Knock it off. Guys!"

I tore away from Mal, trying desperately to catch my breath. He was panting too, his green eyes dilated. Stunned was probably a good word. Sordid wasn't too far behind. After all, we were mauling each other's mouths in public.

I stood there staring at him, shaking. Holy shit. What the hell had just happened?

"That was fun!" He grinned, looking at me like he'd just discovered a new game. One that he really, really liked.

No.

Fuck no.

My heart was trying to burst out of my chest, *Aliens* style. I couldn't blame it for wanting to run for cover. This was insane. I had to keep this shit locked down. What if he'd been able to tell what it did to me? He'd call off our arrangement in a heartbeat.

Time for some damage control.

"It was nice." I gave him a pat on the cheek.

His arrogant grin slipped.

People all around us continued clapping. They were also all facing the other way, though many gave us sideways glances. I turned and went up on tippy toes, to see what was going on. In the open front doorway stood Ev in a simple ivory gown. I saw the whites of her big surprised eyes from across the room. Beside her stood David in a suit similar to what the rest of the guys wore. Slowly, he got down on one knee. I was too far away to hear what he said, the room too noisy. But then Ev was nodding and crying and mouthing the word "yes."

"Davie wanted to do a surprise second ceremony," Mal said, joining in with the clapping. "She doesn't remember last time—it was a quickie drunken Vegas wedding—so he's doing it over for her."

"Th-that's sweet." I licked my lips, ignoring the lingering taste of him. So good.

His arm slipped around my waist and it was all I could do to keep still, to not try and move away. Some breathing room would be great. Just until I got my body back under control.

"I think everyone saw us, yeah?" he said.

"Mm." Without a doubt, we'd established ourselves as a couple. We'd probably managed to momentarily upstage the bride and groom. Excellent. They'd be inviting us back here for sure.

A man dressed in a bling-covered Elvis jumpsuit burst out of the hallway, sporting a big black wig and all. He began to sing "Love Me Tender" as played by the string quartet. Everyone laughed and smiled. Ev started laughing and crying. They repeated their vows and even my eyes misted up after I got myself back under control. It was so wildly romantic. Jimmy moved quietly through the crowd and slipped his brother a ring. The gentle smile on his face surprised me just a little.

Ever so damn slowly my heart rate returned to something nearing normal. I glanced over my shoulder at Mal. At first I couldn't work out what he was looking at. His attention was fixed on an older couple on the other side of the room, Ev or David's parents, perhaps? He looked unhappy. The distance was back in his eyes, the line between his brows. Then he caught me watching. He frowned and returned his gaze to the front.

"Can you believe Davie got her another ring?" Mal whispered in my ear. "He is so fucking wrapped around her finger. It's ridiculous."

"They're in love. I think it's sweet."

"At the rate he's giving her diamonds, she's going to have a tiara by Christmas."

It was one thing for me to be caustic within the sanctity of my own skull. But I hated hearing Mal be so against the idea of love or coupledom or whatever it was that had set him off.

"What?" he asked, seeing my down face.

"I can't decide if you sound jealous, bitter, or what."

"I was making a joke," he said, eyes wounded. "Tiaras are funny. Everyone knows that."

"Right."

Mal just blinked. His mouth, those gorgeous wicked lips of his, did not move.

Another round of applause thundered through the room as the remarkably swift service wound up. Though they were already married, no point dragging it out. Or maybe it only seemed fast to me. They kissed and flashbulbs lit the room. People crowded in to congratulate them.

Happy, happy times. What a joyous occasion.

"Back in a minute," I said, squeezing out of Mal's embrace. I needed air, space, shit like that. I needed to get my head on straight. My overreaction to his kiss had unnerved me big-time. Things were cooler and calmer out on the balcony. I knew having Mal cozy up to me at events would be weird. I'd expected feelings, sensations. Nerves, awkwardness, even mild titillation I could understand, but blow my mind, swamp me with lust, and make the world disappear? Not so much. He'd been right, there was every chance Fatal Attraction loomed large around the corner.

"What's wrong?" he asked, coming up behind me.

"Nothing. Everything's fine."

"Bullshit."

"If I say its fine, its fine," I gritted out.

"You're acting weird." He walked toward me, hypnotic eyes messing with my mind. "That was an awesome kiss," he said.

"It was okay," I lied, giving him a serene smile.

"It was okay?" One of his brows arched skyward. "That's it?"

I shrugged.

"Anne, you nearly tore off my clothing. I think it was better than okay."

"Oh, sorry. Was that overkill? I figured with the way you were going at me we were aiming for over the top."

He stopped. "Going at you?"

"Well, it was pretty full on."

"Was it, now?"

Another shrug. "You have to admit, there was a lot of tongue."

He stepped closer, getting into my personal space. My heels needed to be taller. This wasn't the sort of situation where I wanted to be looked down upon. I clenched and unclenched my fingers behind my back, flustered as fuck but trying not to let it show. This was not me. I didn't allow my life to get messed up by men. Been there, done that, had bought the T-shirt and worn it until it had ratty little holes in it.

"I warned you there'd be tongue when we were making our agreement," he said.

God help me, had there been tongue. Lots and lots of it. I could still feel his, sliding against my own, turning me on. Phantom tongue. There was every possibility Malcolm Ericson was driving me insane. He needed to be stopped. But the best I could do right then was to steer this conversation the hell away from all things oral, stat.

"Yeah, about our agreement . . . why did you say you needed a fake girlfriend?"

"We already talked about that."

"You didn't tell me anything."

"Told you as much as I'm going to." He paused, glowering down at me. "Why are you trying to turn this back onto me? What's wrong, Anne, not feeling defensive over one little kiss, are you?"

"No. Of course not." I crossed my arms. "But we agreed to keep sex out of this. Generally, people not having sex don't need to talk about tongues."

"I disagree."

"You really want to keep talking about this? Really?"

"You have no idea how much, pumpkin."

"Great. Let's discuss it." Maybe I should just throw myself over the balcony. It couldn't be that far down. The laws of physics aside, I might bounce. You never know. "You said you'd put your tongue in my ear, Malcolm, not halfway down my throat."

"I didn't put it halfway down your throat." His eyes narrowed. "I've never had any complaints about the way I kiss before."

I said nothing.

"This is bullshit. You liked it. I know you did."

"It was nice enough."

"Nice enough?" he asked, tendons tightening in his neck like he intended to Hulk out on me. "Did you just call my kiss 'nice enough'?"

"We're just pretending, Mal. Remember? Why don't you calm down?" I stepped back, giving him a calm smile.

He stepped forward, his green eyes blazing bright. "That kiss was not just fucking 'nice enough.'"

"Don't you think you're overreacting just a little?" I tried to laugh it off.

He was not appeased. "No."

"I guess we just don't click that way. Which I think is pretty lucky given the situation, right? It keeps things uncomplicated, just the way you wanted them, right?"

"Wrong."

"Careful there. I think your ego's showing. Not every girl needs to fall at your feet."

"You do."

"Ha. No, Mal, I don't."

"Do."

"Don't."

"Do."

"Stop it." I glared at him. Good god, rock stars were so childish. Spoiled brats.

The silence between us was deafening, the depths of space couldn't compete. We had the bubble thing going on again. Inside the condo didn't exist, there was no party, no music, light, and chatter. But I could control this situation. No way would my head be getting messed up by some rock star who'd be gone in no time.

"I want a do-over. Now," he demanded.

"No way." I put a hand to his chest, trying to hold him back. It didn't help. His heart beat hard against the palm of my hand even through the layers of clothing.

He loomed ever more threateningly closer, licking his gorgeous lips. "Right now, Anne. You and me."

"I don't think so."

"I can do better." And closer.

"You don't have to prove anything to me, Mal."

"You'll like it this time, promise."

If I liked his kiss any more I'd have heart failure. "Truly not necessary."

"Just once more," he said, his voice intoxicatingly low and smooth, lulling me into compliance. Damn him. "No big deal. Just give me one more chance."

His mouth hovered above mine, the anticipation tying me in knots. Damn it, I wasn't going to stop him. Not even a little. I was the worst.

"Trouble in paradise?" Jimmy Ferris stepped out onto the balcony, his trademark sneery smile in place. I could have kissed him for his timely intervention. Except kissing was what had gotten me into this mess.

"Hiding from Lena?" asked Mal calmly.

Jimmy flicked his dark hair back. His gaze slid to me before moving on to the city lights below. There was a non-answer if I'd ever seen one.

"Yeah, that's what I thought." Mal snorted. All of his intensity had evaporated into thin air, thank god. "We're all good thanks, bro. Just picking out names for our future children. Anne wants Malcolm Junior for a boy but I said no, absolutely not. Kid should at least have a chance at a life out from underneath the shadow of his old man."

"That's real big of you," said Jimmy.

"I know, right? Being a parent is all about the sacrifices."

Mal slid his hand behind my neck, rubbing at the tight muscles. "Relax," he ordered. "It isn't good for the baby."

"I am not pregnant."

"Ah, shit, that's right. We were s'posed to be keeping it quiet. Sorry, pumpkin." He smacked himself in the forehead. I would've been happy to do it for him.

"Don't worry," said Jimmy. "We've been friends since we were kids. I know when he's talking shit."

I wish I did.

"Who's pregnant?" asked David Ferris, wandering out onto the balcony with his wife in one hand and a beer in the other. Ben sauntered out after them.

With a look of great pride, Mal rubbed my belly. Any roundness was far more likely due to a weakness for cake than any acts of procreation.

"I'm not—"

"We were keeping it on the down low," said Mal. "We didn't want to upstage you two lovebirds."

"Fast work," said David with a hint of a smile.

"My boys can swim." Mal winked.

"I don't think you can actually tell that soon, dickhead." Jimmy crossed his arms, leaning against the wall of windows. "Science and stuff, right?"

"A real man *knows* when his woman is knocked up, Jimbo. I don't expect you to understand."

"A real man, huh?" Jimmy pushed off the window, walking slowly toward Mal. His smile would've given a shark second thoughts. Hell, they were both smiling. What was it about males that they felt this primal need to beat the shit out of each other for the fun of it? Why?

"Guys," said Ev. "No punching at my do-over wedding, playful or otherwise."

"What about bitch-slapping?" asked Mal, swinging his arm in Jimmy's direction.

"Let's not." I grabbed his hand and dragged it down by my side before he could do anyone any damage. "And Jimmy is right. Forty-eight hours is a bit too soon to tell. Not that we're trying," I hastened to add.

Mal's brows drew in as he gave me a wounded look. "I can't believe you'd side with him against me. That really hurts, Anne. You, of all people, should know my sperm is of superior quality."

"You wouldn't believe how long I could go never hearing you talk about your spunk, man." Ben shook his head.

"Don't be down, dude. It's only natural my alpha sperm would make you feel pitifully inadequate."

With a long groan, Jimmy covered his face. "You should have just let me hit him. If anyone ever needed some fucking sense knocked into them . . ."

"I'll hold him down," Ben offered.

"Knock it off," said David.

Mal opened his lips, eyes alight with glee. So I slapped my hand over his mouth, quick smart.

"Mal, why don't we discuss your sperm later?" I suggested. He kissed my palm and slowly I lowered my hand. "Thank you. And we are not having a baby."

"Okay, Anne. Whatever you say, Anne."

Ben laughed. "What, you pussy whipped now?"

Without comment, David reached out and smacked the bigger man over the back of the head.

"Hey!"

"Thanks, Davie." Mal drew me back into his arms.

"That was for Anne," said David. "Enough embarrassing shit while the girls are around. Act your fucking age, guys."

"A shovel, Malcolm. A rusty old shovel. That's your fate if you upset my friend. Keep it in mind." Ev stepped forward to give me a kiss on the cheek. "I wish you all the luck in the world with him. You're a brave woman."

"Yes, I'm beginning to think so."

"I like the way he looks at you," she said quietly. "That's new."

"Your second wedding was beautiful." I gave her my biggest, brightest smile, sidestepping the subject of my new fake boyfriend entirely.

Ev threw an arm around her husband's neck, smacking a kiss on his cheek. "Yes it was. It was amazing."

"Love you, baby." David kissed her back.

"Love you too."

He whispered something in her ear. Something that made her giggle. "We can't—my parents are here. Later."

David's mouth turned downward.

"Does this mean you're coming on tour, Anne?" asked Ev. "Please say yes."

"Absolutely!" Mal hugged me to him, squeezing me tight enough to make me wheeze. My feet even briefly left the ground.

"I don't know about that. I haven't had a chance to ask for any time off yet." I wiggled around until Mal gave me breathing room. He didn't allow me much beyond it, however. No biggie, I could ignore him and the crazy feelings he inspired, both. It would've been cool to experience life on the road, but I wasn't actually invited. Plus work, Lizzy, real life, and all that. "When does the tour start, by the way?"

"First show's in Portland in five days' time."

"Five days?" I hadn't been able to afford tickets when they went on sale a few months back. And of course they'd sold out in a matter of minutes. Denied attendance, I'd deliberately ignored what the bulk of the city was buzzing about. Call it petty jealousy, if you will.

My time with Mal was so short. My stomach dropped and my heart ached. The knowledge hurt. No matter how scarily stupid his kisses made me, I didn't want him to go. He made life better, brighter. How idiotic of me to have gotten attached. I hadn't meant to, but the evidence was clear.

"Don't look so sad, pumpkin." He gently cupped my chin, eyes serious. "We'll work something out."

"Guys, they're ready to do photos." Lauren stood in the doorway, a full champagne flute in hand. After some grumbling, Jimmy headed inside. Ev and David, arm in arm, followed behind him.

"Great acting," whispered Mal, laying a soft kiss upon my neck. "I honestly thought you were about to burst into tears."

Funny, I'd thought I might too. I huffed out a laugh and gave him my best fake smile. "I played one of the wicked witches in my middle school's production of *The Wizard of Oz.*"

"That explains it."

"It was basically just lying down dead at the start, pretending to be squished while wearing cool red shoes."

"Bet you were the best squished girl ever."

"Thanks. And pregnant? Really?"

He rolled his eyes and pressed a kiss to my cheek. "I'm sorry, I'm sorry. Just got carried away. Do you forgive me?"

I held out for all of two seconds. "Yes."

"Thank you. That's very kind of you. I really didn't mean to stress you out in your delicate condition."

I growled.

He laughed.

"Coming?" asked David, looking back over his shoulder.

"I'll just wait out here," I said, stepping back from Mal while I still could. Immediately the cold evening air rushed in, chilling me.

David shook his head. "No, Anne. You too. If you're with him, you're family. Let's get it done with so we can kick back and relax."

"You heard the groom." Mal grabbed my hand, drawing me in again. "Just one thing first."

"What?"

With the gleam in his eye, I should've known. His lips descended, pressing against mine. His arms wound around me, hauling me up against him. My gasp of surprise was just the entry into my mouth he needed. Turned out he knew how to evil laugh and kiss me senseless at the same time. I shouldn't have been surprised about that either. Despite that, the kiss was soul-shatteringly gentle. He kissed me sugar sweet until my head spun and my heart pounded. My knees knocked and my girl parts cried mercy.

And still he kissed me.

"How was that?" he asked eventually, staring into my undoubtedly dazed eyes. "Better?"

"Um, sure?"

He breathed out through his nose, his brows drawn tight. "Shit, I'm still not getting it right. I'm going to figure this kissing thing out. I am. We just gotta keep trying. Never say die!"

I was done for.

CHAPTER TEN

I studied my reflection in the hallway mirror as the party continued out in the living room. One side of my bottom lip was slightly bigger than the other. Honestly, it was. I looked ridiculous. The drummer was nuts. He'd always been riding the edge of needing immediate admission to a nice, soft, padded white room. And for a while, it had even been kind of charming in an offbeat fashion. But now he'd officially lost all semblance of control.

Did I like biting? No. No I did not. Same went for nibbling and most especially hickeys. The mark on my neck did not impress and I'm pretty certain there was a bruise just above my ass from him grinding me into the kitchen counter.

Needless to say, his rough lovin' experiment hadn't been a success.

"God damn maniac."

"Sorry?" asked the woman waiting beside me for the main bathroom.

"Nothing. Just cursing out loud." I gave her a bland, social smile. "Don't mind me."

She nodded and reapplied her lip gloss with the precision of an artist before proceeding to positioning her breasts. What were the chances of me having an early-twenties growth spurt and developing breasts like those? I wished.

"You're with Malcolm Ericson, right?" she asked.

"Right." I wouldn't say that I preened exactly, but I did run my fingers through my hair.

The smile she gave me seemed less than sincere despite being blindingly bright. "I think that's really brave of you."

"How so?"

"Dating out of your weight range like that." Her eyes met mine in the bathroom mirror. They were a dark, evil, pretty hazel kind of color. "I mean, you're clearly not at his level. But why not enjoy him while you can, right?"

I checked in the mirror. But amazingly enough, there was no steam coming out of my ears. My mouth opened, but it took a moment for me to find the words. "Did you really just say that?"

"What?" She did a nervous giggle, hair-flicking thing. "I'm a complete stranger to you."

"Hey, I think it's great. Go sister and all that."

What petty jealousy bullshit. No way was I giving this bitch the power to make me feel little. "I'm not your sister. I have a sister and she would never say something like that to me."

The woman's perfectly glossy lips popped open.

"Seriously, honey," I said. "Your manners are appalling. Go fuck yourself."

The bathroom door opened and I took my turn, closing the door with a little more zest than needed. My shoulders were up around my ears when I strode back out to the party, the slight throbbing in my lip almost forgotten. I did not look back at the bitch.

People. God damn it.

Hard rock music thumped through me, keeping my agitation fresh. I wanted to hit something. Not someone, but something. Just give an innocent wall a smack with my hand to let out some of the pressure building inside me. I slowed down my breathing, tried to quiet my ranting mind.

Everything was fine.

Mal, Jimmy, and Ben stood to the side, sipping their drinks, ignoring the hopeful glances of the girls nearby. Crap, was this what it was like for them all the time? It had to get old. A few paces away, Lena chatted to a woman her own age. Her gaze kept sliding back to Jimmy in a way that didn't exactly express professional interest. Imagine that.

Out of the confined space, I could breathe again. It was all good.

"What's up?" Mal asked when I got closer.

Behind us, the woman strutted out of the bathroom, throwing my fake boyfriend a big fake grin. Not a hint of shame about her.

"Promise me something," I said.

"Sure."

I stopped, smiled. "You didn't even hesitate."

"You're pissed about something." He leaned down, making our conversation private despite the packed room. "What's wrong?"

"Promise me you won't sleep with her." I nodded to the beast in question. She was now busy talking to an elderly man, smiling and nodding. In all likelihood, she was Ev's cousin or something equally harmless, not the Harpy Queen of Darkness. Still didn't make her behavior right.

Also sometime soon, I should try to not insult someone every time I entered this building. A great idea.

"I won't sleep with her," said Mal.

"And you won't have sex with her either."

He rolled his eyes.

"Just to clarify."

"What'd she do to you, Anne?"

"She insulted me. But it's fine." I just needed to know

she'd never get near him. Now my soul was at peace. "Carry on with your partying."

Mal's face hardened, his mouth drawing tight. "What the fuck did she say?"

"Doesn't matter. I might get another drink. I have no idea where I left mine and suddenly alcohol sounds like a really good idea. I feel I need the social lubrication." I started toward the kitchen, all well once again with my world. Justice would prevail. Mal's pants were closed to the woman.

A hand hooked my elbow, drawing me back into the bathroom. It was a nice bathroom. Dark gray stone surfaces, shiny chrome features. A great bathroom, really, but I didn't need to spend quite this much time in it.

"Mal?"

He slammed the door shut. Whoa, his eyes. There was not a single hint of happy. "What did she say to you?"

"Hey, really, it's okay." I rested my hip against the counter, setting the right example and trying to play it cool. This level of emotion had not been expected.

"Anne."

"I just needed to know she wasn't going to get what she wanted, namely you. Blame it on my little black vindictive heart," I joked.

He did not laugh.

Face still set in furious lines, he stalked toward me, backing me into the counter. The hard gray stone edge connected smack bam with the bruise on my back from earlier. It hurt.

"Ouch." I rubbed at the sore spot, wincing.

"What?"

"I think I've got a bruise from the kitchen bench. Your fault."

He harrumphed in a strangely sexy manner (it had truly never occurred to me that noise could be a turn-on). "I already said sorry about that."

He picked me up by the waist and set me on top of the counter. His able hands pushed my knees apart as far as my skirt would allow and he stepped between.

"Ah, hey there." I put my hands to his shoulders, pressing against the cool material of his suit jacket. "Ease back a bit."

"Tell me what she said."

"Why? You going to challenge her to a duel? Pistols at dawn?"

"You read too many books."

"No such thing!" I cried, aghast.

"No duel. But I'll sure as hell have her ass thrown out of here."

"Mal, seriously. I dealt with it. It's okay."

He just stared at me.

"I very politely thanked her for her opinion and told her to go fuck herself."

The tension in his face eased a little. "You told her to go fuck herself?"

"Yes, I did. I channeled my inner Scarlet O'Hara and took none of her crap."

"Good. Liking that boundary. And you're okay now?" He set his hands on the counter either side of my hips, meaning we were damn close. Much closer with some clothes missing and we'd almost be together in the biblical sense.

"I'm all good. Though my bottom lip sort of hurts. No more biting."

He huffed out a laugh. "Yeah, yeah. I figured that when you pulled half my hair out to get me off of you. You know you can be kind of vicious, pumpkin. I like that."

I smiled and he smiled and everything was fine and dandy.

"You're definitely not going to sleep with her though," I said, just to be sure. I really didn't like the woman. "Seriously."

"My dick doesn't go near anyone that's rude to my friends. That's not cool."

"Your dick has good taste, then."

His eyes went kind of hazy.

"Mal?"

"Hmm? Sorry. I like the way you say 'dick' and 'taste' in the same sentence."

"Right." So not going there. I squirmed ever so discreetly on the countertop. "Thank you for worrying about me. But we should go back out and join the party. People probably want to use the bathroom."

"There's four more." Soft as a feather, he brushed his lips across mine. Every nerve in my body kick-started at the contact.

"I'll make you feel better, Anne."

"Ah, yeah. I already said I was feeling fine. And you remember that line in the sand you drew about us not getting involved in a sexual manner and stuff? You're messing with it big-time tonight."

"It's not a problem."

"It kind of is. I don't want to be your joke, Mal."

"My joke? What the hell are you talking about?" His hands slid around to my butt and suddenly I was pulled in against him. All of him. And by the feel, there was a lot of him in a good and hard mood.

I squeaked and wrapped my legs around his hips. Honest to god, I didn't mean to. It was an accident. When he pressed his cock against me it made thinking impossible. My hormones were seizing control. All of this talk of babies had obviously given them ideas. Still, I made a token effort to resist. "Okay, big guy. That's enough."

Gently, he kissed my bottom lip. "Still hurting?"

"Totally cured." Oh I hurt, I ached. A bit more of the pressure from his pelvis, making my mind reel, would do the job, however. I rocked against him, unable to stop myself. My eyelids slid half closed. Damn, he felt good.

"You're not my joke, Anne. You're my friend. One I am very fucking into for lots of reasons."

I couldn't help but smile. "You're my friend too."

"But you know, it's okay for us to relax and have some fun." He demonstrated this point by kneading my ass. "You don't have to be so wound up all the time. I'm not going to let anything bad happen."

Malcolm Ericson might have been a lot of things, but omnipotent wasn't one of them. Bad things happened. It was a fact of life.

"What are you thinking about?" he asked, grinding himself against me once more, derailing my sadness.

"Nothing." Sex. Stress. A bit of both, really.

"I really like your dress."

"Thanks. The suit's nice; you look incredible."

"I been thinking about this kissing problem we got."

"There's no kissing problem. Everyone believes we're together so . . . job well done Team Mal and Anne." I raised a fist high. "Yay."

He chuckled softly. "See? You can be funny."

I gave him what had to be a dazed smile. Man, he was beautiful, especially up close like this. He angled his head and nudged my cheek with his nose, kissing the corner of my mouth. Fingers toyed with the zipper on the back of my dress. Not moving it, just casually threatening me with its imminent descent. Good god, did I enjoy being threatened in this way by him. My nipples hardened, more than ready to be on display. They so had no sense.

"Been thinking," he said. "Maybe you need to be kissed in other places."

The man was a fucking genius.

Ever so slowly, he tugged the zipper down an inch or two. His smile dared me to stop him. Pity I'd lost all power over my limbs. The zipper went lower, loosening the bodice of my dress, making the front gape. Mal slipped a finger in the neckline, drawing the black lace out a ways.

"You not going to stop me?" he asked in a soft voice.

"Any minute now." Not a chance.

Then he looked down. Hopefully, he appreciated breasts of all types. If he was a size-based guy, this would not end well.

"Anne. Fuck." He swallowed hard. A very good sign. Softly, his fingers traced over the hollow at the base of my throat.

"Yes?"

"You are so damn—"

Somebody hammered on the door, knocking me out of my lust fog.

"Mal, it's time," a voice hollered.

No. NO!

"Wha—?" Mal turned, scowling, while I got busy frantically holding my dress in place.

The door opened and Ben stuck his head in.

"Fuck's sake, man," said Mal, voice tight and furious. "Anne could've been naked."

Ben scoffed. "You never cared who saw what before. And if it's an issue, there's a lock on the door, dickhead."

"Rules have changed."

"Shit, man," said Ben, flashing his teeth in a big smile. "You're actually serious."

"Of course I'm fucking serious. This is my fucking girlfriend, you moron."

Ben's gaze flitted over my body. "Yeah well, your *fucking* girlfriend's pretty cute. You know what? I think I like her."

Every part of Mal tensed. There was fire in his eyes. "You—"

"No." I grabbed hold of the lapels of his jacket. "No fighting."

He looked at me, nostrils flaring. What was it about weddings that invited so much drama?

"I mean it," I said. "This is Ev and David's special night."

But Ben was apparently having far too much fun to stop now. "Remember that time we shared a girl in Berlin? That was good . . . real good. Always thought I'd like to try that again. What do you say, Anne? Up for a bit of fun? Promise we'll take good care of you."

Mal snarled and I lunged, getting him in a strangle hold. I was basically hanging off him. Damn, the man was strong. Ben might be huge, but given Mal's current mood, I wouldn't bet against him in a fair fight. The muscles in his neck were bulging.

"Mal?" I said his name in my super calm and in control voice. Under different circumstances I'd have probably made an awesome therapist. "Are you listening to me?"

"Yeah." His hands gripped my ass, taking some of my weight. A good thing. Dangling from someone's neck was harder than it looked.

"Everything's fine. Ignore him," I said. "Ben, get out." The jerk waggled his eyebrows at me.

"Now."

"Sure, Anne. No worries." He winked at me, closing the door.

"Be calm, Mal. The bad man is gone."

"I'm calm," he growled, holding me to him.

"He didn't mean it. He was just messing with you."

"Didn't you see the way he looked at you? Idiot meant it." Mal hugged me tight. "Piece of shit's bad as Jimmy sometimes. Should have kicked his ass."

"Hey now, harness that inner caveman. You're very aggressive tonight."

"I don't like people saying stuff about you. You shouldn't have to put up with that."

"Well, that's sweet. But I don't need you beating up anybody for me."

"Four of us have been beating each other up since we were kids. It happens." One handed, Mal tugged my zipper back up into place. Then he pierced me with a hard look. "You didn't want to, did you?"

"Generally, I do prefer one penis at a time. It's a failing of mine, I guess . . ."

"Good."

I gave him a kiss on the cheek because a jealous Mal was an awesome sight. "What was he talking about 'it's time'?"

"Davie wants to play a few songs for Ev. We gotta go back out." He sighed and sat me back on the counter. His hands rubbed over my sides. "You okay?"

"Yes."

Still he frowned.

"You know, you can be kind of intense, Malcolm Ericson."

His watched me in silence.

"You come across as this happy-go-lucky-type dude most of the time, but you are in fact a man of many layers. You're kind of complicated."

"Surprised?"

"Yes. And no."

"And you call me complicated. You gonna dance with me later?" he asked, shaking off the bad mood.

"I'd love to."

"You wanted another drink, didn't you? C'mon, let's go get that before I set up." He lifted me down, his hands on my hips, treating me with the utmost care.

"You're the best boyfriend ever. Fake or not."

"How many you had?"

"Boyfriends? Two." I held up a couple of fingers, just in case he wanted a visual aid. It was good to be helpful.

"So I'm number three?"

"No, you're number two. Relationships aren't my specialty."

"No?" He lifted his chin, looked down at me. "You're doing real good, Anne."

"Thanks, Mal."

CHAPTER ELEVEN

I had a nice buzz by the time we stumbled home. We shared a cab with Nate and Lauren at around three in the morning after an amazing party.

I'd finally heard Stage Dive play live. They were awesome playing acoustic. Jimmy's and David's voices melding together beautifully. Each one of those men was so damn talented it made my teeth hurt. Ben, with his bass, and even Mal, deprived of his full drum kit, made his presence felt in amazing ways. They were all in perfect balance, integral to the music.

It might have been way past my bedtime, but I didn't want the night to end. Not just yet. I lay on my back, staring at my bedroom ceiling. It'd stopped spinning a short while ago. The gap in my curtains provided just enough light from the street to see by. A few years ago on nights like this when sleep wouldn't come, I'd often talk to Mal—I mean, the poster version of him. Sad and psychotic, but true. Now the man himself slept next door.

Life could be a strange and beautiful thing sometimes.

Other times it was just a disaster. But sometimes beauty won out.

I ran my fingers over my poor, sore lips. They'd almost been kissed into extinction. Once Mal got an idea into his head, he was unstoppable. And apparently dancing with him meant indulging in a mini make-out session. It had gotten more and more difficult to feign dissatisfaction every time he tried something new. So many ways to kiss, I'd truly had no idea. Soft and hard, with or without teeth, the varying depths of penetration by tongue had featured largely. And hand placement. Whoa, the hand placement. He'd done everything from gently stroking my neck to kneading my ass. A man who knew what to do with his hands was truly a force to be reckoned with. I'd only just stopped him from slipping it up my skirt at midnight.

Such a great night.

He'd stripped down to boxer briefs again once we got home. I'd gone into the bathroom to grab a hairbrush and there he'd been, brushing his teeth. A man brushing his teeth had never been such a turn-on, even with the white bubbly drool slipping out of the corner of his mouth. My guess would be he didn't own pajamas. Nope, a guy like him must sleep in the nude. A brilliant scientific deduction based on the hot and hard man currently occupying my couch. All too readily I could imagine his warm, tanned skin exposed. Did he sleep on his back, stomach, or side? Aesthetically, on his back would be most pleasing . . . for various reasons.

But if he did lie on his stomach the long line of his spine would be on show with the bonus addition of his ass. I'd sell something important to see his bare ass. My books, my e-reader, my soul, whatever was necessary.

And I could think about something else anytime I wanted to. But why would I?

No, masturbating was a much more sensible course of action. I was all wired and awake, my nipples hard and breasts aching. The time had come to take matters into my own hands.

"Mm, Nate."

More moaning.

Some groaning.

A thump.

"Baby, yes."

"Lick it, Lauren."

No. Fucking. Way.

I covered my face with my pillow and silently screamed. If I put on music to drown them out (my usual course of action for dealing with Nate and Lauren's nocturnal passions) I'd probably wake Mal.

Two more thumps. The bed next door started creaking. It was so loud I almost didn't hear my bedroom door being opened.

"Pumpkin, am I in hell?" Mal walked in, sat on the edge of my bed.

"Yes. Yes, you are. I'm sorry. This is the first and worst level of all, the one where you can hear your neighbors fucking through paper-thin walls."

Lauren made some screechy noise she was particularly prone to during such encounters. I cringed.

"Make it stop," Mal whispered, mouth opened wide in horror. "Oh, fuck no. This is horrible."

We both started quietly laughing. It was the only sensible response.

"Let's go to a hotel," he said, moving farther onto my bed.

"It's four in the morning."

"How long do they normally take?"

"They've been drinking, so this could go on for a while." I drew up my knees, hugged them tight to my chest. He didn't need to know about my nipple situation. The sad truth was that listening to people having good, noisy sex wasn't helping. Lucky I was wearing my best comfy cotton jammie pants and an old T-shirt. They were so baggy they hid everything. Otherwise, having Mal sitting on my bed so close might have been a touch embarrassing.

"Isn't there something wrong with this picture?" said Mal, scowling at the wall as if it had personally offended him. "I'm the drummer from Stage Dive. I don't get kept awake by other people having wild sex. I keep them awake. I keep entire fucking neighborhoods awake."

"Damn, baby. You're so good at this," Nate snarled through the wall.

"Did you hear that?" asked Mal.

"Yep."

"Right. That's it." Mal climbed up onto his feet, standing tall on my bed. There was only a foot between him and the ceiling at most. "He's taunting me. He's challenging me."

"He is?"

"The bastard."

"And I always thought Nate was such a nice guy."

He reached out his hand to me. "C'mon, Anne. We must defend our fake sex life."

"Shit." I took his hand, letting him pull me up too. "Don't let me bounce off the side. And don't hit your head."

"I'm not gonna hit my head. Would you stop being such a grown-up for a minute? Relax, have some fun."

"Harder, Nate!" Came from next door.

Mal's cleared his throat, loudly. "Anne!"

"Mal."

"Louder," he hissed, as we started to bounce. The wooden frame of my bed made startling creaking noises. The kind it hadn't made in a very long time, if ever. If only it were due to us being horizontal and naked. That would be so great.

"Mal!"

"You're such a nice girl, Anne," Mal projected for the sake of our neighbors. "I really like you a lot."

"Seriously? That's your version of sex talk?"

"Let's hear you talk dirty, then. C'mon."

I shut my mouth. It stayed shut.

"Coward." Mal turned his face to the wall we shared with Nate and Lauren. "You taste so fucking good."

"Like what?" I asked breathlessly, thigh muscles tightening. The man was lucky I didn't just attack him with my vagina. "What do I taste like?"

"Well, like honey and cream and . . . I dunno, bread?"

I scrunched up my nose. "Bread?"

"Yes. Sexy bread that I could eat all the time because you are so delicious and full of wholegrain goodness."

The next round of giggling made my stomach muscles seize up, but I kept bouncing. How weird to be laughing and jumping and turned on at the same time. Some friends of Lizzy's and mine had a trampoline when we were growing up. It'd never been as much fun as this, however.

Then Mal jumped particularly high and hit the ceiling with his head.

He dropped onto his much-coveted ass, rubbing the top of his skull. "Fuck. Ouch."

"Are you okay?"

The bed suddenly collapsed, one end of the wooden frame crashing to the floor. The noise was most impressive. As was the sudden silence from next door. I stumbled and slid and wound up landing half on his lap. Fortunately, an arm went around me, stopping me from bouncing further. We sat there, basically chest to chest, with one of my legs thrown over both of his.

"We've broken my bed," I said, stating the obvious.

"In battle, sacrifices must be made, pumpkin."

"Is your head okay? Do you need an ice pack?" I pushed his mess of blond hair out of his face. Maybe he needed sexual healing. I was so up for that. It was right on the tip of my tongue to suggest it. Drunken bravado was the best.

"It's good." His smile came ever so slowly.

Someone knocked on the wall from Nate and Lauren's side. "You two okay?"

"We're fine," I called back. "Thanks. Carry on."

I could hear barely subdued laughter. My face felt hot. Flame-worthy hot. You could probably cook a steak on that sucker. Crap, everybody would hear about this. And I do mean everybody. We were never going to live this down.

"They're mocking us," I said.

"Nonsense. We just fucked so hard we broke your bed. They wish they were us. The natural order of sexual status has been restored."

We both laughed. It was all so ridiculous.

But then the laughter kind of dwindled away to nothing and we were sitting there staring at each other. His face was in shadows. It was impossible to read him. But his thickening cock made its presence known against my thigh. What I wouldn't have given to know what he was thinking. All of my awareness went directly to between my legs and oh shit, it felt good. I wished he'd do something because I wasn't sure I could. He reacted to me but what did that mean? Dicks did stuff. Mysterious stuff, like getting hard for no reason. Sex was most definitely not part of our agreement. He'd been specific. And yet, all the kissing and teasing tonight . . .

I'd never been so confused in my entire life. Confused and horny.

Next door, the noises started up once more as they took my advice and did indeed carry on.

"I'm pretty sure they're not thinking about us at all," I said.

"Just out of interest, how drunk are you?"

"The room is kind of spinning. Why?"

"Nothing. We better move," he said, voice guttural. Carefully, he lifted me off of him and then climbed out of the ruin of my old bed. We both stood there, collectively ignoring the bulge in his pants. Not awkward at all. It had to be said though; a damp crotch was far easier to hide.

"Let's go watch a movie," he said. "No one's getting any sleep anytime soon."

"Good idea," I lied and let him haul me out of the wreckage. "Poor bed. But that was fun."

"Yeah, it was. Not as much fun as actually fucking, but still, not bad."

My curiosity got the better of me. Either that or I had no manners and was indeed still drunk. "Speaking of which, what happened to your hook-ups? I thought you might go visiting a lady friend after we got back from the party."

"Meh."

"Meh?" He had a half-on and he was giving me 'meh'?

"Between getting ready for this tour and being in a serious fake relationship, I haven't had the time."

"Fair enough." I didn't believe him at all.

Instead, my alcohol-addled mind made giant leaps of logic. Little to no reason was involved. What if his lack of libido had to do with his need for a fake girlfriend somehow? Maybe he had a mysterious real girlfriend hidden away down in L.A. and I existed solely to put people off the scent. Actually, no. That theory hurt. But maybe this was all about the bet he'd made with Ben. He'd backed himself into this ridiculous corner with his insane jokes and now his pride would be wounded if he tried to back out. And that theory hurt even more. Neither probability covered his being sad sometimes, though. I let him lead me into the living room, my head and my heart a not-so-sober mess.

"What about you? You weren't seriously keeping your legs crossed until douche came to his senses, were you?" He sat in the middle of the velvet couch, pulling me down beside him, keeping me close.

"No, I've dated. Just not recently."

"How not recently?" He picked up a remote and the

huge TV came to life. His arm rested on the back of the
couch behind me, the flat of his hand beating out a fierce
rhythm.

"What do you feel like watching?" I asked.

"Not going to tell me?"

"A few months."

Some old horror film was on. From the eighties, if
the big hair and spiral perm were any indicators. A pair
of barely concealed breasts bounced their way across
the screen. A woman screamed.

"This looks good," Mal said.

"Mmm-hmm."

"You don't scare easily, do you?"

"No. Though it does make me sad when Johnny Depp
gets turned into tomato soup."

"Bet it does." He smiled. "You know, I meant what I
said."

"About what?"

"About you." He looked straight ahead, never meeting
my eyes. The light from the TV lit the angles and planes
of his perfect face. "I like you."

"Thank you, Mal."

Then why weren't we having sex? Obviously, he didn't
like-like me. He just *liked* me, like he'd said.

My mind starting spinning all over again.

"You didn't say you liked me back," he prodded, sounding the tiniest bit insecure if my ears weren't deceiving me.

"Oh, well." I turned to look at him, squinting, ignoring
the screaming still coming from on screen. "You are . . ."

"I'm what?"

"So . . ."

"C'mon, pumpkin, you're taking too long. Spit it out."

"Very . . ."

"Fuck it. I'm just gonna compliment myself."

I sighed long and loud, enjoying this immensely.

"You're hopeless at this," he bitched.

"How about stupendous? Does stupendous work for you?"

"Hmm." He gave me a small, satisfied smile. "Yeah. That's not bad. I mean, it definitely starts to cover the glory that is me."

"And egotistical. So very egotistical."

"You lie." His fingers danced over my sides, making me giggle and squirm. "I am humble perfection."

"No. Don't tickle me."

"Admit I'm your reason for being. Admit it!" His arm came around me, pulling me back into him as I tried to escape. "Shit, don't fall off the chair again. I can't take any more hits to the head to save you."

"Stop tickling me, then," I huffed.

"Tickling you. Please. As if I'd be so immature." A hand came up and gently pushed my head onto his shoulder and the arm around me tightened. "Shh, quiet time now."

The warm buzz filling me was ten times better than anything alcohol could ever provide. No, a million times better, because it came with the added bonus of smelling and feeling like Mal Ericson.

"Relax," he said.

"I'm relaxing." Stuff happened on the big screen. None of it mattered. My eyes drifted closed as I concentrated on him. Whatever his reasons for being here, there was little chance I'd ever get what I wanted. It was the human condition to always want more. That being said, what I had for the moment was pretty damn good.

CHAPTER TWELVE

People were arguing again when I woke up. Only this time, there was no yelling. Heated whispers passed straight over my head.

"Why is my sister asleep on top of you?" asked Lizzy.

"Because I'm her boyfriend," Mal answered. "Who are you? Anne didn't say anything about having a sister."

"She didn't?"

"No. And how many people have fucking keys to this apartment, anyway? You forget the sliding bolt for a moment and it's open city."

"With Skye gone, just me and Lauren as far as I know."

"Don't say that name. She gets upset when you mention it. Her eyes go all sad and it totally bums me out."

"What, Skye?"

"Yeah," he growled.

"Fine, fine." A pause. "You're kinda hot, aren't you?" A disinterested grunt.

"I'm not hitting on you, idiot. She's my sister and this is my suspicious voice. Don't I know you from somewhere? Your face is very familiar."

The fingers connected to the big hand cupping my ass tightened. What it was doing there, I had no idea. But did I like it? Yes. Yes I did. I was sleeping on a bed of Mal. Talk about heavenly. I couldn't even remember falling asleep. Obviously, it had happened sometime during the gory horror movie because we were still on the velvet couch in the living room. My sister was here so it had to be Sunday morning, our day to do our duty and call mom. We always performed this unpleasant task together.

I did not want to move. Not until Wednesday at the very earliest. I was mildly hung over.

But more than that, I didn't want to get off of Mal.

"What the hell did you do to her? Her lips are all puffy and bruised."

"Are they?" Mal's body moved beneath me as he no doubt lifted his head to check out the damage. "Shit. Ah, yeah. She's a bit of a mess, isn't she? But how was I to know if she was into biting or not if I didn't try it out?"

"She's not," said Lizzy. "Or at least, I don't think she is. Anne's never seemed like the biting type to me. She's more . . . restrained."

"Restrained?" Mal laughed softly. "Yeah. Why don't you go check out her bed, then tell me how restrained she is."

Footsteps followed by a gasp. "Fuck me. It's totaled."

"My pumpkin's an animal when she gets going."

"You call her pumpkin?" My sister's voice was filled with awe. "Does she actually answer?"

"Well, she pretends to hate it. But secretly, I know she loves it. Her face goes all soft and everything."

Oh good god, enough. I'd basically raised this girl; she didn't need to hear this sort of shit. Any authority I'd once had would be dust. I cracked open an eyelid. "Quiet, Mal."

"I am your servant in all things."

"What time is it?" I asked as a yawn almost cracked my jaw in two.

"Mal? Did she call you Mal?" asked Lizzy, coming up close beside us. My sister and I didn't look much alike. Her hair was a pretty caramel color as opposed to my carrot. Her features were more delicate than mine, though we both had mom's strong jawline. "No. Way."

Ha, this would be fun.

"Strangely enough yes, way," I said, my voice ever so slightly smug. "Mal, this is my little sister, Lizzy. Lizzy, this is Malcolm Ericson." My sister hadn't been quite as big a Stage Dive fan as me. Doubtful it would stop her from fangirling out, however.

As suspected, Lizzy squealed like a loon. Both Mal and I winced. "Oh my god, Anne loves you. She had an entire wall of her bedroom dedicated to you."

"No!" Shit, how had I not seen this coming? Fear choked me. Someone had to tackle my sister, now. Take her down and lock her in a cupboard. It was absolutely for her own benefit, but mostly mine. I tried to lunge at her, but strong arms held me trapped. "Lizzy. Shut up. Please shut up. He doesn't need to know that."

"Tell me more, Lizzy," demanded Mal. "A whole wall, did you say? That is fascinating. I definitely need to know more."

"No you don't."

"Hush, Anne. I'm listening."

My arms weren't long enough to cover Lizzy's mouth. I had to settle for Mal's ears. I fought him, but he shook off my hands far too easily, the wily man.

"She used to write your name on her thigh in permanent marker," my traitorous wench of a sister reported. It was official: Lizzy sucked. There was a good chance I'd soon be an only child if she kept talking. Given mom rarely noticed she had children at all, the loss shouldn't be too debilitating long-term.

"That's a lie!" I cried, breaking out into a cold sweat.

"Did she write it on her inner thigh? I bet it she did, the minx." Mal grabbed my wrists, holding them against his chest. An effective means of stopping me from beating him bloody. "Did she draw little hearts with arrows sticking out of 'em too?"

"I don't know." My beloved sister settled into the wingback, crossing her legs. "But she did practice signing her name as Anne Ericson *all* the time."

"I am so touched you'd take my name, pumpkin." Mal attempted to smooch my fists. "No shit, that's awesome of you. Means the world to me. My family is gonna love you."

"La-la-la-la," I sang at the top of my voice, drowning them both out as best I could.

"And she'd watch Stage Dive videos over and over. Except for the one where you kissed that girl." Lizzy clicked her fingers, her face tensed in concentration. " 'Last Days of Love', that was the one. She flat-out refused to watch it, would leave the room if it came on."

Beneath me, Mal's body shuddered because he was laughing his ass off. The man was in hysterics. Even his eyes were bright with unshed tears, the douche canoe. A big hand curled around the back of my head, pressing my face into his neck. "Aw, Anne. Were you jealous?"

"No." Yes. Horribly, horribly jealous. That kiss had ravaged my teenage soul and made me listen to sad songs for almost a year.

"My poor girl."

"Shuddup."

"I didn't mean to kiss her. My mouth slipped," he said, trying for earnest and failing. "I swear I was trying to keep myself pure for you. Tell me you believe me, please."

I called him something foul.

He laughed even harder, making the whole couch shake.

Given he wasn't letting me go any time soon, I hid my hot face in his neck as invited. Everyone in the room, I hated them. I hated them hard. It was tempting to bite him but he'd probably enjoy it. He'd certainly spent quality time nibbling at my lips and jaw after cornering me yet again at the party last night. His kissing crusade had almost undone me, but it had taken my sister to do the real damage, my own flesh and blood.

Now Mal knew everything. I was doomed.

"Lizzy, be a good girl and fetch me a pen," said Mal. "I need to write your sister's name on my junk, right now."

Honest to god, I tried not to laugh. I tried so hard.

"How about I go make coffee instead?" Lizzy hauled herself to her feet. "You know she usually has breakfast cooked for me by now, every Sunday at ten o'clock on the dot. You're a bad influence on her, Mal."

"Let me get dressed, I'll take you both out." He smoothed his hand over my back. "Can't have my future sister-in-law getting mad at me already."

"Won't you get hassled?" Lizzy hollered from the kitchen.

"People have usually been pretty cool around here when I've visited. But I'll wear a hat and sunglasses. And I can call up some security if needed."

"Why don't I cook us something? It's got to be my turn by now," said Lizzy. The clanging of pots and pans and the running of water accompanied her statement. Maybe my sister wasn't so bad after all.

"Thanks," I said.

"Soooo." Mal smacked a kiss on the top of my head. "You weren't just a little into me. You're my biggest fan. You love me."

"I don't love you."

"You totally love me." He gave me a squeeze. "I'm your everything. You'd be lost without me."

Thankfully, this time when I scrambled off of him, he didn't try to fight me. I pulled down my old T-shirt and smoothed back my bed hair, getting myself together. "It was just a stupid teenage crush. Don't let it go to your already swollen head."

"The big one or the little one?"

I groaned.

Mal just lay there, his fingers sitting steepled atop his bare chest. He watched me without comment. His eyes, they saw far too much. After a moment, he sat up, his feet hitting the floor. He yawned and then stretched, cracking his neck. "You know, that's the first decent sleep I've gotten in ages."

"With me passed out on top of you? It can't have been comfortable."

The shadows beneath his eyes had faded and he seemed more relaxed, stretching out his long limbs. Still, he rubbed at the back of his neck. "No, it wasn't really. Go figure. Guess we should be sleeping on the couch every night from now on."

"My bed is broken."

He pushed back his hair, gave me a smile.

"You've been having trouble sleeping?" I asked.

"A bit, I guess."

"Something on your mind?"

"Dunno. It's nothing." He avoided my eyes.

"It's something." This was the first real in he'd given me. Or first vague in. Either way, I needed to take it. "What's going on with you? What's wrong? Sometimes I look at you and you seem so . . ."

"What? I seem so what?"

"Sad."

His face blanked, his hands settling on his hips. Tension radiated from his body like a force field. "Nothing's going on. I told you that shit wasn't up for discussion."

"Sorry. I just thought maybe you'd like to talk about it."

"Not up for discussion kinda means, I don't want to talk about it. Got it?" His voice was hard and he used it like a weapon. Accordingly, it hurt.

"Okay," I said quietly.

Anger thinned his lips. "You know, Anne, you're the

last fucking person who should be pushing me about anything. We had a deal, an understanding."

Oh no, he did not. My chin jutted out. "And you've stuck
to it so well."

"What the fuck is that supposed to mean?"

"I went to the party. I played my part."

"Yeah? And?"

"And you spent the night trying to prove you're the
world's greatest lover or something. There wasn't anyone
around to see some of those kisses, Mal. They were all
about you proving you're the shit because that's what you
decided to do."

"They were about more than that." A muscle popped
in his jaw. It was kind of impressive and a little scary.
But screw him.

"Were they?"

"'Course they fucking were."

I stared at him, taken aback. "Okay. I didn't realize.
But don't rip my head off for crossing a few lines because
I'm worried about you. I don't like seeing you sad either."

"Fuck," he swore and his face stilled. He linked his
hands behind his head, muttering some more expletives.
Then he let out a long breath, never taking his gaze off of
me. His mood had shifted, the anger gone from the air.
Ever so gently he reached out and traced my swollen bottom lip. "Looks sore."

"It's okay." My voice wavered.

"I overdid it. Sorry."

I wilted, the anger seeping straight out of me. His eyes
were sad again and this time, it was all about me. I had
no defense for that. "If the worst thing to happen to me is
that you think it's fun to kiss me and lie to people about
me being pregnant with your child, my life will probably
be pretty sweet."

His smile lacked commitment, there and gone in an
instant.

"Mal, if you ever want to talk, I'm here." I should probably have shut up but I couldn't. "It's okay."

He looked away.

"To be honest, I'm not exactly great at sharing either." My hands flexed and fisted, flexed and fisted, as if to demonstrate the point. Awkward as all hell, I hated feeling helpless. Why couldn't he just spill so I could try and fix whatever was wrong already?

"Can we stop talking about this now?" he asked the wall.

"Sure."

"Thanks." He reached out, tugged on a strand of my hair. Then his hand slid around to the back of my neck and he drew me in against him. Damn, he smelled good. I got giddy. Maybe there was also a little relief over the argument ending, hard to tell which. With my cheek pressed to Mal's chest, my brain malfunctioned. I wrapped my arms around his waist, getting a solid hold on him just in case he changed his mind and tried to peel me off of him.

"That was our first fight," he mumbled.

"Yeah. I won."

"Did not."

"Did too."

"Pfft. Okay." His arms tightened around me. "I'll give you that one. But only because you're being so childish about it."

"Thanks."

He breathed out hard. "I don't want to fight again."

"No," I agreed wholeheartedly.

"Is it safe to come out yet?" Lizzy asked, peeking around the kitchen door. She gave Mal a quick once-over and then realized what she was doing and looked away. I didn't blame her, but I didn't like it. Man, now I was getting jealous of my own sister. Ridiculous, especially given the man had an army of women after him. If I planned to hang out with a rock star I'd need to get used to this.

"Your sister and I have to go have make-up sex now. It's very important for the long-term health of our relationship." Mal started forcibly stepping us toward the spare room. "But you have a good breakfast and a very nice day. Just leave the dishes; I'll take care of 'em later. It was lovely to meet you, Lizzy."

"Mal, you're strangling me." Or that's what I tried to say. With my face pressed up against his hard chest, it came out garbled. Most likely my words were completely unintelligible.

"What was that?" He loosened his octopus hold enough to allow me to take a good deep breath. Phew, oxygen, my dear old friend.

"Why don't you put some clothes on? I'm going to help Lizzy cook breakfast," I said.

Lizzy watched us with eyes popping out of her head. Fair enough, really. We'd apparently entered some alternative universe where Mal Ericson was all over me like a rash. How mind-bendingly breathtakingly amazing. I needed to make the most of this before he went on tour. Soak up all the memories I could.

"You're the worst girlfriend I've ever had." He pouted. It shouldn't have been charming. But of course it was.

"Am I?"

"Yes. The very worst ever."

"I'm the only girlfriend you've ever had." Fake or not, it was the truth.

"Yeah, you are." He held my face in his hands and covered it in kisses. Everywhere but my poor, sore lips. I don't know what I'd done exactly to earn such an outpouring of affection, but I was profoundly grateful for it just the same. My heart up and keeled over; gave up the war. Hopefully my panties were made of sterner stuff. Given last night, I highly doubted it, however.

"We good?" he asked, lips brushing against my cheek.

"We're great."

"Okay."

"Clothes, Mal."

He laughed and wandered into the spare room, kicking the door shut behind him with some faux Fred Astaire dance move. The man was all class in his snug boxer briefs.

"I've never seen you smile like that." Lizzy leaned her shoulder against the kitchen door, watching. "You look kind of stoned."

"Ha. Yes, he has that effect."

She had her careful face on. I rarely liked anything I heard when she had her mouth set like that. What with me being the older sibling, I didn't see it often. But when I did, it was never good. "I um, I didn't mean to hear what you guys were saying. But your apartment is pretty small."

"I need you to not ask me any questions about this, please."

"Just one."

I agreed to nothing.

"Whatever is going on between you two, this deal you have, is it going to end up hurting you, Anne?"

I hung my head, scuffed the sole of my foot against the floor. My sister and I didn't lie to each other. It was a rule. One we stuck to without fail. No matter the crap Mom peddled, Lizzy and I were always straight with one another. "I don't know."

"You think it'll be worth it?"

"That's two questions," I said with a small smile.

"Call it an early Christmas present."

"He's great, Lizzy. He's so great. I've never met anyone like him."

She nodded slowly, dusted off her hands, and then squeezed them tight. More nervous traits we'd inherited from our crackpot of a mother. "It's like he's turned you back on. Getting away from home helped but . . . he's found you again or something."

"Found me? I've always been right here, Lizzy."

"No, you've been gone a long time."

I stared at the floor, lost for words.

"So, I thought you were inviting Reece to join us this morning."

My mouth dropped open in surprise. Talk about a first time for everything. "Shit. I said I'd call him. I totally forgot."

"Poor Reece. You know, I think this is going to be character building for him." Lizzy grinned then stopped and sniffed at the air. "Bacon's burning!"

We rushed into the kitchen in time to see smoke rising out of the pan and blackened strips of bacon that had shriveled away to nothing. What a waste. I turned off the burner, emptying the remains of breakfast into the sink. Normally, the fridge would be full for our Sunday brunch. But this week I'd been too busy. "Never mind, we'll have toast instead."

"Sorry."

"You two are coming to band practice, right? The guys won't mind." Mal walked into the kitchen, still zipping up a gray hoodie. The man belonged in a jeans ad he wore them so well. And I was still hanging out in my elegant sleepwear, unwashed, and with what had to be greasy hair. He peered at the charred mess in the sink. "Lemme guess, I'm taking you out for breakfast after all?"

"No, we're having toast. You have practice today after that party?" I asked. The merriment of last night had lasted into the early hours. "That's dedication."

"Only four more days till the tour kicks off. Time's a-wasting." Mal paused. "And we're going out. You can't expect me to live on bread and water. You gotta feed your man better than that, woman."

I did my best not to get weak at the words "your man" and thereby set the feminist movement back fifty years. Proximity to Mal was a dangerous thing. "Sounds great. Let me grab a quick shower."

"Good idea. I'll wash your back," he said, following me into the living room.

"Why don't you keep Lizzy company?"

"Why don't I keep you company?" His voice dropped in volume. "I could clean that special place for you with my tongue. Promise I'll do a good job."

"Wow. That's really sweet of you." Oh, boy. I clutched at the bathroom door handle for support. "Two words for you, Mal. Fatal. Attraction."

His smile was huge as he waved away my concerns. "Hello, I don't even own a rabbit. And let's face facts, you're not that strong, pumpkin. I could easily disarm you if I needed to. We've been getting along so well. Come on, it'll be fun."

"Gah! Stop," I whisper yelled at him. "I can't tell if you're serious or not. You're hurting my head."

He leaned down, getting in close. "Look at me; I am totally serious. You're not drunky Anne today, you know what you're doing, and I feel like fucking. Let's renegotiate. This agreement is no longer working for me. I wanna talk to my lawyer!"

"Oh, you feel like fucking?"

"Well, yeah. I'm not used to going more than a day or two. It's making me antsy." He did a little jig on the spot to demonstrate. "I don't like it. C'mon, Anne. Help a friend out. It'll be good."

"Hands down, that's the most romantic thing I've ever heard. I can pretty much feel my legs just falling wide open for you right now."

"What do you want, some bullshit about love?"

"No." *But maybe* something terrible whispered deep inside of me. It needed to shut up.

"You want a song? No problem. I'll ask Davie to write you one later." He put a hand to either side of the bathroom doorway. "I know you wanted to go for it last night. But I wanted you sober. Now you are. I want you. You want me. Let's fuck."

My heart went into overdrive, but I forced myself to calm down. "You're right, I did want to last night. I still want to. But this is not the time, Mal. My sister is here."

"I'll come quick." His brows bunched up. "Wait, I didn't mean it like that. It'll be fast but great. Anne, you might diss my kissing but I'm telling you now, my oral sex skills are off the chart. I know all about getting dirty down under. Let me show you, pretty please?"

"Mal . . ." I couldn't even think what to say when he gave me pleading eyes. He had me bouncing between emotions as fast as he changed moods. Angry, horny, and amused all blended into one. "Lizzy is just in the kitchen. She can hear every word we're saying."

"We'll shut the bathroom door, turn on the shower. With the water running she won't hear a thing."

"God, you confuse me. I don't think my head has stopped spinning since you walked in the door."

"You can be confused later. But come on my face now, please?"

Which is about the time I started panting. Horny was definitely winning the race. Fortunately my baggy T-shirt hid the worst of the hard nipple evidence. I pushed him back with a hand while I still had the strength. "We'll talk about this later when we're alone. Go bond with your supposed future sister-in-law. Please."

"Fine." His whole body drooped. "But you're missing out big-time."

"I don't doubt it."

"I might not even be in the mood later, Anne. You could completely miss out and that'd be it, life ruined."

"I consider myself duly warned."

"Last chance." He rolled out his big pink tongue like a dog. Though that was probably being mean to dogs. In all likelihood, canines showed more discretion. "Thee? Iths really long."

"Will you please put that away?" I laughed.

Instead he grabbed the back of my head, dragging the length of his warm, damp tongue up the side of my face. I froze against the onslaught. "You did not just do that."

"It's a sign of affection. You think I salivate on just anyone?"

"You . . . I can't even."

"There are women who would kill to have me licking their face. You do not even begin to appreciate just how lucky you are to have my spit. Now lick me back." He pointed to his jaw, demandingly. "Anne, do it. Do it now, woman, before I get offended."

I giggled, my whole body getting in on the act. Which was getting dangerous. "I need to go to the bathroom. Go away. Stop making me laugh."

"I like making you laugh."

"Yeah, well, me peeing my pants would be less cool. Go on."

"Hold up." He grabbed my wrist, his voice quieting. The way he could switch from clown to calm in an instant was nothing short of amazing. "One, that was too much information. Two, you and Lizzy coming to band practice with me?"

"You're sure that's okay?"

"Yes."

"Then we'd love to." I nodded. This had to be the most insanely perfect moment ever. Me with a full bladder and a full heart both at once. "We just have to make a phone call first, then we can go."

"Good. Three, admit you lied about not liking my kisses last night." His gaze held me fast.

No point denying it any longer; I liked him and I wanted him so much it hurt. The minute I had him all alone, it was on. His fingers were still wound around my wrist as I cupped his jaw. The scratch of his stubble against the palm of my hand and the warmth of his skin was divine. But it wasn't enough. I needed to give something back. Some small part of the crazy, confusing, lusty joy he gave me. He held perfectly still while I reached up and pressed a careful kiss to his cheek. "You're right, I lied."

The tension lines around his mouth eased. "You did."

"Yes. I'm sorry. You just kind of overwhelmed me and . . . anyway, you're the best."

He pumped his fists into the air. "I knew it! I'm the best."

"You are."

A simple statement of fact, but it lit up his eyes just the same. "Thanks, pumpkin."

His smile . . . I had no words.

CHAPTER THIRTEEN

We called Mom from my bedroom, perched on the edge of my downed mattress. Mal was busy watching TV in the living room, a cup of coffee in hand.

I nodded and Lizzy took out her cell, selected the contact, and set the phone to speaker. Then she held it between us. My skin prickled. The air seemed cold and hot all at once. Fuck, I hated this. I hated it with a passion. But in my head, Mom was so closely entwined with anger and frustration I couldn't separate her from the emotions. One day, it wouldn't be this way.

"Hi, Mom," said Lizzy, sounding cheery as sunshine in a bottle. She'd forgiven Mom already. I was still getting there.

"Hi, girls. How are you?" Just the sound of her voice brought it all back. Sitting in the dark with her, begging and pleading with her to eat just another spoonful, to get out of bed and have a shower maybe, act like a human being. To start being an adult and look after her daughters so I could go back to being a kid.

"We're great, Mom," I said, doing my best to sound normal. "How are you?"

"Good. Work's been fine."

I nodded like she could see me, relieved she was holding down a job still, being responsible for her own finances. That was good. For years I'd made do with the remains of the savings account, then whatever Dad saw fit to send.

"School's going well." Lizzy swapped her cell over to her other hand, talking on about college all the while. Then she put her arm around me and started rubbing my back. A sweet gesture, but honestly, being touched right then didn't help.

My sister excelled at these conversations. She could babble on for a good ten minutes. And really, ten minutes was a long enough time frame for a weekly call home, right?

"What about you, Anne?" she asked once Lizzy had exhausted herself.

"I'm fine."

"Anne is seeing someone," Lizzy supplied.

I shot her a glance. "It's not that serious."

"He's really great, Mom. He's so into her, you can just see it in his eyes."

"Oh," said Mom, followed by a moment's silence. "You're being careful, aren't you, Anne?"

It could mean so many things, but I knew exactly what my mother was saying. Had I not forgotten men were the sworn enemy? Why, look how our dad had just up and left us! Funny, men being evil wasn't the lesson I'd taken away from my teenage years, no matter what Mom might have intended.

"Yes, mom." I tucked my newly styled hair behind my ears, sat up straighter. "Everything's fine."

Mom let out a little sigh. "Good. I wouldn't want—"

"He's actually waiting to take us to breakfast, Mom. So we better go."

"Alright, I wanted to ask if you girls would like to come home for Thanksgiving, maybe?" Her voice sounded hopeful, pleading. "It would be lovely to see you both."

"Thanksgiving?" Lizzy asked, like she'd never heard of the occasion. "We'll think about it . . . sure."

Like hell.

"I don't think I can get the time off work, Mom," I said. "Sorry."

Mom made a sad little noise and the heart I'd hardened toward her a long time ago paused. There was a twinge of guilt, but not enough to make me go back. Never even remotely enough for that. I had my own life now.

"But, Anne, you never take time off," she said. "It can't be good for you."

"Reece depends on me, Mom."

"Surely you're entitled to some holidays. Are you certain he's not taking advantage of you?"

I just stared at the phone.

"Oh, crap, Mom," said Lizzy. "My cell's about to die. I'm so sorry."

"You're always forgetting to plug it in."

"I know. Look, we love you. Great to talk to you. We'll talk again next week."

"Alright, girls. Take care."

"Bye," cried Lizzy, carrying the show.

I mouthed the word. It was honestly the most I could manage. Thank fuck, we'd made it through another week.

Lizzy ended the call, her hand rubbing up and down my back somewhat frantically. Like I needed nurturing. I'm the one who sat her down and explained what a period was. Oh, and sex too. I'd looked over her homework, making sure she got assignments done on time. I could keep my shit together. So I hadn't quite moved on yet from this issue I had with Mom. I'd get there.

"We're not going home," she said.

"Not a chance." I crawled back up onto my feet, smoothed down the gray sweater dress and straightened my tights. I opened the bedroom door. Mal sat on the wingback, staring at the TV.

"Hey, you good to go?" he asked.

"Yeah. All done."

He cocked his head. "What's up, pumpkin?"

I forced a smile, walking toward him. He made me want to smile. It wasn't a complete lie. The concern didn't fade from his eyes, however.

But my mother wasn't ruining this for me.

I leaned over him, setting my hands on the back of the chair, getting close. "Hey."

"Hi," he said, gripping my upper arms. Despite the feeling of not wanting to be touched, something in me unwound at the contact. At his nearness.

"I need a kiss."

"Do you, now? Then you're in luck. For you, I have an endless supply."

God, he was so sweet.

I pressed my lips to his, kissing him lightly to start with. His hand slid into my hair, supporting my head. Then his tongue slid into my mouth. Warm, glowy, happiness filled me. This man, he had magic. At the very least, he had a magical tongue. And really, wasn't that what life was all about? No, okay. Don't try to follow that logic.

"Mm." My happy place had been found.

"An okay effort," he said, rubbing his lips together. "You could probably use a little practice though."

"Haha."

"You get bad news?" he asked.

"No. My mom just hurts my head." There, let the record show, I'd officially shared.

"Yeah?"

"Yes. Let's go get breakfast. Don't want you to be late for rehearsal."

He wasn't so easily distracted. "Don't have sad eyes, Anne. I can't fucking stand it when you're sad."

"You make it better."

"Dude, of course I do. Have you seen me lately?" He grinned and I laughed. "That's better. C'mon, let's go. Otherwise, we keep kissing, we ain't going anywhere but to bed."

CHAPTER FOURTEEN

We were ten minutes late to band practice and eggs
Benedict could take the blame. Mal had sat at the table
with his back to the room, a baseball cap on his head.
Only the waitress recognized him and quietly asked for
his autograph. He'd tipped her big-time. I'm pretty sure I
saw love shining in her eyes when we left. Lizzy couldn't
be far behind with the sentiment. Sure as hell, he'd gone
out of his way to win her over, asking questions about her
degree and her life in general. He'd been sincere in his
interest, sitting forward, listening carefully to her answers.
She'd also been highly impressed with his big black Jeep
featuring every accessory known to mankind.

But fancy SUVs aside, Mal Ericson was a man to be
proud of. My heart and my hormones both took him very
seriously. Beneath the surface, all caution had fled. He
had me and if the hand fixed to my knee during breakfast
was any indication, he knew it. Strangely enough, I didn't
have it in me to worry.

Screw being stressed about Mom. With Mal smiling at
me, none of it mattered.

Stage Dive practiced in an old building by the river. Mal
switched into business mode the minute we walked into
the massive space. The difference was fascinating. He gave

the side of my face a quick kiss and then continued on to where the guys waited. A stage had been erected at one end of the place. Amps and equipment sat thick on the ground. Cables snaked out in every direction. A couple of roadies, or sound technicians, or whatever they were, rushed about.

Mal stretched his fingers and rolled his wrists, warming up his muscles. Then he stripped off his hoodie and sat behind a shining drum kit, twirling a stick in his hand. The man was clearly in his element, his focus complete. David and Ben were messing around with their instruments, plucking and strumming strings. Interestingly enough, Jimmy was doing push-ups. Lots of them. Then he climbed to his feet and motioned the guys to gather around Mal's kit.

Lizzy and I joined Ev and Lena sitting over on some storage boxes near the back of the hall.

"Hello, fellow Stage Dive groupies and hanger-oners. How is your Sunday morning?" Ev said, sitting on her hands, kicking her feet.

"Good." I smiled back at her and Lena in greeting. "How are you feeling, Mrs. Ferris?"

"I am feeling very very married, thank you for asking. How are you and Mal doing?"

"Ah, good. All good." Everything was good. I parked my butt on the edge of a box. "This is my sister, Lizzy. She goes to school at PSU. Lizzy this is Ev, David's wife, and Lena, Jimmy's . . ." I faltered.

"Assistant. Hi." Lena did the chin tip.

"Hi." Lizzy waved.

"Nice to meet you," said Ev. "Anne, quickly before they start playing. Tell me the story of you and Malcolm. I still haven't heard how you got together, exactly. But Lauren mentioned he basically invaded your apartment."

My mind scrambled. In the next life I was definitely

going to stress less and prepare more. "Ah, well, we met at your place the other night and hit it off."

Lizzy gave me a long look that I ignored.

"That's it?" Ev asked, eyes incredulous.

"Yes, that's pretty much it," I said.

She did not appear pleased.

"What is this, Ev, a grilling?" I laughed.

"Yes, this is a grilling," said Ev with a hopeful smile. "Give me information, please?"

"He's really great and yes, he kind of moved himself in with me. But I love having him there. He's wonderful, you know?" God, I hoped that would do. Definitely time for a subject change. "So, why are you still working in a café?"

"Touché," she said. "It's complicated. I owed my parents money, it was important that they saw me earning it as opposed to my hot, rich husband just handing it over. Things have calmed on the family front now and I'm moving on to other things. Always find it funny the way people react to me working. Like I should sit at home and spend David's money, be the trophy wife. Screw that. I'd be bored as hell inside of two minutes."

Ev shook her head. "Not saying it's been all smooth sailing. We've had to get restraining orders against one nut of a fan and one ass of a photographer. For a while, Sam the security man had to come hang out with me at work. I did not like that, but them's the breaks. After I failed to do anything interesting the paparazzi moved on. Anybody that bothered me got banned from the shop. Not saying it was easy, but I'm entitled to my own life."

"Yes," I said. "You are."

"You'll probably find out for yourself someday soon. Dating one of these guys can be a headache, but they're worth it. Now back to you. Mal is suddenly living with you. I've never even seen him with the same girl twice.

Didn't think it was possible." She paused, eyeballing me to add emphasis to this information. Inside my chest, my heart just sort of shriveled. What would happen when the novelty wore off and Mal got tired of playing house with me?

"Anne? Hello? Please give me more."

"Um." I was tempted to flail, but that would give away too much. "He's very persuasive. And . . . he's Mal Ericson. So, yeah. How could I say no?"

She paused. "This is your tale of true love? That's the worst story ever. To think I spilled my guts to you."

"Their eyes met across a crowded room." Lena supplied, busy playing with her cell.

"Was it love at first sight?" asked Ev.

"Absolutely. Didn't you feel the ground move?"

"So that's what that was. Got it." Ev huddled down into her gray jacket. "Alright, I'll mind my own business. I'm just happy you two are happy."

"Thank you," I said, ignoring the continuing sad state of my heart. I just had to live for the moment. Enjoy being with him while I could. Sure. Not a problem.

Meanwhile, Lizzy hadn't sat like me. Instead, she stood staring at the stage, transfixed by something. Or someone. To be fair, it was an awesome sight. The band finished their talk and separated, moving to their own areas. Then Mal counted them in and bang! Music poured out, filling the hall. No wonder Ev had wanted to talk before the boys started playing. The guitar screamed and the bass thumped, rattling my rib cage. Drums pounded and I felt the rhythm of the music beating in time with my heart. Then Jimmy sang. "I've got this feeling that comes and goes, ten broken fingers and one broken nose . . ."

It was an old song off the *San Pedro* album, one of my favorites. All thought of what the future may or may not hold for me and Mal slipped from my mind. Mal's playing and the music owned me, the smoothness of his move-

ments and his absolute focus. His energy. My face hurt
from smiling by the time they reached the chorus. All four
of us jumped to our feet and broke out into applause at
the end. Jimmy laughed softly and bowed. A group of
people huddled by the side of the stage took turns giving
us bad looks. No idea what their problem was.

"That's their manager, Adrian, and some of the record
company people," said Ev, her voice far from warm. "Piece
of advice, steer clear of them."

"Adrian's an asshole." Lena settled back onto one of
the wooden boxes. "But he's a hell of a manager."

The man in question was middle-aged, wearing a
business shirt with a thick gold chain around his neck.

"Was he there last night?"

"Nope." Ev flicked her hair over her shoulder angrily.
"Adrian and I don't get along. He prefers the band to be
focused on their music rather than wasting time on relationships."

"Like your sexing up David didn't inspire the last album," said Lena.

"Exactly. He should be thanking me." Ev huffed out a
laugh. "If he gives you any crap, Anne, let Mal know. He'll
deal with him."

Four hours later the band finally stopped playing and
handed their instruments over to roadies. My throat was
raw from yelling, my hands red from clapping. God help
me if I ever made it to an actual concert. There had been
some stopping and starting as they worked on perfecting
various parts of songs. Then they'd held meetings, just the
four of them and also with some of the record company
people. They also toyed with effects via the sound guys
with their panel of buttons and dials. Us ladies had danced
and hollered and had a great time all around. Each and
every member of the band was so talented.

But Mal . . . we needed to get back to my apartment
and ruin the remains of my bed.

His hair was dark with sweat and he'd long since lost his T-shirt by the time he approached. "Have fun?"

"Yes, I did," I croaked.

"You losing your voice? I thought that was you screaming." He pulled on his hoodie.

"Oh my god, is that *the* David Ferris?" Ev stood atop one of the boxes we'd been sitting on. Her husband just shook his head and held out his arms, eyes amused. She launched herself at him and with no difficulty at all, David caught her. Her legs went around him and their mouths fused.

"Get a room," groaned Ben.

Mal handed me his drum sticks. "A memento of your first Stage Dive concert."

Someone laughed, but I didn't care. I held the sticks tight to my chest. "I'll treasure them always."

"She heard us play last night." Jimmy hung back from the group, arms crossed. His good mood was apparently gone.

"That was acoustic," said Mal. "And I'm not going to give my love a set of flimsy fucking brushes, am I? Only long, hard, phallic shaped things will do for a girl of her appetites."

"I heard about you two." Carefully, David set his wife back down, keeping an arm around her.

My head snapped up. "What?"

"Ooh, what happened?" asked Lena, ears practically perking up, puppy style.

"They broke the bed." The look on Ev's face—hell, we were never going to live this down. "Can you believe that?"

"Of course we broke the bed. They're just lucky we didn't break the building," announced Mal proudly, taking a bow.

David shook his head. "You two do anything interesting and I get Lauren calling at the crack of fucking dawn to tell my wife. Move already."

"Anne likes it there," said Mal. "No rush."

"You got shit security. People get to know you're in the area, you'll have no privacy. And how fucking small are those apartments?"

"Relax, Davic. We'll think about it. You guys, all so addicted to your mansions and fancy livin'. Why, Anne and I could live in a cardboard box and we wouldn't even notice, our love is so epic. Isn't that right, pumpkin?"

"Um, yes?"

"See?" Mal crowed. "She's insanely psycho crazy about me. Material things mean nothing in the face of such worshipful adoration."

David just shook his head.

"Whatever." Ben ran a hand over his short hair. "I'm starving. We finding somewhere to eat and drink?"

"YES." That was Lizzy. A very loud and determined-sounding Lizzy.

The bass player's eyes moved over her with sudden interest. A slow, salacious smile curled his lips. "Well, okay then."

Red alert. So not okay. My baby sister was not hooking up with a player who had to have eight or more years on her. If I wanted to be stupid with my heart, that was on me. I'd let Lizzy get hurt over my dead body.

"Don't you have to get back to school, Liz?" I asked.

"No, I'm fine."

"I thought you had an assignment to do?" I communicated much with my eyes.

She ignored it all. "Nope."

"Lizzy." I forced her name out through gritted teeth.

"Ladies, ladies," Mal said, sensing the rising hostilities. "We got a problem here?"

A woman who'd been hanging with the record company executives approached, her high-heeled boots tapping across the floor. Her smile was tentative. The woman was gorgeous, breasts about a billion times the size of mine (granted, not hard to do) and blond hair in a cool pixie cut. "Mal?"

He turned and his entire face lit up at the sight of the girl. My insides knotted. Yes, fine. I might have been a bit jealous.

"Ainslie, when did you arrive? Looking good." He sounded super happy. They hugged. Then they hugged some more. The girl giggled and sighed, pressing herself against him. Holy shit, was that bitch actually feeling up my fake boyfriend in front of me? She was practically humping his leg. Given the dynamic between the two, there could be no doubting what their relationship was about. I'd finally met one of Mal's fuck buddies. It had to happen. Surprise was stupid and I had no real right to hurt feelings. Pity that didn't make the pain disappear.

I could feel the other women's eyes on me, boring holes into my skull. No way was I returning their stares. Mal had obviously found someone to scratch his itch. Meanwhile, my face was heating up. The entire scene was fucking horrible and embarrassing.

"Hey, Mal," said Lizzy, interrupting the lovers' reunion. "Should we invite Anne's friend Reece along to eat? He often does stuff with us on Sundays."

Oh the wonderful loyal little shit stirrer. I appreciated the thought, but her intentions were misplaced. I didn't need protecting.

"I think Reece said he'd be busy," I said.

My sister played the wide-eyed innocent so well. "No, really? Why don't you give him a call and check, Anne?"

I shook my head. "Maybe another—"

"Fuck no, Lizzy. I mean, I don't think there'll be room." Mal's arms remained around the woman. Then he noticed the faces of his friends, the disapproving and the curious both. For a moment he looked confused, blinking, his forehead creased. Then he stepped back from her, shoved his hands into his jeans pockets. Talk about compromised. Our fake relationship had entirely slipped his mind. His Chucks shifted restlessly.

Also, apparently the thought of making Reece jealous no longer appealed to him. But I hadn't wanted to call Reece either. I'd been perfectly happy as things were. Either way, right now, it didn't much matter. This woman had changed everything.

Ainslie put a hand on his arm. "Is something wrong?"

"It's cool," I said, not on the verge of tears. The air was just really dusty in the old building. "Why don't you go for a drink with your friend and catch up?"

"I thought we were gonna do something," he said.

"Yeah, but . . ."

Eyes guarded, Mal looked at me. Then he looked right through me. I wasn't even there. Whatever he was thinking, it didn't show on his face. It couldn't be easy for someone who was used to getting what they wanted when they wanted it to back down from an obvious offer of sex. Let's be honest, his impulse control was limited at best.

"I'm sorry, you are?" Ainslie asked. Perfectly polite, I couldn't fault the woman's manners.

"Ainslie, this is Mal's new girlfriend, Anne. Anne, this is Ainslie." Fucking great, even Ev knew her. This one was a regular. What had happened to never seeing him with the same woman twice?

"Girlfriend?" Ainslie laughed uncertainly, eyes darting around the group. No one laughed with her. Christ on a crutch, this was awkward.

Mal stepped closer. "I was just saying hi to a friend. What's the big deal?"

"There isn't one. It's fine."

"Yeah, there obviously is or you wouldn't be looking at me like that," he said, his tone fierce and pissed off. Like I was inconveniencing him or something.

"You need to not talk to me in that tone of voice," I said. "Especially not in front of other people. Go out with your friend, have a nice time. We can discuss this later."

"We can, huh?"

"Yes."

Ainslie took a big step back. Poor woman.

But Mal looked around the group, pissed and confused. A vein looked about ready to pop in his neck. "Fuck it."

He turned and strode back toward the stage, barking an order for sticks at one of the roadies. Soon the pounding of drums once again filled the warehouse. Everyone was looking somewhere else. What a clusterfuck.

Davie looked to Jimmy. His brother nodded, wandering off also in the direction of the stage. Ben followed while Ainslie just sort of drifted back toward the record company people.

"Crap, I forgot." Ev grabbed at her head dramatically as if struck by a sudden thought. "We women all have to go meet Lauren. Girl's night out."

"You do?" asked David.

"Yep." She gave him a piercing look. "We're starting early."

He got the drift. "Right. Yeah."

I don't remember much about us leaving. Between Ev and Lizzy, I was hustled out of there damn fast to a big black Escalade waiting outside. The beefy, bald man standing beside it was strangely familiar.

"Hi," I said. "Didn't you put the bolt on my door the other day?"

"Yes, ma'am."

"That's Sam. Sam, this is Anne. She's one of us." Ev slid into the backseat and buckled up, while Lizzy jumped in the front. She bounced her butt up and down on the plush leather. It was good to know someone was enjoying the lap of luxury. I could have given two shits if we were in some smelly old cab.

"Lovely to meet you, ma'am," said Sam. "Good to see you as always, Mrs. Ferris."

I climbed in and buckled up.

"I don't understand," said Lizzy.

"About?" I asked.

Lizzy twisted in her seat so she could see me. "This. He makes you happier than I've ever seen. It's like you're a different person. He looks at you like you invented whipped cream. Now this. I don't understand."

I shrugged trying my best to keep my face calm, neutral. "Whirlwind romance. Easy come, easy go."

"I'm going to need a rusty shovel, Sam," said Ev.

"I'll get right on that, Mrs. Ferris." He pulled out of the parking lot.

"Excellent. We better go pick up Lauren. She'll want to be included in this."

"And what is this?" I asked. "We're not really doing girl's night out are we?"

Her face let me know that hell yes we were.

"You know, I'm not really in the mood right now. But that's very sweet of you."

"Sam?" Ev sang out almost merrily.

"Yes, Mrs. Ferris?"

"If I needed your help kidnapping our Anne here and making her drink with me, would that be a problem?"

"Of course not, Mrs. Ferris. Anything for you."

"You sweet dear man," she cooed. "You know he used to be a Navy SEAL. I wouldn't mess with him, but you do whatever you feel you need to, Anne."

"You're kind of evil when you get going." I stared out the window, letting the scenery slip by.

Ev held her peace. For all of a moment. "I don't know what the hell Mal was thinking back there letting that skank climb all over him."

Lizzy snorted. "I'm not sure he was thinking."

Me, neither. But I didn't say that.

The truth was, Mal and I might have broken up. Our fake relationship could be over. Who knew? What a truly god-awful horrible fucking notion. I blinked profusely. Must have had something in my eye. Honestly, I wasn't the crying type. So my crush had been crushed. Life goes on. Whatever Lizzy knew, or thought she knew, she wouldn't say a word. And me, I had no comment to make on the subject.

Nothing.

Though, this was exactly why getting overly attached to people wasn't smart. If there was a chance their absence would make things heartrending, walk away. No one should have the power to make you want to throw some manic-depressive episode and swallow a truckload of gin (my mom's favorite method for dealing with such disappointments). I guess you needed to learn these lessons over sometimes. Well, I had it now. All good.

Mal didn't come home Sunday night. Not that my apartment was home, but you know what I mean.

Despite the drinks poured into me, I didn't get much sleep.

CHAPTER FIFTEEN

By the time I fired off the fifth text for the day, lunchtime had come and gone.

> Anne: I can drop your stuff at David & Ev's if you want. Just let me know.

Like the previous ones, this text garnered no response. Zip. Nada. Nothing. I couldn't help myself. I had to try again.

> Anne: I hope we can still be friends.

The minute I sent it regret swamped me. It was such a dumb-ass standard boring thing to say. Why didn't smart-phones come with an "undo" button? Now that would be an app worth having. I should've tried to be more original. Maybe if I'd been funny about it, thrown in something witty about his drum kit or something, he'd respond. But again I got nothing.

"Still texting him?" asked Reece from where he was busy reshuffling books in the action/adventure section.

"Mm-hmm."

"No response yet?"

"No."

Worst Monday ever. I'd managed to talk Reece into letting me tidy up out back all morning, thus eliminating any need for conversation. With only two, maybe three, hours of sleep under my belt, I wasn't human. Not really. I was a nasty, bitchy, ball of heartache. Had Ainslie soothed Mal's man pain? Images of them entangled filled my head. I'd seen almost all of his body, so the details were vivid.

Yes, my delicate little feelings had been well and truly hurt. Thank god Mal left when he did. Any more time together and I'd have become completely devastated when he went on tour.

Still nothing from my cell. I checked it twice just to be sure.

He was right on with the Fatal Attraction. So far I'd only stalked him via text, though. Lucky he'd kept his dick in his pants. His mere presence had inspired me enough. The thought that I might lose him entirely made me want to both burst into tears and break shit (preferably over his head). Anger and sadness owned me.

How many days had it been since I met him? Not many.

"Fucking ridiculous."

"What did you say?" asked Reece, casting a nervous eye toward the hipster couple browsing in home renovation.

Crap. "Nothing. Nothing. Sorry."

Reece approached the counter. I kept pounding on the computer keyboard regardless, pretending to process invoices. Maybe if I ignored him he'd go away. A couple of days, and I'd be fine again. Today, however, I kind of needed some space. I didn't want to hear the details about whoever my boss banged over the weekend. Please understand, I wasn't jealous, for once. Or was it twice, now? My crush on Reece had mysteriously (or not so mysteriously) disappeared. Mal Ericson fever was a potent thing.

"You're really upset about this guy, aren't you?" he asked, sounding like the concept defied logic.

"I don't really want to talk about it, Reece."

"Listen." He sighed, bracing his hands on the counter. "How about I take you out tonight for a few drinks? There's a new bar down in Chinatown. We can check it out."

"That's really great of you. But how about another night?"

"You got plans?"

"Sort of." Because sitting alone brooding while wearing one of Mal's T-shirts constituted plans.

Reece rubbed his chin with the palm of his hand, his brows drawing downward. "Anne, realistically, you had to know this was coming. He's Malcolm Ericson. The guy's a living legend."

"Yeah, I know." My shoulders caved in on me. In standard measurement, I stood about two-feet tall. I couldn't have felt any smaller.

"Guys like that don't have a reputation for stable relationships."

"I, ah . . . I get that. I do."

"Hey, you're great. It's his loss."

"Thanks."

Ugh. The pity in Reece's eyes . . . kill me now. A bottle of tequila was now included in tonight's plans. Rock on. This was why I never much bothered with dating, this whole moment right here. Penises were out and self-love was back in. Not that it had ever really left.

I needed to put my life back into context. Mal was the one being a jerk. I'd done nothing wrong. Except for having no idea how to handle a difficult situation, of course.

"Guess we should get back to work." I wasn't really achieving much, but still, a token effort should be made what with him paying me and all.

Reece crossed and uncrossed his arms, watching me.

"Listen, why don't you take the rest of the day off? I'll close up."

"Really?"

"Yeah." He smiled, dimples popping. "God knows I owe you some hours. You've never even taken a sick day."

"Thanks, Reece."

My big old claw foot tub was the best place in the whole wide world. Nothing could compare. Life seemed so much better from within its warm, soapy watery confines. If I ever had to move, it's what I'd miss the most. I'd been in there, soaking, for a good solid half hour. Frankly, I had no plans to ever get out. I was perfectly content to laze around, staring at the tiles on the wall and thinking of nothing.

Raging, great open seas full of nothing.

Right up until the front door crashed open. I bolted upright, adrenaline pumping through me.

"What the fuck?"

"Anne?" Mal yelled.

Then the bathroom door crashed open too. I grabbed the white towel hanging off the rail overhead, holding it against my chest. Straightaway, the material started soaking up water.

"Anne." Mal stomped in, electric with rage. It spiked out his hair and darkened his eyes. The bathroom door slammed shut behind him.

"Mal?"

"What is this?" he growled, shoving his cell in my face.

"Um, your phone? What the hell are you doing in here?"

"The fucking texts you've been sending me, I mean."

"What?" I stared at him, flabbergasted. "Get out."

"No."

"You want to discuss my texts, you can wait till I'm out of the tub and have some clothes on."

"We'll discuss them now."

For this conversation, I needed armor. The damn towel wasn't working at all. I crossed my arms over my chest, huddling in on myself. "Those messages are me trying to be friendly after yesterday. You barging in here like this, though? I'm not feeling so friendly anymore. Get the fuck out, Mal."

"You're breaking up with me by text." Not a question, a statement. One that made me just a small part livid, though the crashing of doors and yelling might have played a part in it too.

Was he insane? No, seriously, was he?

"That little asswipe Reece push you into this?"

"No," I snapped. "Reece has nothing to do with this. And I can't really be breaking up with you because remember the part where we were never really together? Where it was all fake?"

"It was, huh?" He squatted beside the tub, hands gripping the edge so hard his knuckles whitened.

"Get out."

"I'm not going anywhere till we talk this out."

The vestiges of self-pity disappeared, replaced by flat-out rage. How dare he?

"If you want to talk this out, then you might want to stop acting like a dick. Busting in here and yelling at me, accusing me of crap . . . not smart."

"That right? Why don't you tell me what I'm supposed to do since I'm not so smart and all." He loomed over the side of the tub, eyes bordering on manic. "Tell me how I'm supposed to handle this, Anne. And use small words, okay?"

I tried to sit up, the water sloshing. Could he have picked a more awkward time and place for this? And how had *he* turned into the victim here?

"I didn't mean . . ." I started, but gah, fuck him. If he wanted to get all insulted, he could, with my compliments. I cleared my throat, tried again. "Big picture. You didn't come home . . . back here, to the apartment last night. I assume you were with Ainslie. Your friends are probably going to know that, right? So our cover is blown."

"I wasn't with Ainslie," he ground out.

Everything stopped. "You weren't?"

"No; I played drums till I calmed down, then I did some drinking with the guys. Davie said to give you some time to cool off. I crashed in Ben's hotel suite."

"Word to the wise, next time when it comes to us, try talking to me instead of Davie."

He let out a slow breath. "Okay."

"You just crashed in Ben's suite?" This version of reality differed so wildly from the hateful version I'd been playing in my head. It wouldn't sink in at first.

"Yeah, I did." His dark green gaze roamed my face. "I didn't think when Ainslie came up to me after practice. How it would look and everything. Didn't think at all and then I didn't handle it right."

He paused, but I had nothing. It was all I could do not to burst into tears of relief. Not that I was a crier. I'd blame it on PMS but it was nowhere near my time of the month.

"I fucked up and I hurt you," he said, deflating. "I'm sorry."

"Oh, no, you didn't hurt me." I held my eyes wide open, trying to keep my shit together. "I mean, it might have been nice if you'd answered one of my texts but . . . yeah, no, I wasn't *hurt* exactly."

His brows rose and for a moment, he said nothing. "You looked hurt."

"Well, I wasn't. I was fine."

He just watched me.

"Really."

The smudges were back beneath his eyes. It seemed Mal hadn't gotten any more sleep last night than I had.

"Everything's good," I said, not believing it but hoping he did. Meanwhile, I was still bare-ass naked in the bath, horribly exposed. "Now can you please leave?"

Mal's brows rose. "You're alright?"

"Yep. There's the door."

"I didn't hurt you?"

"Noooo."

"Okay," he said eventually, thumb rapping out a beat on the edge of the tub. "So the deal is still on and everything's cool?"

"Sure, I guess so. Why not?" I gave him my very best big, brave smile, clutching the wet towel to my breasts, my knees drawn up to help cover downstairs.

He breathed out hard through his nose, sat back on his heels. This was good. He was accepting it and we were moving on, thank god.

"We're fine. No worries."

Then he slowly shook his head. "Christ, Anne. You're so full of shit I don't even know what the fuck to say to you right now."

"What?" My screech bounced off the tiled walls, echoing around us.

"You heard me."

"But—"

His hand held firm to the back of my neck and he slammed his mouth down on mine. My words were forgotten. His tongue slid into my mouth, teasing me. His hand cradled my head, holding me out of the water. I gave myself up to it, the demanding press of his lips and the scratch of his stubble. I angled my head, getting closer, going deeper and pulling him into me. If I drowned, it'd be worth it.

There was no finesse. Raw hunger took over.

I didn't realize he'd started climbing into the tub with me until half the water sloshed over the sides. No more of this splashing nonsense, we made a god damn waterfall. He got in, jeans, T-shirt, Chucks and all, his legs tangling with mine. One strong arm wrapped around my waist, holding me to him, the other he braced on the top of the tub. Someone had to keep us afloat because I was too busy getting my hands beneath his T-shirt. I could've kissed him for days, but getting him naked was important.

"Off," I demanded, dragging the material up.

"Hang on." He pulled back onto his knees. With one of his hands and two of mine, we got rid of that sucker.

The feel of his hot skin and hard flesh was so fine. My fingers couldn't travel far enough fast enough. I wanted to learn every inch of him. My mouth found his again and *yes*. I groaned and he clutched me harder. We were pressed together, skin on skin for the most part. My pebbled nipples rubbed against his chest.

Fuck yeah, friction.

Friction was beautiful, but wet denim sucked. I wiggled a hand under the back of his waistband, grabbing onto his tight ass. His hips flexed, pushing against me, grinding into me. There was every chance the bath wasn't big enough for this. We'd make do. My elbow clocked the side, vibrating my funny bone. It hurt like a bitch. He must've noticed, because the next thing I knew we were rolling. More water cascaded out onto the floor.

"On top," he grunted.

"'Kay."

His hands slid over my skin, trying to keep hold. "Fuck, you're slippery."

The man knew how to use his body. All I could do was hold on, my hands tangled in his long hair. His mouth traveled over my collarbone, up my neck, finishing with his teeth at my jaw. Every inch of my skin broke out in goose bumps. My tummy tensed. A large hand palmed my ass, squeezing. Wet denim wasn't so bad after all. Grinding my pussy against the ridge his hard-on felt rather nice. Not as nice as he'd feel bare, but still.

"You hear that?" he asked.

"What? No." The only thing I could hear was my heart pounding. And anyway, who cared? Now wasn't the time for listening. It was the time to feel and I felt fucking fantastic sitting astride him. Luckily I knew how to prioritize. I fit my lips to his, kissing him deep and wet.

He broke away, turning his head aside. "Wait," he said, followed shortly by, "shit."

Distantly, from ever so far away (like the next room), there it was.

"Malcolm? Honey?" It was a woman's voice, accompanied by several sets of feet. We had company.

What on earth?

"Mom?" he answered, his face skewed with disbelief. Oh shit, he'd left the front door open.

"We got an earlier flight," his mom called. And for the record, she sounded like a very nice woman. But shit, I didn't want to meet her like this. What a wonderful first impression.

"You did?" asked Mal.

"That's not a problem, is it?"

"Your parents are visiting?" I queried in a furious whisper. "Right now?"

He squeezed his eyes shut and whispered back, "Did I forget to mention that?"

"Mal? Honey?" his Mom called. "Everything okay?"

"No, no. Not a problem at all, Mom. Everything's good."

"We were just so excited when you told us about Anne."

"She is pretty damn exciting." He gave my breasts a long look. "Got to agree with you there."

"We really wanted to just get here and meet her. I guess we should have warned you."

His grin was pure evil. Hell itself would have been jealous. "Oh, you want to meet Anne? Because she's right—"

I slapped my hand over his mouth. "Don't you fucking dare," I hissed.

Crap, the things he thought were amusing might just get

one of us killed. In this situation, it was most definitely his life on the line. Despite the laughter in his eyes, he nodded, pressing a kiss to the palm of my hand. Slowly, I removed it, my eyes narrowed on him.

"What was that?" asked his mom.

"I was just saying she'll be home from work soon, Mom."

"Wonderful."

"Sorry," he mouthed to me, laughing silently.

"Asshole," I mouthed back.

He grabbed the back of my head, bringing my lips to his. If only I didn't love kissing him so much.

"Son," a deep voice said from the other room.

"Hi, Dad." Mal rested his forehead on my shoulder. "Don't come in."

"No, no. We won't do that."

"There's a lot of water on the floor," his mom said, matter-of-factly. "Aren't you a bit old to be splashing around like this? What on earth were you doing? Where does Anne keep her mop?"

"Kitchen cabinet," I whispered.

"Ah, kitchen cabinet, Mom. Thanks. Guess I got carried away." Mal rested his head against the back of the tub. He rolled his eyes to the side, checking out the floor. "Look what you did, young lady."

"You're the one that climbed into my tub," I replied quietly. Sure enough, the bathroom was pretty much flooded. Water had spread across the floor, a stream of it leading out beneath the door and into the living room. "What a mess. We better clean this up."

"Sorry, pumpkin. I don't mind picking up my shit and all, but I'm a rock star. Rock stars don't mop. It's just not done."

"You help make the mess, you help clean it up. Boundaries, Mal."

"You don't understand." He shut his eyes, face tight with

fake despair. "These are the hands of an artist. Would you expect Bonham to mop?"

"Who?" I asked in confusion.

"John Bonham."

"Right. Well . . . if John Bonham got water on the floor, yes, I would expect him to mop."

"Well, he can't. He's dead."

I cocked my head. "What . . . who are we even talking about?"

"You don't know who John Bonham is?" Mal asked, his voice rising.

"Shh. Your parents are going to hear us."

"Sorry. But c'mon, pumpkin, you have to know who Bonham is. You're fucking with me, right?"

"Sorry."

"Ah, man," he sighed, shaking his head slowly, mournfully. "I'm not sure I can stick my dick in a woman who doesn't even know who John Bonham is."

" 'Stick your dick in'?" I asked, my brows probably touching. "Did you actually just say that?"

"Make love. I meant make love . . . of course. I would never just stick my dick in you. I would make mad, passionate love to this sweet, sweet body of yours for days, no, weeks. It would be beautiful, pumpkin. There'd be little angels, and birdies, and you know . . . all just hanging around, watching. Perverts."

"Right. You are so full of shit." I smiled, cautiously, climbing to my feet.

"What about Kerslake, you know him? How about Wilk, never heard of Wilk?"

"I know Grohl. He's great."

"Oh, no. Fuck, honey. Not Dave Grohl. I mean, he's a good guy and there were flashes of definite genius back in the Nirvana days, sure." His hands slid from my waist down the sides of my thighs, holding me steady. "Whoa, where'd they go?"

"Hmm? Mal, stop."

He stared straight at my sex, studying it. A little line sat between his brows. Deep down inside, I could live without him doing that right now. The man's parents were on the other side of the door. The woman who'd given birth to him was busy cleaning up the mess we'd made. So not the time to be getting familiar with me. Quizzing me on famous drummers could probably also wait.

"Can you not, please? And where'd what go?" I threw a leg over the side of the bath, stepping down carefully onto the slippery floor. Getting the hell away from his overly intrusive eyes. My robe hung on the back of the bathroom door, fortunately. I hadn't thought to bring in a change of clothes and my work wear sat in a soggy heap in the corner.

"Your pubes," he said, angst filling his voice. "Where are they?"

"I wax."

His nose wrinkled up in obvious disgust. "Well, stop it. I want cute carrot-colored pubic hair like on the top of your head. I deserve it."

I bit back a smile. "You've given this a lot of thought, haven't you?"

"It's been almost a week. I had to have something to beat off to."

"You've been masturbating to the thought of me?" I asked, thrilled. Clapping would probably be uncool, plus his parents might hear.

"Do I have a dick, Anne?" Mal climbed out, water running out of his soaked jeans, flowing out of his Chucks. What a beautiful wet disheveled mess.

"Given the size of the bulge in the front of your jeans, I'm going to answer yes to that question, Malcolm."

"Then, yeah, of course I've given this a lot of thought. I've been thinking about your pussy constantly, what it looks like, what it tastes like, how it'll feel." He towered over me, half naked and dripping wet. The dripping-wet part was definitely going around. "Why do you think I was on Ben's couch last night? No one else I wanna fuck. It's gotta be you."

"Wow," I whispered.

"You gonna give me shit about not being romantic like you did last time?"

"Nope."

"Nope?" His fingers toyed with the collar of my robe. Not undoing it, just hanging on.

I gripped the waist of his jeans and lifted my face, pressing my lips to his. "All I heard was blah blah I've been thinking about you constantly. Blah blah it's got to be you. It was perfect, pure romance."

He grinned. "You're crazy."

"We might have that in common, yes."

"I definitely need you to know I have a dick." He rubbed his lips over my jawline, making me shiver.

"Show it to me later?"

"Since you asked so nicely." He drew back slightly. "Shit, we're not going to start acting all nauseating like Davie and Ev are we?"

"Isn't that how we're supposed to be behaving?"

"Yeah, but it was funny while we were faking it. If we're doing it for real . . ." He left the thought hanging.

My lust cooled significantly, chilling me. Because *for real* meant people getting hurt. And *people getting hurt* most likely meant me. It might also mean him, yes. But the odds were not in my favor. I already knew how much it would sting when our fake relationship ended. But a real relationship? That would be so much worse.

"I, um . . . why don't we just take it easy? See how it goes," I said.

"Can't stop now." He rested his forehead against mine. "We really fucking need to have sex, Anne."

"Yes. But things don't have to change if we start sleeping together."

"They don't?"

"No. It'll be fine." God didn't smite me. Who knew, it could even be the truth.

"Cool," he said, cocky grin back in full force. He held one big hand aloft, waiting for me to high-five him. "Damn, we're good."

I slapped our palms together, before slipping my fingers between his and holding on tight. "We so are."

CHAPTER SIXTEEN

When it came to his parents' visit, Mal went all out.

He threw on dry clothes and mopped out the bathroom while I hid in the tub behind the curtain. All in all, he got his parents out of the apartment quite quickly. I heard his mom asking about my decimated bed (because the bedroom doors were wide open too). Our on-and-off, real-and-fake relationship was slowly destroying my apartment and its contents. Though hopefully the water spillage hadn't done too much damage.

Mal mumbled an explanation about the bed and his father changed the topic of conversation. What the hell had he told them? Now they probably thought I was some sort of sex fiend, knowing him. Though the real reason, that we'd been jumping on the bed like a pair of idiots, wasn't something I wanted his parents knowing either.

I got dried and finished up the mopping. Fifteen minutes later Mal texted me.

Mal: Car will b there in 15
Anne: Where are we going?
Mal: Surprise
Anne: I don't like surprises. Where are we going?

Anne: Answer me or I will hurt you while you
    sleep. I need to know what to wear etc
Mal: Wear nothing
Anne: . . . Try again
Mal: Restaurant in town. Wear a skirt
Mal: Plz?
Anne: Your wish is my command
Mal: HAHA I fucking wish

I stood on the curb, freezing my knees off in the bitter
cold wind. Also panicking ever so slightly about what his
parents would think of me, barely educated and broke.
Then a sleek stretch limousine pulled up.

Oh, wow.

My eyes had to be as wide as the wheels. This was a
first for me. I'd missed out on prom. I'd missed out on a
lot of things. My first boyfriend had moved on to someone who had time to go to games and after-parties.

A young man in a snazzy gray suit and hat stepped out.
"Miss Rollins?" he asked.

"Yes." I pulled open the door, eager to check out the
inside. Then paused. "Crap. I was supposed to let you do
that, wasn't I?"

"That's alright, miss." He took up his position by the
door, waiting for me to get in. Luckily my skirt went to
my knees. Given the size of the vehicle, there wasn't really any dainty way to make an entrance.

Glossy leather and a shining crystal decanter and
glasses set greeted me. Talk about luxury. The limo
dropped me at an up-market steak place in the Pearl District. We always seemed to end up in that part of town. I'd
never been to the restaurant before, but I'd heard all about
it. Once upon a time, Reece had taken a woman there in
hopes of impressing her. It did the job. This place reeked
of style, with its red booths and low lighting. Honestly, the
lighting fixtures looked more like art installations. There

were these giant, sparkly orb-type things. I really needed one for home just as soon as I made my first million.

I mentioned Mal's name and the cool guy acting as the host gave me several once-overs. Though I guess after the first time, the look ceased to be a once-over and turned plain rude.

"Whenever you're ready," I said, not bothering with friendly.

Mal was sitting with his back to the room, his hair in a short ponytail. Asking him if his mom had made him tidy it up was tempting but in any teasing war of words, I usually wound up the loser. My nerves were frayed enough from meeting his parents so I kept my mouth shut and admired the cut of his cheekbones.

"Here she is." The pride in Mal's voice both startled and warmed me in turn. He slid out of the booth and put an arm around my waist. "Mom, Dad, this is Anne."

Mal's mom was petite and her smile lit up her entire face. Neil, Mal's dad, stood at my approach. Tall with golden blond hair, he appeared to have Viking blood in him. It made sense once you'd seen the son.

"Lovely to meet you," I said, trying my best to project bright, bubbly, trustworthy . . . shit like that. I'd never been introduced to a man's parents before. Mal and I were forging new ground. Fingers crossed, I didn't let him down.

His mom held her delicate hand out to me. The bones in her fingers felt fragile, obvious to the touch. "Hi, Anne. I'm Lori. And this is Neil. We're so happy to meet you."

"Hi, Lori. Nice to meet you too."

Pleasantries done with, I slid into the booth, Mal following close behind me. His jeans-clad thigh pressed against the length of mine and a hand covered my bare knee. After dithering around in my wardrobe, I'd gone with a navy long-sleeved top, black skirt and ankle boots. A touch of conservative mixed in with a dash of ass kicking for good measure. Maybe it'd been a poor choice. What did I know about the families of rock stars? Neil wore a dress shirt and tie, Lori a white linen top and pants. I hadn't exactly expected piercings and leather, but white linen? I'd have spilled something on myself within the first two minutes given the way my hands were shaking.

"Hey," Mal said, leaning closer.

I definitely didn't want to fuck this up, but a heavy lump of dread sat in my stomach. Things weren't great with my own mother, so what were the chances I'd manage to charm his? My hands were clammy, sticky with sweat. Honestly, put me in a stressful situation and I could rival a rhino for perspiration issues. Assuming rhino's had perspiration issues.

Mal laid a gentle kiss beneath my ear. "Breathe, pumpkin. All good."

"Yep." I gave him two thumbs up.

"Yeah, okay. Not good." He looked around, held out a hand. A waiter rushed over. "Hi. Can you get her a . . . look, whatever you've got that's potent, okay?"

"How about Rocket Fuel, sir?"

Mal clapped his hands together. "Why, that sounds delightful! Excellent, Rocket Fuel it is. Make it a double."

The waiter's eyes went wide. "Uh, yes, sir."

Photos had been spread across the table, a veritable sea of blond-haired babies. Chubby faces and starfish hands were abundant. Lori gave me another warm smile. "These are all our grandchildren."

"I didn't realize Mal was an uncle."

"Eight times over, sweetie." His mother started pointing out faces, naming names. Given his three sisters were such prolific breeders I made a mental note to stock up on condoms. Wherever he and I were at, we definitely weren't ready for Mal Junior, despite his joking. I didn't even know if I wanted to have children. They fell firmly under the "maybe someday" label.

Lori's anecdotes about her grandchildren saw us right through ordering and dinner. She talked while we all ate. Sips of Rocket Fuel loosened me up considerably. So far as I could taste, it consisted of every kind of white liquor with a dash of lemonade. The drink should probably be either illegal or set on fire to burn off some of the alcohol. I laid off it after an inch or two, leaving it for Mal. He stole from my plate and sipped from my drink and I loved it, the intimacy and sense of togetherness. It probably was just plain old thievery but the way he did it, fake distracting me with a smile or wink, made the game worthwhile.

I was so easy for him.

"So you have three older sisters," I said. "You know, I can definitely see you as the youngest child."

His mother guffawed. She might have been little but she laughed big. It spoke well of Mal's childhood. The adoration in her eyes when she looked at her son just backed it up. I couldn't even remember what my mom sounded like laughing. It'd been too long.

"Why?" Mal asked, glaring at me down the length of his nose. "Are you saying I'm loud and immature? Because it's just plain rude to point that shit out, pumpkin."

His mother cleared her throat in an obvious language warning.

Mal sat with his arm stretched across the back of our bench. He'd put on a black Henley to cover his tats, and a dry pair of Chucks. I tried not to look at him too long, terrified of going crazy eyed in front of his parents. Memories of what we'd gotten up to in the bath simmered too near the surface.

"Explain yourself," he ordered.

"All I'm saying is that you're a natural performer. It just makes sense you'd be the youngest."

"Right." He cocked a brow, his gaze shifting to his folks. His hand, however, shifted higher on my leg, sliding up beneath my skirt. I grabbed hold of his fingers, squeezing them hard in warning, before he could make a move for anything important. Only a quirk of his smile betrayed him. "Anne's the oldest. You should see how she is with her sister, Mom. Protective doesn't cover it. I'm surprised the girl isn't bubble wrapped."

His mother smothered a smile.

"I am not overly protective," I said. "She's twenty. She's an adult now. I respect that."

"Do you?" Damn, I liked him teasing me. I liked the familiarity in his gaze. "Ben said he was afraid for his life when you caught him checking her out. He was wondering if he needed to protect the family jewels."

Lori made another admonishing noise at the mention of testicles but Mal just charged on. "He said you looked ready to annihilate him."

This information I liked much less.

"He talked about Lizzy?" My eyes narrowed, all good humor long gone. I didn't even want Ben Nicholson to know she existed. "She's too young for him. She needs to be concentrating on school."

"Relax, momma bear. So happens, I agree." Mal smiled broadly, rubbing the back of my neck, soothing me instantly. Christ, his hands. As much as I liked his parents, hopefully this wouldn't be a long, drawn-out dinner. Short and sweet was the way to go. Mal and I had things to do.

"We'll keep Benny boy away from your baby sister," he promised quietly. "Don't worry."

"What about your mother, Anne?" asked Lori. "Where is she?"

I flinched and Mal's fingers paused against my neck. I didn't need to see what look he was giving me. What I needed was to move the conversation onward and upward. "She's, um . . . she's back in So Cal. She's fine."

"And your father?"

"He left. Many years ago." It was better than saying "Fuck knows." And why sugarcoat it, right? Facts were facts. I picked up my remaining half slice of sourdough bread, nibbled at the crust. It was nice but I was full. We needed something neutral to talk about but the now-empty dinner plate offered no inspiration. My brain wouldn't cough up a damn thing.

"You two staying for the first few tour dates?" asked Mal. I could have kissed his feet for the save.

"We'll see," said his dad.

"Of course we will. At least the first," Lori corrected. "We love seeing you and the boys play. How are they all? Jimmy feeling better?"

"He's good, Mom. They're all doing good. Davie wants to introduce you to Ev as soon as possible."

His mom happy sighed. "I would love to meet her. I always knew David would settle down first. He's such a sensitive soul, more so than the rest of you."

"I'm sensitive. I'm nothing but a big ball of mushy sensitive stuff inside. Tell her, pumpkin."

"Your son is very sensitive," I dutifully recited.

"That didn't sound believable." He gently tugged on a strand of my hair, moving in closer. "My feelings are hurt. You've wounded me. Kiss it better."

"Apologies." I gave him a brief but sweet kiss on the lips.

"That the best you got?" He rubbed his lips against mine, trying to lure me in deeper. "You should be ashamed of yourself. I think you can do much, much better than that. Why, you missed my mouth entirely."

"Later," I whispered, doing my best to keep things below an R rating in front of his parents. But damn, it was hard.

"Promise?"

"Yes."

"Such a pity you weren't home when we dropped by your place earlier, Anne," said Lori. "But you have a lovely little apartment."

"Thank you."

"Malcolm just needs to stop breaking your furniture and causing floods."

Mal groaned. "A man needs to be free to bounce on beds and bathe as he sees fit, Mother."

"You're twenty-seven years old, honey."

"And?"

"Isn't it time to start acting like a grown-up?"

"I pay my bills, see to my responsibilities. Beyond that, does it really matter?" Mal sat up straighter, staring his mom down with a smile. You couldn't help but get the feeling they'd had this conversation many times before.

"Funny," said Neil, talking for the first time in forever. "Could've sworn I heard two voices in that bathroom."

"Thin walls," Mal and I both said at once. Yeah, my smile . . . I highly doubt it was even the tiniest bit believable. Excellent.

His dad grunted.

Lori tried to cover her smile by dabbing her lips with the napkin.

Shit. We were so busted.

"Eat more, hon." Neil pushed Lori's plate closer to her. The rest of us had wolfed the excellent food down, but Lori had barely touched hers.

"I'm not all that hungry." She patted his hand.

The fingers rubbing my neck froze.

"But . . ." Neil leaned in, whispering in her ear.

After a moment Lori shut him down with a quick kiss. She put on a bright smile, a fake one. It was an expression I knew well. Hers wasn't bad, but it still jarred. I guess I hadn't expected it from her. What was going on here? Of course, there could be a hundred and one explanations. Couples fight.

A rousing rendition of "Happy Birthday" broke out on the opposite side of the room. A large group of people around Lizzy's age were starting to get seriously loud. The host on the front desk watched them with wary eyes.

"Malcolm, you have to bring Anne home for the party so she can meet your sisters," she said. "We're having a big family get-together next week in Coeur d'Alene and you both have to be there. It's between the Seattle and Chicago shows, so the boys all have time to come."

"That's where you're from?" I asked Mal without thinking. A real girlfriend would know these things. But Mal and I hadn't gotten around to discussing normal everyday stuff yet. Though the past wasn't a topic I tended to encourage. Fortunately, Lori didn't appear to be concerned.

"Yeah." He nodded, eyes fixed on his dad.

"What's it like?" I asked.

His gaze stayed on his parents and he wasn't smiling. "Trees, lake, a couple of good bars. It's nice enough."

"It's lovely, especially in fall," said Lori enthusiastically. "You have to come, Anne."

"I'll see what I can do." I moved restlessly in my seat. Something had changed. Both Mal and his father seemed subdued, preoccupied. Neither would meet my eyes. The atmosphere in the booth had cooled and I didn't understand why.

"You'll make sure she comes, won't you, sweetie?" Lori reached over and squeezed Mal's hand, ignoring whatever weirdness had come over the table. If anything her smile was larger than before, like she was making up for the lack. "We'll have a wonderful time showing you around."

"Sure," Mal said, his voice hollow. Someone had flicked a switch and turned him off. He simply wasn't there anymore. I recognized that too.

"We better get back to the hotel," announced Neil. "Don't want to get tired out."

Lori smiled glumly. "I suppose so. Say, do you think

it's really haunted, Anne? I saw something about a ghost tour. Wouldn't that be a blast?"

"It sure would."

From his pocket, Mal pulled out his mobile and fired off a text. "They're bringing the car around."

His arm disappeared from around my shoulders and he slid out of the booth. Suddenly, a pair of girls, maybe eighteen years old, appeared out of thin air. Mal took a step back as if startled.

"Oh my god, we thought it was you," gushed the first, giggling.

"We're your biggest fans."

"Ah, hey. Thanks." Mal took the pen they held out and signed their napkins, notebooks, and whatever else. His hand was a blur. Clearly, he'd done this a million times or more. I climbed out after him as Neil helped Lori, his hand to her elbow.

Heads turned and soon more people from the rowdy table joined the two girls circling Mal. The crowd gathered incredibly fast. Flashes went off, blinding me, and I raised a hand to guard my eyes from the glare. There were two, three people between me and him now. Hands pushed me aside and I stumbled into the end of a table, hitting it hard with my hip. A glass smashed on the floor at my feet and suddenly Mal was there.

"You okay?" he asked, steadying me.

"Yes. It just caught me by surprise." If anything, I was embarrassed.

"Let's go." He tucked me in against his side as people around us started to complain and press in once more. One guy tried to shove his phone number at Mal. Mal ignored him, moving us through the crowd mostly by force. When someone yelled right in my face, my heart went boom and I broke out in a cold sweat. These people were fucking insane, well off or not. What would have happened if he'd been recognized at a fast-food joint?

We rushed out of the restaurant, shouts coming from behind us. Neil ushered Lori into the limousine, and we followed fast behind. Hands hammered on the windows as the driver struggled to close the door without maiming anyone. A minute later the limo pulled out into traffic and I could breathe again. We were on our way.

No one said anything and the silence was killing me. Even Lori could only raise a thin smile, apparently running out of steam as Neil had predicted. In the rush to get in, Mal hadn't wound up sitting beside me. A pity; I could have done with some hand holding.

"That was exciting," I said.

"Mostly they're content to just look. But now and then they get carried away," said Lori. "Don't let it scare you, Anne."

No one spoke again.

She kissed me on the cheek before climbing out of the limo once we reached the hotel. The mood from dinner hadn't shifted. I stared at Mal, willing him to look at me. He hadn't had time to shave, and the hint of a beard framed his jaw, his mouth. The need to kiss him, to cover the distance between us, made my heart race.

"Are you alright?" I asked.

"Yeah. You?" he asked, sitting across from me on the seat stretching along the back. He was the picture of cool, calm, and disconnected. "Sorry about the scene at the restaurant."

"I'm fine. Not a big deal."

He scrubbed his face with his hands. "It happens."

"The food was wonderful. Thanks for inviting me."

"Mm."

"Your parents were lovely. I really like your mom."

"Great."

"Your dad was nice too."

He nodded, staring off at nothing.

"No, seriously, Mal. What's wrong?" I blurted out. We

needed to go home and get back in the bath. Things had been better there.

"Nothing."

This conversation sucked. Somewhere along the line, things had turned to shit and I had no idea how to salvage them. I lacked the skills.

I so badly wanted to go sit beside him, but something held me back. For some reason, I wasn't sure of my welcome. Tonight was meant to be the night, skin on skin, sweaty sex, the whole shebang. Now I wasn't so sure. Not about whether I wanted him or not, because I did, the need I had for him made me a foolhardy mess. I just didn't want to be there alone.

Outside, it started to rain.

"I'm going to go play the drums for a while," he asked. "I'll drop you back at the apartment first."

"There's a practice session tonight?"

His smile didn't even get close to his eyes. "No. I just feel like hitting the drums."

"You didn't want to come home with me?" I asked, and he knew to what I was referring; he had to know.

Mal shrugged.

Oh, no. No way. He did not just shrug off us finally having sex. This was not a situation where ambivalence could be considered cool in any way, shape, or form. The limo pulled into the nighttime traffic, awaiting notification of our destination, no doubt.

Mal pulled out his cell and started flipping through the screens. I crossed my arms over my chest. Fine, if that was the way he wanted to play it. Outside, downtown Portland passed us by in all its beauty. The trees in one of the little parks were lit up. Everything glistened in the wet weather. Tiny streams ran down the car windows, obscuring the view.

Fuck it; if he really wanted to go and drum he could

just go. Obviously, he wasn't in the mood for company. I opened my mouth to agree to the plan but nothing came out. This wasn't working. Truth was, I could be a stubborn bitch and horny didn't really sit well with me. Might be best if I had some space.

"Can you ask him to pull over?" I pushed a strand of carrot-colored hair out of my face. "There's no need for you to go out of your way. I'll find my own way home. Catch up with you later."

His eyes narrowed. "I'm not dropping you on a street corner in the rain, Anne. I'll take you home."

"Alright. Thanks."

He opened his mouth and then shut it again.

"What?"

He said nothing.

Ugh, avoidance. I knew it so well. I couldn't keep demanding that he share with me when I had no intention of spilling my whole sorry history to him. No one needed to hear that.

Still, we were better than this. Or we should be.

"Fuck this," I muttered.

"What did you say?"

"Fuck. This."

He cocked his head.

"Safety in moving vehicles is highly overrated."

"Wha—"

I crossed to the seat beside him. Then went one better, climbing onto his lap, straddling him. He blinked, his hands hovering over my hips as if unsure where to set down. His cell fell to the side, forgotten apparently. Thank god I'd worn a skirt. It was shortish and made of a stretchy material, useful for so many occasions but particularly this one.

"Anne."

"Mal."

"What's going on?"

"The night isn't ending this way," I told him, perfectly calm. "I won't let it."

He looked at me like I'd started speaking in tongues. Which was actually an excellent idea, given I had no real idea what the problem was here.

I slipped my hands around the back of his neck. Now I got why he always did this, the skin was so soft and warm there. In all honesty, I had no idea what to say; kissing him made much more sense than blurting out the wrong thing again. I brushed my lips against his, plump and perfect. His swift intake of breath was music to my ears. Given half a chance, I could have paid homage to his lips all night. Hooker lips. No other man was this kissable.

"I hate seeing you sad."

We stared at each other, our faces close. Whatever was going on with him, hurting him, it needed to stay away from the here and now. Mal and I had earned this moment. He'd just forgotten it somewhere along the way, gotten sidetracked. Lucky for him, I hadn't.

"Whatever it is, let me fix it. Just for a little while . . ."

I angled my head and kissed him, tracing my tongue over his lips. He tasted wonderful. Already my hips shifted restlessly in his lap, seeking more. I was in heat and it was all his fault, so he'd just have to deal with it. With a groan he gave up and opened his mouth. Fuck, I loved the feel of his tongue, the sweet taste of him. It went straight to my head, making me giddy.

He didn't hesitate. His hands slid up my legs, under my skirt, going straight for the kill, god love him.

"Need something?" he asked, fingers stroking over my thighs.

"You."

"Fuck. Anne." His mouth chased mine, pushing for more, deeper. And holy hell, was I happy to give. The tips of his clever fingers stroked the crotch of my panties, making every corner of me light up in response. If anything stopped us this time, I couldn't be held responsible for my actions.

"Keep doing that," I panted, tugging the tie from his ponytail to loosen his hair.

"You don't want this instead?" The pad of his thumb pressed against my clit, moving in small circles.

"Oh, god." My head fall back, sensation rushing through me. I was so turned on it was embarrassing. The damp fabric of my panties told the tale. But we'd had days and days of foreplay, really. Long before I'd met him I'd wanted him, though reality far exceeded my expectations. Mal Ericson was my dream come true. The kissathon at David and Ev's, lying awake missing him last night, these things had already pushed me to the edge. Safety and sensible be damned. I'd get as much of him as I could for as long as I could.

"That's it," he murmured.

I pushed forward against his hand, seeking more. He cradled the back of my skull, holding up my head so he could see. "You are so fucking pretty. Have I told you that?"

No idea. And if he expected me to answer, he'd be waiting a while.

"I should've told you that," he said.

I just stared at him, dazed. He was, without a doubt, the most beautiful man I'd ever seen. The elegant lines of his face made me want to write bad poetry. And the sound of his voice, his words, they were all so perfect and good. But then my insides tightened, and there was nothing there to hold on to. I was so horribly empty I ached.

"I need . . ." Forget talking. I started tearing at his belt buckle instead, ripping into the button and zip of his jeans. My thigh muscles burned from gripping him and if the car stopped suddenly I'd be in serious trouble.

"You can have whatever you want, Anne. Just ask for it."

"I want you."

Fingers traced the seam of my sex, making my head swim.

"How do you want me?" he asked, his hand coaxing a moan from me. I rested my cheek against his, lungs struggling for air. "Hmm?"

"Inside me." Words were a hassle and so was his zipper. "Mal, please . . . stop playing with me."

"But you love me playing with you."

I held his face in my hands, my mouth rigid. "Enough."

Just as well I was sitting down, otherwise his smile would have floored me. Arrogant, gorgeous bastard.

"Okay." Mal pulled his hand out from under my skirt. I could have wept for the loss of the lovely pressure. Much more important, however, to get him into me as soon as humanly possible.

"Hop off a sec," he said.

He lifted me aside and pushed down his jeans and underwear, dug a condom out of his pocket. I stopped dead at the sight of his cock, jutting out large and loud. I needed more time to look. How mad would he get if I tried to take a picture? It would be purely for my own personal use, of course.

"Anne," he said, breaking my concentration. "Panties off. Now."

"Right." My skirt had already bunched up around my waist. I hooked my thumbs in either side and shimmied them down, kicking off my ankle boots at the same time. Coordinated and cool I was not, but only getting myself bare from the waist down mattered.

He opened the condom wrapper with his teeth and rolled it on.

"C'mon." Big hands gripped my hips, pulling me back

over his lap. I grabbed hold of his shoulders for balance and stared at his face, memorizing him. This moment needed to go down in history with every last detail imprinted for all time. From the curve of his cheekbones and line of his jaw to the small dip in his top lip that I was dying to kiss and lick, I didn't want to forget a thing.

He slipped a finger into me and my muscles spasmed in shock at the intrusion.

"Okay?" he asked, holding still.

I nodded. "Just caught me by surprise."

Slowly, he eased in deeper, making me squirm. Ever so skillfully he worked me higher and higher. His thumb rubbed around my clit while he stroked over some sweet spot inside of me. Someone somewhere had given up the secrets of my pussy; the man knew everything. I couldn't remember anyone ever turning me on so effortlessly.

"Fuck, you feel good, my finger's in heaven."

"Mal, please . . ." I wasn't even sure what I was asking for. I wanted his fingers, his cock, his mouth, his everything. The man made me greedy.

His finger slid out of me, teasing over my lips, spreading me gently open. My pelvis moved of its own accord, grinding against his hand. My moans were so loud the driver had to have heard them despite the divider. Did I care? Nope.

"We're ready," Mal announced.

We so were.

One hand held my hip while the other moved his cock into position. The press of him sliding against my labia had me seeing stars. I didn't know how I'd survive more. Slowly, steadily, I sunk down on him. His nostrils flared as I took him deep. I didn't stop until I sat atop his bare thighs, the hair on his legs tickling me.

"There we go." His focus on me was complete, his gaze searching my face, taking in everything. It left me no room to hide. A problem, given I had the stupidest impulse to burst into tears or something.

Since when did sex mean so much?

"I want to move," I said. But the hands on my waist held me down. The feel of him filling me couldn't be described. It bordered on being too much.

"Wait." He reached up, kissing me soft and slow. "Just gimme a minute. Fucking perfect. Been waiting to feel you for forever."

I rocked against him, getting past desperate.

We were still dressed up top, but oh man, the things we were doing down below.

"Mal," I breathed. "Now."

Fingers dug into my ass, drawing me up his hard length before easing me slowly back down, letting me get used to the feel of his thick cock. That same motion, over and over, again and again, was heaven. The slide of him into me made my blood run red hot. Slow was too good. It melted my mind.

Gradually, I started picking up the pace, his hands helping me along. Faster and harder, I rode him. Nothing could compare to the solid heat of him dragging over sweet places inside of me, turning me liquid. I slammed down onto his hard length, working us both into a frenzy. Sweat slicked our skin. My spine tingled; my whole body was shaking with need. This was life and death and a billion other things I never even knew existed. The tension inside me grew to exquisite gigantic proportions. His thumb slid back and forth over my clit and the whole wide world burst open. My hips bucked and I hid my face against his shoulder as I came hard, biting down through his Henley. A mouthful of cotton tried to muffle the noise escaping my throat.

It went on and on until I fell limp against him, lost and found and everything in between.

Mal groaned, holding me down on his cock. He was

growling something. It might have been my name, in which case I appreciated the sentiment. The minute I could, I'd be sure to tell him thanks.

I never wanted to move. Never ever. Or at least, not until the next round.

We sat slumped on the limousine's backseat in silence. Sweat and body fluids glued our thighs and groins together. Every muscle in me trembled. Holy fucking hell. That had been epic.

"You alive?" he asked after a while, brushing my hair back behind my ear.

I gazed up at him, slack jawed and fuck drunk. Best feeling ever. "It was okay, I guess."

Crap, my words were slurred. My tongue had turned thick and dumb.

"Yeah?" He didn't bother to hold back the smile.

"I'm sure you tried your hardest."

"I appreciate the vote of confidence."

I kind of grunted at him in a completely ladylike manner, out of energy.

"Sweetie pie? Pumpkin? You screamed so loud my ears are still ringing. I can't actually hear whatever bullshit you're peddling right now. Tell me later after I get a couple of stitches put in my shoulder, okay?" He chuckled, the sound rumbling through his chest in the nicest way. "A biter and a screamer. And you seem like such a nice, quiet girl. I'm shocked."

I pushed the neck of his shirt aside, inspecting his shoulder. "You're not bleeding. There'll be a bruise at the most."

"I'll wear it with pride."

Damn, he smelled good. The limo should just keep circling the city until it ran out of gas so I could keep breathing him in. Sex and sweat and man.

"Did you still want to go to practice?" I asked, mostly being polite. The desire to keep him all to myself kept my arms around his neck in something close to a strangle hold. But if he wanted to go, I'd go. Orgasms tended to leave me in a pretty benevolent mood. "I could hang out, listen to you play again."

"Fuck, no," he said.

"Fuck, no?"

He snorted, his lips twisted like I was lacking in the mental department. "Home. Bed. Now."

"You got it." I grinned.

CHAPTER SEVENTEEN

We fell out of the limousine, still tugging our clothes into place. Things between my legs were sticky and swollen. Upon reflection, I don't think I'd make a very good cowgirl because my thigh muscles still hadn't quite recovered from the ride. I really did need to get back into going to Pilates. A mild bit of muscle strain wasn't wiping the stupid smile off my face, however. More practice was required and odds were, the way Mal kept putting his hands on me, he wouldn't mind.

"There's so many stars. Look how clear it is." I let my head fall back, inspecting the heavens. Fresh from a great orgasm with Mal Ericson at my side, the world was a pretty fucking awesome place.

Mal kissed my chin. He tucked a finger in the waistband of my skirt and towed me toward our apartment building's front door. "C'mon, your shirt looks uncomfortable. You need to get it off."

"But nature, it's beautiful and stuff."

"Your tits are beautiful and stuff. I'm more than willing to spend serious time looking at them. Will that do?"

"Yes."

He laughed.

I fumbled the key in the door, clumsy in my haste. The lock turned, the door swinging open, slamming into the wall. Crap, what a noise. It echoed through the hall, up the stairs. We really would break the building before we were through. Mrs. Lucia was going to give us hell for being so loud. She lived on the first floor and considered herself the sheriff in these here parts. No one had the nerve to tell her otherwise. But if I had to, I'd pull up my big-girl panties and deal with Mrs. Lucia.

What I didn't know was how to deal with the sight of Reece sitting on the stairs with a bunch of flowers in hand. They were every color of the rainbow. I stumbled to a halt, Mal beside me.

Reece bought me donuts now and then. A bottle of wine when we went out for my birthday or his. He didn't bring me flowers. And he sure as hell didn't sit on my stairs looking forlorn, a lock of hair hanging over his forehead.

"Reece . . ." I climbed the stairs toward him.

Mal stayed put, his hand slipping from my grasp.

The color had fallen out of Reece's face. He looked as white as a blank piece of paper. My and Mal's disheveled state couldn't be interpreted too many different ways. Reece looked like a child who'd lost his favorite toy. I don't think I'd fully appreciated the differences between Mal and him before now. But for all of his joking, Mal was in his head and heart a man. Reece was a boy. I'm not even sure I could explain the distinctions. They simply played in different ways.

"Anne." Reece gave the flowers a perplexed look, like he wasn't quite sure how they'd come to be in his possession. "Didn't realize you'd have company. Sorry."

I silently held my keys out to Mal. His mouth flatlined. He gave me a harsh little shake of the head and I shoved the keys at him. What the hell did he expect me to do? I couldn't just leave Reece sitting on the fucking stairs. Mal stared at me and I stared back, silently willing him to understand. God, this was basically my best friend.

After a moment he snatched the keys out of my hand and went ahead, stepping around Reece. Mal went inside, closing the door (not slamming it, thank god).

Reece offered me a stiff smile. "This is awkward."

What an understatement. I sat down beside him, resting my elbows on my knees. "Nice flowers."

"They're for you." He handed them over, the scent sweet and heady. He didn't meet my eyes.

"Thank you. They're beautiful."

"I was worried about you."

The statement sat there like an accusation. I didn't know what to say. Emotion had never been my strong point. I was woefully unprepared for this mix of sadness and guilt and whatever the fuck else he'd bought in on his boot heels. Mom had taught me a long time ago to play it safe and keep your mouth shut.

"You two worked things out," he said.

"Yes." On the other hand, my mom was a beyond-shitty role model. Reece deserved better. "What's going on here?"

"I got to thinking about things. About us." He shoved a hand through his hair, pushing back the floppy fringe. I'd always adored the way he did that, the accompanying toss of his head. But my heart didn't roll over and give it up to him. Not like it did for Mal. Reece had waited too long.

"Us?" I prompted, both angry and bewildered.

His smile was far from happy. He nodded toward the upper floor. "Thought he was gone."

"So did I. Apparently, I misunderstood."

"Guess that's good for you. Think it'll last?" His voice

wasn't unkind exactly. But the question garnered an immediate reaction.

I sucked in a breath, an honest answer eluding me. My happy-sex high hadn't dissipated enough for brutal honesty, not with Mal waiting upstairs. My mind didn't want to know. Mom had always said love made you stupid. Guess I hadn't learned that lesson yet after all. "I don't know. But I hope so."

It was still relatively early but the building sat in silence. Our voices barely made a dint.

Reece rose to his feet, moving slowly like he'd been hit. "I'm going to go. See you tomorrow."

"Reece," I said, my voice tight and high. Something was breaking right there beside me and like so much lately, I didn't think I could fix it. I couldn't give Reece what he'd finally decided he just might want. "I'm sorry."

He hung his head. "It's my fault, Anne. I was an asshole. I was too stupid to see what was right in front of my eyes until it was too late."

I had nothing. Absolutely nothing.

He waited a moment, lips skewed with disappointment perhaps. Then he started moving.

"Night." He jogged down the stairs, taking them two at a time, obviously eager to get gone.

"Bye."

I sat there, holding my flowers, staring into space. I just needed a moment to get my head together. The world was so strange. Nothing made sense. A minute later Mal came out and sat down beside me. He leaned over, sniffed at the bouquet. His hands bashed out a beat against his thighs, but he said nothing. Finger tapping seemed to mean restless or busy thinking things out. This savage piece of percussion was something altogether different.

"Reece left," I said, breaking the silence.

"Mm."

"This has been a strange day," I said, quite possibly making the understatement of the century.

"Strange good or strange bad?"

"Both."

"Mm." He grabbed the back of his neck, sucked in a deep breath. "You breaking up with me here or what?"

My head shot around. "You want to break up?"

He didn't respond. For a minute or more, I said nothing and neither did he. We had apparently entered into some messed-up contest of wills. When I gave him a questioning look, he simply raised a brow, waiting me out.

"I couldn't just leave him sitting here. He's my friend." Mal jerked his chin.

"Was I supposed to let you two arm wrestle over me or something? Because that was never going to happen."

"We screwed and then you sent me on my way with a pat on the head." The low, cold way he said it didn't help at all.

"No," I answered, matching his tone of voice. "Come on, Mal. You know that's not what happened. I sent Reece on his way. You I asked to wait in my home. To give me a chance to speak to him."

He stared at me and I stared straight back.

"Don't do this," I said.

"God!" He scrubbed at his face with his hands, growling in frustration. "I fucking hate being jealous. Hate it."

"Tell me about it." I threw up my hands in equal frustration. "You are aware that a healthy portion of the vagina-owning population wants to do you? Don't even get me started about the penis-wielding people, because there's quite a few of them into you as well."

"The shit you say . . ." He sputtered out a laugh. "Fuck."

The storm seemed to be over, thank god. I leaned my head on his shoulder, needing to get closer. Happily, he let me.

"I don't usually fight with other people," he said, rubbing his cheek against the top of my head. "In the band, I usually keep the guys from ripping into each other over stupid shit. Tell a joke, get 'em smiling again."

"You're the peacekeeper. But you were ready to rip into Ben the other night."

"About you. You're turning out to be kind of a mind fuck for me, pumpkin."

I frowned.

"Not saying you mean to be."

"Yeah, that doesn't make me feel any better."

We sat in silence. Eventually, he lifted the flowers out of my arms, stood, and headed down the stairs. The only noise the entire time was the soft thud of his shoes on the worn wooden steps. Carefully, he placed the flowers on Mrs. Lucia's doorstep, before returning to sit beside me. A statement had been made by confiscating those flowers, but what exactly did it mean? That was the question. Mal Ericson was quite the mind fuck himself. And he went on tour in a couple of days. It'd be foolish of me to ignore this oh-so-salient fact. I tugged at the buckles on my boots, all agitated. Too many emotions were stirred up inside of me.

He did that.

"When I was sitting up there, waiting for you, a couple of things occurred to me," he said.

"Yes?"

"Well, you're my girlfriend for real now."

I stopped breathing for a moment, thrown. "I think I needed to hear you say that."

"You have been for a while. Didn't mean for you to be, but you are. I just have to get used to it."

Of course, when he put it like that I sort of wanted to physically hurt him. Instead, I sat and waited to see where he was going with this.

"Don't get mad," he said. "Just stating a fact."

"I'm not mad."

"Liar. See, now this is why we should have gone to counseling when I suggested it right at the start."

"What?" I scrunched up my nose. "When did that happen?"

"Day after I moved in, when we were sexting."

"We weren't sexting, we were just texting. You said you wanted to get a dog too, if I recall correctly. So I really didn't think you were serious about counseling."

The slow curl of his lips made something hot and delicious unfurl deep in my stomach. "Pumpkin, I'm always serious when it comes to you. Even when I'm messing around, I'm still serious as shit. Whatever you need, whatever I have to do. It's been that way since we met. Haven't you noticed yet? We're fucking destined or something. I can't help myself. It's pathetic, really."

"Huh." I stuffed my hands beneath my thighs, giving his words a moment to sink in. "That's what you figured out waiting upstairs?"

"Yep." He shuffled closer, pressing his hip to mine. "Think about it. Things were shit and then I met you at the party and you amused me. I wanted more time with you and then I saw Ev's side boob and Davie threw me out so I had to move in with you. I wanted to sleep with you and we accidentally broke your bed jumping around on it so you had to crash on the couch with me. I wanted to have sex with you and you got bored on the ride home and jumped my bones. See? Destiny."

I burst out laughing. "That's beautiful. But I'm not sure it completely makes sense."

"It's fate, Anne. Written in the stars. Leave it the fuck alone."

"You're crazy." I hung my head and sighed. What else could I do?

"That's better. Can't stand it when you're sad either." His arm slipped around my shoulders, drawing me in against him. I grabbed hold of his fingers, just hanging on.

That was better. Everything would be okay. But there was still an issue I was curious about. "Why did you ask me to be your fake girlfriend?"

He shrugged, looked away. "I wanted to spend time with you. You make me happy."

I scrunched up my forehead. "That's all it was?"

"That's pretty fucking important. Guess with Davie pairing up I was feeling a bit lonely or something. I thought we could be friends."

I just stared at him.

"Needed a chance to get to know you a little better, just you and me alone. Moving in seemed a good way to do that. And you needed the help. Okay?"

"Okay."

We sat in silence for a moment.

"Whatever shit you're telling yourself, stop it," he said.

"What? What are you talking about now?"

"Reece." He rested his head atop of mine. "You're worrying about him. Stop it."

"Mal . . ." How could I explain this to him? The words were weighted in lead, impossible to get out. I hadn't been thinking about Reece, but now that he mentioned it . . .

"You didn't do anything wrong."

I wiggled out from underneath him, needing to see his face. Since when could he read me and why couldn't I do the same? He appeared calm and sure, beautiful as sin. His lips sat slightly apart, his eyes serene. Suddenly, the words weren't so impossible to find after all.

"I hurt him."

"Maybe. But he's the one that left you hanging on. He hurt you too."

"But I fix things," I said. "It's what I do."

"You can't fix this." He toyed with my hair, wrapping the short strands around a finger.

"Why not?"

"You going to dump my ass? Send me packing?"

"No. Absolutely not."

He smiled and shrugged. "There you go."

"You make it sound so simple."

"It is. I'm your boyfriend now, which means there's no room for your hipster admirer. He'll just have to lick his wounds while we lick other things." He raised a devilish eyebrow.

My head filled with so many needy questions. A hundred and one ways to beg him for reassurance. No god damn way any of it was getting past my lips. He was so insanely perfect and I'd had him inside of me. My body buzzed with the memories, sliding straight toward overload. I wanted him again. Maybe I should just shackle myself to his ankle and be done with it. This could be the answer.

"I didn't want to upset you," I said. "But I needed to talk to him alone."

"Yeah, I know. I was being a dick." He moaned, looked to the heavens. "That enough of an apology?"

"You're sorry?"

"Yeah. I get Reece is part of your life. I'll try to be nice to him."

"Thank you."

His hair was in his face again. Carefully, I tucked some behind his ear and then cupped his cheek.

"Hey, crazy eyes. Operation Fake Girlfriend is off," he murmured. "In case you were wondering."

"It is, huh?"

"Way I figure it, we're together until we decide we're not together anymore. Let's not put too much thought into it. Let it sort itself out, yeah?"

It was a sound plan, considering we'd only started sleeping together less than an hour ago. "I approve."

"Glad to have you on board, Miss Rollins." He covered

my hand with his own, pressing it against his face. "I don't wanna be unduly crass or any shit like that, but I'm worried about something."

"What might that be?"

"Your shirt."

I opened my mouth, shut it. "My shirt?"

"I think it's chafing you. Subconsciously like." His eyes were intense, his expression grave.

"My shirt is chafing my subconscious?"

"No, I believe it's chafing the delicate skin of your nipples and the area around . . . what's it called?"

"The areola?"

"Yeah, that bit. 'Cause it's all pink and sensitive, you know? It's delicate, so I believe my concern with regards to the harsh and unyielding nature of your shirt is real important even though you have yet to acknowledge the discomfort it's causing you."

"You know you could have been one hell of a salesman." He was so convincing, I almost felt bad for the soft cotton of my long-sleeved top. "I'm wearing a bra. But my nipples really appreciate your concern."

"Yeah, your bra's in on it too. They're both against you."

"No way!" I said. He made it damn hard not to smile.

"I know, right? Thank fuck I'm here to deal with these things."

"How about we go upstairs and I take my shirt and bra off, would that ease your mind?"

"I'd definitely feel a lot better if you did that, yes."

"Well, alrighty then. Race you." I jumped to my feet, barreling up the stairs, giggling. Mal's arm came around me from behind, lifting me off my feet, pulling me back up against his chest.

"I win," he said, and carried me into the apartment where we both won, big-time.

CHAPTER EIGHTEEN

Fingers were playing with me. Clever fingers.

My alarm hadn't gone off for work yet. It was just before dawn. Sleep, however, wasn't an option with him stirring me up the way he was. Since when was Mal a morning person? Answer, since he wanted sex.

God bless him for his base desires.

I lay on my stomach with him beside me, the hardness and heat of his body a wonderful thing to wake up to. Ever so gently, he stroked me between my legs. He trailed his knuckles softly back and forth along the seam of my sex. Everything low in me tensed in approval. I arched my pelvis, giving him better access to my pussy. We'd dragged my mattress out into the living room, away from the destruction of my wooden bed frame, and gone at it again last night.

"You awake?" he asked, voice husky from sleep.

"No."

He trailed kisses down my spine, making me get all quivery. The graze of his stubble made for a delicious tactile sensory whatever. Yeah, I was still half asleep.

"Okay, don't mind me. I just need something. Shouldn't take too long . . . I'll try not to disturb you."

"Mm, thanks."

His hard-on prodded my thigh. Then a strong hand slid beneath my hips, lifting. "Up," he said, sliding the soft bulk of a pillow under me. "This is sweet. Anne, really, your ass looks great raised up like this."

Wet fingers slid around my clit, turning me on like nobody's business. He circled and stroked and tickled in turn, touching me just right. My thigh muscles tensed, knees digging into the bed. Damn, the man knew what he was doing. I clutched at the sheets, already breathing hard. It would be futile to try and express exactly how much I enjoyed having him touch me. Especially when my brain had shut down for the duration. I moaned in disappointment when he took to kneading my butt cheeks instead, trailing his fingers up and down my thighs.

"Wider," he murmured, pushing my legs farther apart. The mattress shifted beneath me as he moved into place. From behind wasn't my favorite position, but I had no doubt Mal could make it work. The man had skills.

There was the crinkle of a condom wrapper as he changed over to teasing me one-handed. Even just one of his hands was pretty damn good. Then the broad head of his cock nudged my sex. I squeezed my eyes shut, pushed back against him, groaning as he slid into me. With his cock filling me, there was no room for thought. I could only feel.

So damn good.

The way he gripped my ass, his fingers digging into my flesh, gave this tiny thrill of pain. He was truly a whole-body experience, quite possibly involving the astral plane. There were all the usual five senses and then something more I couldn't begin to describe. Something addictive only he could give me. If my brain had been working, I would have been worried about this.

Big hands stroked over my back. Then the heat of his body covered me. Teeth nipped the lobe of my ear, stinging. My shoulders hitched and my muscles clenched.

"Ah, yeah. Fuck, that's hot." Mal pushed himself hard into me. Like he could get any deeper . . . as if. "You're a lazy lay in the morning, Anne."

"Hmm. I did all the work last night in the limousine."

He chuckled, his chest moving against my back. Then he flexed his hips, pushing in, then drawing out, making every inch of me tremble. With his arms set on either side of me, he proceeded to fuck me leisurely into the mattress. My butt jiggled and it didn't matter one iota. Not with Mal buried inside me. It seemed to take forever for him to pick up the pace. And he called *me* lazy. I needed more. Pushing my hips back against him, I urged him on. He got the message, moving faster, going harder. Sweat dripped off of him, onto me.

Gray noise filled my ears and white light filled my head. So damn close I could taste it. The sublime knot of tension drew tighter, but it wasn't quite enough.

Yes.

YES.

But no. Shit. Damn it.

Mal ground himself against me, groaning. His cock jerked deep inside me.

I hadn't even realized I'd been holding myself tense until I collapsed facedown on the mattress. Made it kind of hard to breathe. I turned my head to the side, concentrated on catching my breath, on letting go of the ache. I'd almost gotten there, a first for the position.

Never mind, I just needed to think happy thoughts. Good thoughts. You couldn't win every time.

Mal pulled out of me and fell onto the bed at my side. Outside, birds were singing. The faint hum of traffic came from not too far away. Nate was clumping around in the apartment next door.

"Anne?"

"Yes?" I rolled onto my back.

Mal was busy pulling off the used condom and tying

a knot in it. Then he rolled off the mattress and walked into the bathroom.

"What, Mal?"

The toilet flushed. He walked back out, face carefully blank. We'd only been sleeping together for approximately five minutes and this felt weird. Like all relationships didn't have their average sex moments. But did he know? I couldn't tell. Maybe he was about to ask about breakfast or comment on the weather.

I pulled up the sheet, covering myself. "What's wrong?"

"Is something wrong there?" he asked, tipping his chin.

"What, with me? No."

"You sure about that?"

"Yes." Mostly.

He knelt at the end of the mattress, watching me. "We need to talk."

"Okay."

"You won't need this." He grabbed the sheet, pulling it down, exposing me.

Right, fine. I started to sit up, needing to be in more of a position of power. The big ape grabbed my ankles, dragging me down. My back bounced on the bed, teeth clattering.

"Hey!" I squeaked.

"Let me explain what I mean by 'talk.'"

His hands moved up my legs, spreading them wide. Cool as can be, he lay flat on his stomach, face level with my sex.

"Mal."

"I'm not talking to you," he said, fingers gently folding back the lips of my sex.

"You're not?"

"No. You had your chance to communicate with me and you chose not to. You let this relationship down. Feel bad, Anne." His breath tickled my still-sensitive pussy. It made feeling bad damn hard, frankly. Impossible when he flicked my clit with the tip of his tongue. My hips shot off the mattress but his hands were there, holding me down. "Hello, Anne's clitoris. It's me, Malcolm, your lord and master."

"Oh, god, no." I covered my face with my hands. "Please don't."

"Shh. This is a private conversation." He brushed hot, feverish kisses up and down the lips of my sex. My stomach tensed so hard it hurt. "Look at you all pretty, pink, and excited. Don't worry, I'll look after you."

"If you don't stop talking to my vagina I'm going to kill you." I put a hand down, trying to cover myself. The bastard slapped it. Hard too. I would get him back for that later.

"You're beautiful, Anne's pussy. Just beautiful. And I'm not mean like her. I'm on your side and I love you very much because you feel fucking amazing wrapped around my dick."

"Malcolm, I mean it. You're ruining oral sex for me forever. Cut it out."

"Bullshit. You're dripping wet. We'll never get these sheets clean."

"Oh, god." My back bowed as he dragged his tongue up the center of me, finishing with a flourish at the top. I saw stars. "Too much."

"Not even close."

I whimpered.

He laughed.

His mouth covered my clitoris and his tongue went to god damn town on me. I writhed, out of control, but it made no difference. Hands banded around my thighs, holding me to him. There was no escaping the terrible, all-consuming overwhelming pleasure. He sucked, flicked his tongue, and generally unleashed an unsurpassed wealth of oral talent upon my unsuspecting sex.

The bastard.

Who even knew teeth could be used like that?

I came in under a minute, crying his name. My heart-beat thundered through my head and my whole body shook. I lay sprawled across the mattress, letting the aftershocks have their way with me. Endorphins had pickled my mind. Tears slid down my face, the orgasm had hit me so hard, so fast. That had never happened before. Hurriedly, I brushed them away. My heart seemed suddenly too big for my chest. The orgasm had engorged it somehow. It couldn't be healthy.

From next door came banging on the wall. "I already knew Mal's name, Anne. But thanks for the reminder."

I used the last of my energy reserves to give the wall the finger. "Morning, Lauren."

Distantly, there was laughter, male and female both. Our neighbors sucked.

"We need to kill them or move," I said. "I'm open to either option."

"You know, you talk tough," said Mal, "but inside, you're all soft and wet and really quite tasty."

I choked back a laugh. "Glad you approve."

Mal crawled up, pausing to wipe his mouth on the sheet. He laid his head on my shoulder, snuggling into me. That was good, I needed him near. The glut of emotions felt more manageable with him close, even if he was the cause of all the chaos.

"I think my legs are broken; they won't work." Not that I'd actually tried yet. My brain was too floaty for any movement.

He pressed a kiss to my cheek. "Next time, just tell me you need more."

"You're a monster," I whispered.

"Okay." He didn't even sound the slightest bit perturbed.

"I mean it."

"Mm-hm."

"But the worst part is, I feel something for you," I said,

because fair was fair. Love was a stupid word. I'd heard it from various people and it rarely meant what you thought it did. Somewhere along the way, that word had turned into a pleasantry, not profound and weighty as it should have been. No, love wasn't what I felt. This was different, more complex. I couldn't even think of a word for it. "I only feel it a tiny bit . . . probably just because of the great orgasm, so it's not like it's a big deal or anything. It'll pass."

With a sigh, he went up on one elbow and put an arm around me, pulling me up against him. When he rolled onto his back, I went too. I lay sprawled across him. There was no better thing. Apart from what he'd just done to me, of course. One hand stroked my back, while the other lay behind his head.

"A miniscule amount, really." My thumb rubbed over his nipple, back and forth, back and forth. I seemed to have entered some stream-of-consciousness state and I didn't have the energy to fight it. "You probably couldn't even see it with a microscope."

Another sigh from the man.

"Well, maybe one of those lab ones, but not a kid's toy one. The magnification wouldn't be—"

All of a sudden we rolled again and I was on the bottom with the weight of Mal's body pushing me deep into the mattress.

"Hi," I said, just a bit discombobulated by the abrupt change in position. He'd barely given my head time to stop spinning from the previous shift.

"Been thinking." He watched me, eyes intense. "Want you to do something for me."

"Okay."

"Need you to come on tour, least for a while. See what you can manage, okay?"

My engorged heart basically burst. My insides were officially a mess. "Need?"

"Yeah, need." His forehead furrowed. "Things are happening and I know you've got questions but I need you to not ask them right now. I just . . . I need you with me. I deal with stuff better when you're around."

"Stuff like the other reason why you wanted me around that you wouldn't admit to last night?"

Guilt slid across his face. "Yeah."

"We're going to have to talk about stuff eventually."

"Yeah, we are. Yours and mine both."

I froze beneath him, not answering. But he just patiently waited me out. The words were stuck inside my chest with the rest of the clutter. It was hard to find them. "You're right. I know. And I'll try and work something out about the tour."

Work would survive. Reece owed me. He wasn't going to like it, but he sure as hell owed me. Between Tara and the new guy, Alex, my shifts could be covered.

"Thanks." He nodded, gave me a small mile. "And it's okay about the feeling something thing. I get it."

"You do?" What a relief, because I still wasn't sure I did. I'd never even said anything close to resembling those words.

"Yeah. You don't need to keep babbling about it."

"I wasn't babbling."

"You were, but that's okay." His fingers toyed with my hair. "The timing isn't great for me, pumpkin. I didn't need shit getting any more complicated. But like I said last night, we see where this goes. Agreed?"

Sounded like a solid plan. "Yes."

"You're good for me. You take me any mood I come in. I don't have to be always happy or on around you. You roll with any shit I say and give as good as you get. You don't let me push you around if it doesn't suit you and you haven't asked me to buy you a fucking thing."

I arched my brows and "ooh"ed. "God, I'm so slow. It hadn't even occurred to me. Can I have a Porsche?"

"Sure. What color?"

Holy shit, he would too. If only to mess with me. I took a deep breath and let it out slowly, shook my head. "You never hesitate when I ask for something."

"You don't do it often. I figure if you're asking, it's something that matters."

My eyes did not tear up again. I had allergies or something, probably to feelings. And you had to know, this man, he made me feel *all* the things *all* the damn time. "I don't really need a sports car. But thanks."

"Let me know if you change your mind." He smirked, obviously having known full and well his agreeing would freak me out. Cunning man.

"Ev wants to organize a dinner tonight with the parents and everyone," he said. "You good with that?"

"Sure. They're nice and their place is beautiful."

He stilled, studying my face. "Yeah, it is nice. Glad you like it there. They mean a lot to me."

"They're great people." In my bedroom the alarm clock blared to life, belting out some long forgotten hit from the seventies. "I have to get moving."

"Your legs working yet?" Mischief danced in his eyes.

"I think so." I laughed.

"Call me today. I wanna know you're okay dealing with Reece and everything."

"I've been dealing with things for a long time." My jaw tightened. "I can deal with Reece."

"Hey, you were into him for over two years. I'm allowed to feel a little vulnerable and insecure about the fuck-face. Stop trying to stunt my emotional growth, Anne."

"I thought you were going to try to be nice to him. And stunt your emotional growth? How do you even come up with this stuff?"

"*To* him, not *about* him. And it's a gift." Given what was making its presence known once more against my hip, love and understanding wasn't all he was searching for. "I have another gift for you."

"We don't have time for you to give me your gift. Plus, your good friend, my vagina, needs a rest."

His mouth turned down at the edges and he rose up on his arms, sitting back on the mattress. He stood and offered me a hand. "Call me. I'm not trying to mess with your boundaries or anything. Just want to know you're okay."

Easily, he pulled me up onto my feet. "Alright, I'll call."

"Thanks."

I cocked my head. "You going to call me if things aren't okay with you regarding stuff?"

The little line appeared between his brows. Now maybe he appreciated how hard it could be letting someone into certain places. He looked away, jerked his chin.

What a pair we were. Sometimes it seemed we'd need a miracle to make this work. But my usually cautious heart had already committed.

"Thanks." I placed my hand on his chest. "You don't need to worry about Reece."

"I know, I know. He's nothing compared to my magnificence." His fingers stroked mine and his eyes softened. "But just out of curiosity, how do you feel about getting my name tattooed on your forehead?"

CHAPTER NINETEEN

I was two blocks from work when I saw Reece walking toward me through the early morning crowd. His face was set in hard lines. Five minutes late. Five. Okay, seven (max) and he came looking for me? I'd even skipped my morning coffee fix to hurry things along. Excuses ran through my mind, backed up by all the times I'd stayed late to close because he had a date. I should have kept actual figures. They would have been so helpful right now.

"Reece, I—"

"About-face." He hooked my arm with his and spun me around to face the way I'd come. "Keep walking. You don't want to go to the shop."

"What's going on?" My cell buzzed in my handbag. Mal's name flashed up on screen. "Mal?"

"Ah, hey. Got good news and bad news. What do you want first?"

"Does this have to do with Reece keeping me from my place of employment?"

"Yeah, he called here a few minutes ago." He made a pained noise. "Listen, photos of us at the restaurant last night got around. Someone recognized you and told a reporter who is currently hanging around the shop waiting to get the inside scoop on our *lurve*."

"Right." Mind officially boggled. Reece rushed me across a road and down another block. "What's the good news?"

"Everyone knows about us now. We don't have to hide."

"We weren't hiding anyway."

"Good point. Sorry, pumpkin, there is no good news. Things are going to be painful for a while."

"You're lucky I'm extremely fond of you. What happens next?" We turned into the entry of a café. A table was available in the corner and Reece and I walked toward it.

"Reporters will probably just scrounge whatever information they can on you or make shit up, enough to have a story to run with. They'll wanna get it out fast, news'll spread, and there'll be more people digging into your life. It shouldn't be anything like what happened with Ev 'cause we haven't done anything crazy stupid like getting married in Vegas." He took a breath. "You don't do anything else too newsworthy, they'll lose interest. Meanwhile, how do you feel about us staying at a hotel?"

"What about work?" I asked him, then shook my head and turned to Reece. It was really a question for the boss. I turned to Reece. "What about work?"

Reece raised his eyebrows in question while Mal cleared his throat. "Well, I figured you'd want to talk to him about that," said Mal.

"Yes, I do."

"But, Anne, for once don't worry about the money, okay? I've got you covered."

Hmm. I didn't know about that. Realistically, though, if I was with Mal, I'd be crashing in his hotel room. My rent was paid up. Apart from the occasional meal, I shouldn't need much.

"Okay. Just give me a minute please, Mal." I moved the cell back a bit. "Sorry. Reece?"

"We talked," Reece said. "He said it'll probably be crazy for the next week or so, but then it should calm down."

"I'm sorry about the reporter. But I was hoping to ask if I could take some time off anyway? I realize this is short notice, but given the circumstances . . ."

Reece flinched and panic rose up like a tidal wave. He didn't seem angry last night, but that didn't mean he wasn't holding a grudge, or he might well decide he'd had enough and fire me. Things could get screwed up pretty fast here.

But he sighed and relaxed once more. "You're going on tour with him?"

"I'd like to. Just for a while. It would give this a chance to blow over."

"I guess it makes sense. Though if you stick with him, this shit could be ongoing. Have you thought of that?"

"Are you asking for my resignation?"

"Of course not."

"I'm not giving him up, Reece."

He looked away. "I can cover you for a week, Anne. With such short notice, I don't think I can do more."

"No, a week would be great. Thank you."

"You're overdue for vacation. And I can't have reporters hanging around, scaring the customers. I'll rearrange the shifts with Tara and Alex."

"I really appreciate it."

He grimaced.

"You're an awesome friend."

"I'm awesome," said Mal in my ear. "I'm so much more awesome than him, I can't even . . . there's no comparison. Why would you even use that word in reference to him?"

"Hush," I told him.

"Be back in time for your birthday, okay?" asked Reece with a hesitant smile. "We're still going to dinner, right?"

"God, I hadn't even thought about it. I'll be back then."

We always went out to dinner on each other's birthdays. It was our tradition. Mal would still be on the road, so I could celebrate with him early. This would be a nice chance to mend bridges with Reece, going out as just friends. "I'd like that."

"What?" asked Mal. "When's your birthday? Pumpkin?"

"Take care," said Reece. "You need anything, call me."

"Thanks. Really, I . . . you're a great friend."

"A great friend . . . right," he said dryly. Then he leaned in, kissing me on the cheek. "Bye."

"Did he just kiss you?" Mal yelled in my ear, making it ring.

I winced, pulling the cell back. "Whoa. Noise levels, buddy."

Reece moved through the crowd and out the door. Maybe we were going to survive this after all. Last night, I hadn't been so sure.

"When is your birthday?" Mal asked.

"Twenty-eighth of October."

"A week and a half away. I'll have to get something sorted for you."

"Just you will do. We'll have to celebrate it early, though. I've only got a week and I was probably damn lucky to get that what with the giving five minutes' notice."

"Can't believe he kissed you. Ballsy, but still, he's dead." He mumbled some more of what I presumed to be idle threats. "Don't come back here, just in case. I'll ask Lauren to help me pack a couple of bags for you. You head to The Benson, okay? There'll be a room ready by the time you get there."

"Thanks."

"You're not mad about me turning your life upside down?"

"I'm a big girl, Mal. I knew who you were going into

this and I saw what went down with Ev. There was always a chance this could happen."

"And if it keeps happening, you gonna get sick of it and leave me?"

My heart rebelled at the thought. "No. We'll work something out."

"Yeah, we will," he agreed. "You're pretty mellow after a night of hot sex. I'm keeping a note of that."

"You do that, my friend."

He chuckled. "See you in an hour or two. We'll break in the hotel mattress, order some room service, and hang out, okay?"

"Sounds great." With a grin, I slumped down in the chair. I was officially on vacation. The last vacation I went on was to Florida with Mom, Dad, and Lizzy. I'd been fourteen years old, the year before everything went to shit. And no way did I need to be dwelling on the past.

Life here and now with Mal was a roller coaster. Scary and elating. No matter how strange the circumstances, I was going to enjoy this time.

The dinner with the band and his parents was lovely.

Afterward, we headed for a dive bar on the edge of Chinatown. It was located down a narrow staircase, underground. Not too clean but not too dirty. There were pinball machines and a pool table, a jukebox blasting out Joy Division. The crowd had the market on slacker-hipster style cornered. Apart from a few double takes, nobody got excited when we came in. I guess they were all too cool to freak out over some boring old rock stars.

Though Sam the body guard was along, just in case.

My cell had been ringing on and off due to my new-found fame. Plenty of messages had been received, but I'd checked in with Lizzy and she was fine. There wasn't really anyone else I needed to talk to. Ev had given me a pep talk about dealing with all the attention. To keep my head down and not feed the monster. Eventually, they'd lose interest and move on.

At the hotel, Mal and I had watched movies and taken it easy. It'd been great. Lori had invited me down to the lobby bar for a drink before dinner. She seemed more concerned about the media attention than I was. Though I'd managed to pretty successfully hide from it so far. I assured her that her son and I were doing fine. Real fine.

It had, all in all, been a great day. And this dive bar was cool and relaxed and all that it should be. We'd spread out around a table against the far wall. With a nod to one of the bartenders, Ben had ordered pitchers of beer (water for Jimmy and Lena).

"Owner's a friend. We come here to play pool sometimes during the day," Mal said, pulling my chair closer to his. He seemed wired, beating out a rhythm on the tabletop with the palm of his hand. The mood was infectious, keeping me on edge too.

I don't think I'd understood how tight-knit the band and their families were. During the dinner, David and Jimmy had doted on Lori. They pretty much treated her as if she were their own mother out for a visit. Even Ben had demonstrated a subdued sort of affection. And they all seemed to respect the mostly silent Neil, Mal's dad. Father and son had kept a close eye on Lori again throughout the evening. They practically hovered at her side. Lori had gotten tired again and Neil had taken her back to the hotel.

Yes, I had suspicions aplenty about what was stressing Mal out and keeping him up at night. But we were getting along so well. He'd asked me not to question him. Not yet. And I wasn't ready to provide him with answers on my issues either. So I kept my concerns to myself for the time being. But judgment day was coming for both of us. I could feel it.

Only a few days out from the start of the tour, everyone

seemed too restless to call it a night once Lori and Neil left. It was too early, only just past nine.

Strange looks were being passed between David and Jimmy. They'd give Mal curious glances and then talk amongst themselves. I had a feeling Mal was very much aware of it, the way he was turned away, giving the pair the cold shoulder.

"Hey," Mal said, his smile twitchy. "Let's go back to the hotel and break another bed."

"We just got here."

"Yeah, I changed my mind. I wanna be alone with you." His foot started tapping out a hyper beat against the ground. "What do you say? We'll just get naked and see what happens after that."

"Sounds like a great experiment. Can I just finish this drink and then we'll go? Be rude to take off right away."

"Pfft. How often do Davie and Ev disappear at things?"

"I'll drink fast," I promised, before proceeding to gulp half of my glass of beer. Only a little dribbled down my chin and wet my tight green sweater. Rushing might not have been ladylike, it's true. But with Mal wanting to get naked and dirty, can you blame me?

Hell no.

With all the whispering of wicked things stirring up my hormones, I hadn't noticed the Ferris brother's heated conversation. Down the other end of the table, they were all but growling at each other.

Jimmy thumped the table, making the beer glasses shake and drawing the attention of surrounding patrons. "Fuck's sake, Dave. Just ask him."

"I said leave it for now," his brother answered.

Ben sat back in his chair and crossed his thick arms, saying nothing, watching everything. A new song came on, the opening chords ear-shatteringly loud.

"Yeah!" yelled one of the long-haired, heavily tattooed men behind the bar. Glad someone was having a good time. The atmosphere around the table had turned decidedly dark.

A muscle started ticking in Mal's neck. He looked back at the Ferris brothers, his face like thunder. "What?"

"You know what," said Jimmy, yelling to be heard over the music.

Mal spread his hands expansively. "Jimbo, I'm a man of many, many talents, but reading your fucking mind ain't one of them."

"What's going on with Lori?"

Ev's gaze darted to mine. I didn't know any more than she did. Still.

"You on something, Jimbo?" asked Mal, sitting forward in his seat. "Tell the truth now."

"Don't be an asshole." David leaned his elbows on the table, staring furiously at Mal. "We care about her. She's lost a shitload of weight. Looks like a breeze could blow her away. You and Neil never take your eyes off her. You know exactly what Jimmy's talking about."

I could almost hear Mal grinding his teeth.

"We have a right to know," said Jimmy.

David sucked in his cheeks. "C'mon, man. Just tell us."

Shit. Mal went rigid in his seat beside me and then he started rocking. We needed to leave.

I placed my hand on his arm. He vibrated with tension. I didn't know how to comfort him, but I had to try. "Mal?"

He shook me off without so much as a glance.

"She had a flu or something," said Mal. "That's all. Don't make a big deal out of it."

Jimmy shot forward in his seat. "It's more than that. Don't you fucking lie."

"This is what's been messing with your head, isn't it?" asked David. "Lori's sick. Real sick."

"I don't know what you two are talking about." Mal's laughter was a horrible thing. "This is ridiculous. Jimmy here's probably back to fucking freebasing, but what's your excuse, Davie?"

Lena pushed out of her seat. She grabbed the remaining half-full pitcher of beer and threw it in Mal's face. Foamy cold liquid splashed me, and Mal snapped back in surprise.

"What the fuck?" he roared, rising quickly out of the chair.

Across from him, Jimmy shot to his feet as well, shoving a belligerent Lena behind him. Everyone stopped, all conversation in the bar falling silent. The few quiet drinks plan had clearly fallen to shit.

"Don't you yell at her," said Jimmy, hands curled into fists.

Mal's shoulders heaved. The two men faced off across the table, both clearly furious. Slowly, Ben and David got to their feet. This was all going to hell in a handbasket.

"Mal, let's go," I said. "Give everyone a chance to cool off."

Again, he ignored me.

"Walk away, bro," said Ben, voice eerily calm.

Beer dripped from Mal's hair. The front of his shirt was soaked. From behind us came a flash of light. A guy stood with his phone, taking pictures. Asshole.

Without another word, Mal turned and bolted for the stairs, almost sending a girl carrying a bottle of something flying. I just stood there stunned for a moment, useless and stinking of beer. Ben and Sam took off after him.

"Anne, let us handle it," said David.

David and Jimmy both left too, jogging up the small, dark stairwell. Like hell I was doing as I was told.

Mal had left his jacket over the back of his seat. He'd freeze out there. I picked it up and a hand grabbed my wrist. Ev's hand.

"Please, give them a chance to talk," she said, getting in my face. "Those guys have been together a long time."

I picked up my purse and held his jacket to my chest. "No."

"But—"

I didn't have time for this shit. What I needed to do was to find Mal and see if he was all right.

I rushed up the stairs, past the ground-floor bar and out the door. The cold night air chilled me, courtesy of the wet patches on my sweater and jeans. My heart beat double-time. Shit. There was no sign of any of them in either direction. His black Jeep was gone from across the street. They could be fucking anywhere by now.

"Shit."

What to do? Where to go? Maybe he'd headed back to the hotel. Yes, of course. A cab cruised by and I held out my arm. Far too damn slowly, it pulled to a stop.

I threw open the back door and climbed in. "The Benson, please."

I'd find him.

CHAPTER TWENTY

The text from Ev came at quarter to eleven. I'd been wide awake, staring at the ceiling because staring at the walls had gotten old. He hadn't come back to the hotel. I'd been waiting for over half an hour.

> Ev: Lauren gave me your number. The guys talked things out with Mal then he took off again. They don't know where to.
>
> Anne: Ok
>
> Ev: Do you know where he might be?
>
> Anne: If I find him I'll let you know
>
> Ev: Thanks

He might have been driving around town. But far more likely, if he was still worked up, he'd want to take it out on his drum kit.

I took a cab. Money might be tight, but I wouldn't be waiting for him to come to me any longer. Hopefully David and co. had talked him down, calmed him. Now it was time to play my part, whatever that might be. I sat in the backseat, trying to think up speeches. All in all, I was out of wise words.

A hazy drizzle began to fall from the sky as I arrived

at the practice hall. My breath misted in the cold. Ah, Portland. It never disappointed. Best weather ever. Mal's Jeep sat parked next to the building. Thank god, he was here.

The frenetic beat of drums hammered through the building's walls, shaking it to its foundation. A few brave bugs circled the dim light above the metal door. He'd left the door unlocked, thankfully. I stepped inside, bracing myself for the noise. Up on the stage, Mal, sitting in a pool of light, was creating an almighty storm of noise.

Closer to him, broken drum sticks littered the area. Mal had snapped an impressive amount in such a short time.

I climbed up onto the stage, making my way around to him. He sat, poised at the drum kit with eyes closed, hands moving so fast they were almost a blur. Sweat shone, already covering his upper body. Blond hair stuck to the sides of his face. A quarter-empty bottle of Johnny Walker Black Label sat beside him on the floor. The lines of his muscles and the angles of his cheekbones were stark beneath the harsh lighting.

He seemed lost in his own world, totally unaware. I hesitated for a moment then sank down, sitting cross-legged. I covered my ears but it made little difference to the deafening thunder of the drums. No matter. The clash of the cymbals cut through me. The heavy thud of the bass hit my heart. He played on and on, moving between rhythms but never slowing down. Not even to drink. He'd pick up the bottle and just hold it, one-handed, his other hand and both feet never missing a beat.

After the second slug of scotch, though, he didn't get the bottle all the way to the floor before letting go. It tipped over, liquid pouring out. I slid over and set it upright, replacing it in its spot beside him. For the first time he seemed to register my presence, tilting his chin in greeting or appreciation or I don't know what. Maybe I just imagined it. Then he was back to the music, powering on.

I pulled out my phone then hesitated. Ev had pissed me

off, holding me up, but these people were also his family. They deserved to know he was still in one piece.

Anne: He's at the practice hall
Ev: Thank you

David Ferris strode in not fifteen minutes later. He nodded to me, then picked up a guitar and plugged it in. As the first strains of noise rang out Mal opened one eye and saw David standing opposite him. Nothing was said. Time moved by, both sluggish and swift at once. The two of them played for hours. I fell into some sort of daze. It took me a moment to realize when they finally stopped.

"Hey," he croaked, the words muted as if we were underwater. The noise might have broken my ears.

"Hi."

He put the almost empty bottle of scotch to his lips and tossed some back. His gaze stayed on me. Carefully, he screwed the lid back on. It took him a couple of tries. "I'm a little bit fucked-up, pumpkin."

"That's okay. I'll help get you back to the hotel."

He nodded, sniffed his armpits. "And I stink."

"I'll help you shower too." I walked over and knelt between his legs. "Not a problem."

His hands curved over my cheeks, molding my face. Slowly, he pressed his lips to mine. "Mm, I feel something for you, Anne. Which is pretty fucking impressive given how numb I am right now."

"It's huge," I agreed.

"I'm not normally like this . . . drinking this much. Want you to know that. It's just . . ." A muscle spasmed in his jaw and he stared off into the distance.

"I know, Mal. It's okay."

No response.

"We'll get through this."

"Anne—" In a flurry of motion, he fell back off the

stool. I grabbed at his jeans, trying to keep him upright. Not the best idea. One of Mal's big-ass Chucks bumped the side of my head, which hurt. His other foot upset the cymbal stands and they clattered to the floor.

"Shit." Footsteps rushed closer.

Mal lay on his back, laughing.

I sat back on my heels, rubbing at the tender spot on my skull. What a night.

"You alright?" asked David, crouching beside me.

"Fine!" called Mal, still laughing like a loon.

"Not talking to you, asswipe. You kicked Anne."

"What?" Mal rolled over, grabbed the stool, and threw it out of the way. He rushed to my side, pushing David away. "Pumpkin, you okay?"

"Yes, you only clipped me. No damage done."

"Fuck. Oh, shit, Anne." His arms went around me, hugging me so tight he nearly throttled me. "I'm so sorry. We have to get her to a hospital and get a brains can. Brain scan. Fuck, one of those."

"I don't need a hospital or a scan. It's just a bump."

"You sure?" asked David, checking out my eyes.

"Yes," I said. "It was an accident, Mal. Calm down."

"I'm the worst boyfriend ever."

"I sure as hell wouldn't date you," said David.

"Fuck off, Davie."

"Party's over. Time for everyone to go home." David wrestled him off of me and onto his feet.

Mal seemed perplexed to find himself there. He just sort of stood and swayed, frowning down at me. "You okay?"

"Yep."

"I'm really fucking sorry, pumpkin. Wanna kick me in the head? Will that make you feel better?"

"Um, no. But thanks."

David got Mal's arm over his shoulders, dragging or carrying Mal toward the short set of stairs leading down off the stage. It was hard to tell which.

"Wait, where's his shirt? He'll freeze out there."

"Serve him fucking right."

"Shut up, Ferris. You're a whiny little bitch."

"Yeah, and you're loaded."

I rushed ahead and held the door open for them. Mal stumbled and they almost fell. But David got them moving forward again instead of face-planting. Just. "I'm fine, man," Mal said, pushing away from him to teeter precariously on his own. I grabbed his hand to support him and he pulled me in under his shoulder, steadying himself. "See, it's all good."

David just nodded, staying close.

"Gave my Ludwig kit a workout tonight. Broke a lot of drum sticks too." Mal threw his other arm around me, holding me close. He really did need a wash. "American hickory. Zildjian. Made to take a beating but I must have broken eight, maybe ten. Happens in concert often but you don't hear it. I just pick up the next one, keep going, never miss a beat. That's how we roll. Shit gets broken, no matter, play on."

He sighed, shifting his weight against me. I moved my feet farther apart, keeping my arms tight around his middle. The man was not light.

"I'm missing a beat, Anne. I can feel it. Shit ain't right."

I looked up into his beautiful face. My heart breaking for him. "I know. But it's okay. We've got you."

He just frowned down at me.

"I've got you," I said.

"You sure?"

"Very."

He nodded slowly. "Okay. Thanks, pumpkin."

"Let's get you back to the hotel room."

The rain had stopped, thankfully. David stepped in again, helping Mal over to the Jeep, leaning him up against it. One of the shiny black Escalades was parked nearby.

"Man, where are your keys?" asked David, digging through Mal's jeans pockets.

"Geez, Davie. I was saving that especially for Anne."

"I'm not interested in your dick. Where's the keys to your car?"

"Don't get me wrong, man. I love you, just not in that way."

"Uh, got 'em." David dangled the keys from a finger. "Anne, you good to drive him? I'll follow you back, help you get him up to your room."

"Sounds good. Thanks."

"Awesome," Mal mumbled. He let his head fall back and closed his eyes. His mouth, on the other hand, he opened wide. "I LOVE YOU, ANNE!"

I jumped, somewhat startled by the noise. "Holy shit."

"I LOVE YOU."

David just looked at me with one eyebrow raised.

"Huh. He is really drunk," I said, and David half-smiled. Best just to ignore my mini heart attack over Mal saying those words.

"I FUCKING LOVE YOU, ANNE."

"Yeah, okay. Shut up now." David tried to slap a hand over Mal's mouth.

"AAAAAAAANNNNNE!" My name was a long, drawn-out howling kind of noise, muffled at the last when David managed to cover his mouth. Muted grunts and snarling came next.

"God damn it," swore David. "He just fucking bit me."

"My love shall not be silenced!"

I did my best not to laugh. "Mal? I've got a headache from you accidentally kicking me in the head. Do you mind being quiet?"

"Oh, shit, fuck, okay. Sorry, pumpkin. So sorry." He stared up at the sky. "Look, Anne, stars and shit. It's beautiful, right?"

I looked up and sure enough the clouds had parted,

allowing a couple of brave stars to shine through. "Right. Let's go back to the hotel now."

"Mm, yeah, let's go. I have something in my pants I want to show you." His clumsy fingers started in on the waist of his jeans. "Look, it's real important."

I grabbed his fingers, squeezed them tight. "That's great. Show me back at our hotel room, okay?"

"Okay." Mal happy sighed. The air around him consisted solidly of scotch fumes.

"Thanks for texting Ev." David pulled open the passenger side door, grabbed Mal's arm, and proceeded to shove him into the car. "You think tonight was fun, wait till we go on tour. Then things'll get interesting. First time ever there's been girlfriends or wives along."

"The way you say that . . . should I be afraid?"

Mal hammered on the passenger side window. "Anne, my pants itch. I think I'm allergic to them. Come help me take 'em off."

We both ignored him.

David scratched his head. "Think it'll be a learning curve for all of us, yeah?"

"Yeah." The future was a big, ripe ball of I had no damn clue what would happen. And for once, that was okay.

CHAPTER TWENTY-ONE

There was groaning, loud, long, and explicitly painful. Most closely it resembled a wounded animal. Though with an animal, there would have been less swearing. These noises coming from behind me didn't speak of fun times. No, what these noises referred to was a special particular level of hell called The Morning After a mother truckload of booze.

"Pumpkin." Mal buried his face in the back of my neck, pressing his hot skin against me. "Fuck."

"Hmm?"

"Hurts."

"Mm."

The hand stuffed down the front of my pants flexed and curled. It pressed down on all sorts of interesting places, making me squirm.

"Why'd you put my hand down your panties while I was asleep? What's that about?" he mumbled. "Christ, woman. You're out of control. I feel violated."

"I didn't do that, sweetheart. That was all you."

He groaned again.

"You were most insistent about having your hand there. I figured after you fell asleep I'd be able to move you. But it didn't happen." I rubbed my cheek into my pillow, his bicep.

"This pussy is mine." His fingers stretched, pushing against the material of my underwear, stroking accidentally over the insides of my thighs. So not the time to get turned on. We had talking to do.

"Yes, that's what you said. Repeatedly."

He grunted and yawned, then rubbed his hips against me. Morning wood pressed into my butt check. "You shouldn't have made me drink so much. That was very irresponsible of you."

"I'm afraid that was all you too." I tried to sit up but his arm held me down.

"Don't move yet."

"You need water and Advil, Mal."

"'Kay."

His hand withdrew from my crotch and he rolled onto his back with much huffing and puffing. I hadn't managed to get him into the shower last night. Accordingly, this morning, we both stank of sweat and scotch.

I got him a bottle of water and a couple of pills and sat back on the side of the bed. "Up. Swallow."

He opened one bleary eye. "I'll swallow if you will."

"You got it."

"You better mean that. A man doesn't like to be lied to about that sort of thing." Ever so slowly he sat up, his lank, blond hair hanging in his face. He stuck out his tongue and I dropped the pills on it, then handed him the water. For a while he's just there, sipping the water and watching me. I had no idea what came next, what I should say. It was so much easier to just crack stupid jokes than to actually attempt to be deep and meaningful. To help him.

"I'm sorry," I said, just to break the silence.

"Why? What'd you do?" he asked softly.

"I mean about Lori."

He drew up his legs, braced his elbows on his knees, and hung his head. There was nothing but the noise of the air conditioner clicking on, the clink of silverware or something from the room next door. When he finally looked up at me, his eyes were red rimmed and liquid. Mine immediately did the same in empathy. There wasn't a part of me that didn't hurt for him.

"I don't know what it feels like so I'm not going to pretend I do," I said.

His lips stayed shut.

"But I'm so sorry, Mal. And I know that doesn't help, not really. It doesn't change anything."

Still nothing.

"I can't help you and I hate that."

Fact was, a part of wanting to soothe another person was making yourself feel useful. But nothing I could say would take away his pain. I could turn myself inside out, give him everything, and it still wouldn't stop whatever was wrong with Lori.

"I don't even have a functioning relationship with my mother, so I have no idea. Truth is, I used to wish her dead all the time. Now I just wish she'd leave me alone," I blurted out, then stopped, reeling at my own stupidity. "Shit. That's the worst thing to be telling you."

"Keep going."

Crap, he was serious.

I opened my mouth and my throat closed up. The words were dragged out kicking and screaming. "She, um . . . she checked out on us, Lizzy and me. Dad left and she went to bed. That was her great solution to the problem of our family falling apart. No trying to get help, no doctors, just lying in the dark doing nothing. She pretty much stayed in her room for three years. Apart from the time Child Protection Services came by. We managed to persuade them she wasn't a complete waste of space. What a joke."

He stared at me, his lips thin and white.

"I came home one day and she was sitting on the side of her bed with all these little colored pills lined up on her bedside table. She was holding this big glass of water. Her hand was shaking so bad it splashed everywhere, her nightie was all wet. I didn't do anything, not at first." That one moment was horrendously clear in my head. Hovering by the bedroom door, torn over what to do. It had to be manslaughter, to stand by and let it happen. Something like that had to stain you.

"I mean, it was so tempting," I said, my voice cracking. "The thought of not having to deal with her anymore . . . but then Lizzy and I would have gone into the foster-care system and probably gotten separated. I couldn't risk that. She was better off at home with me."

His gaze was stark, his face pale.

"So I stayed home to watch her. She tried to kill herself a couple more times, then gave up on that too, like even dying was too much effort. Some days, I would just wish I'd been five minutes too late. That she'd managed to finish it. Then I'd feel guilty for even thinking that way."

He didn't even blink.

"I hate her so much for putting us through that. I get that depression happens and it's a serious, terrible illness, but she didn't even try to find help. I would make her appointments with doctors, try to get brochures and information and she just . . . you know, she had kids, she didn't have the fucking luxury of just disappearing up her own ass." Tears slid down my face unchecked. "Dad wasn't much better, though he did send money. I guess I should be grateful he didn't forget us entirely. I asked him 'why' when he was leaving and he said he just couldn't do it anymore. He was really quite apologetic about it. Like he'd ticked the wrong box on a form or something and now sorry, but he was opting out. Family? No. Oh shit, did I say yes? Oops! Fucking asshole. As if saying sorry changes anything when you're walking out the door.

"You don't appreciate how much time it takes, running a house, paying the bills, doing all the cooking and cleaning until it's all down to you. My boyfriend stuck with me for a couple of months but then he became resentful because I couldn't go out Saturday nights to games and parties and things. He was young, he wanted to go out and have fun, not stay in to look after a manic-depressive and a thirteen-year-old kid. Who could blame him?"

I ducked my head, trying to line up the important details in my mind. It wasn't easy, considering how much time I'd spent trying to forget. "Then Lizzy rebelled and that just made everything so much worse. She hated the whole world, and who could blame her? At least when she behaved like a selfish, immature kid there was an actual reason behind it, what with her being one. She got busted stealing from this store. I managed to talk the owner into not pressing charges. The scare seemed to snap her out of it. She settled down, got back into her schoolwork. One of us had to make it to college because I tried, but there was no way I was keeping up with school on my own."

What a fucking scene I was making. I blinked furiously and scrubbed away the tears. "You know, I actually wanted to cheer you up or something. Anything."

His silence was killing me.

"So that's my tale of woe." I gave him a smile. Doubtless it looked as shitty as it felt.

"Mom's got ovarian cancer," he said, his voice rough. "They're giving her a couple of months at best . . ."

It felt like my heart stopped. Time stopped. Everything.

"Oh, Mal."

He pushed back his hair, lacing his fingers behind his head. "She's so fucking happy you're around. Kept going on about you at dinner, how wonderful you were. You're her dream come true for me. She's been wanting me to settle down for a while now."

I nodded, trying for a better smile. "She's really great."

"Yeah."

"Fuck, Anne. That's not the only reason why, though . . . I mean . . . at first that was a big part of the reason." He gripped the back of his neck, muscles flexing. "There's more to it now than making her happy before she'd—" He paused, his lips twisting, unable to say the word. "You know there's more, right? We're not pretend anymore. You know that, don't you?"

"I know that." This time I totally aced the smile. "It's okay."

So our start had been dubious. It didn't change where we were now.

"Come have a shower with me?" He held out his hand.

"I'd love to."

He gave me a gallant attempt at a smile.

The bathroom was spacious, white marble with gold trim. We even had a grand piano out in the living room, should the mood strike. Apparently his parents were up in the presidential suite so we'd had to make do with second best. Second best was pretty fine.

He stripped off his boxer briefs. I got the water running at the right temperature, letting the room slowly fill up with steam. Hands slid over me from behind, tugging down my panties, drawing up my old Stage Dive T-shirt. It was the only thing he'd okayed me wearing to bed last night in his drunken wisdom. We were our own small, perfect world in the warmth of the shower cubicle. Mal stepped under the water and it soaked his hair, ran down over his beautiful body. I slid my arms around his waist, resting my head on his chest. The arms he put around me made everything right.

We could deal with things alone. Of course we could. But it was so much better together.

"Worst fucking thing is the morning," he said, resting his chin on the top of my head. "For a few seconds, everything's alright. Then I remember she's sick, and . . . it's just . . . I don't even know how to describe it."

I held him tighter, hanging on for dear life.

"She's always been there. Used to drive us to shows, help us set up. She's always been our biggest fan. When we went platinum she got a Stage Dive tattoo to celebrate. At the age of sixty, the woman got inked. And now she's sick. I can't get my head around it." His chest moved against me as he breathed deep, let it out slow.

I stroked his back, the length of his spine, up and down, smoothing my hands over the curves of his ass, drifting my fingers over the ridges of his rib cage. We stood beneath the hot water and I soothed him as much as I could. Let him know he was loved.

I picked up the bar of soap, running it over him, washing him like a child. First his top half, from the lines of his shoulder blades to the muscles in his arms, every inch of his chest and back. Washing his hair was tricky due to the differences in height.

"Lean down." I poured some shampoo into my hand then rubbed it in, massaging his scalp, taking my time. "Let me rinse it."

He did as asked without comment, hanging his head beneath the showerhead. Next came the conditioner. Carefully, I finger-combed it through.

"You're not allowed to cut your hair," I informed him.

"Okay."

"Ever."

He gave me an almost smile. It was definitely getting closer.

Once his top half was done I knelt on hard stone tiles, soaping up his feet and ankles. Spray from the shower drifted down over me, keeping me warm. Face to face with it or not, I ignored his thickening cock. It wasn't time yet. The muscles in his long, lean legs were so nice. I really needed to look up their names. He flinched when I did the back of his knees.

"Ticklish?" I asked, grinning up at him.

"I'm too manly to be ticklish."

"Ah." I dragged the soap over the hard length of his thighs, back and forth. Damned if he wouldn't be the cleanest, sparkliest rock 'n' roll drummer in the whole wide world. Water slid over his body, highlighting all the ridges and dips, the curve of his pecs and the satin of his skin. I should just call him cake and eat him with a spoon.

"You going higher?" Desire deepened his voice.

"Eventually." I soaped up my hands and put the bar of soap aside. "Why?"

"No reason."

The "no reason" was pointing right at me all large and demanding. I held it aside with one hand, slipping the other between his legs. His hard dick warmed the palm of my hand. A woman with more patience wouldn't have curved her fingers around it, squeezed tight. I was so crap at waiting.

Mal sucked in a breath, his six-pack contracting sharply.

"I love your ass." I said, tracing soapy fingers along the crack before cradling his balls. Every part of him was sublime, body and soul. The good and the bad and the difficult. The times I wanted him to be serious and the times I didn't have a fucking clue where he was at. He always made me want more while making me profoundly thankful for what I had at the same time.

Because I had him, it was right there in his eyes.

"No idea how I got so lucky." I nuzzled his hip bone, sliding my fingers over the smooth skin of his cock.

"You love my ass that much?"

"No, it's more of an all-of-you kind of thing."

I gave his cock another squeeze and his eyes went hazy

in the way I liked so much. Things had definitely woken up between my legs, but this was all about him. The tips of his fingers drifted over the sides of my face, his touch gentle, reverent.

Enough playing around.

I guided the head of his cock into my mouth and sucked hard. Hands dug into my wet hair, holding on tight. My tongue flicked over the top of him, teasing the sensitive rim before dipping below to rub against his sweet spot. I took him in deeper, sucking hard, again and again. His hips shifted, pressing him farther into my mouth. I'd never perfected the art of deep throating, sorry. Mal made me want to learn. Something told me he wouldn't be averse to some practice time. With one hand I cradled his balls, massaging. The other stayed wrapped tight around the root of his penis, stopping him from going too far and gagging me. But I took him as far as I could, pulling back to lavish him with attention from my tongue. Tracing the thick veins and toying with the slit.

The fingers in my hair drew tight, stinging ever so slightly. But it was fine. It was all good. I fucking loved being able to do this to him.

I drew him in deep and sucked hard, working him. He came with a shout, pumping into my mouth as far as my hand would let him. I swallowed.

And they said romance was dead.

He stood, panting, arms hanging slack and eyes closed. Fuck, he was perfect. I slowly stood, my numb knees shaky. After oral, there always seemed to be this moment of shyness. Maybe I should have been smug, thrown in some swagger. There wasn't really the space for it in the shower, however.

Mal opened his eyes and stared at me, his arms going around my shoulders. He drew me in, placing soft kisses on my face.

"Thanks," he said, the word muffled against my skin.

"You're welcome."

"I'm sorry about your parents, pumpkin. So fucking sorry."

My fingers tightened on his hips, involuntarily. One day, I'd stop reacting like that and I'd let it go. "I'm sorry about your mom."

"Yeah." He rubbed my arms briskly, smooched the top of my head. "We need to think happy thoughts. And order a shitload of bacon and eggs. And waffles too. You like waffles?"

"Who doesn't like waffles?"

"Exactly. Anyone who doesn't like waffles should be put in the fucking penal system. Lock 'em up and throw away the key."

"Absolutely."

"No more sad stuff today," he said, voice gruff.

He picked up the soap and started washing me, paying particular attention to my breasts.

"There's just one more thing I think we should talk about," I said, as he worked hard at rubbing some imaginary spot from my left nipple. It felt rather nice, truth be told.

"What's that?" he asked.

"Well, about what you said last night when we got back here. About starting a family."

His hand paused, covering my right breast. "Starting a family?"

"Yes. You said you were really serious about it. You even threw all the condoms out the window and flushed my pill down the toilet."

"That's pretty damn serious. Did we fuck?"

I batted my eyelashes at him and gave him an innocent, if somewhat evil, look. "No. Of course not."

The whites of his eyes blazed bright. "God . . . you nearly gave me a heart attack."

"Sorry." I kissed his chest. "You did throw all of your

condoms out the window. You couldn't find where I kept my pills, though. Then you lay down and proceeded to name all of our children."

"All of them?"

"I take it we're no longer having a brood of lucky thirteen?"

His brows arched up. "Shit. Um, maybe not, huh?"

"Probably for the best. You were going to name three of them David. It would've gotten confusing."

"How much crap did I speak last night, just out of interest?"

"Not too much. You fell off the bed a couple of times, trying to lick my toes, and then you went to sleep."

He washed the soap off his hands and reached for the shampoo, massaging it into my hair.

"Ouch," I gasped. "Gentle."

"What's wrong?"

"You don't remember?"

He turned his face slightly and gave me side eyes. "What now?"

"You might've accidentally kicked me in the head ever so slightly when you fell off your drumming stool."

"Oh, no. Fuck. Anne . . ."

"You didn't hurt me. It's just a little bump."

Face drawn, he carefully washed the shampoo from my hair, starting in on the conditioner. He kept shaking his head, frowning hard.

"Hey," I said, grabbing his chin. "It's okay. Really."

"I'll make it up to you."

"You already did." I placed my hand over his heart, feeling it beat against my palm. "You listened to my story without judging me. You told me what was up with you. Those two things are huge, Mal. They really are. We're good."

"I'll make it up to you more. That won't fucking happen again."

"Okay."

"I mean it."

"I know you do."

He gave me cranky eyes and then suddenly smiled. "I know what I'll get you. Been thinking about it for a while now."

"You don't need to get me anything. Though waffles really would be good, I'm starving." I finished washing off my hair, ready to get out.

"You're getting more than waffles." His arms came around me from behind, a hand sliding down between my legs. Lightly, he started stroking his fingers back and forth along the lips of my sex. "First, you need to come too."

"Okay."

He chuckled in my ear. "So obliging about your orgasms. I like that."

I wound my arms up around his neck and held on tight. He raised his hand to his mouth, wetting some fingers. Then one finger slipped through the seam of my sex, tantalizing me. I tingled from top to toe. Slowly he pressed a little inside, then drew back to trace my entrance, spreading the wetness around. He worked me up in no time, my breathing coming fast and shallow. I writhed against his hand.

"You have to stand still, Anne," he chided me, laying a hand flat against my stomach. Two fingers slid up into me, rubbing at something that felt amazing inside. "C'mon, you're not even trying."

"I can't."

"You have to. I can't do this right if you don't stay still."

"Oh," I gasped as his thumb slid over my clit, sending lightning up my spine.

"See? You made me slip."

The way he loved to tease me was both a blessing and a curse. Fingers drew out, leaving me empty, and all of his attention turned to my clit. He rubbed both sides at once, making me moan.

"Stay still."

"I'm trying."

"Try harder." Lightly, he slapped the top of my sex. The reaction was immediate, my hips kicking forward. No one had ever done that before. Every nerve ending in me felt about ready to explode.

"Like that percussion?" he asked.

"Fuck." It was the only word I had.

He hummed in my ear and went back to working my clit even faster. The pressure just kept building. So close.

"Mal. Please."

He slapped me again and I broke. I cried out, my body caving in. If he hadn't been there to hold me up I'd have hit the floor. The man probably needed to be locked away for the safety of women everywhere.

The water stopped. He wrapped me up in a towel and placed me like a limp rag doll on the bathroom counter.

"Hey, look at me," he said, standing bent before me.

"Hi."

He carefully tucked my wet hair behind my ears.

"I feel like we should touch base about this relationship stuff. And I should probably say something profound here. But I'm not really up to it. Especially not this morning." He exhaled hard. "You're an awesome lay, a great girl, I fucking hate it when you're sad, and I don't like it when you're not around. I'm even getting used to the fighting and drama now and then, because the make-up sex is rockin'. And besides, you're worth it to me."

The tip of his tongue rubbed over his top lip. "That's basically it. Not necessarily in that order, though. Okay?"

"Okay." I laughed, but only a little. He was, after all, being sincere.

"You're my girl. You gotta know that." He grinned and put his hands on my knees. "Need anything else from me?"

I paused, gave it some thought. "We're monogamous?"

"Yep."

"We're seeing where this goes?"

"Mm-hm."

"Then yeah, I'm good."

He nodded, gave my knees a squeeze. "You need anything from me, I expect you to let me know."

"Same goes for you. Anything."

"Thanks, pumpkin." He smiled, leaned in, and kissed me. "Ready to go on tour, Miss Rollins?"

"Absolutely."

CHAPTER TWENTY-TWO

The first day of our official vacation/tour time together, we spent mostly in bed. Waffles were ordered and consumed. In the evening, we left the sanctity of our hotel room to have dinner with his parents up in their suite. Once more, Neil was stalwart and silent, staying close to Lori's side at all times. Lori was the life of the party. The stories she told about Mal as a kid annoyed him and had me howling with laughter.

My favorite was the time an eleven-year-old Mal and his dad had built a small skate ramp in the backyard and he'd broken an arm, two fingers, and a leg within the first two and a half months. Lori made Neil turn the ramp into kindling. Mal staged a hunger strike that lasted approximately two and a half hours.

To make up for the loss of the ramp, his mom promised him a drum kit.

And so the legend began.

It was a great night. His mom didn't mention her illness, so neither did we. If Lori weren't so thin and fragile, and the men so on edge, you could've almost imagined nothing was wrong. The more time I spent with her, the more I understood Mal's devastation. Skate-ramp destroyer or not, Lori Ericson was great. Now that I knew, the quiet despair in Neil's eyes seemed obvious. He was dying inside, going through this with her.

That was the problem with love, it didn't last. One way or another, everything came to an end. People got hurt.

When we returned to our room Mal was withdrawn, silent. I put on an action film full of explosions. We watched it together, his head in my lap. When the movie ended was when the night really began. The sex was slow and intense. It went on and on until I barely remembered my own name. He stared into my eyes, moving above and inside me like time didn't matter.

Like we could do this forever.

The second day, all of their equipment and instruments had been moved from the practice hall to the venue. Mal had a sound check, then a business meeting to attend. I had my own plans. Lizzy came over to keep me and my low profile company. Apparently a couple of reporters were staking out the bookshop and my apartment, still hoping for the inside scoop. An old, fuzzy high school photo of me was the best they'd been able to do. It'd run in the local paper yesterday to no particular acclaim.

Fortunately, given her fascination with Ben, Lizzy already had a date lined up for tonight and couldn't make the concert.

That night, the tour kicked off.

I had barely a week before I had to return to work.

We hung out backstage with the guys until Adrian, their manager, came in, clapping his hands loudly. "Five minutes, guys. We good to go?"

He was followed by a man with a headset and a clipboard or computer of some description. I'd seen quite a few people outfitted this way around. Exactly how much was involved in bringing Stage Dive to town, I had no idea.

Ev and I were watching the concert from the side of the stage beside a collection of massive amps. Holy fucking hell, the roar of the crowd and the energy filling the massive space was amazing. I wasn't particularly deep or spiritual, but standing there, looking out over so many thousands of people, was an impressive thing. There was a definite vibe.

Stage Dive had sold out the largest concert venue in Portland in record time. Their tour was nine cities stateside, then on to Asia. They'd be hitting several festivals in Europe next spring and summer along with doing more concerts. Somehow during all of this, they'd also spend time in the recording studio. David had apparently been busy writing more songs about the glory of doing his wife.

Ah, true love and stuff.

The music was amazing up this close and personal. I enjoyed myself immensely until I noticed a woman in the front row had my boyfriend's name written on her tits in big red letters. Kind of hard not to notice when she kept insisting on flashing them.

"Suck it up and smile," said Ev, her teeth on show.

"Screw her." I turned my attention back to the drummer, going hard at it. He was flinging his head about, blond hair wild and sweat flying off him. My heart went thump. Let's not even go into what my loins did.

After an hour and a half or so, Lori and Neil joined us. Both were sporting earplugs and smiles. The looks of pride they gave their son made my eyes mist up ever so slightly. Lori must have noticed, because she slipped her arm around my waist, leaning into me. I put my arm around her shoulder as the band played another song, and then another. Gradually she gave me more of her weight. She didn't weigh much, but when she started to sway on her feet I gave Neil a nervous look.

He put a hand beneath her elbow, leaning down in front of her with his subtle smile. Lori perked up, waving him away, standing taller. Then her knees buckled and gave out. Both Neil and I grabbed for her, keeping her off the ground. Unfortunately, all of this happened between songs.

Jimmy was smooth talking the screaming audience up front of the stage. And despite all of the bright lights, Mal saw Lori stagger. He rose from his stool, standing, watching us. Anxiety lined his face.

Without further ado, Neil swung Lori up into his arms and carried her off. I held my hand up to Mal and nodded, hoping he'd get the message that I'd follow them and do what I could. He must have, because he nodded back at me and then sat down again.

"Come on," said Ev, grabbing my hand. We ran after Mal's parents, ducking and weaving around people and equipment. Lena met us just outside the room we'd been in before, backstage. Beside her stood an unhappy Adrian, but then I doubted I'd ever see a happy one.

"Let me know if you want me to call a doctor," she said.

"Thanks."

Neil had lain Lori down on a couch and was holding a glass of juice to her lips. A bird would have drunk more than she seemed to. Her skin was pale and paper thin, her eyes dazed.

"There's no need to fuss," she said chidingly to Neil. When she saw me, her mouth fell open in obvious dismay. "Oh, Anne, you didn't need to come. You were enjoying the show."

"They must be nearly finished. And Mal would want me to come and check on you, I'm sure."

"Well, you've checked. I'm fine. Go on back now."

Fuck. I knew all about *fine*. Care of my mom's early example, I was the Queen of fucking fine. I perched on the edge of the couch while Neil squatted near the end. Up this close, her face was tinged gray.

"I know you're sick, Lori. Mal told me."

The air hissed out of her. "I told him I didn't want everyone knowing and carrying on. It's life, sweetie, we all have to go sometime."

"He said you had a month or two," I said. Lori and Neil

shared a look I did not like one tiny bit. "Is there something you need to tell your son?"

"It might be less than that now. We saw the doctor in Spokane before we left to come here." Her chin hiked high. "But it makes no difference. I'm not spending my final days in a hospital."

Something stuck in my throat. "Your final days?"

"Weeks," she amended. "They think another week or two at best. We'll head home tomorrow afternoon. I'd like to be there . . ."

Neil inhaled hard and turned away. His hand slid over his wife's, fingers intermeshing.

"You have to tell him," I said. There were razor blades in my throat, barbed wire, nails, assorted hardware, and sharp implements. It was wildly uncomfortable.

"I suppose you're right."

With a grunt, Neil gave her fingers a final squeeze and rose to his feet. "I'll let him know when he comes off-stage. Can't ask Anne to keep it from him."

"No," agreed Lori. "Just, help me sit up. Everyone will come in and I'll be lying here like a fool."

This wasn't happening. Shit.

Carefully, Neil and I helped Lori to sit upright. Then he went off to wait for his son. I took over juice duties. At least holding the glass gave me something to do.

"I'm glad he has you," said Lori, straightening the skirt of her pale green dress. "I know I've said it before. But my going will hit him hard. He acts all loud and tough, but he's got a soft underbelly, my son has. He's going to need you, Anne."

She took my spare hand in hers. Mine was sweaty, hers was not.

"I really like your son," I said. Because I had to say something. So, of course it was woefully inadequate as per the ordinary when it came to feelings.

"I know you do, sweetie. I've seen the way you look at him."

"Crazy eyes?"

"Yes." She laughed softly. "Crazy eyes."

Out front, the crowd roared and the stamping of feet almost shook the building. Funny, back here, the music was a mild thrumming sort of noise at most. Negligible. Or maybe it was care of the pounding in my skull. I could feel a headache coming on. This whole situation was beyond heavy, the weight of it crippling. There was no making this right or fixing it.

People started flowing into the room. A long table full of drinks and food had been set up. Apparently an after party was planned for right here. Adrian stood by the door, shaking hands and laughing loudly at the shit people said. It was all so surreal. Somewhere out there, Neil was probably telling Mal, right now.

"Everything will be fine." Lori patted my hand. Funny, the way she clung to my favorite word. Perhaps there was something to the belief of finding a partner who reflected your parent. Which was fantastically creepy and wrong. I really didn't want to think about it after all. Mal was nothing like my father.

Then he stormed in. Mal, not my dad. A T-shirt was wrapped around his right hand, blood dripped from his fingers.

"What the hell happened?" I jumped out of my seat, running toward him.

Neil returned to Lori's side. Jimmy headed straight for the table laden with booze and gourmet goodies. He dug into the big bucket filled with foreign beers with a single-minded dedication.

"Jimmy. What are you doing?" Lena grabbed at his arm.

With a look of pure annoyance, Jimmy leaned down,

whispered in her ear. Lena's gaze darted to Mal and then dropped to his hand. She looked up and down the table, searching for something.

"Mal?" The scent of him was a kick to my gut, same as always. But what the hell was going on?

"Hey, pumpkin. No big deal." He didn't meet my eyes. He also studiously avoided his mom's concerned gaze.

Jimmy returned with his hands full. He and Lena had turned a linen table cloth into an ice pack. "Here."

"Thanks." Slowly, Mal unwound the bloody T-shirt. Beneath it, his knuckles were raw, open wounds. His jaw clenched as he held the ice to his hand.

The managerial jerk, Adrian, elbowed his way into our circle. "Mal, buddy. I hear there was an incident upstairs?"

"Ah, yeah, Adrian, you mind getting that straightened out? Mal accidentally put a hole in the wall. Just one of those things, yeah?" David put a hand to the man's shoulder, leading him away.

I highly fucking doubted it was an accident, given the timing.

"We need to get someone in to look at his hand," said Adrian.

They kept talking but I tuned them out. I put my hand to Mal's face, willing him to look at me. "Hey."

His eyes were going to give me nightmares, the misery in them. He leaned forward, caught my mouth with his, kissing me fully, frantically. His tongue invaded my mouth, demanding everything. And I gave it to him. Of course I did.

At last he calmed, resting his forehead against mine. "'S'all fucked."

"I know."

"She's only got a week or two at most."

There was nothing I could say.

He squeezed his eyes shut. Sweat from his face dampened my skin. He was bare from the waist up and the room was cold, the air-conditioning working overtime for some reason. Not so necessary this time of year.

"Let's get you hydrated," I said, grateful for anything I could do for him. "Find another T-shirt for you to put on. Okay? You're going to cool off fast in here."

"'Kay."

"Stay with him," said Ev, her hand on my shoulder. "I'll go."

"Evvie." Mal looped his arms over my head in an awkward hug, still holding the ice to his hand. "Hard stuff."

Her forehead creased.

"Scotch or something," said Mal. "Please."

With a sigh, she turned away, headed off into the growing crowd. Worst damn timing for a party ever.

"We better go over," said Mal, turning to face his parents.

Neil perched on the arm of the couch, an arm around his wife. Lori's lips were pinched with worry.

"Hey, Mom," said Mal, keeping me tight against him. "Glad you guys could make it. Had a little accident with my hand."

"Are you alright?"

"Oh, yeah. No worries."

The guys stood nearby, holding back spectators, keeping industry and other types at bay from our corner of the room. Soon, Sam arrived with another black-suited guy and took over this duty. Ben and Jimmy kept close, talking to people, doing their job, and socializing. But their gazes kept returning to Mal.

Ev must have run, because she returned with a Stage Dive Tour shirt for him to wear, a bottle of Smirnoff vodka and another of Gatorade. "They didn't have scotch."

"It'll do." He handed me the sopping wet ice pack while he pulled on the shirt. It had a big candy skull on the front. "Thanks, Evvie."

"Son," said Neil. There was a lot communicated through just the one word.

"Dad, all good," crowed Mal, suddenly switching mood to exuberant. It didn't give me a good feeling. "This is how we roll after the show. You know that!"

Neil said nothing. The latest Stage Dive record and the chatter of a hundred or so party people filled the air instead. Mal downed half of the bottle of green Gatorade. Then he passed it to me to hold and downed big mouthfuls of vodka.

Ah, shit. This was going to be like watching a car wreck.

"Baby," I said, slipping my arms around his waist, drawing him closer. "Just stop and breathe for a minute."

"You called me baby." He smiled.

"Yes."

"You called me sweetheart the other day."

"You're the one that wanted a stupid romantic nickname."

"Yeah. My Anne." He rubbed his cheek against mine like he was marking me. Stubble scratched my skin and my whole body glowed like embers. The emotion was too much, completely overwhelming.

"Mal."

"Don't frown, there's no need to worry. Do me a favor and go talk to Mom okay?" he asked. "Keep her happy. I can't, ah . . . I can't talk to her right now. Not yet."

He put the bottle to his lips again, tipped his head back and drank, while I swallowed hard. The booze was him self-medicating regarding this situation. But I'd be lying if I said it didn't scare me just the same. His eyes popped wide open and he exhaled. "That's better. That's fucking better."

"I think Adrian's going to get someone to come check your hand," said David, sidling up next to us.

"No need."

I tried to clear my sore throat. "Let him look at your hand, Mal."

"Pumpkin—"

Enough of this shit. "You want me not to worry? You get your hand looked at. That's the deal."

His gaze ever so slowly sized me up. "I love it when you get all hard assed on me. Okay. If it'll make you happy, I'll let them look at it."

"Thank you."

Another big swig from the bottle.

Ev situated herself beneath David's arm, both of them watching him with anxious eyes. There was strain and stress on everyone's faces and Mal just kept right on drinking. Bottom of the bottle, here he came. For some reason, it just made me mad.

"That's enough." I tugged the bottle out of his hand. He obviously hadn't been expecting it because he didn't put up a fight. Big green eyes blinked at me, then narrowed into anger.

"What the fuck?" he said in a low voice.

"Find another way to deal with this."

"That's not your call."

"You really want one of her last memories of you to be watching you get drunk?"

"Oh, please. Mom's been around since the beginning. She knows what parties are like backstage, Anne. She wants normal? I'm giving her normal."

"I'm serious, stop this."

He gave me more of the angry stare. No problem. If he wanted to do glaring competitions all night, fine by me. I'd said I had his back. It meant protecting him even from himself if need be.

"Look around you," I said. "They all just watched Jimmy go through this. They're scared shitless for you, Mal."

"It's not like that," he growled.

"Not yet."

"Not your job to tell me what to do, pumpkin. Not even remotely."

"Mal—"

"We've been together what, a week? And you know best now, huh?" He looked down at me, his jaw shifting from side to side. "Yeah, Anne's in charge."

"Ah, for fuck's sake," said David, stepping forward. "Shut up, you dickhead, before you say something you really regret. She's right. I got no interest in watching you go through rehab too."

"Oh give me a break," said Mal. "Rehab? A bit over-dramatic there, Davie."

"Really?" asked David, getting right up in his face. "You're getting so drunk you're accidentally kicking your girlfriend in the head. So mad you're putting your fist through walls. How's that sound to you, hmm? Sound like someone who's got it all under control?"

Mal flinched. "Stuff is happening."

"I get that. We all get that. But Anne's right, you fucking yourself up every other night isn't the answer."

Mal's shoulders dropped, the fight leaving him. "Fuck you, Ferris."

"Whatever. Say sorry to your girlfriend and mean it."

His sad-eyed gaze turned to me. "Sorry, pumpkin."

I nodded, tried for a smile.

"Come on, you need a breather." David grabbed Mal by the back of the neck and towed him off into the crowd. Fortunately, Mal didn't fight him. I watched them go with relative calm. Sure, everything would be alright. Whatever happened, however, I didn't want to turn around. I could feel the weight of Lori's stare burning a hole in the middle of my back. Her and Neil had to have heard and seen it all. What could I possibly say?

I was so terrible at this family and relationship stuff. I

wish Lizzy were here. She'd know what to do. She was so much better with people than me.

"It'll be okay," said Ev, taking my hand in hers.

A nice sentiment, but I highly doubted it.

CHAPTER TWENTY-THREE

"PARTY!" An hour later, Mal was in loud, manic mode.

He only had a bottle of water in his hand. Our words had gotten through to him at least. Just like the first night I met him, he stood on top of a coffee table, doing his groove thing. There were a lot of women willing to heed his party call. Plenty of slick, shiny women watching my man with avarice in their eyes. It was something I'd have to get used to. I couldn't kill all of them. I mean, where on earth would I hide so many bodies?

This dating rock stars business was harder than it looked.

One such young lady tried to climb up onto the table with him and no. Not even a little.

I grabbed her arm. "Not happening."

"Get your hand off me," she spat.

"PUMPKIN!" shouted my drumming delight from above.

Holy hell, my ears. They were ringing.

The woman gazed up and gave Mal a foxy grin. Her facial expression when she turned back to me was not as warm.

"Sorry," I said (blatant lie there). "He's taken."

"Who the hell are you?"

"I'm pumpkin." The "ha, bitch" was silent, but make no mistake, it was most definitely there.

She did some strange squinty-eyed thing and then about-faced, disappearing into the crowd. There was a flash of shiny silver stilettos and she was gone. Awesome shoes. I'd worn my usual boots and a skirt, denim this time, a black long-sleeve shirt and some chunky resin jewelry finished me off. Deep down inside, I had no idea how a rock star's girlfriend was supposed to dress, but for comfort would do. Those shoes though, I'd really like to know where she got them. Chances of her telling me now had to be somewhere between nil and none.

Lori and Neil were still stationed on the couch in the corner. David and Ev kept them company while I guarded my man from other women. Or something like that. Honestly, I wasn't having a very good time. The argument earlier had left me on edge and I didn't fit with this crowd. There were music reporters and industry types, a mixed assortment of the rich and famous all gathered together to kick off the tour.

"Pumpkin?" Mal called again.

I turned to face him.

"Oh, there you are. Hey. I have an announcement to make," hollered Mal. "Everyone. Yo!"

The crowd quieted, all heads turning his way. I didn't have a good feeling about this.

"Lot of shit's been happening lately. Got me thinking about things." He gazed over at his parents. "Life's short and you gotta make it count, take the time to be with the people you love. Keep 'em close to you. So I, ah . . . I've come to a decision. Right here, right now."

He stared down at me, his brows nearly meeting above the straight line of his nose. And then, he sank down on one knee, on top of the coffee table. His hand reached out for mine and I took it, fingers numb with surprise.

"Marry me, Anne."

My heart stopped. Holy fucking hell. He couldn't be serious.

"What?"

"Yeah, marry me tonight," he said, his voice clear to one and all. "We'll fly down to Vegas on the red-eye. Be back in time for breakfast."

Flashes went off around us, blinding me. But nothing else existed. There was only his beautiful, hopeful face, fading in and out of view.

". . . So romantic," whispered someone nearby.

"We can take the guys with us," he said. "Go pick up Lizzy on the way. Even bring Reece if you want."

I couldn't breathe.

"I'll buy you the biggest fucking ring you've ever seen."

No, really, was there no oxygen in this room?

"I know this is soon. And I know you've got some issues with marriage, but this is you and me. We're solid."

No, we weren't. We'd just had a fight. We were always having fights and it'd only been . . . fuck, how many days? Yes, we could be good together. But we were only beginning; no way were we ready for this.

"C'mon, Anne."

"It's only been a week . . ."

"I need you to do this for me."

"I'll marry you, Mal!" Some bitch at the back of the room shouted. Others muttered their agreement.

"Why?" I searched his face, my heart beating overtime.

"Lots of reasons."

I shook my head, stupefied.

"Please," he said, staring into my eyes.

Neil was supporting Lori, they were standing right there, not four feet away, watching the whole thing. My stomach turned upside down. There was such hope on Lori's face. She had her hands clutched to her chest, her eyes shining with unshed tears. Ev stood just past her with

David and her lips were drawn, but her eyes . . . Fuck, they all actually thought this insane idea might work. Well, I guess Ev would, she'd done some crazy stuff in Vegas herself.

But this wasn't romance. This was insanity.

"I need you to do this for me," he repeated. "Take a chance, Anne."

Take a chance on heartbreak and abandonment. All the pain and suffering I knew so well. I barely had a grip on being in a relationship and he wanted to make it legal and binding forever and ever until someone up and decided they'd had enough.

My shoulders curved in. "Mal . . . don't."

His gaze darted over my face. "You and me in Vegas. C'mon, it'll be fun."

I stepped closer to him, trying for privacy. "I can't marry you just to make your mom happy."

"It's more than that."

"It's not. If it weren't for her being sick, there's no way you'd be asking me this right now."

"But—"

"I'm sorry. No."

"Anne . . ."

I could see the exact moment he realized he wasn't going to talk me into it. That he wasn't going to get his way. His jaw hardened and he dropped my hand. In one smooth move he jumped off the coffee table and headed for the door. Any possible words stuck in my throat, choking me.

There he went. Going, going, gone.

He was gone.

Every eye in the room was on me. David followed Mal, and Ev appeared at my elbow. They really did have this shit down by now, managing drama the Stage Dive way. Jimmy and Ben stopped Adrian from following David and Mal. The manager gave me a look strongly encouraging me to curl up and die. I was so sick of this.

Something broke inside. The pain was excruciating.
It was really best just to get this dealt with.

Lori's look was hesitant, sad. "Oh, Anne . . ."

"I'm sorry," I said, and then I got the fuck out of there.

Mal didn't return to our hotel room that night. There was
no message from him the next day either. I went home.

CHAPTER TWENTY-FOUR

I spent the remaining days of my vacation spring cleaning the apartment. Lizzy and Lauren took turns sitting on the love seat, watching me go berserk. Berserk being their word, not mine. I was fully functioning and fine given my heartbroken status. No way had I crawled into bed like Mom and refused to come out. I was stronger than that and my apartment was very, very clean.

"Look at that bowl," I said, gesturing toward the bathroom with my pink, rubber-gloved hand and toilet brush. "You could eat out of it."

"Babe, all power to you, but I am not inspecting your toilet." Lauren crossed her legs, swung her foot back and forth.

"No shit, it's sparkling."

"I believe you."

The front door opened and Lizzy walked in. "She still at it?"

Yes, during particularly unlucky times, they'd both be there, commenting and getting in my face. So helpful. Friends and family were the worst. They were also the best, seeing me through this temporary insanity.

"Yes, she is. Please knock before you come in uninvited," I said.

Mal would be pissed. He hated people just waltzing in. Not that he would ever be here again or cared, so whatever. Maybe I should scrub the kitchen one more time. Going back to work tomorrow would be good. It'd help keep me busy. Reece had dropped off a couple of new bottles of environmental all-surfaces cleanser and a scrubbing brush for me yesterday (I'd worn my old one out.). He got my drive to keep busy right now. Or, if he didn't get it, he at least had the sense to stay out of my way and not mention any famous drummers.

"And you didn't close the door properly, Lizzy."

My sister looked at me over the top of her sunglasses. "That's because you have another guest about to arrive. Hopefully you'll be nicer to this one."

"I'm nice to everyone."

Lauren winced. "No. Not really. You're kind of pretty fucking painful lately. But we love you and we get that you're hurting, so here we are."

My frown did feel permanently pressed into my face. Perhaps they had a point. It might be time to move on. If I'd only been with him a week, then mourning him for half a week was probably about right. Too bad my heart disagreed.

"Helllooooo!" cried Ev, appearing around the door frame. "Yeah, okay. Wow, Liz. She needs help."

"Told you," said Lauren, standing up to give Ev a hug.

"Um, Anne?" Ev approached me with extreme caution, slowly slipping out of her woolen jacket. "Take the gloves off and go put on clothes that don't have holes in them. You might want to shower first, wash your hair, maybe? Wouldn't that be nice?"

"I've been cleaning," I explained, holding the brush up as evidence. "You don't wear good clothes to clean in."

Lizzy turned me in the direction of the bathroom. "About the time you're waving a toilet brush around exclaiming about the beauty of your bowl, it's probably time to stop and rethink your life."

"Go back in there and clean you this time," directed Lauren. "I'll find you some clothes."

"Wait." I turned back to Ev. "Why are you here? Why aren't you on tour?"

She grimaced. "The tour's been cancelled. Put off until next year. It's for the best. They're saying Lori only has a couple of days left so the guys have all gone to Coeur d'Alene."

Oh, god. Poor Mal. My ribs squeezed breathtakingly tight.

"Why aren't you with them?" I asked.

"I'm flying there this afternoon." She spoke slowly, carefully. "But I wanted to be here for your intervention. And to ask if maybe you wanted to come with me."

I just stared at her blankly.

"I think he would really appreciate you being there, Anne. I know things got left in a bad place between you two. But I think he could really do with your support right now. Lori would probably like to say good-bye."

"I turned down her son's proposal of marriage, so I highly doubt that."

Ev gave a one-shoulder shrug. "She was sad, but . . . I don't think she was mad at you exactly."

"It doesn't matter anyway. I can't go." I wandered into the bathroom, put away the toilet brush, and peeled off the rubber gloves. Ev, Lauren, and Lizzy huddled in the doorway, watching me. I washed my hands, soaping them up super well. "Look, guys, I appreciate the intervention, not that I believe I needed it. I was just keeping busy before I had to go back to work."

"Sure you were," said Lizzy. "That's why you scoured the ceiling."

"It was dusty."

"Focus, ladies." Lauren clicked her tongue. "Anne, you need to go with Ev. Talk to him."

I dried my hands with a towel. The girl in the mirror was a bit of a mess, hair lank and skin greasy. They were right there, I had looked better.

"You two were good together," said Ev. "He got carried away with the wedding idea, but I think he gets that now."

"Oh, I don't know. I don't think there's so many good ways to take someone refusing to marry you." I huffed out a laugh. "Not sure there's any coming back from that one. Thanks for the thought, Ev. But he doesn't want me there."

She shook her head. "You don't know that—"

"Yes, I do." I put my hands on my hips. It didn't feel quite right so I swapped over to crossing them over my chest instead. "I texted him the other day, asked if there was anything I could do. If he wanted me there even just as a friend. He said no."

And yes, Mal's one-word, two-letter answer had pissed me off and hurt. The fact that I bought myself a new phone for my birthday was somewhat related. As was the mark I needed to paint over on my bedroom wall. Turns out I had a better throwing arm than I was aware of.

Ev, Lauren, and Lizzy just stared at me. Awesome. I could do without yet again having my heartbreak on display for one and all. And that was a shitty, stupid thought. "Seriously, thanks anyway, guys. For everything. I'm going to take your advice and have a shower."

"That took balls, reaching out to him," said Lizzy.

"I had to try."

Lauren frowned at the floor. "We need booze. Food."

"Yeah," sighed Lizzy.

My smile started twitching at the edges. I couldn't quite make it. "Sounds good."

Ev nodded somberly. Then she paused. "Anne, be

smarter than him. If he means something to you, if you get another chance . . . don't give up so easily."

I had nothing. I just stared at her, lost, not a clue how to react or what to do with myself. It was the same damn way I'd been feeling since the night Mal walked out on me.

"Go get cleaned up." Lizzy hugged me from behind, wrapping her arms around me and squeezing tight. "I'll organize some food and drinks."

"Oh, I can do that after I—"

"Anne, please. Let me look after you for a change."

I nodded slowly, on the verge of tears yet again. "Okay. Thanks."

Lizzy set her chin on my shoulder, not letting go. "You're my amazingly strong big sister and I love you. But you are allowed to need help now and then. You don't have to fix everything on your own anymore, you know?"

"I know." I didn't know it exactly, but I was beginning to feel it. And it was warm, wonderful, and everything it should have been. Not being alone in this, having them all here was a beautiful thing. "Thank you."

My birthday didn't feel like my birthday. The last two had been nice, shopping with Lizzy and going out to dinner with Reece. But this year's? Not so much. It was a lot like being back with Mom and pasting a smile on my face for Lizzy's sake. Making a cake and then getting sick after eating half of it because it was what you did.

I'd been back at work for three days now. The "intervention" had stuck. I hadn't indulged in anymore crazy cleaning marathons. To be fair, the apartment couldn't get any more hygienic if I tried. I hadn't heard from Mal again and I didn't expect I would. End of story.

My stripy jersey dress was definitely the go-to look for dinner with Reece. It made me happy. Heartbreak could be covered over by a million and one things including cake and happy stripy dresses.

Fucking rock stars with their fucking ridiculous marital demands and their fucking incredible smell, face, body, voice, sense of humor, mind, generous spirit, and all the rest (Not necessarily in that order.).

Fuck them all. But especially fuck Mal.

Reece was fifteen minutes late. I tapped my knee-high brown boots on the scuffed wooden floor, beating out a hectic rhythm. No need to mention whom I might have picked up the habit from. Maybe waiting outside was a better idea, out in the cold wind. I trudged down the stairs and out the door while firing off a text message to Reece making sure he hadn't broken down or anything.

He hadn't.

I knew this because he was rolling around on the small patch of front lawn with someone. Not in ecstasy so much as agony. Lots of agony, if the groans and grunts were any indication. A battered bouquet of roses lay tossed aside. What the hell?

"Reece?"

No response.

I blinked, double-checking my vision. Was that really . . . "Mal?"

Yes, Mal and Reece were fighting on the front lawn. Blood wept from a cut on Mal's brow and on Reece's lip. A dark mark covered Mal's cheek and Reece's shirt was ripped open. They wrestled on, throwing punches and making animalistic-sounding noises.

"Motherfucking little . . ." Mal's drove his fist hard into Reece's stomach.

Reece grunted and countered by attempting to kick him in the groin. He caught Mal's thigh instead. Given the way Mal's face twisted, it obviously stung.

"You're the asswipe that left her," sneered Reece.

They came clashing together again, fists and blood flying. Bile stung the back of my throat and I swallowed it back down. Shit, shit, shit. What to do? I fished out my cell phone, dialed Lauren's number.

"Hi, Anne."

"Are you guys here? I need Nate out front now, please. Hurry."

"What's going on?"

"Mal and Reece are trying to kill each other."

There was swearing and muttering. "On our way back. We'll be there in five minutes."

I hung up. Five minutes. They could hurt each other worse in five minutes and do some real damage if they hadn't already. I couldn't wait five minutes. I needed to do something now.

I cupped my hands over my mouth, standing on the front step. "Hey! What the fuck do you two idiots think you're doing?"

Reece looked my way and Mal clocked him on the chin. Beyond enraged, they fell on each other again.

Well, that didn't work.

Then Reece swung hard, catching Mal in the face, knocking him back a step. Mal stood, stunned for a moment. And no damn way could I stand there and watch him get hurt any more. It just wasn't in me. Reece pulled back his arm, his bloody lips drawn, baring his teeth.

"Reece, no!" I didn't stop and think. Instead, I made like a fool and rushed in, hell-bent on defending my man.

Mal turned. "Anne."

I ran straight for him. Reece's fist hit me in the eye and I dropped. Pain filled my world, blanking my mind. Fuck, did it hurt.

"Are you okay?" asked Mal.

"Ah . . ." was about the best I could do.

"Anne, oh fucking hell, I'm so sorry," Reece babbled.

"Easy," said Mal. My head was carefully lifted and placed upon a firm jeans-clad thigh.

"Hey. Hi," I said, somewhat dazed and confused. I covered my battered eye with both hands, breathing through the exquisite agony.

"Pumpkin, what the fuck were you thinking, running in like that?"

"I was saving you. Or something. You know . . ."

They had stopped fighting. It was sort of a success.

Excited whimpering came from the box beside me. A little head popped up, then disappeared. What the hell? To the whole scene basically, I couldn't restrict the question to any one thing happening tonight on the front lawn. The grass was cool and damp beneath me. I lay on my back, staring up at the night sky. My brain pounded. Mal stared down at me, his eyes tight with concern, his face a bloody mess.

"How you feeling?" he asked.

"Ouch."

"Anne, I'm so damn sorry," said Reece, looking about as contrite and torn up about it as possible. "Are you alright?"

"I'll live." Mostly. "Advil and ice would probably be good."

"Yep, let's get you upstairs." Mal carefully brushed the hair back from my face.

Panting this time came from the box, along with a high-pitched yelp.

"It's alright, Killer. Mommy's okay." Mal put a hand in the box and lifted out a wriggly little body covered in black-and-white fur. A fancy, studded collar sat around his neck, topped off by a big red bow. The bow was bigger than the dog. "Mommy was trying to save Daddy from evil Uncle Reecey, wasn't she? A nice thing to do, but Daddy is still going to spank Mommy for being so silly and jumping into a fight. Yes he is, because Daddy's the best."

"Oh for fuck's sake," mumbled Reece.

"Happy birthday; I got you a puppy." Mal held the puppy near my face and a wet, pink tongue darted out, licking my chin. He had the darkest, sweetest little eyes. "I named him Killer."

"Wow." God, he was cute—the man and the dog both. "Mal, you can't call something that small Killer."

"He earned it. Killed one of my Chucks right after I picked him up this afternoon. Chewed a hole right through it."

The puppy licked me again, nearly getting me on the lips this time.

"Gross, little dude." I smiled. "I know what you do with that tongue."

Mal smiled, then handed the puppy to Reece. "Here, carry him up. Don't drop him."

"I won't drop him."

"You better not."

More grumbling from Reece and some yips from Killer the puppy. Truly, this night was surreal.

"Wait, Mal. What about your mom?" I asked. "How is she?"

His mouth firmed and his brows descended. "Not good. She doesn't have long now."

"What are you doing here?"

His bloody face screwed up and gave me a pained look. "That's kind of a long story too. I'll tell it to you upstairs."

A car pulled to a screeching halt at the curb, and Nate and Lauren rushed out. I waved groggily at them. "It's okay. They stopped fighting."

"Ooh, look at the puppy!" cried Lauren.

"You two fucking idiots. What did you do to her?" Nate squatted down next to me, scowling, studying my rapidly swelling shut eye. The world was a blur on that side. "How's your head, Anne?"

He turned back to Lauren, who was still busy petting and cooing at Killer. "Lauren, leave the dog and call that nurse friend of yours. If we take Anne anywhere like this people will ask questions I'm assuming she won't want to answer."

"Sorry. Yes. Good idea." Lauren pulled her cell phone out of her purse.

"No, please don't," I said. "It's fine."

Lauren hesitated, looking between me, Mal, and Nate.

"Really," I insisted, trying to look perky. "I'm going to have a shiner, but I'm okay."

"I'll carry her," growled Mal when Nate tried to pick me up.

"I'll walk. Just help me up." I held up my hands and Nate gently pulled me to my feet. Behind me, Mal jumped up. He gripped my hips, holding me steady as the world slipped and slid.

"Whoa." My head spun round and round.

"Easy." Mal stood at my back, letting me lean against him until I found my feet. "Fuck, Anne. I'm so sorry."

"I've never had a black eye before."

"Could have lived without you getting one now because of me." His lips brushed against my ear. "Let me carry you."

"Okay." Fighting was dumb. Mal and Reece fighting, and me resisting being carried.

Mal picked me up in his big, strong arms while I swooned like a proper romance-novel heroine.

"I'm thinking my career as a prizefighter has come and gone." I rested my head on his shoulder, breathing in his familiar scent. Man, I'd missed that. Mal just shook his head. I don't think he was quite ready to see the humor in my getting hit just yet.

Nate opened the front door to our apartment building and the rest followed behind me and Mal, Reece carrying the puppy, and Lauren still trying to pat the puppy.

"You're back and you got me a puppy?" The concept

still seemed strange. It might have been my recent brain injury. I looped an arm around his neck, taking liberties with him while I could. Who knew how long he'd stay this time. Or why he was even back.

"You never had one as a kid."

"I can't have pets in this building, Mal."

"Yeah, I know. I got you a new apartment too. No point doing things halfway, right?"

"Riiiight." I had the worst feeling he wasn't joking.

Up the stairs we went. Nate rummaged in my purse and pulled out my keys, opening the door.

"Just put me on the couch, thanks," I directed. "Ah, there's an ice pack in the freezer."

Without a word, Mal deposited me as told then went to find the ice. It didn't hurt too badly to let him go. Not in comparison to my eye. I kept one hand over it, shielding it from the too-bright overhead light.

"Thanks for coming back, guys," I said to Nate and Lauren. "Sorry to mess with your night."

They just looked at me, sort of stunned still. Lauren had on heels and jeans, clearly ready for a night on the town.

"I'm sorry I interrupted your date. And Reece, relax," I said, moving right along. "It was an accident."

He gave me eyes full of guilt.

Mal came bustling back in with an ice pack wrapped up in a towel, a bottle of water, and a bottle of Advil.

"Thanks." I swallowed two of those suckers straight down and held the ice pack over my eye. "Reece and Mal, you need to stop fighting. Can I have that for my birthday, please?"

Without delay, Mal stuck out his hand, ready for shaking.

"Yeah, okay." Reece moved the puppy to one arm and shook Mal's hand.

"Thank you."

"Here," he said, holding my new dog out to me. The big, red bow had flopped down over Killer's face and he was growling and tugging on it with his teeth. Cutest thing ever. I hadn't even realized I wanted a dog but despite my eye throbbing like a bitch, I couldn't stop smiling. Reece placed him in my lap. Immediately he tried to climb me and lick my chin. Out of the three males present, he was definitely my favorite, despite being the jumpiest.

"Chill, little guy." Mal sat beside me on the love seat, placing a restraining hand on Killer.

"You sure you're okay?" asked Lauren, reaching in to give Killer a final scratch behind the ears.

"Yeah, I'll be fine. Thanks."

"You want us to go so you can kick Mal's ass?"

"Please."

She nodded, grabbed a scowly faced Nate, and dragged him out the door. Because girls got it. Men, not so much.

"Listen, Anne," said Reece. "I'm sorry about the scene out front. About you getting hit and everything."

"I know you are, Reece. But right now, I need to yell at Mal. Can we do dinner another time?"

"You're not going to yell at me?"

"No. I'm going to yell at him, because I'm in love with him."

Mal stiffened beside me, the hand petting Killer missing a beat.

"Right," said Reece. "Which means you're definitely not in love with me, and I need to give up and back off."

"I'm sorry, Reece."

"All right." Reece gave me a sad smile, then leaned in and kissed me on the cheek. "I'll remember that next time. Just do me a favor? Don't come to work for a few days. Stay home and give your eye and my guilt time to heal."

"You got it."

"So damn sorry about that."

"I know. It was an accident, Reece. No hard feelings."

"Yeah, no hard feelings," he repeated softly. Then he gave me a halfhearted wave and left, closing the door behind him. And here we were, me, Mal, and Killer. The apartment was eerily silent apart from the snuffling, panting puppy. Mal picked him up and put him carefully on the floor.

"I want to yell at you for leaving me the way you did, for disappearing on me," I said, moving the ice pack from my face. "But I can't because the situation with your mom is terrible and I know you're hurting. And for some stupid reason I still feel guilty about not agreeing to marry you even though you asking me was an insane, ridiculous stunt that had next to nothing to do with me."

"That's not true. And keep the ice on your face."

I covered my war wound back up. "I can't see you clearly if you sit on that side."

He sighed and knelt before me, his hands on my knees. "Can you see me now?"

"Yes. Why aren't you with your mom? That's where you should be."

"She wanted me here with you on your birthday. I wanted me here with you on your birthday. Neither of us wanted some other guy taking you out. Just the thought of it drove me nuts." His face tensed up and his hands smoothed up and down my woolen-tight-covered thighs. "Mom and I talked . . . about you and about everything. She helped me figure a few things out."

"Such as?"

"You just told Reece you were in love with me."

"Yes. But what did your mom help you figure out?"

There was growling going on down by Mal's shoe. We both ignored it.

"I dunno, what a relationship is, what love is. Lots of things. Seeing her and Dad together these last few days . . ." He pressed my knees apart, getting closer. "You know, I'm in love with you too. I just, I pushed too hard on the wrong thing, at the wrong time, for the wrong reason. I was a whole lot of wrong, pumpkin."

"Yeah."

He nodded. "Right girl, wrong everything else."

My good eye teared up. My bad one had never really stopped, but that was something else altogether. "Thank you. But things went to shit and you disappeared on me again. You need to stop doing that. That's a boundary, Mal. It's not the sort of thing I can keep taking from you."

"I won't disappear on you again. I promise. We'll sort things out together."

"Okay." I sniffed and smiled. "You better get back to your mom."

"In the morning. I hired a jet to take us back. She, ah . . . they think in the next day or two." He shut his eyes tight and pressed his forehead into my lap. "Hardest fucking week of my life. Hardly gotten any sleep at all. Will you sleep with me, Anne? I really need you to sleep with me."

I placed my hand on his head, rubbing at the soft strands of hair. "Whatever you need."

Eleven-forty glowed green on my alarm clock when I woke. We'd turned out all the lights and lain down together on my bed (still a mattress on the floor). The Advil had knocked me out like it always did. Where Mal was now, I had no idea. Distantly, there were footsteps on the stairs, the door opened, and little nails were clicking across the floor. Next thing I knew, Killer was jumping all over me, being psycho energetic. Having greeted me properly, he then bounded over to my stripy jersey dress.

I'd tossed it at the set of drawers but they'd failed to catch. It lay on the floor, a perfect puppy bed, apparently.

"Our son needed to take a leak," said Mal, stripping off his hoodie and toeing off his boots.

"You're a good father."

"I know, right? I'm the best." His jeans went next and there was nothing but him beneath. If only there was more than ambient light from the street to see him by. He crawled underneath the blanket next to me. "How you doing, pumpkin? Your eye's looking a little messed up."

"I know. I can't see out of that side at all. But you're supposed to tell me I'm beautiful, no matter what."

"You are beautiful no matter what. You also have an awesome black eye. In the future, no running into fights." He kissed me, soft and sweet. Then he kissed me deep and wet, sliding his tongue into my mouth. His taste was home, the feel of his hands cradling my head perfection. I ran my fingers over his rib cage and up over his thick shoulders, getting familiar with him once again. My thighs tensed, between my legs turning swollen and wet for him. His thickening cock nudged my hip bone. So damn nice not to be alone in this.

"Happy birthday," he whispered.

"It is now that you're here."

"Fuck, I missed you."

"Missed you too."

"You fell asleep so fast. What's under here?" He toyed with the hem of my sleep shirt.

"You've forgotten already?"

He dragged my T-shirt over my head and tossed it aside. "Oh, breasts. Best present ever. Thanks, pumpkin."

"You're very welcome. I'm all about the giving on my birthday." I sucked in a harsh breath as he licked across first one nipple, then the other. They hardened, aching in the best way possible. "Wait till you see what else I've got for you."

"In here? Show me." His fingers hooked in the waistband of my underwear, dragging them down and off. "Nice. I need a closer look."

He crawled between my legs, his fingers drifting up and down my thighs featherlight. Torturously slow, he licked a path from the top of my sex up to my sternum. Every part of me he touched tingled. His mouth covered mine and his hand massaged my pussy, a finger sliding deep inside with ease. "I think you like me."

"Shut up and kiss me."

He laughed. The finger inside me moved and he rubbed at some sweet spot that drove me out of my fucking head. I gasped. My neck arched and my eyes opened wide, staring sightlessly up at the ceiling.

"Christ, Mal."

"That's it." His thumb circled my clit, making my leg muscles tremble. This was going to be fast and hard, no doubt about it. I might have somewhat neglected my orgasms during his absence. My libido had been on vacation. Now, it was back and then some. A hot mouth closed over one nipple, sucking hard, teasing with tongue.

I moaned and held him to me. "More."

A second finger joined the first, stretching me slightly, making the contact on my sweet spot so much more effective. My heels dug deep into the mattress. He might just kill me this time, but it would be worth it.

"Tell me you love me," he said, still toying with my nipple.

"I love you."

"No you don't. You're just saying that 'cause you want to come." He rose to look me in the eye with an evil grin. I was done for. "I don't believe you at all."

I grabbed his face, mashing our lips together, kissing him hard. Showing him how I felt. Between my legs, his hand never stopped working, driving me out of my mind. Fingers pumped into me again and again. It was almost

enough, but not quite. God, the knot building inside of
me. So close.

"Do you love me, Anne?" He sat back on his heels,
sliding his fingers in and out of me, making the pressure
grow.

"Yes."

From the edge of the bed he grabbed a condom wrapper, ripping it open with his teeth. "Lots?"

I nodded, fighting for breath.

"Like, lots and lots? Or just a little lots?"

"What?"

With a grin, he rolled on the condom. "How much do
you love me? How many lots?"

"Mal . . ." I couldn't make sense of the question. My
hands fisted in the pillow behind my head.

"See, this is what I mean." He set his arm beside my
head and lowered himself over me. Slowly he slid his
fingers out of my sex and lined up his cock. I tried to keep
my eyes open, but it was a losing battle. My eyelids drifted
down. I was lost to the sensation of his thick length pushing into me, making a permanent place for himself. We fit
just right.

"I love you more," he said. Then his fingers slid around
my clit, giving me what I needed, applying the perfect
pressure to set me alight. I exploded. The fire inside of me
burning out of control. But so long as I held on to him, it
was okay. My legs held him tight, my hands anchoring him
to me, bound around his neck. The muscles in my pussy
grabbed at his cock, greedy and needing.

And he groaned, pressing his cheek into mine.

I drifted back to reality, awareness returning ever so
gradually. Mal started moving, slowly at first, sliding in
and out. Little shudders wracked me with each stroke.

"Liar," I whispered, remembering what he'd said. "I
love you more."

He smiled, thrusting into me. "Prove it."

I wrapped him up in my legs and arms, bringing his mouth to mine, giving him everything. Trusting him with everything. Because I'd finally found someone who could take both the good and the bad, the sad and the happy. I wanted to do the same for him.

He was being so careful, but there was so much emotion built up inside of him. I could feel it, coursing beneath his skin, raging behind his eyes.

"Harder," I urged him.

He picked up the pace.

"Stop holding back."

"Anne . . ." His jaw was tensed, his green eyes ablaze.

"Do it. Give it to me. I can take it."

Mal didn't need any more prompting. He gathered me up against him, our skin slapping as he pounded into me. Our hips hit hard, his cock driving deep into the heart of me. It was like standing in a storm, frightening and beautiful both. I'd never trusted anyone to be this rough before, to take things this far. He hammered into me. His teeth fixed on my neck, marking me, as his hand gripped my ass cheek, holding me to him. The whole of him shuddered against me as he buried himself deep and came. He shouted my name, his mouth still pressed against my skin.

I kept my arms and legs tight around him, making him collapse on top of me. The heavy weight of him pinned me to the bed. I could hold on to him forever.

We lay there in silence. My face was wet where he pressed his cheek against it. His sweat or tears, I don't know, but he shook for a long time. I petted his hair and stroked his back, running my fingers up and down his spine.

"I love you," I said. "So much I can't say."

He trailed his lips against my jaw. "I believe you."

EPILOGUE

A MONTH LATER ...

"I'm not sure about this." I sat on the side of our bed, cuddling Killer. He'd tolerate it for short periods, but the way his butt was wriggling my time was nearly up. Puppies tended to only have two speeds in my limited experience. Stop and go. It wasn't unusual to find him fast asleep face down in his food bowl now and then after a hard day's playing.

"What do you want to do?" asked Mal.

"I don't know."

He looked around our bedroom, leaning a hip against the end of our brand-new gigantic four-poster bed. Mal had insisted we needed it and gone into great detail regarding plans for its usage. Apparently I was to play the part of the sacrificial lamb, regularly tied down and offered up to the gods of oral sex. As a fate, I found this to be not even remotely dire. Also, the bed was a far sturdier structure than the one from my apartment. If and when we decided to do more bed jumping, he assured me this one wouldn't die on us.

Mal made living fun. But today was a different matter entirely.

"They'll start arriving soon," he said. "You've been

working your ass off. The food's all ready. Everything's organized and you wanted to do this. This was your idea. But if you really think turning tail and running away like a cowardly little lion is best, then that's okay with me too. I'll even help you live with the shame and regret for the rest of your life."

I slumped. "Oh god, you bastard."

"I love you, pumpkin."

"I love you too. I'm just not very good at this stuff." I set Killer down and he immediately chased down the empty Diet Coke bottle. It was his favorite toy since being forced to give up eating Mal's Chucks. His unofficial aunts, Lizzy, Ev, and Lauren bought him every dog treat and toy under the sun, but he would not be swayed from his redneck ways. Best dog ever.

Someone knocked on the door out in the living room area.

Killer might have been my first birthday present. But the real one was the condo opposite David and Ev's, where Mal and I now lived together. Pets were allowed there. What did you say to a guy who bought a condo so you could have the dog you missed out on as a child? Actually, I didn't say anything. I gave him a blow job once I stopped crying. He seemed to appreciate it. Besides, he already knew I loved him. I pretty much told him constantly.

Someone knocked on the door, again.

My shoulders jumped.

"Ready?" he asked.

I nodded. He held his hand out to me and I took it, letting him lead me through the hallway, into the living room.

"You won't leave?" I asked, hating the way my knees were knocking.

"I won't leave. I'll be at your side the whole time."

"Okay." I smiled. "Not that I'm some pathetic weakling using you for a crutch or a safety blanket or anything."

"Hey," he said, grasping my chin gently. "You've been

my crutch for the last month and a half. Given me whatever I needed whenever you could. We lean on each other, pumpkin. It's all good."

"Thank you."

He sketched a bow. "Thank *you*."

It was ridiculous really, what a monster I'd made of this situation in my head. But I could slay dragons with him at my side. Without a doubt. I stood up straight, took a deep breath. "I'm fine."

"Yeah, you are. All of our friends are coming. Everyone's got your back, Anne," he said. "This will be the best day before Thanksgiving dinner ever."

We were spending the actual Thanksgiving at his eldest sister's place in Idaho. Lori had died not long after we flew back to Coeur d'Alene, the day after our reunion It had hit Mal hard. It still hit him hard, but there'd been no more slamming his fist into walls or wiping out a bottle of Jack Daniel's every other night. He did get quiet and withdrawn sometimes. He always came back to me, though.

"You can do this," he said. And I believed him.

He opened the door and there stood Lizzy and Mom. Mom gave me a cautious smile. Her carrot-colored hair had more gray in it than I remembered and lines softened her face. If anything, she seemed more nervous than me, the way her fingers were clasped tight in front of her.

"Hi, Mom." I stepped forward, almost kissing her cheek but not quite. It was a really close call. Maybe next time. "Mom, this is Mal. Mal, this my mother, Jan."

"Hey, Jan. Nice to meet you." Mal moved forward to greet her, all smiles. But his hand never left mine.

Worry lined Mom's face further at the sight of Mal. Her words were nice enough, however, as they exchanged pleasantries. Everything would be fine. We'd get through this. Because the fact was, my life here was good. It had been before Mal came along. And now it was even better.

Astronomically so. If my mom and I could move forward and have some sort of functioning relationship, then that was great. If not, I'd survive.

"Come see their place, Mom. It's gorgeous. Mal bought it for Anne for her birthday." Lizzy winked at me, ushering Mom past us and into the condo. Giving me a moment to catch my breath, bless her.

I was extremely fortunate because our home was, indeed, gorgeous. The floor was covered in a very cool, slightly sparkly, black Italian tile. Our walls were pristine white and the furniture gray with splashes of turquoise. Despite the layout being the same, it had a different feel to it than Ev and David's place. Speaking of which, they made excellent neighbors. They loved puppysitting Killer. Or at least Ev did. David still bore some resentment over my dog's chewing of a leather guitar strap or two and peeing on their rug. Some people were so judgy.

Mal and David hung out often, with Ben and Jimmy drifting between their own places and the two condos. The Stage Dive Family never blinked at my inclusion. Something I was profoundly grateful for. They'd even made sure Lizzy felt welcome. Though her continuing crush on Ben still gave me pause.

"Check out the size of their bathtub, Mom." Lizzy's voice drifted down the hall along with Mom's answering words of admiration. It was a big tub. And Mal and I made full use of it. I hardly missed the old claw foot tub from the apartment at all.

"All good?" he asked me quietly, ignoring Killer's scratching at his jeans-clad leg.

"Yes." I turned my face up to his and slipped my hand around his neck. Without a word, he leaned in, fitting his mouth to mine and giving me everything and then some. By the time he finished I was breathing heavy, feeling flushed.

"Break it up." Ben groaned, swinging a bouquet of

bright flowers in one hand. "You've got guests, for fuck's sake."

"Aw, that's sweet. You bring me flowers, Benny?" Mal asked, rubbing a hand up and down my back.

"Hell no. I bought your hot girlfriend flowers." He handed the heavy bunch over to my waiting arms.

"Thank you, Ben." I smiled, charmed.

"Well, your hot girlfriend and her equally hot little sister."

I narrowed my eyes at him.

The big man smiled. Such a shit stirrer.

"Where's the rest of them?" asked Ben. He scooped up Killer and then settled himself in the corner of the couch, turning on the TV. With one hand he flicked through channels, with the other he proceeded to rile up my puppy. Soon crazed baby-sized barks, snapping, and growling filled the air. Killer adored Mal, but Ben wasn't too far behind in his doggy affections.

"They'll be here soon," said Mal.

"You heard Lena quit?"

I just about jumped. "What? No. When?"

"Couple of days ago. Jimmy is not pleased."

Mal gave a low whistle but otherwise didn't comment. His gaze went to the hallway, where Mom and Lizzy were winding up their tour on account of them running out of places to look.

"Quick," Mal said, bringing his face close to mine.

"What?"

"This." He covered my mouth with his, sliding his tongue into my mouth. Generally kissing me stupid. Whatever mocking statement Ben made, I missed it. Only kissing Mal mattered. His hands cupped my ass, fingers kneading. My toes curled and my senses went wild. By the time he pulled back, my lips were wet and most definitely so were things downstairs. It took a long minute for me to catch my breath.

"Can't make out in front of your mom," he explained. "Oops. I kinda fucked up your lipstick. More than last time even. Sorry."

"It was worth it."

"Was it?" he asked, heat and affection and a hundred other things shining in his beautiful green eyes.

"Oh, yeah. You're the best." I grinned back at him.

"Pumpkin, hello. Of course I am!"